Books by Robert Bidinotto

Nonfiction

Criminal Justice? The Legal System vs. Individual Responsibility

Freed to Kill

Fiction

Hunter

HUNTER

A Thriller

ROBERT BIDINOTTO

Chester, Maryland

HUNTER
ROBERT BIDINOTTO

Published by
Avenger Books
P.O. Box 555
Chester, Maryland 21619

Published in the United States of America

Cover design by **Allen Chiu**

Formatting and layout provided by **Everything Indie**
http://www.everything-indie.com

To the forgotten victims of crime,
to the unsung heroes who protect us and our freedoms,
and most of all
to Cynthia—
for encouraging me to chase a dream.

"Most of the harm in the world is done by good people, and not by accident, lapse, or omission. It is the result of their deliberate actions, long persevered in, which they hold to be motivated by high ideals toward virtuous ends."

—Isabel Paterson, *The God of the Machine*

PART I

"Justice is that virtue of the soul which is distributive
according to desert."

—Aristotle, *Metaphysics*
"On the Virtues and Vices: Justice"

ONE

T oday she would finally nail the bastard.

Annie Woods watched the traitor's cab thread through the jam of courtesy vans and pull to the curb. The right rear door opened and he emerged. She slowed her own tailing car to a crawl.

Looking edgy, the man scanned the vehicles around him. Masked only by her sunglasses, she held her breath as his gaze slid right past her. Then he leaned back inside the cab, pulled out a rolling carry-on suitcase, and slammed the door shut. He wheeled it behind him, heading into the terminal. Through the building's soaring windows she saw him make his way to the rear of a long line of passengers snaking toward the ticket counter.

She squeezed the Agency's Taurus in behind a departing vehicle and leaped out. She flipped open her CIA credentials and held them in her outstretched hand as she approached a young state trooper directing traffic.

"Sir, we've got a national-security situation here," she said. "I'm Ann Woods, with a federal task force following a criminal suspect. He's just entered the terminal."

He squinted at her ID. "Nobody told me anything about this."

At that moment, two midnight-blue Crown Vics and a black Suburban pulled up beside them. Doors flew open and nine men in dark suits spilled out, quickly assembling behind the SUV. The trooper's mouth fell open.

"Please alert airport security," she continued. "Tell them they're not to interfere or approach the ticket area until we give the all-clear."

The startled trooper nodded, then moved off, radioing it in.

Rick Groat, the FBI's special agent in charge, trotted over. His dark brown mustache was meticulously trimmed, and his eyes gleamed with an adrenaline rush. "Where's he now?"

She nodded toward the building. "In line at the Aeroflot counter."

They joined the others behind the SUV. "Okay, listen up," Groat said. "You guys"—he pointed to three agents— "go in over there on the left and hold that entrance. You two—and you also, Ms. Woods—block the other door on the right. The rest of you, follow me in here. We'll approach him and I'll make the arrest."

"But he knows you, Rick," she said. "He'll spot you as soon as you enter. Especially if you take in a team."

Groat frowned, clearly not happy to be challenged in front of his men. "So? We'll have him surrounded. Where could he go?"

"That's not the point. Remember, he's probably armed—at least until he gets near security, when he'll dump his weapon somewhere. But if he sees you, this could go south, fast. Maybe somebody gets hurt or taken hostage."

"So, how would *you* play it?"

"Give me a second." She went to her car, grabbed her shoulder bag from the passenger seat, then rejoined them. She drew out a curly blonde wig, pulled it over her short brown hair, then put her sunglasses back on. From their sudden smiles, she knew the transformation was striking.

"I've used this in investigations. I can get right next to him without being recognized, then take him down before he knows what's happening."

"*You?*"

"Why not?" She saw his uncertain look. "Look, here's what you can do. Cover the far entrances, so he can't escape. You stay outside this one. I'll go in and wait until he's left the ticket counter and heads toward the gates. I'll radio you a *'mark,'* then count down from ten. On *'two,'* you come in fast, from all directions. Yell, make some noise. When he turns your way, I'll grab him from behind—right at *'zero.'* If we time this right, he'll never see me coming."

He still looked unsure.

"Remember," she added, "come in only when I say *'two.'* No sooner. Don't alert him before I can reach him."

"I don't like it," Groat said. "The *Bureau* has the lead on this arrest.... Okay, you do the initial approach. But since *I'm* the SAC here, it's *my* responsibility to make the collar and read him his rights."

She forced herself to speak evenly. "Of course. It's your operation."

She shouldered her bag and headed toward the entrance. Inside, she took position behind another line. She pulled out her cell and raised it to her ear, feeling the tug of the pistol rig under her tailored jacket. "Six in position," she whispered into her throat microphone, pretending to be chatting into the phone.

"Control copies."

Out of the corner of her eye she kept track of her quarry.

*

James Muller was chubby, baby-faced, and fifty-three. He wore rumpled gray slacks and a wilted white shirt beneath a navy blazer. For a veteran manager in the CIA's Office of Security—where Annie worked as an investigator—Muller's tradecraft left much to be desired. He fidgeted, checked his watch constantly, and stole furtive glances at fellow passengers. He kept running his fingers through his lank, thinning gray-blond hair.

She watched him shuffle toward the front of his line. She tried to suppress her anger and focus only on him. But she couldn't help thinking about the absurdities that had put Groat in charge of Muller's arrest. The FBI, not the CIA, wielded authority over counterintelligence activities on U.S. soil. And Groat was the FBI's chief liaison with Langley's Counterintelligence Center.

As the security officer who first suspected, then investigated, and finally exposed Muller's treason, Annie had worried for months about Groat's interference. That's why she waited until after she'd already done the critical leg-work before telling her boss about her investigation. Impressed, he'd pulled strings to allow her to remain involved to the end.

But now, it was clear that Groat intended to cut her out and hog the glory of the arrest.

*

Muller reached the front of his line, then wheeled his carry-on bag toward a waiting ticket agent.

"Six," she whispered. "He's at the counter. Stand by for my count."

"Control copies. Guys, get ready!"

Her silent cell phone pressed to her ear, Annie threaded her way to the back of her line, then moved to position herself for the intercept. She reached a point between Muller and the corridor leading back to the boarding gates. He'd have to pass her here.

She set her shoulder bag on the floor and pretended now to send a text message.

And waited.

She felt a drop of sweat trickle down her back.

Felt the weight of the holster under her jacket.

In her peripheral vision, Muller took his ticket from the counter woman, grabbed his rolling bag, then turned in her direction.

"Mark," she whispered in her throat microphone. "Ten...nine...eight...seven...six..."

"Go! Now! Now! Now!"

The sudden shout in her earpiece startled her. Then noise, to her right. She looked.

Groat was charging through the entrance alone, gun in hand.

"Freeze!" he was shouting. "Freeze! Freeze!"

She couldn't believe it. She wheeled. Saw Muller still twenty feet behind her, staring wide-eyed at Groat. Then he whipped around, looking for someplace to run.

And spotted her looking right at him.

She dropped her cell and hurtled toward him.

He released his grip on the suitcase. His right hand clawed inside his blazer.

"Freeze! Freeze!"

Beside Muller, a young couple froze in place.

"Down! Everybody down!"

Behind him, other agents, yelling and pushing through the milling mass of passengers.

Can't let him shoot....

She sprinted toward him as he looked down, fumbling inside his jacket.

She reached him just as his gun pulled free.

Her left hand seized that wrist and her right palm drove into his throat and she slammed against him, her momentum driving them back over his suitcase and onto the floor.

She landed on him hard. Heard him gasp. Heard his weapon clatter across the marble floor.

Then something massive smashed into her, knocking her aside.

She lay sprawled on her back, sucking in air, reeling from the impact.

"Got him!" A beefy young agent straddled Muller, knees pinning the traitor's arms, a .40 caliber Glock pressed to his captive's forehead.

"James Muller...you...are under arrest!" Groat's voice, quavering. He stood over Muller, panting, legs splayed too far apart, pointing his own service pistol in extended hands. The muzzle was wavering.

She forced herself to sit up. Other agents retrieved Muller's weapon and suitcase, then established a perimeter. The young agent atop Muller flipped him onto his stomach, slapped cuffs around his wrists behind his back, and began to pat him down. He glanced over at her sheepishly.

"Sorry," he said. "Hey, you okay?"

She wasn't in the mood to reassure him. Her right shoulder felt like it had been clubbed with a baseball bat. She hauled herself slowly to her feet and took stock. Her own Glock was still in its holster. Her favorite sunglasses lay next to Muller, crushed. He remained curled up on his side, fetal position, coughing and retching, his hands secured behind his back. Around them, scores of passengers, some whimpering, huddled against walls or lay terrified on the terminal floor; others hurried away down the corridors.

Rubbing her shoulder, she stepped toward Groat, who lowered his weapon. His eyes were too wide; they held both fear and relief.

She got right in his face. "You jumped my signal."

He took an involuntary step back. "You...are you all right?"

"No thanks to you, you stupid son of a bitch."

*

They jammed into a small airport security office. State police milled outside the door. Another trooper, a sergeant, sat at a gray metal desk barking into the phone. Muller slouched in a chair next to the desk, hands still cuffed behind his back, two Bureau agents looming over him. They'd wrapped a towel filled with ice from a soda machine around his rapidly bruising throat. His cheeks were red and he was still coughing.

Groat entered the room. His eyes darted at her, then scurried away. He marched straight to Muller. Drew an envelope from inside his suit jacket, then unfolded a document from it.

"Okay. To finish the formalities. James Harold Muller, you are hereby under arrest for violation of Title 18, United States Code Section 794(c), conspiracy to commit espionage. You have the right to remain silent. Anything you say—"

Muller shot a glance up at him. "Not another word, Ricky," he interrupted, his voice hoarse. "I know my rights."

"Look, I have to—"

"If you shut the hell up, Ricky, I might even be willing to make a statement without the presence of counsel."

Everyone stopped what they were doing and looked at him. This was too good to be true.

Groat nodded. "Okay. We're listening."

Muller coughed and shook his head. "No, Ricky. Way too many people here. You want my cooperation, we do this my way."

"Exactly what way is that?"

The traitor sat back in his chair, taking his time. His gaze drifted over to where Annie stood leaning against the wall in a corner, arms folded across her chest.

"I see you're back to brunette, Annie. Good. Blonde just isn't you."

She just looked at him, refusing to take the bait. She knew he loved to grandstand.

"Tell me the truth, now, Annie. You're the one who sorted it all out, right?" Muller nodded scornfully in Groat's direction. "Certainly not this bozo. Groat couldn't find his ass with a GPS."

The FBI man's face reddened. She saw the other agents struggle not to smile.

"Yeah, I figured as much," Muller went on. "You know, Annie, I always worried that it would be somebody like you who'd get on to me."

"You've got something to say, say it," she said.

He coughed again. "Sure, Annie. I'll tell *you* everything. But not the G-Man here. In fact, not anybody from the Bureau."

"What do you mean?"

"You heard me, Ricky. I only talk to people I respect. *Agency* people." He paused again, making a show of it. "I think Annie's earned the right to be in on this. And I think, maybe...how about Grant Garrett? Yeah, Garrett, too."

"You're in no position to dictate terms!" Groat shouted. "This is *FBI* jurisdiction, not—"

"Ricky, Ricky. You just don't get it, do you? I *am* in a position to dictate terms. Uncle Sam very badly needs to know what I did. But if Uncle wants to hear it, he's going to have to do things my way."

Nobody said a word. James Muller leaned forward and smiled.

"Come on, now, people. Do I chat alone with Annie and Garrett? Or do I get lawyered up?"

TWO

WASHINGTON, D.C.
Monday, March 17, 1:45 p.m.

The man left the elevator and emerged into the underground garage. Traffic noise from above echoed faintly around the cavernous gray walls. Like all downtown parking facilities, it was crammed with vehicles this time of day. But he saw no one else around; only his shadow marched before him as he approached his SUV.

He tossed his briefcase over onto the passenger seat as he settled in, snapped the belt across his corduroy jacket, and turned over the engine. The digital clock on the dash lit up, reassuring him that it was still before two o'clock. A relief that his meeting had ended so early; he'd beat the rush-hour traffic.

Still, District streets were never predictable, what with unexpected road closures and VIP motorcades creating constant bottlenecks. He reached over and clicked on the radio, set to the local news station, to catch their traffic report.

"...*according to a CIA spokesperson. And the* Washington Post *is reporting on its website that the dramatic capture of this 'mole' within the Agency came after a nearly two-year investigation—*"

The seat beneath him seemed to be falling away.

"*—a* Post *source at Langley, the individual taken into custody caused, quote, 'serious harm to national security, including the betrayal of numerous CIA assets and sensitive operations over a period of years.'*"

His hand, still extended to the volume control, fell to his thigh.

"*Meanwhile, the Agency spokesperson tells us that more information about the arrest of James Harold Muller today at Dulles Airport will be released at a joint CIA-FBI news conference, scheduled for 3:30 p.m. That's it from here. Richard, back to you.*"

"*Thanks, Mark. We'll have a lot more on this breaking story at the top of the hour.... Now, let's find out what's happening on the area roadways—*"

Muller.

For a moment, he couldn't think of anything beyond that name. The rest of his mind was an empty hole.

Then the man's face floated up into his consciousness. Smooth, round, moon-like. Pale blue slits for eyes. The wispy hair. The little smirk.

A blast of rage tore through him.

Muller.

Now it all made sense.

He hammered the steering wheel with his fist, once. Twice.

Then gripped the wheel. Hard. Squeezed his eyes shut. Took a slow, steady breath. Tried to impose order on the churning images in his brain.

All right. What happens next? What do they do with him?

Well, what would *you* do if you had just captured a traitor? Somebody who had—

Immediately, he knew. Knew what they'd do.

Guessed where they'd go.

He turned to fasten his seat belt. Straightening, he noticed his eyes reflected in the rearview mirror. Hard and glittering, like marbles.

Then the anger melted away.

His hands now rested lightly on the steering wheel. As always after he'd made a decision, he experienced a sense of icy physical tranquility and heightened mental clarity.

He shut off the radio. Began to roll it around in his mind. Options. Details. Implications.

It occurred to him that he should be concerned. After all, he might be about to wreck everything he'd been working so carefully to establish during the past two years. Yet that stray thought now seemed an irrelevant intrusion, like a scarecrow hanging impotently in some distant field.

He would deal with any remote consequences, if and when. The only thing that mattered is that he could not let this go, here and now.

Would not let this go.

He sat in stillness for another minute, taking comfort in the low, reassuring purr of the engine. Then he shifted smoothly into reverse, backed from his parking space, and eased forward through the garage, prowling slowly toward the ramp that curved upward toward the exit.

He would make a few calls, change some plans.
He would not go home tonight.

THREE

The tall hills—as a Colorado native, she couldn't think of the Blue Ridge chain as real mountains—rose and rolled around them as their trio of CIA vehicles sped west on Route 66. They'd been on the highway since the early-morning meeting on the seventh floor at Langley.

"Nice briefing."

She lowered the copy of the *Washington Post* that she'd been reading and glanced at the man beside her in the rear seat of the armored Lincoln limo.

Grant Garrett, the CIA's deputy director of National Clandestine Services, wasn't given to compliments. Nor had he looked at her as he said it; he was staring off at the hills. He was a study in gunmetal gray, from his close-cropped hair, to his well-tailored suit, to the pen he tapped idly against the slate-colored note pad on his lap.

As always, Garrett looked morose. It wasn't a matter of his mood, typically inscrutable. His flinty features exuded an unforgiving toughness. But the sagging skin beneath his pale blue eyes also suggested world-weary sadness, born of decades of ruthless victories and regretted losses.

"Thanks," she said tentatively, taking her cue from his terseness.

Garrett glanced at her. "Boss didn't rattle you."

"Not particularly."

He grunted. Looked back at the passing hills. She took that as another compliment.

"Lucky that asshole didn't get you killed," he added.

"Which one—Muller or Groat?"

He grunted again. In Garrett, that passed for knee-slapping laughter. The grunt turned into a cough. The man was an incorrigible chain smoker. The only thing keeping him from lighting up here and now was gentlemanly courtesy.

They were quiet while she finished reading the *Post* story about Muller's arrest. The media frenzy about his chaotic airport takedown was to be expected. But a "high-level CIA source, speaking on condition of anonymity," had leaked a few sensitive background details to a *Post* reporter, a guy to whom Agency higher-ups often fed self-serving propaganda. The most disturbing detail was that Muller was "being held for questioning by the Agency at an undisclosed location outside of Washington." Garrett, who had scanned the paper first, circled that paragraph before he handed her the paper.

She folded and dropped it on the seat, then pressed back into the soft black leather. She was physically drained. Her right shoulder throbbed. She needed sleep badly. She turned to the passing landscape. A power line running parallel to the highway rose and fell rhythmically between poles, like the soothing pulse of a cardiograph. She struggled to keep her eyes open.

"You happy working for Randy, Ms. Woods?"

She looked at him; his face was unreadable, eyes forward. She thought about her supervisor in the Office of Security. "He's a good guy to work for," she said carefully. "And I like investigations."

"You're good at them. As everyone now knows."

More compliments?

"Thank you, sir."

"Please. Grant."

"Okay. Thank you, Grant."

A pause.

"I spoke to Randy about you last night," he continued. "Says you've maxed out, as far as promotions in OS."

"Yes. Unfortunately. Well, we don't work at Langley to get rich."

"Tell me about it."

Another pause.

"Ever think of transferring?"

Where is this going?

"As I say, I like investigations. And, as you say, I'm good at them."

"Well, it's clear to us that your investigative talents are being wasted on stuff like background clearances. NCS certainly could use your skill set. In counterintelligence."

It startled her. "That's...very flattering, sir, but—"

"Grant."

"Yes, sorry. Grant. Very flattering. But frankly, I don't think I could stand working in CIC and having to suck up to Rick Groat every day."

"I wasn't talking about the Counterintelligence Center. I meant working directly for me."

She shifted around to face him.

"Here's my problem," he went on. "Yeah, Groat is a royal pain in the ass. But I can't get the Bureau to replace him. Long as he's their liaison at CIC, my people there are hog-tied. They spend more time justifying what they do than just doing it."

"Which is exactly why I wouldn't want to be there."

"Which is exactly why I wouldn't want you to be there, either. I need somebody to function independently from the Center. To help me run special CI ops directly. The old-fashioned way."

She knew exactly what he meant. Before ascending the food chain in National Clandestine Services—which veterans still called by its old name, the Directorate of Operations—Grant Garrett had been a legendary case officer, one of those "cowboys" that some congressmen despised and some Langley managers feared. But he survived because he got results, and he got results because he wasn't afraid to get his hands dirty.

She wondered why Garrett bothered to stick it out in a bureaucracy that was risk-averse to the point of paralysis. She thought she knew *how*. Randy once hinted to her in an unguarded moment that Garrett "had stuff on some guys on the seventh floor." That didn't surprise her. Garrett was a bare-knuckles guy, heir to the operational style that prevailed in the CIA's predecessor agency, the OSS of World War II, under its legendary founder, "Wild Bill" Donovan. These days, Garrett was the only reason that

Langley still produced any valuable HUMINT at all. They relied way too much on satellites and drones.

"Think of it this way, Ms. Woods—"

"Annie."

He actually smiled. "Okay—Annie. Think of it this way. If we had a fully functioning counterintelligence section in NCS, we might have picked up something about Muller from the Russian side. But we don't, and we didn't. We were completely blindsided. That bastard has cost us dearly. Think of the officers and agents blown or killed. Strauss, Kilwalski, Sokolov, Malone, Ayyad. God knows who else." He looked down at his hands, his expression even more dour. "I shudder to think what he's fed to the SVR."

"Let's hope he tells us today."

"Yes. Let's hope. But over the longer haul, I still need to beef up our CI. And after this, I don't know who I can trust anymore." He lifted his eyes. Looked into hers. "Except somebody who's proved her loyalty and competence."

She didn't know what to say.

"I've already taken the liberty to get Randy and the Corner Office to sign off on this—but only if you want it. Look, I know that CI officers aren't the most popular people at Langley. But what you've done has won you lots of respect. Anyway, it would be a promotion and a considerable jump in pay. Down the road, it might lead to some foreign travel. Young woman like you, that could— Oh, that's right. You're married. I forgot. But no kids yet, right?"

She felt her lips tighten. "No. No kids. And no marriage anymore."

She saw that it caught him off-guard.

"Sorry, Annie. That should've been in the file."

She looked away, out the tinted window. Recalled Frank's heart-stopping admission of his affair. The months since—a smear of ugly, painful images involving lies, leaving, and lawyers. Nothing she'd wanted to share with colleagues.

The Muller investigation had been a diversion, a blessed obsession that forced her to focus on betrayals less intimate. But the case was winding down. She'd no longer have the cushion of that distraction. She'd go home each night to the now-too-big Tudor in Falls Church. Lie alone in the now-too-big king bed.

"It's okay. The divorce went through only a couple of months ago. I didn't broadcast it."

"I understand.... Well. Maybe you don't need another major disruption so soon. How about you sleep on it?"

She faced him again, forced a smile. "Thanks. I'm flattered. Really. I'll think it over."

Maybe another major disruption is just what I need.

FOUR

CIA SAFE HOUSE, LINDEN, VIRGINIA
Tuesday, March 18, 10:15 a.m.

They turned off 66 at exit 13, just west of the small rural community of Linden, Virginia. Their limo followed close behind the lead car—a Grand Cherokee loaded with a security team and communications gear—onto Route 55, running parallel to 66. A short distance past the volunteer fire department and a bottling plant, they turned south onto a narrow side road posted "No Trespassing—U.S. Government Property."

The road took them into the wooded hills. Within a couple hundred yards, they approached a guy standing at the roadside in jeans and a denim jacket. He spoke into a walkie-talkie as they passed. After about a mile, the road curved left into a tiny valley—a flat depression, really, between a couple of thousand-foot-high hills.

It dead-ended at the gate to a driveway that looped in front of a modern, three-story house. The gate was part of a white rail fence that surrounded the property, which looked to be about three or four acres. The house had multiple gables and was wrapped by a broad porch filled with scattered white wicker tables and chairs. A young woman in a green windbreaker and brown slacks sat in a rocker near the front door, a magazine on her lap. Not far from the house, a man in a plaid shirt was raking a patch of bare earth. Several smaller wooden structures stood not far from the main building. A gravel parking area held three vehicles; next to it rose a two-story, four-car garage.

Fearing that the Russians might now come after him to shut him up, Muller had insisted that his debriefing take place somewhere both secret and secure, but also away from Langley. When told about the Linden site, he quickly agreed. Garrett explained to Annie that the Agency had established this covert safe house four years earlier, after left-wing "journalists"—he pronounced the word with disdain—had blown the locations of other CIA facilities much closer to HQ, even posting detailed satellite photos on the Internet. But this one remained secret. Any lost tourist or deer hunter who wandered near the property would see little to arouse his suspicions before politely being sent on his way. There were no signs of security obvious to an untrained observer, but Annie knew better. The innocuous rustic rail fence would be loaded with sensors. She also noticed small communications antennae and multiple satellite dishes on the house and garage roofs.

Because of today's special guest, security would be much tighter than usual. The woman on the porch and the man in the garden would be part of a detail of about twenty armed, highly trained members of the Office of Security. Most would remain hidden in the house, in the garage, and on the road leading to the residence. A sniper team would be perched on one of the hills overlooking the property. And their arriving convoy would add eight more officers to the protective detail.

As their lead car pulled up to the gate, the young woman on the porch stood and moved her hand onto the porch railing. The gate section blocking the driveway slid aside electronically, allowing them to enter. The Cherokee and their chase car peeled off toward the parking area, while their driver pulled their limo around to the front door.

"This," said Grant Garrett, unfastening his seat belt, "should be interesting."

*

"Why us?"

At the question, James Muller looked up from his cup of coffee, which was steaming in the surprisingly chilly room. His soft, almost cherubic features flowed into a smile. His hands were no longer cuffed, but a security officer stood nearby.

"Why me, anyway?" Garrett continued. "I know you've worked before with Ms. Woods. But you and I have never met. So, why do you want to talk only to her and me?"

They sat on sofas and stuffed chairs in the spacious, maple-paneled den of the safe house. In addition to the cool temperature, the room seemed dreary and impersonal, as if the home's occupants had not yet fully moved in. Annie noticed that the big stone fireplace was unused; no metal tools around it that might be employed as weapons. Nor were there candy dishes, ashtrays, photos on the walls. Even the built-in bookcases were empty. Thick, bark-colored curtains were drawn over what she knew would be bullet-resistant, laminated windows.

Muller chuckled. "Why you? Because I want to tell my story to *the best*—that's why. And you're *The Man*. Nobody at Langley holds a candle to the great Grant Garrett."

"So, do you want to talk, or do you want to be president of my fan club?"

Muller roared with laughter, sloshing coffee into the tan, high-pile carpet. "Sure, I'll talk. I just figured it was only proper to tell my tale to the only people at Langley still worth a damn. You and Annie. You—because you're the guy holding operations together. Annie—well, because fair's fair. She's the one who caught me." He looked her up and down, grinning. "And because she's hotter than hell."

Annie had long ago pegged Muller as a narcissist, if not a sociopath. He loved every minute of the grandstanding and attention. She sighed, put down her cup, leaned forward.

"Think you're flattering us?" she said quietly. "You sold out your country. You ended the careers and lives of some great people. So before we get down to specifics, you mind telling us why?"

He lost the grin. His pale blue eyes blinked rapidly. Narrowed into slits.

"Why. You want to know *why*. Well, maybe because after thirty years in the Company, doing *damned* good work, my pay still sucks. And maybe because that—plus all the nights and weekends, year after year—cost me my marriage.

But hey, at least I could always take solace in the complete *lack of recognition*. Did you know I was security admin for the CI team that nailed Nicholson? That's right, *Nicholson*. How could anyone do better than that? But what the hell did it get me?"

He began to rise from his sofa, but sat back down when the security officer stepped forward. He took a long breath. When he spoke again, he was subdued.

"Look at me. I'm fifty-three. And what do I have to show for it? My whole life is *crap*. I would've retired in a few more years. But to what? I'm alone. She took the kids, even the dog. I'm broke from the alimony. Where could I go? What could I do? Be a security guard at Wal-Mart?"

"So—you approached the Russians, not the other way around?"

Muller looked at Garrett and nodded. He tilted his cup to his lips and drained the last of the coffee.

"How long ago?" she asked.

"Three years, January."

"Where? In D.C.?"

Muller nodded, put down his cup. "Okay, I'll get into all of that. But look, I haven't had a smoke for over twenty-four hours. I was so goddamn jittery last night I couldn't even sleep."

"You can't smoke in here."

"Come on, man, give me a break. Can't we go outside?"

Garrett looked at Annie. "I could use one myself. Okay. Out on the porch."

*

They went through the kitchen and out the back door, led by the security officer, who slipped on mirrored sunglasses and stepped down into the yard. Two more members of the detail followed, then fanned out to flank them. Annie donned her own sunglasses—a spare pair she kept in her car—before stepping out into the dazzling morning sun.

Garrett fished a pack of cigarettes from his suit jacket, flipped it open. Thumbed one out and between his lips. Then offered the pack to Muller.

The traitor held it up, displaying the familiar red bulls-eye label.

"Ha. Look at that. *Luckies*. Ironic, isn't it?"

He shook out a cigarette and returned the pack.

The spy chief drew out a silver lighter. Fired up the other's cigarette, then his own.

Muller stepped to the porch rail. She and Garrett moved to either side of him. She watched the prisoner take a deep drag. Hold it. Slowly release a white cloud from between his lips. It coiled and drifted off, then was torn away by a sudden gust. He leaned forward to catch the sun on his face. Braced his arms on the rail, the butt dangling from his lips.

"Damn, that's good.... Thanks. I was dying for a smoke."

He squinted, looking up at the forested hillside rising before them.

"Pretty out here. I—"

A bee sound and hollow *smackkk*—an explosion of red mist and his face gone and warm spray hitting her face and hands—his body jerking back, legs buckling—a distant echoing *crack*—

"Down!"

Garrett diving over Muller's collapsing body, slamming into her, knocking her down, sprawling across her—gasping, crushed under his weight—muffled shouts—pounding steps vibrating through floorboards pressed painfully against her skull—twisting her face under Garrett's shielding arm—

Muller's body. A few feet away. On its back. Face toward her, what was left of it, barely half of it, one wide pale blue eye staring at her, the other somewhere inside a ragged crater of crimson pulp.

Blood streaming from his mouth around the smoking cigarette, still clinging to his lower lip....

FIVE

CIA HEADQUARTERS, LANGLEY, VIRGINIA
Wednesday, March 19, 4:30 p.m.

They gathered again around the table in the director's conference room, at the end of a painfully long day that had begun the night before. Their purpose: to assess the magnitude of the national-security catastrophe.

Annie, arms crossed, shifted in one of the chairs against the wall. Feeling like hell, despite all the ibuprofen. Pulsing pain behind her right eye. Ribs aching when she breathed. Stiff left knee. Sore purple bruises on her right shoulder, forearm, both legs. She reflected that in the past two days, she'd tackled a guy, been slammed into by another, then knocked down by a third.

Most action I've had with men in almost a year.

She wished she felt like laughing about it.

Nobody in the room knew how the Kremlin had found out about the safe house.

"Maybe Muller learned about it somehow, then told them during the past year or so," the FBI director ventured.

At the head of the table, the CIA boss rocked back in his gray leather chair. "Or maybe they trailed the transport team out to the site. We can't be sure about anything right now." He took off his rimless glasses, rubbed his eyes. "What have your people found out about the sniper or snipers?"

"I'll let our special agent in charge, Steve Sully, fill you in on what we know so far."

The red-haired, middle-aged man seated next to the FBI director took a sip from his water bottle, then spoke.

"Our investigators talked to the CIA's protective sniper team, situated on the opposite hillside. Those guys never saw the shooter. He had set up to the southeast, almost directly into the morning sun from their position. The rest of the detail at the house couldn't tell the precise direction of the sniper either. Not that it would have mattered. Our people triangulated from the witness reports, then did a grid search to determine his exact location. It was behind a fallen log up in the trees near the ridge line, over twelve hundred yards from the house. That's over two-thirds of a mile."

Somebody whistled. Sully nodded.

"Yes. And the shooter didn't even take the safer shot and go for center-mass. I don't know why, but he went for the head. You don't have to be a marksman to know that a head shot at that range is one hell of a shot. There was some wind gusting around out there, and the bullet hit Muller's face off-center, on its right, blowing away half his skull. If it had hit dead center, it would've probably exploded the whole head. Decapitated him."

Annie stared at a pattern on her sleeve to block the image in her memory. She heard people stirring uncomfortably.

"Ballistics retrieved a piece of the bullet from inside the house. *Way* inside. After going through Muller's skull, it passed through the outside wall, a kitchen cabinet, a coffee pot on the table, a hallway door, a sofa back, and another interior wall before lodging near the bottom of a bedroom wall. We were lucky to get a big fragment. We figured it had to be a .50 caliber. But the lab determined it came from a Barrett .416 cartridge. That particular cartridge propels a high-velocity, 400-grain, solid-brass, boattail spitzer bullet." He noticed blank looks and smiled sheepishly. "Okay, sorry, that's a sniper round, fairly new and relatively rare. It was designed by the Barrett Firearms Company in 2005. Currently, the only sniper rifle chambered to handle it is the Barrett Model 99."

This was all Greek to her, but she noticed that Grant Garrett leaned forward.

The SAC flipped through the papers spread on the table before him. "Forensics found no shell casing. Obviously, he took it with him. No footprints worth a damn, either. It looks like he had some kind of covering, maybe canvas or plastic, over his shoes or boots. And no hairs or fibers. Probably wore a coverall, probably camo. From his stride and foot impressions, we guess medium-to-tallish—six feet, maybe a little more—weight not more than one-ninety, max. But those are just rough guesses, given the terrain. In sum, about as clean a crime scene as you could find—unfortunately."

The CIA director shook his head slowly. "Great."

Sully nodded and glanced down at his papers again. "Reconstructing the sequence of events, it appears he left his vehicle a short way down the far side of that hill. There's a paved road up there, running in from Route 55. It leads south to some summer homes a couple of miles back in the hills. They're vacant this time of year, so no traffic. Being a pro, our shooter no doubt reconned the area and knew that. He probably left his car or truck right on the pavement, knowing it wouldn't be bothered by anybody. In any case, we found no tire tracks. So we have nothing to go on for a vehicle, either."

He took another sip of water. "From where he set up, we figure that after taking the shot, he trotted down the slope to his vehicle. We clocked it and estimate he could've made it in less than three minutes—then be back on 55, or more likely 66, within another minute or two."

"You keep saying 'he,'" Garrett broke in. "A single sniper? Not a team?"

The agent shook his head. "One set of footprints, in and out."

Garrett grunted.

"Anything else?" the CIA director prompted.

"Our theory is that after the Russkies heard about Muller's capture early yesterday afternoon, they guessed— or were told, or watched—where he'd be taken. Then they dispatched their shooter to the area. This guy could have set up and stayed in place overnight. Except then, his parked car might have been spotted by patrolling cops or neighbors. More importantly, we don't think he would've wanted to risk a long-distance night shoot using an infrared scope, because he needed to positively I.D. his target."

The FBI director interrupted. "So instead of staking out the safe house overnight, our guess is he waited to take position sometime before dawn. Which means he might have stayed somewhere nearby last night. On that theory, we checked local hotels and motels for anyone suspicious. Almost all the names checked out. We got two dead ends, though." He nodded at Sully to continue from there.

"Unlike the rest, both of these men paid cash," the agent continued. "One guy signed in as 'R. Lasher' at a cheap motel about ten miles east. The other guy registered in the Hampton Inn right off 66 near Front Royal, under the name 'B.J. Stoddard.' We ran both names through the databases. Nothing."

"Annie—did you want to say something?"

Garrett, looking at her; he must have seen her react. Everyone else turned to her.

"I—I'm not sure. Something in what Agent Sully said. But I can't put my finger on it.... Let me think about it."

"Maybe these were just guys cheating on their wives," the FBI boss interjected. "Maybe not. We're interviewing the hotel night staffs to see if we can get useful descriptions or leads."

The meeting didn't last long after that. After agreeing on an action plan and defining responsibilities, everyone got up and began to filter out.

Garrett caught up with Annie. "Let's talk," he said.

*

In his spacious seventh-floor office, they sat in big club chairs around a small mahogany coffee table, sipping from water bottles they'd brought back from the conference room. She detected the faint aroma of cigarettes—a Langley no-no.

"This stinks," Garrett said eventually, staring at the carpet.

"Sure does," she said, suppressing a smile.

"I don't mean Muller selling us out. Or even getting whacked before he talked to us. I mean, *how* he was killed. It doesn't add up." He glanced up at her. "Look—would you rat me out if I smoked?"

She laughed and shook her head.

"Thanks." He went to his desk, fetched a blockish, battery-operated ventilation gadget from a drawer, got it purring, set it on the coffee table. Then fired up one of his Luckies. The smoke drifted toward the contraption. He looked at her. "A toymaker buddy down in DS&T put this thing together for me."

"Nice to know the right people."

He sat back. "Let's start with the gun."

"What about it?"

"The Barrett 99 is American manufacture. So is the .416 ammo. More significantly, that cartridge is uniquely suitable for very-long-distance sniping—I think even better than the .50 caliber." He flicked a look at her. "Don't ask me how I know this."

"I won't. But what's the significance?"

"One: The Barrett isn't the Kremlin's sniper weapon of choice. It's only been around three years—not enough time for the Russkies to become really proficient with it, anyway. They train their people on the Dragunov SVD and the SV-98. Good enough weapons out to about six hundred meters or so. But our shooter nailed Muller through the face at twice that distance."

He inhaled, leaned forward, blew a stream of smoke toward his humming little machine.

"Two: Russian snipers also tend to operate in teams, not as lone shooters. Almost everybody else does these days, too. The idea of a lone-wolf sniper, especially on an op this important, bothers me.

"Three: There's the business of knowing where we'd be taking Muller. Annie, let me tell you, we've worked damned hard to keep the Linden site secret. Only a few people in the Agency, top people, and a handful of case officers and interrogators, knew about it. If Muller *did* find out about it and told Moscow its location, then it isn't logical that he showed no hesitation about going there. Knowing they'd want to silence him, wouldn't he have insisted on going someplace else?"

"Makes sense."

"So we can probably rule that out. Four, and finally: I have to disagree with The Boss. I just can't imagine our people could have been tailed transporting Muller there, not without picking up the surveillance."

"You're right. OS protective teams are just too good for that." She paused a moment. "So then, exactly what are you saying?"

He leaned forward, tapped some ashes into a navy-blue Agency mug.

"I'm not entirely sure. Except that this just doesn't smell like a Russian hit."

She put down her water bottle. "Then who?"

"Damned if I know. Because the only other possibilities I can think of are insane. And scarier. Such as: Maybe there's *another* mole here who tipped off the Russians about where Muller was being held. Or, even crazier: Maybe the *hitter himself* is somebody inside Langley. Maybe somebody from the Special Activities Division, who might have turned—"

She smacked her forehead. "I just remembered."

"What?"

"Something that FBI guy, Sully, said. Remember those guest names from the hotels? A man registered as 'R. Lasher,' another guy as 'B.J. Stoddard'?"

"What about them?"

"That second name. Grant, do you read thrillers?"

He scowled. "Little lady, I *live* thrillers. Why would I need to read them?"

"Well, I do. Love them, actually. And one of my favorite series is about this guy from Arkansas, named Billy Joe Stoddard."

"Okay. B.J. Stoddard—Billy Joe Stoddard. I see it. But so what?"

She leaned forward, hands on knees, holding his eyes.

"Billy Joe Stoddard is a former American military sniper."

He stared back at her. "Jesus Christ."

*

Garrett draped his suit jacket across the back of his desk chair, then called the cafeteria to send up a fresh pot of coffee and chicken salad sandwiches. After these were delivered, the pair ate in silence. Beyond the window, flesh-colored clouds faded to gray, as if life were bleeding from the sky. He didn't bother to turn on the office lamps. They sat in the gathering gloom as Garrett torched his way non-stop through the last of his Luckies. The periodic flare of his lighter cut deeper fissures into his stony features.

For an hour they discussed meanings, possibilities, ramifications. They didn't like their conclusions.

"This is certainly going to blow away the task force at tomorrow's meeting," she said at last.

"Not so fast."

The aging spymaster mashed out his last glowing butt in the mug, got up, moved to the window. He stood there, hands clasped behind his back, a dark gray silhouette against the lighter gray rectangle. He stared out past the parking lot, out somewhere into the shadow world surrounding the sprawling complex.

"Annie, we agree that we may have another mole. Somebody high enough in the pecking order here to know that we took Muller to Linden. Maybe somebody with the clout to send out someone else, maybe an SAD guy, to hit him. That would mean somebody right here on the seventh floor, right?"

"I suppose so."

He turned to face her. "So, do you want to alert this person that we're looking for him?"

She hadn't thought of that. She shook her head.

"If we're going to nail him, we can't go through normal channels."

She nodded. After a moment, she stood. Walked over to face him.

"You're right," she said. "I don't want to alert him. I want to be the one to *find* him."

"Oh?" The lights from the parking lot revealed a glimmer of amusement in his eyes.

"Look, sir. I did what you said. I slept on it. And I'd like to accept that transfer offer and work for you." She hesitated, then added: "But only if my job is to hunt that son of a bitch, sir."

He looked down at her and, incredibly, actually smiled again.

"Grant. Call me Grant."

SIX

WASHINGTON, D.C.
Monday, September 1, 1:25 p.m.

"*Hell-o*, Mr. Hunter!"

The pretty receptionist sang out the greeting as he entered the suite and approached her desk.

"And to you, Danika." He had to smile back, in spite of his foul mood.

She pushed her lips into a playful pout. "I was thinking you forgot the address here. What's it been? Two weeks?"

"I've been out of town. On assignment." A half-truth.

She rubbed her chin, mock-serious, appraising him. "Now, that's a bold fashion statement. Shades are nice, though."

Hunter removed his Oakley sunglasses and followed her gaze down to his reversible windbreaker. He now wore it garish-orange-side out, the side with the snarling black panther leaping across his chest. He'd meant it to be a point of focus, a distraction. It seemed to be working.

"Well, Danika, I guess I just don't have your taste and refinement."

She tsk-tsked. "What you need is *daily guidance* from a woman of taste and refinement." She leaned forward, the top two buttons of her pale-yellow silk blouse strategically unbuttoned. Whatever she wore underneath must have been spun from a single spool of gossamer.

"No woman of taste and refinement would possibly want me," he said, careful not to let his eyes drift south.

"Don't you be so sure, now." She grinned, settling back and rocking her swivel chair so that he could get a good look at the rest of her. "You'd be an interesting project."

"'Project.' How romantic. How's Tyrone?"

She beamed. "He just had his fourth birthday party on Saturday. Ten neighbor kids showed up. They had a ball, but I spent all afternoon yesterday getting chocolate cake and ice cream out of the carpet." She laughed. "That boy's something. You know, before he opened his presents, he insisted on reading all his birthday cards out loud. Didn't miss a single word."

"Such a bright little guy. Takes after a lovely lady I know. And how's Melvin treating that lady?"

She wrinkled her nose. "That man, he's the most infuriating— Oh, don't you get me started, now."

"Any mail?"

"Nothing in two weeks. Just one call, this morning—Mr. Bronowski. That's your editor, right?"

"So he believes."

"He asked you to return his call today, if possible. And your one-thirty arrived early. Mr. Diffendorfer." She tried to keep a straight face. "He's occupying office number eleven."

"All of it, I'm sure."

She laughed, the dimples deepening in her smooth coffee skin. "You bad."

"Danika, you have no idea."

*

Hunter left her and headed down the hallway of the suite. It was a perfect set-up: a "virtual office" lease arrangement from a national chain that provided him a downtown address, mail and call-forwarding, and time-shared space whenever he needed it. Anybody who wished to find Dylan Lee Hunter could try to contact him here. But anybody whom he did not wish to find him would reach a charming but unyielding stone wall named Danika Cheyenne Brown.

The conference room was empty, so he ducked in. From the thigh pocket of his cargo pants he pulled a cell phone. It was one of the many cheap, prepaid models that he bought anonymously, with cash, from drugstores throughout Maryland and Virginia, then dumped after brief use. He reinstalled the battery, thumbed the number for the managing editor's line at the *Capitol Inquirer*, then sat on the edge of the conference table as the call rang through.

"Bronowski." The voice was harsh and harried.

"Hunter."

"Finally! Dammit, Dylan, you're harder to get ahold of than a virgin on a first date. Don't you check your messages?"

"Annually."

"Very funny. Why the hell don't you give me a direct number where I can reach you?"

"I've told you. I don't share my personal contact information."

"But this is stupid. I'm your editor."

"Not stupid. What I write upsets people. Powerful, nasty people. I need to protect my privacy."

"What, you don't even trust *me* with your number?" Silence. "Well. I guess not, then. Dylan, this whole goddamned arrangement is weird. You realize we still haven't met, even though you've been working for me for a year?"

"Not for you, Bill. Not for anybody. I work for myself."

"Know something? Even for a writer, you're an uncooperative, egotistical, insufferably arrogant prick."

"Hey—who are you calling 'uncooperative'?"

Bronowski laughed in spite of himself. "Well, you're right about one thing. What you write does upset people. Wanna know who you've pissed off now?"

"No."

"The frickin' *governor of Maryland*, that's who. He was none too happy with your feature about his inmate commutation policy."

"Tough. I'm none too happy about his policy. Neither are the victims of all the thugs he's turned loose."

"Yeah, easy for you to say. You weren't the one who had to take the phone call last night."

"Did you give the guv my regards?"

Bronowski snorted. "Call wasn't from him. It was from Addison. Our dear publisher was not amused. You've simultaneously pissed off both a governor and our boss."

"*Your* boss. Remember?"

"Okay, *my* boss. Regardless. He wasn't pleased about having his Sunday golf game down in Lauderdale interrupted by a call from Annapolis. He got an earful, and last night he returned me the favor. Now he wants to know what I'm going to do about you."

He paused. Hunter said nothing.

"Don't you care what I'm going to do?" Bronowski demanded.

"No."

The editor dropped a cluster of f-bombs. Then stopped. Hunter heard a sigh.

"Dylan, what the hell *am* I gonna do with you? You know what kind of position you've stuck me in? Look, I'm not gonna lie to you. You're the best investigative reporter I've run into in a long time. I don't know where you got your training—but that's the point! I don't know a goddamned thing about you. Where you come from. Where you went to J school. Who you worked for before, where you live, whether you have a wife or kids or a dog—"

"Cat."

He snorted again. "How nice. You know, after you started freelancing with us, I Googled your name. I figured, your talent, a thousand links would come up. But nothing. Not *one*. You're like the Invisible Man."

Hunter was studying a wall photo of the Washington Monument. He spoke quietly. "My past doesn't matter to me. Why should it matter to you?"

Bronowski was silent a moment. "Okay. I won't pry anymore. Hell, I don't care if you flunked English or were Saddam Hussein's press secretary. Only thing that matters is, you keep delivering the goods. Right now your freelancing generates more mail than anything my staff here produces. Which reminds me—the circ audit just came in. I checked back. Since you started pitching me stories last year, we're up eight percent. That's while the competition is bleeding readers and advertisers."

"So what did you tell Addison?"

"*That's* what I told Addison."

"Good for you, Bill."

"Yeah, well, since you're gonna cost me my job any day now, you damned well better make your next piece worth my while."

It reminded him of why he had come here today. He felt his jaw tighten.

"It will be the talk of the town."

He removed the battery from the cell again as he left the conference room, then rounded a corner and opened the door to number eleven.

*

Freddie Diffendorfer perched like an enormous Buddha on the armless visitor's chair next to the desk. His legs were splayed far apart, unavoidable given the size of his thighs. An open box of a dozen assorted doughnuts covered much of the desktop—at least, it used to contain a dozen. Three were left.

He looked up at Hunter, a semi-circle of white pastry poised in his hand. His cheeks were streaked with powdered sugar.

"Hello, Dylan," he mumbled as he chewed.

"Hello, Wonk." Hunter barely managed to squeeze past him to get to the chair behind the desk. "What's this? Late lunch?"

His visitor shook his head. A crumb hiding somewhere in one of his chins came loose and landed on his lap. "No, I had lunch at McDonald's. But on my way through Dupont Circle, I observed that the hot light was on."

"I understand. Opportunity of a lifetime. So, do you need some time to finish up?"

"No, I shall save the rest for a snack later, thank you."

Hunter watched with a mixture of awe and disgust as Wonk crammed the remaining half of the doughnut into his mouth. Barely chewed before he swallowed. Then licked his fingers. Then clapped his fat palms together, raising a small white cloud. Then wiped his hands on stained, unpressed slacks the size of a circus tent.

Hunter closed the sticky lid of the box and slid it aside to clear space on the desk. "Now that you're amply, if not properly, fortified, what do you have for me?"

Wonk leaned forward; the chair's metal legs creaked ominously. He couldn't bend more than a few inches, but his chubby arms somehow managed to reach past the curve of his belly to grip the green canvas bag at his feet. He lifted it laboriously and balanced it precariously on what little remained of his lap. Then he poked around inside and extracted three thick manila folders, held together by rubber bands.

"Here they are," he said, panting from his heroic exertion. He pushed the folders across the desk. "All three files that you asked for."

They bore official Department of Corrections stamps and labels. Hunter whistled softly. "Amazing. How do you manage to get your hands on all this stuff?"

Wonk looked like a puppy tossed a treat. "Trade secrets. That is why I am the highly paid professional researcher, while you are the high-profile professional journalist." He hesitated. Hunter knew Wonk was waiting to be begged for details. Amused, he ignored him, and instead took his time removing the rubber bands.

"The *only* thing that I can tell you," Wonk blurted finally, "is that an administrative assistant in the DOC owed me a *huge* favor. But Dylan, please understand that you cannot keep these for more than two hours. I *must* get them back to her before the end of the business day."

"No problem. I'll look through the files and have Danika photocopy whatever I need. Did you find out anything else about these guys? The things I wanted to know specifically?"

"Certainly. I ran a Lexis-Nexis search." He pulled out another file folder and placed it on the desk. "You can keep that one."

"Just the headlines."

"You already know from the news reports on Friday that the two younger perpetrators were quietly transferred last month from the juvenile facility into what the DOC calls their 'reintegration track.' Specifically, that refers to a community-based vocational training program called Youth Horizons, headquartered in Alexandria. That is what caused that victims-rights group to become so upset. They are really on the warpath about it."

"What do you know about the program?"

"I am still compiling information. Supposedly, it accepts only nonviolent offenders, so I am not certain how these two qualified for admission. I can only surmise that because they were convicted as first-time offenders, the department's psychologists may think they constitute promising candidates for rehabilitation."

"But that doesn't make sense." Hunter took a slow breath, tried to keep his tone matter-of-fact. "What they did to...the Copeland woman. They couldn't have just decided one day, out of the blue, to assault a total stranger. Violently, sexually assault her. Predators start very young, with petty offenses. Then they escalate over the years. By the time they're caught and convicted for violent adult crimes, they've already got long rap sheets."

"And that is precisely what we see with these young men. The challenge for me was that their juvenile histories have been sealed."

"So tell me."

Wonk leaned back, delighted to expound. "My sources in various prosecutors' offices inform me that it happens all the time. Everyone wishes to grant a juvenile delinquent a 'second chance.' A police officer I know has labeled it the 'Father Flanagan myth'—in other words, 'There is no such thing as a really bad boy.' So, in most states, the legal system minimizes a child's crimes. They usually are not charged with the actual offense that they committed, but with something far less serious. In addition, their juvenile records are sealed, sometimes even expunged, so that the public can never discover their true backgrounds."

"I know. It's insane."

"Perhaps. But prevailing theory is that most youths eventually outgrow their impulsiveness and stupidity; therefore, if their criminal histories are kept confidential, the stigma of juvenile indiscretions will not follow them into adulthood."

"'Indiscretions'? Are you serious? We're not talking about stealing hubcaps, here. We're talking about violent rape. And probably a lot more—if only we had access to their juvie records."

His visitor folded his pudgy hands across the globe of his midsection and smiled serenely.

Hunter stared at him. "You didn't."

"Well, I was not permitted to take them *with* me. But a person who shall remain nameless did allow me to take a peek."

"And?"

Wonk removed his black-framed eyeglasses carefully; one temple clung to the frame by white adhesive tape. He gazed toward the ceiling and, in the staccato of bureaucratese, began to recite chapter and verse from memory. Hunter wondered for the hundredth time if his research assistant was some kind of savant.

"William Michael Bracey, a.k.a. 'Billy B.' Age twenty. That is the individual in the top file. Born in Arlington. Raised by a single mother. Three half-brothers by different fathers. The others turned out reasonably well. Not William, however. Truancy at age eleven. Shoplifting arrest at twelve. His mother paid restitution, so nothing happened to him. Associating with gangs since the age of fourteen. Left school before his sixteenth birthday. Arrested several months later for stealing a car, but the victim did not wish to prosecute. Suspected in a violent gang attack that put an honor-roll student in the ICU for weeks; but when the young man came out of the hospital, he either could not or would not identify his attackers.

"William and several other gang members then were arrested for the robbery of a corner grocery in the District, during which the owner was shot several times and later died. There were eyewitnesses to that incident, which is what led to the initial arrests. In fact, William— "

"Don't call him that. We're not on a chummy, first-name basis with this dirtbag."

Wonk blinked. "Sorry. Anyway...Mr. Bracey?" Seeing no objection, he continued. "Mr. Bracey was initially identified by both witnesses as the one who actually shot the store owner. In their initial statements to the police, they said the shooting was entirely unprovoked; the victim had already surrendered the contents of his cash register."

"Tell me about him."

"He was a gentleman in his forties, an immigrant from Japan, with a wife and four children. The *Post* clipping in the file reports that Mr. Takahashi was a beloved local resident, very hard-working. He was a huge baseball fan and quite active sponsoring Little League teams. His family and the community were absolutely devastated.... Is something wrong?"

"Nothing. Everything. Continue."

"When Mr. Bracey came to trial, neither of the eyewitnesses would testify. You'll see a note near the back of the file, written by an assistant prosecutor who comments about likely witness tampering. But without their testimony, there was no case."

Hunter didn't say anything.

"There is nothing further in his official record, not until the Copeland attack. Believe it or not, Dylan, that was his first criminal conviction."

Hunter flipped open the file folder. Bracey's photo was paper-clipped inside the cover.

Hollow cheeks, thin lips, dirty-blond hair, empty eyes the color of ice.

"So, that makes this piece of crap a 'first-time offender.'"

"As far as the courts and the DOC are concerned— yes. And that is probably why they admitted him into that rehabilitation program.... That is the extent of what I learned, but there is more detail in the file about his family, past associates, addresses, and so on."

"That should be helpful." Hunter took a last look at the photo, burning the image into his memory, then slapped the cover shut on it and slid the folder aside.

He flipped open the second file. Saw a broad, leering face with dark curly hair and a wispy mustache staring back at him from black shark's eyes.

"That next fellow is John Joseph Valenti. 'Jay-Jay' is his street name. Anyway, Joh— Mr. Valenti hails from a nice Philadelphia working-class family. His father is a heavy-machine operator. They all moved to the Virginia suburbs ten years ago, when the builder for whom his father works landed a major paving contract in the District."

Wonk paused. "Believe me, Dylan, this one is a real weirdo. I had a brief look at his social services report. When he was a child—a really young child—he liked to hurt animals. They caught him drowning a litter of kittens in a stream. Slowly, one at a time. He was only six years old. Can you imagine that?"

"Indeed I can. What else?"

"He was caught...exposing himself to other children."

"No need to be embarrassed, Wonk."

"Well, I just find that positively *creepy*. And not just to children. Later on, to a neighbor, an adult female living in the house next door. He stood naked in front of his window, doing...things. He was only ten."

"Precocious little bastard, wasn't he?"

Wonk winced. Dylan had forgotten that he didn't like raw language.

"Anyway, there was more of that sort of thing as Mr. Valenti entered his teen years. So he was placed in a psychological counseling program. However, there were no legal consequences when he stopped attending."

"Why am I not surprised."

"Things grew considerably more serious when he was accused of molesting a fourteen-year-old girl."

"His first known rape?"

The researcher's plump cheeks reddened. "Well. Not rape, exactly. It was—what do they call it?—a kind of a fetish assault."

"Say no more. I'll read the file. So, what happened to him?"

"Nothing happened. As with Mr. Bracey, nothing of consequence *ever* happened to this individual, either. In this case, the girl was too embarrassed to pursue charges. Or perhaps it was her parents who were embarrassed; the report is ambiguous on that point. But Mr. Valenti—he was fifteen at the time—was urged again to seek counseling. He did not."

"I am reeling in shocked incredulity. Anything else?"

"Only rumors. Very disturbing rumors, however. During the summer that he turned sixteen, Roberta Gifford, a college coed who lived on his block, went missing. Her body was discovered a week later, two miles away. She had been tortured...with various objects."

He fell silent for a moment. Hunter stared down at the shark's eyes in the photo.

"He was questioned about it," Wonk continued, "but nothing came of it. He had an alibi, and so the case is still listed as unsolved."

"What was his alibi?"

Wonk pointed at the third file folder. "Him."

Hunter looked at it. Drew it closer. Flipped it open to the photo.

Older man, early forties.

Strong face. Large, hawkish nose.

Longish, slack sandy hair, tossed back roughly.

Eyes like an overcast November sky.

Hunter tapped the face in the photo with his forefinger. "This," he said softly, "is the one who interests me most."

"Adrian Dalton Wulfe," Wonk announced. "He had hired Mr. Valenti to help him with home renovations at the time of the girl's disappearance. Or so he claimed to the authorities." Hunter didn't say anything, so he went on. "And not long afterward, he also hired Mr. Bracey to assist with the yard work. That, apparently, is how the trio met."

Hunter rocked slowly in his chair, holding the file folder level with his eyes.

"Dylan?"

Hunter remained silent. Rocked. Studied the photo before him.

"Why have you asked me to research these individuals?"

Silence.

"I gather that this is all about Dr. Copeland's suicide this weekend. Am I correct?"

Silence.

"I assume that you intend to write about it, then?"

He stopped rocking. Lowered the file folder and met his researcher's eyes.

"Among other things," said Dylan Lee Hunter.

SEVEN

ARLINGTON, VIRGINIA
Monday, September 1, 6:45 p.m.

They stood in the hallway of the funeral home. Susanne Copeland, clutching a tissue, stared at the open door of the parlor just ahead of them, on the left. Her eyes were red-rimmed and swollen; her dark-red, shoulder-length hair bordered a pretty face now lined with pain and fatigue, a face that seemed to have aged ten years in the past three days.

She breathed deeply. "Okay. I guess it's time."

Annie took her arm gently and they began to walk slowly toward the room, followed closely by about a dozen of Susie and Arthur Copeland's closest family members.

The funeral director who had greeted them at the building entrance had walked ahead, and now stood to one side of the parlor door. On the opposite side of the entrance a small, marble-topped table supported a spray of white roses, the visitors' register, and a golden pen. The director smiled sadly as they approached, his hands clasped before him like a maitre d'.

"Mrs. Copeland," he said, placing a consoling hand on her shoulder, "please take all the private time you need, and let me know if you require anything, anything at all."

She blinked and swallowed. "Thank you, Mr. Reynolds."

He moved to greet the relatives following them. She glanced at Annie, then at the door yawning open before her, as if it were the entrance to hell. Annie gave her arm a supportive squeeze. Susie took another deep breath, let it out, and they entered.

Soft string music was playing over the intercom—some banal, bittersweet religious hymn. She felt Susie's arm go rigid at the first sight of the casket. Illuminated by hidden lights, it rested in a recessed alcove to their right. It was a gleaming bronze thing lying on a bier draped in cascades of rich white fabric, surrounded by what seemed to be a solid wall of floral wreaths and displays. The sickly sweet scent of hundreds of flowers was almost overpowering.

Arthur Copeland's face and folded hands were visible against the white satin of the casket's open lid.

As they neared, Susie's pace slowed; then her steps became halting, each punctuated by a little gasp. The gasps became sobs. She sank onto the kneeling pad at the side of her husband's body.

"Oh God. Oh God. *Oh Arthur!*" she cried out, her voice high and thin. She reached out a trembling hand, touched his sleeve. "Oh Arthur!"

Annie found hot tears running down her own cheeks. She knelt beside her friend, wrapped her arm around her quaking shoulders. Susie turned into her, and they hugged and cried together.

Annie didn't know how long they remained like that. She became dully aware of the family members around them, sobbing and praying.

Eventually, Susie regained her composure. Annie helped the young widow to her feet and then stepped aside to let her lean in close to her husband's body.

It was a cliché, she thought, but Arthur looked as if he were merely asleep. The man's face, so anguished during the past two years, was serene now—unlined, unmarked, bespectacled, just as it had been earlier in his life. She had dreaded seeing his body tonight almost as much as Susie had; but she marveled now that there was no sign of the gunshot wound that he had inflicted to his own skull. Clearly, the funeral director was as skilled at his own reconstructive craft as Dr. Arthur Copeland had been at his. At just forty-four, Arthur had been one the nation's most renowned plastic surgeons.

"I can't believe it. I can't believe it," Susie said, shaking her head. "Oh, Arthur, *why?*" She touched his clasped hands, flinched a bit—the shock of the hard coldness, Annie realized—but then let her palm rest on them. She touched his wedding ring with her forefinger. Then she leaned her face over his, and began to talk to him so quietly that Annie could no longer hear what she was saying. As she spoke, she patted his loose blond strands.

Smoothed the lapel of his charcoal suit. Ran her palm down his tie.

Annie had to turn away. Each of her friend's tender gestures felt like the thrust of a knife.

At last, Susie bent and kissed Arthur's forehead. She straightened and hesitated, swaying slightly.

"Susie dear, would you like to sit down, now?"

Her cheeks were wet, her eyes dazed; she was beyond exhaustion. "Yes. Thanks. And maybe a little water."

They took seats in a line of chairs positioned not far from the casket. Annie fetched a paper cup of water from a cooler in the corner and found a box of tissues. The rest of the family members joined them, consoling each other quietly as they took their seats. After a while, the director entered, closing the door behind him, and approached.

"Mrs. Copeland, many of your friends and family have already gathered outside. Just let me know when you feel ready to receive them."

"I'm ready. Ready as I can be."

He smiled gently. "He obviously was a beloved man. We haven't had this many visitors here for a very long time."

He returned to open the door, and people began to file in slowly. They first approached the body to kneel and pray, then turned to the waiting family, most of whom stood to receive them. Annie stood beside Susie, who remained seated. The visitors, some in tears, leaned over to hug her and whisper the painfully trite things that people always struggle to say to those who have lost a loved one. Once past the receiving line, many stayed for a while, taking seats in the rows of padded folding chairs that filled the rest of the parlor.

Annie was not surprised to recognize and greet a number of those filing past her: They were co-workers from Langley. Susie was a long-time European analyst in the Directorate of Intelligence, and Arthur had worked for the Agency on a consulting basis for over a dozen years. She was astonished, though, when the CIA director himself entered, flanked by several top Agency people, including Grant Garrett. Nobody had told her about this. But then again, they wouldn't announce in advance the itinerary of such a group. She knew the two OS security officers flanking the door; many more would be outside, forming a protective cordon around the building and the armored limos.

The intelligence chiefs paused as a group at the casket for a solemn moment, then made their way to Susie. Each of them hugged her and expressed sadness that Annie knew was heartfelt. When they reached her, they greeted her quietly and by name. Garrett, his face stony, nodded, said a terse hello, and gave her a brief hug before moving on. After they passed through the receiving line, they wandered among the seated guests, exchanging handshakes with some of those whom they recognized and—she had to smile to herself—pointedly ignoring others whose identities it would be unwise to acknowledge.

Susie stared at them in wonder. "I never knew how many friends we had there."

Annie leaned close to her ear. "Whatever its faults, you can say this for Langley: It's family."

Her eyes roamed the endless line still wending its way into the parlor. Then rested on a man framed in the doorway.

He was not exceptionally tall, but his lean physique made him look so. He had an arresting face: dark, curly hair and craggy features—a somewhat broad nose, gaunt cheeks, and eyes that moved constantly and seemed to be taking in everything. Upon entering, he glanced at the two OS men at the door. Then his eyes wandered and rested on the Agency bosses circulating among the seated visitors. She saw or imagined some fleeting expression cross his face before he turned and moved toward the casket.

Susie asked her for another cup of water, so she headed back to the water cooler. As she returned, she noticed that the man was standing over Arthur Copeland's body. He did not kneel; he simply remained there a long time, motionless, hands jammed in the pockets of his long, dark cloth coat. Finally, he turned away to join the procession approaching the receiving line. His glance met hers and she looked away quickly, as if she'd been caught.

When the man reached Susie, he leaned over and took her hand in both of his.

"Mrs. Copeland," he said in a soft baritone, "I join your husband's many friends and admirers in sharing your grief."

"Thank you so much.... Forgive me, Arthur knew so many people. You are—?"

"I'm sorry. Dylan Hunter."

"And how did you know my husband, Mr. Hunter?"

He hesitated, just an instant. "I met him in a professional capacity."

"You're a doctor, then?.... Oh!" She glanced knowingly toward the CIA chiefs, now heading toward the exit. "I think I understand—"

"I'm a journalist, you see," he interrupted smoothly, "and your husband was helpful to me, once. With some medical research. It was for an important story that I was working on. I regret that I never had the opportunity to tell him just how grateful I was. I came by to pay my respects to him and to you. He was a—" The man paused. "He was someone I can't forget."

"Thank you. It's so kind of you to tell me that. Arthur touched so many people."

He smiled at that. He lifted Susie's hand gently in both of his and kissed it.

Then he turned to her.

"Hello. Dylan Hunter. I'm so terribly sorry for your loss."

His eyes were hazel-green and locked onto hers. She suddenly felt awkward.

"Actually, I'm just a friend. Of Susie's. I mean—of course, it is a loss. A great loss to all of us. Thank you."

Her words felt clumsy, but he nodded, still holding her eyes. She suddenly felt aware of her body. Found her hand moving instinctively toward her hair before she caught herself and extended it to him instead.

He took her hand. His was big and warm and strong. He held hers and he held her eyes.

Then he released her hand and her eyes and was gone.

She watched his receding figure as he strode toward the exit. He wore black, low-cut boots. His long, loose cloth coat tapered down from his shoulders, falling cape-like behind him.

ANNANDALE, VIRGINIA
Tuesday, September 2, 11:35 a.m.

The slow procession of cars, led by the hearse and the black limos bearing the family members, rolled down the narrow, meandering lane through the cemetery. It pulled up and stopped beside a broad, open-sided tent. Not far away, beneath a stand of several weeping willows, a pile of rich brown earth amid the gray headstones marked Arthur Copeland's final resting place.

Annie parked the Accord she'd taken from the motor pool, then walked across the spongy grass to the tent. Wooden folding chairs awaited the party, as did the minister. She remained just outside the tent. It was a beautiful early fall day—temperature in the seventies, light breeze, not a cloud in the sky. Birds twittered somewhere off in the trees.

She thought about the church service. The Copelands were not religious, but Arthur's siblings had converted from Judaism to Christianity, so for their sake Susie had allowed the service to be held at a local Methodist church. It had been a difficult hour. The fact that Arthur died by his own hand was not easy to square with church teachings. But the pastor did his best to skirt that issue and focus instead on all the good he had done for so many people during his short life.

The pallbearers removed the casket from the hearse and wheeled it to the front of the tent. There were about forty people here, mostly family. She was surprised to see Grant Garrett standing off by himself, on the other side of the tent. She had no idea that he knew the Copelands that well.

The burial service was brief, about ten minutes. The custom at this cemetery was not to lower the casket into the grave while the family was present; instead, it would remain under the tent with the cemetery workers, for burial a little later. After the pastor gave his final blessing, Susie stood first, approached the casket, kissed it, and left a red rose on top. Then she left. The rest of the family filed by silently, touching the casket as they passed, many crying softly.

Annie caught up with her a few moments later, as she neared her limo. "How are you managing, girlfriend?"

"Okay, I guess. For now."

"Do you want to ride with your family, or would you like me to give you a lift?"

"That's a great idea. I need to get away from them for a few minutes."

They got in Annie's car, then followed the line of cars to leave. The lane continued a little farther into the cemetery, then curled around and doubled back on itself toward the exit.

As they drew abreast of the tent, Susie gazed for the last time at her husband's casket.

"Annie—who's that?"

She slowed the car. She had time only for a brief glimpse.

A dark-haired man in a gray suit stood beneath the tent, his back toward them. His hand rested on Arthur Copeland's casket.

"I'm not sure."

EIGHT

BETHESDA, MARYLAND
Friday, September 5, 9:45 a.m.

"*Maaooww.*"

"Not now."

"*Maaaaaooooww.*"

"Let me finish this."

"*Mrrraaaaaaoooooow.*"

Hunter sighed, folded the newspaper and tossed it aside on his small dining table. "Yeah, yeah. I'm coming." He took another sip of coffee from an oversized brown ceramic mug.

Luna was strutting back and forth across the kitchen entranceway like a furry black-and-white sentry. Then she stopped to glare at him impatiently.

He got up, cinched tight the belt on his white terrycloth bathrobe, and padded in his bare feet past her into the kitchen. She pranced after him eagerly, her tail standing straight up like a wobbly periscope. He pulled off the lid of a large tin can he kept on the floor beside the refrigerator. The fishy scent assaulted his nostrils. He grabbed a handful of the dry food and dumped it into her empty metal dish.

"There. Crunchies."

She sniffed the contents, then looked up at him expectantly. The black patch of fur over one eye made her look like a feline pirate.

"Maaaaoow."

He sighed again and bent to pet her. At that, she happily plunged her face into the brown spirals and stars. His petting elicited a combination of contented purring, crunching, and snuffling noises.

"Okay. You've eaten. I've pet you. Now let me alone."

He returned to his coffee and the morning *Inquirer* and finished reading his article. To his inner ear, as he thought of it, his writing sounded different in newsprint than on the computer screen.

"All right. Listen up and tell me what you think of this:

> *"What happened in the Copeland case is not rare. Today, eighty to ninety percent of all convictions stem from pre-trial guilty pleas, invariably to reduced charges, negotiated between prosecutors and defense attorneys, and rubber-stamped by judges. These cynical*

maneuvers let criminals evade the full penalties of their crimes; permit lazy prosecutors to enhance their political careers by boasting of high 'conviction rates'; let defense attorneys quickly handle a large number of clients (and collect a large number of fees) without having to prepare for trial; and help harried judges clear clogged court calendars and jammed jails.

"In short, plea-bargaining is the triumph of expediency over justice. Everyone leaves the courtroom smiling—except for crime victims like Susanne and Arthur Copeland. Ignored by all during the proceedings, they can only look on in shocked disbelief. And too often, at the end of their day in court, they discover that they have been mugged again."

He lowered the paper, looked at the cat.

In the kitchen entranceway, Luna raised her front paw and started to lick it.

"Once again you fail to appreciate the nuances of literary craftsmanship."

He poured himself another mug of coffee from his four-cup pot and took it into the bathroom. While he showered, he thought of Arthur Copeland's funeral.

He dressed and stepped out onto his bedroom balcony. It overlooked the courtyard pool area inside the apartment complex. Because it was past Labor Day, it was deserted down there now. A green tarp covered the pool. White plastic reclining chairs were folded up against the walls. He glanced at the sky. Overcast. The weather guy had said today's outlook was uncertain.

For sure.

He came back in, closed the sliding glass door, went into his small den. Removed the false front below the bottom shelf of his wooden bookcase, reached in, and extracted a small pile of file folders. He tossed them onto his computer desk and slid into his swivel chair.

The first three files were copies of the ones Wonk had obtained. He spread them apart.

Bracey. Valenti. Wulfe.

He rocked back, closed his eyes, and could still see their faces.

You can still walk away, you know.

He remembered the faces of Susanne and Arthur Copeland.

He opened his eyes. Saw his reflection in the blank gray of his computer screen.

No. You can't.

You've never been able to walk away.

He moved the three folders aside and opened another. It contained over a dozen sheets, each listing a name and related biographical data. He studied them for a while, then pulled out five.

Something touched his leg. The cat had followed him into the den and now was stropping back and forth across his shins.

He reached down, picked her up, put her on his lap. Started to scratch her head.

"So, what do you say, Luna?"

She purred and closed her eyes while he rocked and scratched.

"It would be a huge step for us, you know. If we do this, there will be no turning back. Ever."

She rubbed her cheek against his stomach.

"So you're okay with this."

She raised her face, looked at him, and blinked.

"But this time Dylan Lee Hunter can't go it alone. It'll have to be a team effort."

He turned the biographical sheets toward the cat and fanned them out. Five names. For all the specialized roles. Planning, logistical support, intelligence, infiltration, and field operations.

"What do you think of these five characters?"

She jumped down from his lap and trotted away, back toward her bowl.

"Nice vote of confidence."

CONNOR'S POINT
MARYLAND'S EASTERN SHORE
Friday, September 5, 9:35 p.m.

Victor Edward Rostand had come home late this afternoon after a ten-day business trip. That's what he told his neighbors, Jim and Billie Rutherford, when they saw him changing a dead light bulb outside his three-car garage and walked over to say hello. Vic explained that he was only stopping in for a few hours to pay some bills and check on things. He had to leave again later that night.

Vic had moved into the brick-faced Colonial on Connor's Point a couple of years earlier. His marketing consulting took him out of town a lot. Business must have been good, Jim and Billie figured, because the man sure liked his toys. He kept three vehicles in the garage: a blue Honda CR-V, a black Ford E-Series SUV van, and his latest: a sweet new Honda motorcycle. He had a boat tied up in his slip at the end of the street—a nice 28-foot Bayliner 285 Cruiser. There was a rumor that he also kept a small plane over at the Kent Island airport, too, but Vic laughed it off when they asked him about it.

If Vic had money, he certainly didn't put on airs about it. He dressed casually, shaved sporadically, bought Girl Scout cookies outside the local supermarkets, ate at unpretentious neighborhood restaurants, and put in brief appearances at cookouts on the Point during the summer, where he cooked up some mean chili. Most of the time, he even cut his own grass with an old-fashioned push-type lawn mower. About the only quirky thing about him was that he wore tinted glasses day and night, because he said his eyes—which Billie guessed might be "a rich, coffee brown"—were overly sensitive to light.

Just a regular nice guy.

Like a few of the other neighbors, Jim and Billie had tried to socialize with him a bit more. He accepted a dinner invitation once, and they had a nice time. Vic brought a couple of bottles, a Syrah and a Chenin Blanc, and mentioned some of his foreign travels to places they'd never been, like Dubai and Cairo. Jim asked him about marketing, and Vic talked a bit about "positioning" and "branding," but stopped after a short time because, he said, he didn't want to bore them. Billie asked if he managed to do any dating. Vic smiled and replied that he was in a long-distance relationship with a business woman in Chicago, but their schedules weren't very compatible, so he doubted it would last much longer. He complained that his work schedule just didn't allow much time for relationships, either social or romantic.

At nine-thirty this evening, Billie sent Jim out to the Safeway to pick up some eggs and half-and-half for breakfast. Backing out of the driveway, he saw that Vic's garage lights were on and he was putting some boxes in the open back doors of his Ford van. Jim shook his head. He'd never seen a guy stay so busy. He tapped his horn as he drove off.

*

He set the box down in the bed of the van, then heard a horn beep. He looked back to see Jim Rutherford's car pulling away. He waved casually at the departing vehicle, closed the rear doors of the Ford, then went to the wall switch and lowered the garage door. For the next few minutes, he would need privacy.

He left the garage by its back door. He paused a moment in the darkness to savor the moonlight shimmering on the water of Connor's Creek behind the house. A few Canada geese were honking out there in the marsh somewhere. Or was it the trumpeter swans? He wasn't sure; he just didn't spend enough time out here, much as he loved the place.

He moved behind a large pine near the house and over to the wooden shed. He opened the padlock and entered, closing the door behind him. By feel, he found and pulled a drawstring; a bare bulb lit the interior. He slid the door bolt, locking it from the inside.

The shed contained nothing but heaps of crumbling storage boxes. They were crammed with old file folders containing billing statements to a variety of companies. None of the paperwork meant anything; he'd retrieved it all from a Dumpster two years ago. He moved aside a stack of the boxes, one by one, clearing a space on the floor. You had to look very closely to see the thin slit across the dusty floorboards. He stuck a screwdriver into the crack, levered it up, grabbed the edge of the hinged trap door, and hoisted it the rest of the way open.

He made his way carefully down a crude set of wooden stairs into a small underground room with concrete walls and floors. He pulled another drawstring down there, and a second, brighter bulb illuminated his armory.

He drew two sheathed combat knives, one large, one small, from a leather-lined wooden case and placed them on a wide bench. He opened a cabinet and selected several makes of handguns and corresponding suppressors and ammo. He assembled an array of electronic equipment, burglary tools, and other useful items. These items he wrapped carefully in lint-free cloths and placed in a couple of olive-green duffle bags. Shouldering them, he turned out the light, climbed from the room, and replaced the trap door and the boxes over it. He left the shed as he had come and re-entered the garage.

He glanced at his watch. The timetable still allowed him plenty of time to get to D.C. and make the weapons transfer to the operations vehicle, so that the rest of the plan could proceed on schedule.

Ten minutes later, he backed the black Ford van out of the garage.

*

Safeway didn't have the small size of half-and-half, so Jim had to go another mile to the Acme. By the time he returned home, he noticed that all the lights were off at Vic's place.

That guy. Never gives it a rest. Always up to something.

NINE

ALEXANDRIA, VIRGINIA
Saturday, September 6, 11:27 p.m.

The bearded man parked his nondescript old Chevy Metro hatchback on a side street just a couple of blocks from the Braddock Road Metro Station. Then he settled in for what would likely be several hours of surveillance outside the target's place.

The Chevy was cramped and uncomfortable, even with the seat pushed back. But so was the motel room he'd stayed in down on Route 1 the night before. The stained, peeling wallpaper, once beige, looked as if it had acquired a case of jaundice over the decades. The cheap nightstands and bathroom sink were criss-crossed with brown scars from unattended cigarettes, and he had to work under the light of the room's single functional lamp. One glance in the bathroom convinced him to pass on taking a shower, just as a look at the carpet convinced him to keep his sneakers on.

He'd had no choice, really. He needed a base nearby to run this op, but it had to be the sort of place where he could pay cash and not have to show a credit card or his New York driver's license. It was out of the question to let the clerk see the name Shane Michael Stone—however unlikely it was that anyone would track him to a place like that. So he peeled off fifty-five bucks for two nights and signed in, using an alias that appealed to his sense of irony.

It had been very late when he arrived at the motel. But rather than get some sleep, he spent the remaining hours before dawn conducting a recon of this neighborhood. When he returned to his room, he covered the stained bed cover with newspapers before lying down fully dressed. He woke in the late afternoon, grabbed a bite at a Wendy's up the highway, then returned to the motel to check his gear and mentally walk through the plan, which included contingency options at every stage.

After that, he dressed for the job with clothes from one of the two duffle bags delivered by the van from Maryland. Then he looked himself over in the cracked, full-length mirror barely attached to the bathroom door.

Scruffy-looking guy. Ragged red hair and beard, oversized blue pullover sweater, baggy jeans, Orioles baseball cap. Where he was headed, he'd fit right in.

As always, he was ultra-careful about leaving any prints behind. Before he left the room for the last time, he wiped down the place. Which was more than he could say for the cleaning staff, such as it was. He also carefully folded the newspapers covering the bed and took them with him....

He'd picked this place to park because it faced the street spur that extended straight back into the courtyard of the project, where it dead-ended a short distance away at a parking lot. That was the only route in, and from here he had a clear view of everyone who entered or left. It was a pretty safe spot, too. Though the cops patrolled regularly, his car was off the main street they mainly used, and it was shadowed from the nearest street light by a tree. In addition, the one upgrade he'd given the Chevy was extra-dark tinted windows. Even the cops were unlikely to spot him sitting inside.

Last night, the target had returned home to the projects with another guy about three a.m. They'd entered the courtyard in a battered silver Honda Civic, pulled into the lot and parked. He watched them through the latest thing in monocular night-vision scopes: the Xenonics SuperVision Digital Viewing System. When the pair emerged from the car about fifty yards away and stood chatting, he was able to zoom in and identify his target in a black-and-white, high-definition image. After a few minutes, they did a fist-bumping thing and parted company. He watched the guy unlock and enter a door in a brick row house on the right, not far from the street entrance to the complex.

Tonight, a bit earlier, he'd walked past the complex entrance and didn't see the target's car parked in the lot. This being a Saturday night, he figured he was in for another long wait. But now, just before midnight, he watched the Civic turn into the cul-de-sac and head back into an empty parking space. He picked up the SuperVision scope from his passenger seat and confirmed that the driver was his man. This time the target was alone; he crossed in the direction of the door to his apartment unit and disappeared inside.

He checked his watch. Decided to give it two hours.

Settled back in his seat and waited.

*

At two a.m. he reached into a blue gym bag on the passenger side floor. Pulled out a black Sig Sauer P229 with a threaded barrel. From a side pocket of the bag he drew an Impuls IIA sound suppressor. Screwed it onto the end of the barrel.

He checked the magazine once again. It held thirteen 147-grain Remington Golden Saber hollowpoints—a subsonic round that would further reduce the noise of a gunshot. Then he replaced the gun in the gym bag. He put on his baseball cap. Tugged the brim down over his eyes. Pulled on a pair of black latex gloves.

He exited the car, carrying the gym bag and leaving the driver's side door unlocked. He crossed the deserted main street in front of him, making sure no cop cars were in sight. He knew from his previous recon there were no security cameras to worry about, but he kept his head down to shade his face from the street lights.

He looked around the courtyard as he stepped quietly into the silent cul-de-sac. The shabby buildings were featureless three-story brick. Only a couple of lighted windows gave evidence that anyone lived here.

The buildings on his left were divided into tiny yards by three-foot metal fences—public housing's illusion of private property. A maze of clotheslines strung across these barren plots, competing for space with plastic chairs, plastic toys, and plastic 55-gallon garbage cans, which stood at parade rest along the curb.

The buildings on his right were different. They were very narrow brick row houses. Their small front yards were set off from the street by a brick wall. It was four feet high, with narrow openings for sidewalks that led back to each building entrance. He scanned the walls of the buildings; no windows were lit.

When he reached the third opening in the wall, he entered the yard and walked without hesitation to the door. He reached into the gym bag and withdrew what looked like a hand-held electric drill. Illuminated from behind by a street light, he perused the locks. One was on the doorknob; the other, in the door itself, would be a dead bolt. Standard stuff, no big deal. He selected one of the metal picks he'd taped to the top of the device and pushed it into the barrel. Then he inserted the pick into the doorknob lock and pulled the trigger, keeping his other hand wrapped around the knob to minimize rattling. There was a low whirring noise as the electronic pick vibrated at high speed, moving the tumblers in the lock. In a few seconds, the knob turned freely in his hand.

He waited. No response from inside the house. No barking dog, no creaking stairs, no lights. His previous recon gave no indication of a dog or someone living with the target, but you never know.

He selected another pick and repeated the process on the deadbolt. This time when he turned the knob and pushed, the door cracked open.

He paused to listen for another full minute. Nothing.

He returned the electronic lock pick to the bag, but when his right hand emerged this time, it held the Sig. He reached in with his left and pulled out the night-vision scope. Flipped it on.

Leaving the gym bag outside, he slowly swung open the door, applying upward pressure on the knob to minimize squeaking from the hinges.

*

He was a rock star and everyone was cheering and he screamed into the mike and leaped around the stage naked between the bass and lead guitars and the lights were flashing on his face and now he was playing the lead guitar greasy fast licks up and down the frets and everyone was chanting his name now he was the drummer and hot chicks ripping off their clothes around him and the lights flashing in his eyes the girls dancing naked in the lights and calling his name they were saying hello William grabbing his arm William hello William wake up lights flashing in his eyes William....

"Hello, William."

Light flashing into his closed eyes. Somebody had his arm in an iron grip. Then jerked him over roughly, onto his back.

"Huh?" He blinked, dazzled by the light in his eyes.

"Back to the land of the living. At least, for about another minute."

He felt a jolt of panic.

"Who the hell are you?" he yelled, trying to see the face behind the blinding flashlight.

Without warning, a hand shot forward, grabbed his hair and yanked hard, pulling him up to a sitting position.

His hair was released but a split second later a tremendous blow crashed across his face, snapping his head to the side. He found himself on his back again, everything spinning, his left cheek and jaw numb.

"Let me introduce myself. I'm a messenger, William," the voice said softly. "Just a fellow here to deliver a message from some people you know."

The blinding light moved away from his eyes, darted around the walls of the dark room. He heard movement.

"Hell you talkin' 'bout, man?" he mumbled, fiery pain now burning his cheek and mouth.

The overhead light to his room flared to life.

He squinted. Next to the light switch at the door, a bearded guy in a baseball cap. Black gloves. Sticking a thin flashlight into his belt.

"I'm a messenger from your victims, William."

He sat up, rubbing his jaw. "Whaddya mean? Don't know 'bout any—"

"Susanne Copeland." The voice was low, quiet, coldly matter-of-fact.

He felt something drop inside his stomach.

The man moved toward him. "How could you forget Susanne, William?"

He shuddered, suddenly unable to speak.

"And then there's Arthur Copeland." The man stopped at the foot of the bed. Looked down at him.

Something in his hand, down along his leg.

William Bracey shuddered.

"I'm also here to deliver a message from Yoshiro Takahashi. Oh, I see you remember him, too. Yet you told the court you weren't even there. Tell me something, William: What do you suppose Mr. Takahashi was feeling when you pointed your .357 magnum at him?"

"*I didn't!*"

"You're lying, William."

The man leaned over him and raised his hand.

A gun with a long, fat barrel.

"No! I didn't—"

"You did." The man glanced down. Shook his head. "And you just peed your pants, William."

"Please!" he whispered, staring into the black hole of the sound suppressor. "Honest to God no I didn't I didn't—"

"And now the one-word message from your victims, William: *Goodbye.*"

Bright light flashed in his eyes again.

Just once.

*

He stood with the gun in his hand, barrel pointing toward the floor.

Stared at the skinny young punk on the rumpled bed. A pool of crimson expanded in a circle around his shattered skull.

He watched the glassy expression fix in William Bracey's eyes.

He felt drained. He didn't enjoy taking a human life. Never had. Even though it was his business.

But sometimes, there is no other way.

He listened once more. Silence. Turned out the light, pulled aside the window shade, looked outside. No lights. No movement. He cleared his weapon, shoved the magazine into his back pocket. Unscrewed the suppressor, stuck it into his front pocket. Jammed the Sig into his belt behind his back. Pulled his sweater down over it.

And sometimes, a death can even do some good.

He approached the body and went through with the rest of the plan.

PART II

"He who refuses what is just, gives up everything to him who is armed."

—Lucanus (Marcus Annaeus Lucan)
Pharsalia (I, 348)

TEN

**CLAIBOURNE CORRECTIONAL FACILITY
CLAIBOURNE, VIRGINIA
Monday, September 8, 9:40 a.m.**

"So, tell me again why I'm doing this."

Susie Copeland spoke so softly that it seemed she was talking to herself. Annie took her eyes off the road long enough to flash a supportive smile.

From the moment Susie had gotten into the car, Annie was concerned about how fragile she looked. She sat stiffly upright in the passenger seat, hands clutched in her lap. No makeup masked the pallor of her skin. Her wine-red hair, every strand, was pulled back and clipped tight behind her head, emphasizing the new sharpness of her cheekbones. She had chosen to wear a conservative navy pantsuit—loose now, given the weight she'd so quickly lost—and Annie also noticed that she kept its jacket buttoned closed, even in here.

"Susie, I never told you to meet with him in the first place. It was your idea. You can still call this whole thing off right now."

Her companion shook her head. "No. I'm going through with this."

They had turned off Interstate 95 some time ago, heading west on a two-lane road that crossed miles of barren fields and bleak villages. The sky was a soiled sheet, and darkening clouds clung to the basin rim of the western horizon, like dirty suds.

"Do you really think he asked for this meeting because he's feeling remorse now?" Annie asked. "Is that what you're hoping for?"

"No. Not really. But whatever he's feeling—that's not the point. This is for *me*. I need to face him."

"Okay. I'm just not sure I understand why."

Susie unclenched her hands, inspected the ragged edges of her unpolished nails. "I'm not really sure, either. I guess it's about control. About taking back control. From *him*." Her voice had an edge now. "When he—when they had me—there was nothing I could do. I was powerless. Nothing I said mattered to them. I begged them to stop. But they just slapped me and told me to shut up."

Susie lifted her eyes toward the road ahead; they appeared to be unfocused—or perhaps focused on things Annie didn't want to imagine. Her voice now was very soft.

"I thought I was going to die. I was sure they were going to kill us. I—" She stopped. "Well, I guess they did kill Arthur that night. It just took us both a while to realize it."

"Susie—"

"No. I'm okay. I guess I was better able to deal with it than he could. Arthur could never forgive himself. For what they did to me. For having to watch and not being able to do anything about it. He felt so helpless. So *worthless*." She lowered her head. "God, I miss him."

"I just wish that there was something I could do for you."

"Oh, Annie, you are. You've been here for me through all this. It means so much that you'd take today off just to be with me. I couldn't possibly do this without you being here."

Annie reached out, touched the clenched hands. The skin felt cold and dry. Susie looked away, blinking.

There was nothing to say for a while.

When Susie spoke again, it was to change the subject. "So. How's that mysterious project you've been working on, what, six months now?"

"To be honest, not so great."

Silence.

"I know: If you told me, you'd have to kill me."

Annie chuckled. "Not quite. Let's just say it's been frustrating. I haven't been able to crack a puzzle we've been working on since I got there. We've been testing a theory that would explain—something that otherwise just doesn't make any sense. I've been running down leads, but finding nothing but dead ends. Grant is really good about it, he's a patient guy. But we're both going a bit nuts."

"I could tell that whatever it is has been worrying you. Overall, though, do you like your new gig in DCS?"

"Sure do. Grant's great to work for. He's— Oh, we're here."

*

They had crested a rise in the road, and a small community appeared before them, about a mile away. On this, its eastern side, they were approaching what looked like an industrial park with a water tower and a vast spread of lawn among the buildings. But as they got closer, the reflected glint of the sun raced along the razor wire atop the concentric fences that circled the compound, sparking like twin strings of fireworks.

Annie slowed as they came to an access road that ran from the complex out to the highway. At the intersection stood a sign, raised gray metal letters embedded in a red-brick wall:

Claibourne Correctional Center
Virginia Department of Corrections

Incongruously, a colorful, well-tended bed of flowers surrounded the base of the sign.

Turning onto the road, Annie sensed the sudden tension in her companion. She drove on toward a parking lot in front of a single-story, tan-brick building whose windowless face peeked from behind the security fence. The flags of the United States and the Commonwealth of Virginia stirred on tall poles on either side of the entrance.

She pulled into a diagonal parking spot marked for visitors and turned off the ignition. She heard a long hiss of expelled breath beside her.

"You okay, girlfriend?"

Susie opened her eyes. "Yes." She unsnapped her seat belt. "Let's do this."

Remembering to leave their purses locked in the car, they got out into the harsh sunlight. The pinging sound of the ropes bouncing against the metal flagpoles tolled in the chilly breeze. They walked toward the shadow of the covered entranceway.

A man sat on a low wall beside the front door. He wore sunglasses, a gray tweed jacket, gray cord slacks, and fashionably low-cut black boots. He stood as they approached, as if he'd been waiting for them.

"Hello again, Susanne." He removed his sunglasses and smiled. "Dylan Hunter."

"Oh!" Susie said. "You were at the funeral home. And you wrote that article in the *Inquirer* yesterday."

"I did. I hope it didn't upset you in any way. That's the last thing I would want."

"No, not at all," she said, extending her hand. "I'm grateful for what you said. I just can't tell you *how* grateful, Dylan."

"I'm relieved to hear that." He turned toward Annie.

"You remember my friend, Annie Woods."

The eyes—in the sun, an even-more-intense hazel green.

"I certainly do. We meet again—is it Mrs. Woods?"

"Not Mrs. And it's Annie." She offered her hand. His—warm, strong, just as she remembered. She felt rattled again. "That article of yours—I read it, too. I was surprised to see your name on it." Wrong thing to say. "I mean, surprised to see your name so soon after we met. What you wrote—it was infuriating."

"That's for sure," Susie said. "I had no idea those two had juvenile records that horrible. That's not what the prosecutor told me. He said they had no prior convictions."

"'Convictions' don't tell the whole story," he said, still holding Annie's eyes. And hand. He seemed to realize it at the same time she did. He released it and turned to Susie.

"I never would have agreed to those plea deals if I'd known any of that," she continued. She nodded toward the doors. "I only wish I could find out more about *him*."

"Me too," he said. "I heard about your meeting him here today and thought I might tag along. Maybe interview him. But it appears that the Department of Corrections isn't as pleased with my article as you are."

"What do you mean?"

"I was just in there," he said, hooking his thumb toward the door. "They won't let me back inside. The Corrections Commissioner sent out an email last night to all his state prison wardens, telling them to refuse any of my future interview requests."

"That's outrageous!"

"I agree, Susanne. So, I gave them fair warning."

"What did you say?"

"I said I don't deal well with rejection."

They laughed. Annie liked his crooked little smile. His stomach looked tight and flat beneath the dark gray shirt, and his shoulders filled the jacket. A few strands of gray caught the sun at his temples.

"Anyway, some DOC muckamucks are waiting for you. Because of the bad press, they seem anxious to make you happy."

"You mean because of your article. Well, if that's the case, then maybe I can change their minds about keeping you out." Susie turned and marched through the automatic doors.

He looked at Annie, a hint of amusement in his eyes. "After you," he said, sweeping his open palm toward the entrance.

She smiled and went in ahead of him.

Felt his eyes on her as she walked.

*

For the next ten minutes, they argued it out in the lobby with the warden, his deputy superintendent, and the security staff's shift supervisor. It took an ultimatum from Susie—a threat to leave and go to the news media—before the warden relented and a compromise was reached. Hunter would not be allowed to interview Adrian Wulfe or to remain in the same room with Annie and Susie during their meeting; however, he would be permitted to watch the proceedings from behind the glass wall of a side observation room, take notes, and then write about their meeting, if he wished.

After being signed in and issued badges, they passed through the metal detector, underwent a pat-down from corrections officers, then were led through a maze of security checkpoints. Every time they reached a door, their escort signaled a guard who buzzed them into a waiting chamber; the door behind them locked shut; then another door was unlocked in front of them, allowing them to proceed.

Hunter had been through this drill two months ago, at a prison in another state, while researching a story about frivolous inmate lawsuits. "Nothing cheap here," his young guide had boasted then, eager to show off the lavish array of inmate amenities. Well-stocked law libraries. A modern gym loaded with expensive workout machines. Infirmaries providing free medical and dental care. A building housing inmate organizations, including a drama club that toured local colleges. A music room crammed with electric guitars, keyboards, drums, and amplifiers. In-cell TVs with access to premium cable channels, for inmates willing to pay for them. Classrooms where thugs could take college courses from teachers moonlighting from local campuses.

"What does this prison offer by way of punishment?" he had asked the guide.

The kid frowned and replied: "People are sent here *as* punishment. They're not sent here *for* punishment."

So, some predator rapes a woman. His taxpaying victim then pays to house him where he can build his body to be even stronger and more intimidating. Where he can fuel his fantasies with cable-TV porn. Where he learns how to file lawsuits against the very system that's pampering him....

Today's escort stopped outside a final door. As they were waiting to be buzzed through, Hunter noticed a memo on a nearby bulletin board. It was signed by Claibourne's policy coordinator:

> *A third softball field will be made in the West Field in order to allow more inmates to play softball. The horseshoe pits will be temporarily relocated near the miniature golf course. The bocce area will be relocated at the site of the new gym. And the soccer field will be relocated to the East Field behind the softball field.*

The escort directed Hunter into a narrow, sterile cinderblock room. It was painted cold white and lit by fluorescent tubes in the ceiling. A row of blue plastic chairs lined one wall. They faced a tinted observation window that ran the full length of the room, made of one-way shatterproof glass. It allowed him to see into the next room without being seen.

The adjoining room was divided into two facing cubicles by a waist-high cinderblock wall, topped by its own thick window. It was the kind of window you see at the teller counters in banks—laminated glass, embedded with a circular speaking grill. On either side of the window, stainless-steel surfaces served as desktops; beneath them twin metal chairs were bolted to the floor. This allowed pairs of seated people to converse through the window grill.

For his part, Hunter could roam the full length of his observation room to watch the occupants in either of the two cubicles. Though soundproof, their ceilings were miked; a speaker in his room let him listen in on the conversations.

After a moment, the door opened at the far end of the cubicle to his left. Annie Woods entered first, leading a nervous-looking Susanne Copeland by the arm. They each took a chair, Annie the one nearest to his window.

He stood there, unseen, looking down at her.

Only once before, in his teens, had a female affected him at first sight like this. That girl had a vaguely similar look. He wondered why each of us, in our youth, seem to fixate on certain physical and stylistic traits that become our "type." He'd never known what his own type was, until he had seen that girl long ago.

Well, you're seeing it again.

Her eyes were what first riveted him. Smoky gray, set wide, crowned by brows that arced up and outward. The subtly feline look accentuated by her mouth—wide, full-lipped, turning up at the corners when she smiled. Short, tousled chestnut hair framing a pale oval face. Her neck, like the rest of her, gracefully long-lined and slender, suggesting an incongruous delicacy.

She wore a short brown suede jacket over a white cotton blouse and jeans. She would have looked just as sensational wearing a canvas sack. If it weren't for the window, he could have reached down and touched her hair.

Steps approaching in the hallway.

Get a grip.

He watched the door at the end of the other cubicle. Saw motion in its narrow window.

It swung open.

ELEVEN

CLAIBOURNE CORRECTIONAL FACILITY
CLAIBOURNE, VIRGINIA
Monday, September 8, 10:15 a.m.

The first man to enter was short and pudgy and wore a red plaid shirt and tan slacks. He had receding, copper-colored hair and a goatee, both wiry and unkempt. Smiling, he moved purposefully across the room to the window where the women sat.

"Hi. I'm Dr. Frankfurt. We spoke on the phone. Susanne, so good of you to come." He took the chair opposite Annie, and they exchanged introductions.

Hunter kept his eyes on the open doorway. A corrections officer stood there waiting, then stepped back.

Adrian Wulfe strode in.

The guy was huge, about six-six, big-boned and lanky. He wore pale blue-gray prison coveralls. His eyebrows drooped downward at the outside, giving him a faintly sad look. His hair was a bit shorter than Hunter recalled from his photo, but still tossed back loosely, indifferently. As he moved to take his seat, Hunter saw that his nose in profile was large and blade-like, reminding him of an American Indian. He didn't speak, but nodded once at Susanne, in acknowledgment.

Her eyes bore into him, wide and unblinking. Her lips were a thin scar, and her fingers gripped the edge of the stainless-steel desktop.

Annie's eyes were filled with contempt.

Frankfurt tried to break the ice. "Let me say: It's so good of you all to do this!" It sounded forced, like a comic trying to warm up a tough crowd. "Susanne, I know this is a big step for you, just as it is for Adrian. I'm so proud of you both. And Ms. Woods, thank you so much for accompanying Susanne. I understand that you've been a central pillar in her restorative support system. That's why—"

"Her what?"

He blinked. "Restorative support system. Friends, family, peer-group members—all those who have been there to help her through the Four Restorative Stages."

"Look, I don't know a damned thing about your 'restorative stages.' I do know that Susanne has some things that she needs to say"—she pointed right at Wulfe—"to that piece of crap that's stinking up your room."

Hunter laughed, wishing that they could hear him.

Wulfe eased back in his chair, staring at her. He smiled slightly; it looked pasted into place and didn't reach his eyes.

Frankfurt didn't notice; he was too preoccupied waving his hands around, as if erasing a student's embarrassing mistake from a blackboard. "Now, I fully understand how difficult this is for all concerned. But we've already taken the first big step, so please let's try to move forward in a mutually positive spirit. Your role here, Ms. Woods, is only as a nonparticipating observer, to lend emotional support to Susanne. So before we begin, let me explain how this Restorative Justice Dialogue will proceed."

He leaned forward, continuing his contrived eagerness. "First, the victim"—he nodded toward Susanne—"will have the opportunity to explain how she feels and felt, and what needs were not met as the result of the offender's actions. Then, the offender must repeat what he has heard, and he must continue to listen and repeat what the victim says she feels and needs.

"Once our victim feels completely heard, then she will be ready to listen to what Adrian, our offender, feels and needs now—and also what he felt and needed at the time of the offense. Susanne then will reflect those feelings and needs back to her offender. At the end of our dialogue, Susanne will make a request to Adrian, and Adrian will do likewise. Our aim is to arrive at a strategy for resolution."

Hunter watched as Annie's expression moved from incomprehension to incredulity to indignation. She got up from her chair and leaned toward Frankfurt, just inches from the glass, her palms flat on the counter.

"Are you telling us," she said slowly, through her teeth, "that Susie is supposed to sit here and *swap feelings* with this—"

"Annie, don't."

They turned to Susanne.

"It's okay. Really. Remember, I get to speak first."

Something unspoken passed between the women. Annie sat down slowly. Crossed her arms. He saw that she and Wulfe locked eyes.

"For the last time, Ms. Woods, I must caution you that you aren't to interrupt the dialogue between Susanne and Adrian. Susanne, would you like to go ahead and say something to Adrian?"

She drew a breath, released it. Placed her hands on her lap. Raised her eyes to Wulfe's.

"Two years ago, on a beautiful July evening, you and two young thugs destroyed my life. I don't have to tell you what you did. But maybe he"—she glanced at Frankfurt—"doesn't know the whole story. So let me tell it.

"Arthur and I were going home from a friend's house, down a country road, when we had to stop because of a flat tire. He tried to change it, but the lug nuts were too tight. And out there, we couldn't get a cell signal. So we were just standing beside the car, waiting for somebody to come along, when the three of you drove up. At first, you pretended that you wanted to play Good Samaritan. You were all smiles. Next thing I knew, your friends grabbed me, and you punched Arthur and knocked him down.

"Then you dragged us into the weeds beside the road. And you held Arthur down, and you made him watch— while they raped me." She paused. "And you know what else they did to me, too.... And through that whole nightmare, I remember Arthur screaming and crying and I heard you laughing and hitting him and telling him to shut up, and then laughing some more at what they were doing to me, and telling them to hurry up, because they didn't have a lot of time, and it was *your* turn."

She stopped. Her eyes were closed.

Adrian Wulfe's face was expressionless.

"It must have made you feel so very powerful to do that to Arthur, didn't it, Mr. Wulfe? I mean, to hit him, hold him down, humiliate him like that? After all, Arthur wasn't a great big guy like you. And Arthur wouldn't have known how to overpower or hurt someone. Because he never wanted to. He was a *doctor*, Mr. Wulfe. A plastic surgeon. Unlike you, he devoted his whole life to fixing people's injuries—not causing them. Sometimes, he even had to repair the horrible damage that monsters like you cause."

Frankfurt squirmed in his seat. Wulfe sat motionless.

"You and I both know you were going to kill us that night, Mr. Wulfe. You wouldn't have wanted to leave us alive to identify you. It was sheer dumb luck for us that you didn't—if you want to call us lucky for surviving. If it wasn't for that pizza delivery kid driving past with his windows down, who heard our screaming and radioed for the cops, I wouldn't be here. Of course—" Her voice caught. "Of course, Arthur *isn't* here. Is he, Mr. Wulfe? No, because he couldn't deal with it."

She turned to Frankfurt, her eyes blazing. "So, doctor. You want me to talk about how I felt. You want me to talk about how I feel. You want me to say what I need. Let me tell you what I need. *I need my husband back.* I need the wonderful man who shot himself ten days ago, to end the hell that son of a bitch put him through. I need the husband he took from me! I need the man he murdered, just as sure as if he'd bashed in his skull with the tire iron that night. So tell me, doctor: How do you suppose he's going to 'restore' my husband? And why in God's name should I give a damn about *his* feelings and *his* needs?"

Frankfurt shifted again uncomfortably.

"You're right, Mrs. Copeland."

They all turned to Adrian Wulfe.

"There's absolutely no reason why you should care about anything I feel or need. Absolutely none. Everything you said about me—you're right. It was monstrous, what I did. Inexcusable."

Susanne just stared at him, as if she no longer had the capacity for speech.

"The only reason I asked for this meeting," he continued, his voice rumbling deep and soft, "was to give you the chance to say these things to my face. Things you need to say, but weren't given the opportunity to say in the courtroom. But there's no reason for you to listen to me. Nothing I can say could ever undo all the suffering I've caused you and your husband. It would be insulting of me to even try to apologize."

Susanne Copeland was trembling. A tear began a thin track down her cheek.

"Do you have anything else that you'd like to say to me, Mrs. Copeland?" Wulfe asked. "I'll stay here as long as you want me to."

She shook her head. Tears were now flowing freely. Annie reached out to touch her shoulder.

"In that case, doctor, there's no reason she should have to endure my presence any longer."

He rose to his feet. Nodded to Susanne. Then met Annie's angry frown with a little smile.

You goddamned manipulative fraud.

Hunter rushed to the door, yanked it open. In the hallway, a few feet away, two waiting corrections officers leaning against the wall straightened when they saw him.

Two seconds later, the door to Wulfe's cubicle opened and he emerged.

Hunter went for him. "Wulfe!"

The prisoner looked his way, startled. The guards jumped between them, one blocking his path while the other pushed Wulfe in the opposite direction.

"Hold on, buddy! You stop right there!" the nearest officer yelled to Hunter, pressing him back.

He stopped. He wasn't about to hurt innocent people just to get at the guy.

"Look at me, Wulfe."

Towering above the head of the other guard, the inmate stared back at him.

"See this face? I want you to remember it in your nightmares. Because someday, it'll be the last face you'll ever see."

*

The three of them sat in a small diner on the outskirts of Claibourne, the old-fashioned kind that looked like a railroad car parked on the side of the highway. She and Susie faced Dylan Hunter on the opposite side of the booth. Annie suspected that he was hungry, but since they were only having hot tea, he stuck to coffee.

"You actually spoke to him, then," Susie said.

"Briefly."

"What did you say to him?"

He took a sip from his mug. "Enough."

Annie studied him more closely. His was a masculine face, not pretty-boy handsome, but rough-handsome. Skin creased and slightly weathered, as if he spent his years outdoors. Deep-set eyes, constantly on the move, seeming to miss nothing. Cleft chin, broad nose, thick tangle of dark brown hair. She thought she saw a thin, faint scar along his jawline. He looked more like a prizefighter than a reporter.

Those eyes caught her watching him; she lowered her gaze to her teacup.

"You think it was all some kind of ruse, then."

"Yes, Susanne, I do."

"What could he possibly hope to gain?"

He shrugged. "Virginia abolished parole years ago. So he can't be trying to suck up to the parole board. But his plea bargain minimized the time he'll stay behind bars."

Susie looked down. "I suppose you wonder why I agreed to that."

"None of my business."

"Well, I want to tell you, anyway. It wasn't so much the ordeal of testifying in court. Yes, I knew it would be hard to face my friends and co-workers if they had all of those...images in their minds. But that wasn't the biggest thing. It was mostly for Arthur's sake. He was having so much trouble with it. I couldn't bear the thought of forcing him to relive it in court."

"I understand."

"And when their lawyers made it clear that they would really go after *us* at trial—well, I told the Commonwealth Attorney's office I wouldn't fight a plea deal. Not as long as they'd be convicted of a sex crime of some sort. I wanted them branded as sex criminals, with their names in a registry. So that other people would be warned that they're predators."

"You figured that if they were convicted for sex crimes, they'd be gone for a long time."

"I still don't understand why not."

Dylan took another sip, put down the mug. Spread his big hands on the paper placemat. "From what I've been able to figure out, Wulfe initially was charged with rape and conspiracy to commit a felony. But because *he* didn't actually assault you—"

"Only because the cops got there in time," Annie interrupted.

"Only because. So they charged him with 'attempt to commit rape.' In this state, that's a Class 4 felony—which means he was eligible for a two-to-ten-year sentence. The conspiracy charge could've added another year or so behind bars. But by the terms of the plea deal, the judge ordered the two sentences to run concurrently, not consecutively."

"So, their conspiracy—their gang attack—added nothing, then?" Annie demanded.

"I'm afraid not. Wulfe received just a little over three years. But with all these early-release programs, who knows what that really means?"

"What about the other two?" Susie asked.

"When they attacked you, Bracey and Valenti were still juveniles, if only by a few months. Still, because of the seriousness of the charges, they were indicted in circuit court. They could have been convicted and sentenced as adults. But again, the plea bargains changed all that. They bounced those two back to the juvie system. Which, as we know, is a joke. Since they didn't have any serious previous convictions, they were eligible for shorter sentences."

"Even though we know they probably both committed *murders* in the past?"

"Even though."

"That's crazy!"

"Crazy. And immoral. Because our so-called justice system has nothing to do with justice."

"So what happens to Bracey and Valenti now?"

Annie thought something moved in his eyes.

"They were in sex-offender 'therapy' in the juvenile correction centers. Then they were transferred to a 'community-based alternative' in Alexandria called Youth Horizons. It is a group home in a residential neighborhood.

When I wrote my article last week, I thought these guys were still living there, locked up."

"They're not?" Susie looked shocked.

Dylan shook his head. "All they really have to do is show up each morning for four hours of counseling. In the afternoons, they're released, supposedly to look for jobs. But at night, those two are out roaming the streets. You can thank the idiots promoting all these 'alternatives to incarceration' programs. They're responsible for— Something wrong, Annie?"

She tried to cover her reaction. "Sorry. I, I just remembered—I have to visit someone tonight."

"Anyway, next year, when they turn twenty-one, they can't be held any longer. But I think they'll be out even sooner, because they get months of 'good behavior' credits that shorten their sentences."

"You're telling me these animals will serve *less than three years*, then be back on the streets?"

"Susanne, I'm telling you they're already back on the streets."

She put her head in her hands. "I can't believe this. They took my Arthur forever, and they lose only three years of their lives."

Dylan turned away and looked at the passing traffic.

"I appreciate your honesty. I wish the prosecutor had been this honest with me."

They were silent for a moment. Then Susie spoke again. "Dylan, for a reporter, you're unusually sympathetic to crime victims. I was thinking. I'd like to invite you to the next executive committee meeting of our Vigilance for Victims group. I think the members would like to meet you."

He nodded immediately. "Susanne, I'd be honored."

"You, too, Annie. I've been inviting you for months, and you haven't shown up yet."

"Well...when is it?"

"Wednesday night, 7:30. I know it's short notice, but—"

"Works for me," Hunter said, looking not at Susie, but at her.

"Sure," she found herself saying, breaking eye contact. "I think I'm clear, too."

"Great. It's at our...it's at my home just off Route 193, north of Tysons Corner. Annie knows where it is, but I'll email you the directions. You'll be glad you came. The people are wonderful. Inspiring. For me, they've meant so—"

"Excuse me," Dylan said, pulling his ringing cell phone from a jacket pocket. "Yes?.... Oh, Danika. Hi. Look, I'm tied up right now. Could I— *What?*"

His eyes widened, his lips parted. She exchanged glances with Susie.

"Sure.... I understand.... Listen, let the detective know I can meet him there about 4:30. Then call Bronowski back and tell him I'll phone in about an hour, okay?.... Thanks."

He closed the phone. "Sorry for the interruption. That was my answering service. Considering what we've just been talking about, you're not going to believe this."

He pushed his cup and saucer aside, reached across the table and rested his hand on Susie's. "Susanne, it seems that you have one less criminal to worry about. William Bracey has just been found shot dead."

Her shoulders began to shake.

Then he was around the table, holding her close as she began to sob.

TWELVE

Dylan Hunter liked Ed Cronin's face.

The Alexandria homicide investigator had a squarish jaw, a fringe of close-cropped blond hair, and blue eyes that sparked with intelligence. He looked to be in his mid-forties; beneath his blue sports jacket he seemed trim and athletic. Maybe a handball player or runner. One of that minority of balding guys that women go for.

"I appreciate this, Mr. Hunter. I won't take much of your time."

"It's okay, Sergeant Cronin. End of the workday. What can I do for you?"

"As I told your receptionist when I called, it's about the murder of William Bracey."

"Right. One of the trio I wrote about last week. I caught the news on the radio on my way here."

"That's the guy."

"Well, I don't think many people will lament his passing."

Cronin smiled, the only editorial he would permit himself.

"But I put everything that I learned about the guy in the article. So if you're looking for more information, I'm not sure I can help you."

The detective leaned back in the guest chair. It didn't creak as it had under the weight of its previous occupant. "Maybe you can. We found something unusual at the crime scene."

He shut up. Waiting for him to fill the silence. The guy was good. But it would seem suspicious not to bite. "Unusual?"

Cronin reached into the large manila envelope he'd brought with him. Extracted a clear, zip-lock plastic bag and slid it across the desk toward him. He leaned over to look at it. Inside was a newspaper clipping with brownish spatters on it.

He looked up at his visitor. "You found *this* at the crime scene?"

Cronin nodded, watching him.

Hunter sat back, frowned, and spread his hands. "I don't understand."

Cronin stared at him for a moment. Then relaxed and sighed. "Neither do we, frankly. We can only speculate. Most likely thing is, somebody read your article, got royally pissed off, and decided to whack the guy. Then leave the clipping at the crime scene. As his justification."

"You think *my article* motivated somebody to kill this guy?"

The detective shrugged. "Sure looks like it. From the way the crime scene was staged."

"Staged?"

"Look, I tell you this, it's not for public consumption, okay? I don't want to read about it in the paper tomorrow."

Hunter didn't like it, but he raised three fingers. "Scout's honor."

"Okay, Bracey was shot lying in his bed. But that's not where we found him. The perp, or perps, dragged him off the bed and perched him in a stuffed chair facing his front door. Then they positioned his hands on his lap. And they put your article in his hands. Like he was reading it."

He blinked, his mouth hanging open. "You're kidding."

"Damnedest thing I've seen in a while."

He stared at the cop. Then began to laugh.

Cronin smiled. "We thought it was funny, too."

Hunter clapped several times. "Bravo! Somebody out there has a sense of—I don't know, what would you call it?"

"Humor, for sure."

"I was going to say 'poetic justice,' but that's not quite right. And I don't pretend my writing is poetic."

"Whatever it is—between us, the guys in the department like it. We're glad somebody's saying this stuff, because we can't. You know how it is."

"I know exactly how it is."

Cronin reached for the plastic evidence bag, returned it to the envelope. "No matter what I think about this privately, though, I have a job to do."

"Of course. We can't have killers walking the streets, now, can we?"

The cop caught the irony and chuckled. "No, of course not. Anyway, we're doing the usual. Looking at Bracey's associates, enemies. Checking out the families of his vics, to see if anybody might have gone over the edge. They'd probably have the most motive. We also talked to your editor, asked him for all the mail that came in about your article. Has anybody really upset contacted you privately about it? Mail, email, calls?"

Hunter looked off into space. "Not really. Certainly no one who sticks out as being unhinged."

The detective got up, pulled out a business card, and left it on the desk. "Well, you let me know if anybody communicates with you that we should check out."

Hunter walked with the detective back to the reception area. Danika looked up and smiled at them both.

"Sorry I couldn't help you."

Cronin turned and extended his hand. "Mr. Hunter, what you do, that's already a big help. To everybody. Please keep it up."

He held the man's eyes. "Count on it."

WASHINGTON, D.C.
Monday, September 8, 7:30 p.m.

She turned off 16th onto a side street that curved back into an upscale residential neighborhood of northwest Washington. In a couple of blocks, she pulled into the driveway of a large, stately home. After turning off the ignition, she remained at the wheel a moment, steadying herself for the conversation to come. They'd had a few such conversations before. They never lasted long. They never got easier. And they never got anywhere.

Maybe this time.

She got out and walked up the tidy brick sidewalk that arced toward the front door. Even before she rang the bell, Gracie, the old Irish Setter, began to bark inside.

Kenneth MacLean peered through the arched window of the door, and a smile spread over his face. The door opened a few seconds later.

"Annie dear! What a lovely surprise." He opened his arms and she returned his hearty hug.

"Hi, Dad."

"Come, sit down." He put his arm around her shoulders and led her into the den. Gracie followed and Annie bent to pat her for a minute until, satisfied, the dog wandered off.

Paneled in dark oak, the room was a gentleman's sanctuary from another era. The wall to the left was lined, floor to ceiling, with bookcases. The wall opposite featured a massive stone fireplace. Family photos adorned the mantelpiece, and a few paintings surrounded the window on the far wall. It had been her favorite place in the house as a little girl. Curled up with a story book in one of the big club chairs, she felt a sense of security, stability, and permanence.

She had not felt that here for a long time. She tried to recapture it now, as she took one of the twin stuffed chairs facing the fire.

"Let me pour some wine, sweetie. You still like Shiraz?" She nodded. "Good. I have something here you might enjoy." He fetched a half-filled Wedgewood decanter and two crystal glasses from a sideboard and brought them to the coffee table between her chair and his.

Looking at him as he poured the ruby liquid, she marveled at how well he had aged. In his youth, Kenneth Martin MacLean had movie-star good looks, a boyish grin, and thick, unruly hair that, on a woman, would be called strawberry blond. Back then, he cynically exploited those looks, aided and abetted by a fortune inherited from the family banking empire. The looks and money had allowed him every advantage of social status, including the ability to break most of society's rules and get away with it.

But that was then, and then was long ago. Today he dressed unpretentiously in corduroy slacks and a cable-knit sweater, both dark brown. The clothes reflected the different man he was now: spiritual rather than materialistic, self-effacing rather than self-indulgent, idealistic rather than hedonistic. He was still a handsome man, though the once-boyish face was lined and drawn; he still sported a full head of hair, though the rusty waves were streaked with gray.

He offered her a glass, tapped his against hers in a wordless toast, and settled into his chair. They exchanged idle questions and answers about each other's work. Then the conversation petered out. For a few minutes they sipped in silence, enjoying the crackling of the fire and the ticking of the grandfather clock in the corner of the room.

He closed his eyes. "What brings you here, Annie?"

He can read me, of course. He knows something's wrong.

"I had a tough day."

He opened his eyes, looked at her. "Tell me."

She did. She told him about the prison visit. About Susie's confrontation with Wulfe. About the news of Bracey's death. About their discovery of Bracey's and Valenti's participation in the Youth Horizons program. For some reason, she found that she didn't want to mention the presence of Dylan Hunter.

"Dad, I'm just trying to understand all these programs that you run. Like this Youth Horizons. All for the benefit of those—*animals*."

"Animals?"

"Well, what would you call the likes of Wulfe and Bracey and Valenti? Give me a name for creatures that could do things like that to decent people like Susie and Arthur."

He stared into his wine glass, swirling the contents; firelight flashed from the crystal facets. "I suppose I'd call them what our Lord and Savior called them: His children." He looked over at her, smiling gently. "They're human beings, Annie. Not animals. Tragically flawed human beings."

"Dad, look. I know how much your faith means to you. And how strongly you feel about compassion, and mercy, and rehabilitation, and all that. Very nice, in the abstract. But it all boils down to one ugly reality: You're talking about letting bad people off the hook. You're helping bad people get away with their bad behavior."

He drained the last of his wine, set the glass on the coffee table. "I just don't accept your premise, Annie. People can change. Look at me: I was a hell-raiser as a kid. But I changed. Rehabilitation is possible. That's why I don't think there is such a thing as a truly 'bad person.' To varying degrees, all of us are just victims of bad circumstances. And sometimes, circumstances drive even very good people to do very bad things."

"You mean that people aren't responsible for what they do?"

"Well, if you put it that way, I suppose I'd have to say—no. Not ultimately."

She stared at him in disbelief. "Are you telling me that Adrian Wulfe isn't responsble for what he did to Susie and Arthur? That he was just driven against his will to rape her?"

He shook his head. "That's overly simplistic. But I can't presume to know what terrible influences in his past could have twisted his thinking and urges so terribly. It must have been awful, though. So I have to feel some compassion for the miserable little kid who grew up to be such an unhappy adult."

"*Unhappy?* I'm not hearing this. How about a little compassion for his victims, Dad?"

"Of course I feel for them, Annie! I feel terrible for them. Because they're victims, too—victims of whatever happened to him early in his life."

"You mean they're—what? Collateral damage?"

"That's a strange way of putting it. But in a sense, it's causally true."

She looked at him, speechless.

"Forget Adrian Wulfe for the moment," he went on. "Let's talk about your friend, Susie. She just can't continue to wallow in anger. You can't live that way. You have to learn at some point to forgive and move on."

Her eyes returned to a photo on his mantelpiece. "Like you forgave Julia?"

From the corner of her eye she saw him wince. A moment passed. When he spoke, his voice was softer.

"Annie, why don't you call her 'Mother'?"

She had to fight down the anger to keep her own tone even. "She's no mother to me. Just like she was no wife to you. Dad, she betrayed you. She betrayed both of us. How can you keep her photo up there?"

He shook his head. "I forgave her long ago. I had to turn away from anger, or it would have consumed me." He hesitated. "Just as you ought to forgive Frank."

"You want to forgive, go ahead. I don't forgive the unforgivable."

"You should try to understand her. And him. Victor Hugo said it well. 'To understand all is to forgive all.' And you should give the Church a try, too. It turned my life around after your—after Julia left."

"You mean, after she betrayed you and abandoned both of us."

"I'm sure she had her reasons."

"For deception? For betraying her marriage vows? Are you saying she had no choice? That she was like some sleepwalker, driven by forces beyond her control?"

"I don't know. I suppose I was to blame. Maybe I didn't give her enough attention. Perhaps—"

She picked up her purse from the floor and stood. "Well, you can believe whatever you want to believe about her. But I'll tell you this: I wasn't to blame for her leaving us. I didn't deserve that. And I sure as hell didn't deserve what Frank did to me, either." She headed for the door.

He rose. "Annie, please, wait—"

She stopped. Faced him.

"Wait? For what? For more excuses? For you to try to convince me that it's acceptable for people like Julia and Frank and Wulfe to do monstrous things to other people?" She looked at him, thinking about it. "Or are you just trying to convince yourself, Dad? Does it make you feel better to imagine that she really didn't *want* to hurt you?"

She didn't wait to see the impact of her words.

THIRTEEN

CLAIBOURNE CORRECTIONAL FACILITY
CLAIBOURNE, VIRGINIA
Tuesday, September 9, 12:15 p.m.

Adrian Wulfe sprawled across the cement steps, letting the mid-day sun dry the sweat from his T-shirt.

The steps led from the cellblock door down into the prison yard. He'd just finished his workout out there. Now a group of Hispanics had moved in to pump iron—grunting, clanking the plates on the bars, and spotting for each other. Most of them were big, some bigger than him. But they'd all gotten out of the way when he showed up. Just as the guys entering and leaving the entrance behind him made sure to pass by without touching him or asking him to move.

He closed his eyes, savoring the memory of his first week here, when he'd settled all that. When that Spic giant in the shower had tried to make him his punk. He'd broken the bastard's nose, right arm, and left tibia.

Nobody ratted him out for it: He knew it was a matter of honor that the Spics would want to settle it themselves. So he was ready when three of them, also big guys, came for him the next day. It happened down in the laundry room, where he worked sorting clothes. He wasn't as nice about it that time. He left them barely alive, two of them with their own shivs sticking out of their guts. The third would never again walk without crutches or see out of his left eye.

Under questioning later, none of the eyewitnesses breathed a word about who had done it. Not after they saw what he could do. Not after he told them—with that little twisted smile that he had perfected in his youth—just what would happen to them if they did. Of course, he himself had no difficulty lying persuasively to the warden or staff. He could pass a polygraph with ease, and had. He'd once overheard his whore mother tell some John that her brat Addie could lie to God and get away with it. He smiled at the memory: It had been the only clever thing the bitch had ever said in her life.

He stretched and shook his ape-like arms, loosening the tight muscles.

So, from the beginning, things had been at least tolerable here. Not that he *wanted* to be here, of course. He wanted out. After all, he had plans. But, for the time being, whenever he told somebody to do something, they did it. Nobody had said no to Adrian Wulfe for decades.

At least, nobody did and lived.

Plans.... He knew that the first things to do when he was free would be to settle some accounts. The call last night from Valenti had especially cheered him. That kid, at least, was reliable—not like the cokehead, Bracey. All impulse, no self-discipline. Little wonder that he'd gotten himself shot. From the story in the paper, there was little doubt he'd tried to stiff someone on a deal. On the other hand, with Jay-Jay, he'd picked well. The kid had come through for him again, this time with the information he needed about the two women.

He remembered every word they'd said to him. Remembered how, with Frankfurt there, he had to just sit there and smile and take it.

He closed his eyes, let his imagination run. First thing when he got out of here, it would be payback time. Especially with that arrogant Woods bitch. But damn, she was hot. She was going to be such fun....

An image intruded. The guy who'd come after him, out in the hallway. He'd gotten the man's name easily enough from a guard who owed him, and he immediately recognized it as the name of the reporter who wrote about him in the *Inquirer*. But Valenti couldn't find an address or much of anything else about him. Like this Hunter was a ghost or something, the kid said.

Strange. And why did this guy have such a hard-on about getting him, anyway? He recalled the guy's eyes and voice. Both ice-cold, not at all frightened. How he moved: fast, smooth. No, not one of the usual pencil-neck reporters you run into.

He raised his hands before his face, opened and closed them. They were big, veined mitts, calloused and hardened from years of hard dojo training.

When he got out of here, he'd have to figure out a way to find him, too. After all, the man had threatened him. And in the presence of witnesses. That would never do.

Nobody threatened Adrian Wulfe and lived.

ALEXANDRIA, VIRGINIA
Tuesday, September 9, 12:45 p.m.

The dented old Chevy van bore the logo of Sorkin Cleaning Services. It was parked on a street in a quiet residential area, across from the entrance to a big, ornate, three-story Victorian sited on a spacious grassy lot. A small plate on the front door of the house, almost invisible to passers-by, bore the name Youth Horizons.

From behind the tinted glass of the van's rear windows, the bearded man watched his target emerge from the house. The young guy had dark, curly hair and a thin wispy mustache. He walked up the sidewalk to a black Mustang that had pulled up a few minutes earlier. The driver, a skinny blond kid, tossed a cigarette out his window as his buddy got in on the passenger side. He'd left his radio on, thumping out rap music loud enough to be felt even here, in a closed van.

The man was back behind the wheel of the van as the Mustang's driver revved his engine a few times, then screeched out of his parking space, laying down some rubber.

He eased the van ahead, made a quick U-turn in a driveway, then followed the Mustang. He kept his distance, staying back just far enough so that they wouldn't spot him. But with the noise and wild gesturing he could see inside the car, he could have probably sat in their back seat without being noticed.

ALEXANDRIA, VIRGINIA
Tuesday, September 9, 7:30 p.m.

"Come on, man. *You* go."

Stretched out on the threadbare sofa, Johnny Valenti tried to ignore his friend. He couldn't take his eyes off the pay-per-view porn. The two babes getting it on were really putting him in the mood for when Jamie and Vicki would show up in just another half hour.

"You hard of hearing, Jay-Jay?" Keith Janiels demanded. Valenti was dimly aware of the sound of the refrigerator closing, then steps approaching. He glanced up and saw his friend, beer in hand, walk to the end table, pick up the remote, then click it off.

"Hey! What the hell!"

"Screw you, Jay-Jay. I got the pizza last time."

"Look, you have the car, and I'm paying. So *you* go get it." Valenti shoved his hands into the pocket of his jeans, emerged with a crumpled twenty, tossed it onto the coffee table. "Come on, dickhead, they'll be here soon."

Janiels cursed, grabbed the bill, and headed toward the door. His baggy, ripped-up jeans hung almost off his ass. "We shoulda just had it delivered."

"You know they don't deliver in this neighborhood."

"Well, leave me a few beers, will you?" Janiels grabbed his worn leather jacket from a chair and left, banging the apartment door behind him.

"Jerk-off," Valenti said, reaching for the remote to click the porn back on. Then he noticed the coffee table was covered with crumbs and empty snack bags. His eyes drifted around the room, taking in the dirty clothes, beer cans, and butts scattered everywhere. Didn't he ever clean this dump? Christ, what are the girls gonna think?

He sighed and rolled off the sofa to his feet. He'd better tidy up a bit. Women were funny about stuff like that. No point in wrecking their mood.

He was cramming a handful of trash into the heaping garbage can in the cabinet beneath the kitchen sink when he heard the knocking.

It had only been a couple of minutes. Goddamned Keith probably forgot his keys again. "Yeah, hang on." He wiped off his hands on the sides of his jeans as he went to the door. "Lock yourself out again, moron?"

He opened it and found himself staring into the eyes of a bearded stranger.

Before he could react, the guy snapped a fast kick into his gut. As he buckled forward, there was another blur and something banged into his skull.

His next memory was feeling his face being slapped, over and over, hard, stinging blows. His eyes flickered open on the face of the bearded dude, hovering just inches above his face. He now found himself on the floor. His head and abdomen hurt so damned much that his body shook with spasms and he couldn't breathe or speak. The guy was saying something to him, words he couldn't put together.

Then the guy got up, leaving him curled on the floor, gasping and quivering. Eventually, the spinning slowed and the dude's words began to come together. He wore a baseball cap and some kind of gray, cover-all uniform.

And he pointed a black handgun right at his head.

"You with me now, Jay-Jay? Did you hear a word I said?"

He could only grunt and shake his head, which made it hurt worse.

"While I hate to repeat myself, it's only fair that you know what's happening, and why. So I'll say it again. Five years ago, you sexually brutalized a fourteen-year-old girl. I hear that she's never been the same since. Four years ago, you kidnapped, tortured, and murdered another girl, Roberta Gifford. You left her in—"

"No!" he grunted.

The guy bent over him, waving the big gun barrel side to side, in a no-no motion. "Too late to lie, Jay-Jay. But I hear that your parents are good people. And practicing Catholics. So, out of respect for them, I'll give you one more minute to confess your sins, before I blow your goddamned brains out."

His throat constricted with panic. He stared at the gun barrel, realizing now that it looked so big because it had a silencer on it. The dude was really going to kill him.

He shook his head wildly. "Not me...swear.... Please!"

"Cut the crap, Jay-Jay. You're down to forty-five seconds. Your dear mother wouldn't want you to die with unconfessed sins on your soul, now would she?"

"Not me.... Wulfe...."

The guy's expression changed. "What did you say?"

He sucked in a long breath. "Wulfe's idea.... I didn't...kill her."

The guy leaned over him, sticking the muzzle right into his face. "Are you talking about Adrian Wulfe?"

He nodded frantically. Then told the tale. It took only a couple of minutes. When he was done, the guy stood over him motionless, holding the gun down along his thigh. His eyes looked hard.

"So you didn't kill her. It was Wulfe."

"Yeah! You gotta believe me!"

"Perhaps. But you and Bracey still helped him, right? You helped him kidnap her. Then you both joined in to rape and torture her. Didn't you, Jay-Jay?"

He couldn't say anything. His eyes began to swim with tears.

"And that other girl, the year before. You did that all by yourself. Didn't you, Jay-Jay?"

He began to cry.

"Then, of course, there was Susanne and Arthur Copeland. We both know what you did to Susanne. Anything you care to say about that, Jay-Jay?"

"I'm so sorry, man.... I...don't...know what—"

"—got into you," the man finished. "I know, I know. Poor Jay-Jay. The devil made you do it."

He nodded, sobbing.

The man raised the pistol, pointed it at his chest. "Then go and take up your complaint with him."

Something banged against his chest, like a hammer. Then the bearded man's face faded away....

*

He didn't have much time.

He unscrewed the AAC Evolution 9 suppressor from the barrel of the Glock 17, shoved the silencer into a pants pocket and the gun into the holster inside his windbreaker.

He went to the door, opened it. Loud music down the hall, but nobody in the hallway. He grabbed the rolling plastic trash container that he had left just outside the door and rolled it into the apartment.

Inside was a folded plastic tarp and a roll of duct tape. He opened it on the floor beside the body. Careful not to get blood on his uniform, he flipped Valenti's body onto it, then wrapped it up, quickly sealing it with a few strips of the tape. He lowered the trash container onto its side, its bottom braced against a wall; then he slid and pushed the body inside. He muscled it upright, closed the lid, and rolled it out of the apartment toward the exit door down the hall.

He was just hoisting the ramp back into the rear of the van when the Mustang pulled into the parking lot and took the space next to him, on his passenger's side. The blond kid, never glancing his way, carried the pizza toward the apartment building.

He slammed the back doors shut, then jumped in and drove off. He didn't want to be in the neighborhood when the kid found nothing of Jay-Jay, except his blood on that filthy gray shag carpet.

ALEXANDRIA CIRCUIT COURT
ALEXANDRIA, VIRGINIA
Tuesday, September 9, 8:48 p.m.

George Crenshaw heard the noise before the cleaning guy rounded the corner and approached his security desk. The noise came from the wheels of the big plastic garbage bin he pushed in front of him.

"Hi," the bearded guy said, smiling at him. He wore a gray baseball cap with the brim pulled low over his eyes, and the gray Sorkin Cleaning Services uniform. "I'm the replacement they sent over."

"You're early." Crenshaw pawed through the papers on his desk and found the memo. "Yeah. Here it is. Your company called it in this afternoon. Said they'd be sending in somebody new tonight."

"That's me." The bearded guy tapped the plastic photo ID clipped to his uniform pocket.

"Let me get the number off your badge. You can sign in here."

The guy didn't use the pen chained to the sign-in clipboard, but instead drew one out of his own pocket and scribbled his name. Crenshaw leaned forward, checked the photo on the badge against the guy's face, then took down the name and number on it and entered them next to the signature.

"Okay, that's all I need Mr. Dantes."

"Just call me Edmond."

Crenshaw glanced at the guy and returned his smile. "Well, Edmond, I suppose you need help finding your way around here."

"No problem. I can figure it out if there's a directory."

The security guard pointed. "Right over there near the elevators."

"Thanks. I won't be long," Dantes said. "I'll leave some things upstairs, but then I have to go back to the office and get some stuff I forgot."

"Sure." Crenshaw reached under his desk, pulled a key off a hook, and handed it to the cleaning man. "Here's a copy of the master. You can just walk right around the metal detector."

"I appreciate your help. Well, I'd better get to it. See you in a bit."

He watched the guy head off toward the elevators, whistling. Crenshaw shook his head. Amazing that anybody could enjoy such a job.

*

This would be tricky.

He emerged from the elevator with his latex gloves on. He rolled the trash bin down the hallway, noting the position and angles of the various closed-circuit cameras. He needed to find just the right spot.

He did. The angle of the overhead camera in the reception area of the Commonwealth Attorney's office appeared to leave a blind spot to the right of the receptionist's desk. He also noticed the very tall, broad-leafed potted plant standing in the corner. He dragged the plant to where it would block even more of the camera's line of sight.

He pushed one of the chairs from the waiting area and positioned it beside the reception desk, facing the entrance. Then he rolled his trash container into the blind spot and carefully tipped it to the floor. After he slid out Valenti's body, he used scissors from the receptionist's desk to cut away the plastic tarp. He heaved the corpse onto the chair, tying it in position with a cord he'd found days ago in a Dumpster.

Then he used tape from the desk to stick a copy of the *Inquirer* article to Valenti's shirt, just above the bullet hole. Beneath it, on Valenti's lap, he carefully placed a much older news clipping.

It reported the tragic discovery of the body of Roberta Gifford. For a few seconds, he looked at the face of the girl in the photo.

Then he pulled a small digital camera from his pocket and began snapping photos.

When he was done, he tossed the tarp, scissors, tape, and everything else he had used or touched into his trash container. Before he left, he checked the whole area carefully. He kept the gloves on as he took the cart back down to the lobby.

"All done?" the guard asked him when he dropped off the key at the security desk.

"For the time being."

*

Across town, in a warehouse area, he stopped in an alley that he had checked earlier. He got out and stripped the magnetic janitorial sign from the side of the van, replacing it with a larger, gaudier one advertising a nonexistent nightclub in Baltimore. He snapped a plastic cover off the license plate, revealing a different, equally phony number from Maryland.

He headed north out of Alexandria. In a few miles, he pulled off the George Washington Parkway into the Gravelly Point parking area near Reagan National Airport. He waited for the noise to subside as a jet glided down the Potomac just a few hundred feet away and landed on the nearby runway.

From the glove compartment he took a hand-held recorder and a disposable cell phone. Replacing the battery in the phone, he powered it on and dialed a second disposable cell, hidden in another location. That one was set for call forwarding, to the night desk at the *Inquirer*. But the call would go first through a "spoof" website, so that a different phone number would show up on the editor's Caller ID. The number was that of Youth Horizons in Alexandria.

He liked that touch. In any case, the police would never track the calls to him—especially after he destroyed and dumped both phones within the hour.

When he heard the night guy at the paper pick up, he pressed the "play" button on the recorder. His voice, electronically distorted by the spoof site, told the astonished editor exactly what would be found in the Alexandria courthouse.

FOURTEEN

ALEXANDRIA, VIRGINIA
Wednesday, September 10, 1:30 p.m.

It wasn't the best of days for the Alexandria Police Department.

As supervisor of the Violent Crimes Unit, Ed Cronin stood beside two of his superiors: the police chief and the deputy chief of the Investigations Bureau. Inside a conference room of their headquarters just off the Capital Beltway, under the TV camera lights and reporters' probing eyes, they manned a podium spiked with microphones, fielding embarrassing questions to which they could give only awkward answers.

He felt particularly sorry for his chief. The man was trying to back-pedal away from the press statement that he had issued earlier that morning. But it was hard to do, because that statement had been a lie, and now he was caught in it.

Last night, a reporter at the *Inquirer* was tipped about the stiff in the courthouse, and he showed up with a photographer. The guard at the front desk had no clue what the hell they were talking about. He made them wait while he went upstairs to check out their crazy story.

Then rushed back to phone it in.

Since it was obvious from the m.o. that Valenti's murder was connected to Bracey's, the investigators didn't want details to leak out, details that could be useful later when questioning suspects. So, this morning—in answer to the front-page story in the *Inquirer*—the chief issued a flat denial that any messages had been left by the killer or killers at either crime scene.

But around noon, the *Inquirer* and other media outlets received anonymous phone calls directing them to envelopes left at various places around the District. Inside, they found photos of Valenti's body posed in the Commonwealth Attorney's office, including a close-up shot of the newspaper clipping taped to the corpse.

Naturally, this caused a sensation, and it forced the chief to call this second news conference to rationalize his deceptive remarks at the first. Cronin was relieved not to be fielding any of those questions—they were the chief's problem. But the reporters finally got around to singling him out.

"Nan Lafferty, the *Post*, for Sergeant Cronin: Have you been able to connect the two shootings as having been done with the same weapon?"

No, two different guns. "I'm sorry, but I can't get into issues of physical evidence."

"A follow-up, if I may," the woman continued. "You have at least one eyewitness, the guard in the lobby, and the courthouse has plenty of security cameras. Will you be releasing a description or video footage of the suspect to the public?"

The commander of the Investigations Bureau leaned into the fountain of mics. "Yes. We're processing the footage and expect to release a clip and some stills for you in another few hours, along with some additional details from the witness."

"Would any of you please comment on the statement just released from the Commonwealth Attorney, in which he blamed 'incendiary media coverage'—specifically, the article in the *Inquirer* last week—for inciting these killings?"

"With all due respect to him, I think that's premature," the commander said. The chief shook his head and added, "We don't have enough yet to speak to motive."

"Darrell Ellis, WTOP. Sergeant Cronin, how about you? As the lead investigator, do you think the killings were motivated by revenge?"

"Well, that assumes the perpetrator or perpetrators were personally involved with the deceased. We aren't able to draw any conclusions like that at this early stage."

"So you think there's a possibility of more than one person being involved?"

Sure as hell looks that way. "We aren't prepared to rule anything out at this point."

He saw another hand waving in the back, near the door. *Oh Jesus.* He pointed. "Yes, Mr. Hunter."

Everybody turned around to look at the guy.

"Dylan Hunter, on assignment for the *Inquirer*," he said. "It seems that I've become part of this story, whether

I want to be or not. So, Sergeant, why don't we simply connect the dots here?"

"What do you mean?"

"First dot: Just after my article outlining their criminal histories appears in print, Bracey and Valenti are both shot, execution-style, within a three-day period. Second dot: A clip of that article is placed on Valenti's body, which is left right inside the prosecutor's office. Third dot: Whoever did all this then notifies the media, and encloses photos of the body and also of the clipping. So, isn't it reasonable to assume that the two killings are connected by a common motive—such as revenge—and that the killer or killers left that clipping behind as their explanation or rationale?"

"We're not in the business of operating on assumptions, Mr. Hunter."

"You don't see an obvious message here?"

The chief interrupted. "We've called upon the FBI's behavioral profiling experts to assist us in interpreting the crime scene evidence. But as Sergeant Cronin said, at this point, we aren't prepared to leap to conclusions."

*

When the news conference ended, Cronin's two bosses huddled with him away from the microphones.

"That *Inquirer* dude," said the deputy chief of Investigations. "What do you know about him?"

Cronin watched as Hunter, brushing off a knot of reporters, left the room.

"Not a lot. Maybe if I ever get some time, I'll find out and let you know."

TYSONS CORNER, VIRGINIA
Wednesday, September 10, 7:25 p.m.

Hunter descended the stairs into the spacious, rustic den of the Copelands' gracious Colonial home. The conversations among the fifteen people in the room trailed off as they turned his way.

The first person whose eyes his found was Annie Woods. He nodded.

She nodded back.

Smiling, Susanne got up from an armchair and approached. "I'm so glad you made it, Dylan. Everyone, this is Dylan Hunter, the *Inquirer* reporter."

She led him into the room and performed the introductions. He filed away their names in memory as he shook hands. The executive committee of Vigilance for Victims was a demographically diverse group: couples and singles, young and old, a mix of races and ethnic backgrounds. Their only common denominator was something he saw in their eyes. He'd seen that haunted look many times in the eyes of victims of violence. It added a tinge of poignancy to their smiles and friendly greetings.

Declining the offer of the punch and cookies spread on their bar, he found a spot in a folding chair against a paneled wall covered with framed vacation photos of the Copelands in various countries. They looked young and happy and in love.

As the group reclaimed their seats, Susanne spoke again. "I know you all share my gratitude to Dylan for the courageous work he's been doing on behalf of crime victims." They began to applaud.

"Thank you," he said. "But you're the courageous ones, not me."

"You're too modest, Dylan."

He shook his head. "My job is merely to chronicle your courage. The word 'crime' means nothing to public officials, except pages of cold, empty statistics. But when you stand up and speak out for justice, you put human faces on all those abstract numbers. I'm honored to be in your presence."

Morgan Jackson, a dignified, middle-aged African-American, and co-chair of the group, took the floor to open the session with a prayer. As he spoke, those in the room bowed heads and joined hands. A frail elderly woman, who had been introduced to him as Kate Higgins, rested a pale, thin hand on Susanne's shoulder.

"And Lord," Jackson concluded, "in Your infinite mercy, please lift the burdens from our hearts. Remember especially in this difficult hour our sister Susanne. Give her comfort, even as You welcome into Your holy presence the soul of her dear husband and our beloved brother, Arthur. And Lord, continue to shine Your grace upon the souls of those whom we have lost. Amen."

The meeting began with reports from various fundraising and project committees. Before long, the agenda turned to new business. Jeri West, a svelte blonde in her early fifties, stood and faced the group with a grim expression.

"I spoke this morning with the chief of staff in Congressman Shipler's office. He told me that H.R. 207 was going to pass favorably out of committee."

The room erupted in protests; she raised a hand. "I know. Last week we were told it wasn't going to happen. But it looks like the 'prisoner rights' lobby finally got to some of the committee members. So did the idea of getting a lot of federal money in their districts."

"Damn the bastards! We can't let them get away with this!" George Banacek's eyes blazed. Well into his sixties, he had the rugged face and rough manner of a man who had worked all his life with his hands. There was no sign of pain in that face; whatever private agony he had endured had long since metastasized into unforgiving anger.

"I'm sorry," Hunter said, "but I don't know the bill you're referring to."

Jeri explained that if passed into law, H.R. 207 would provide states tens of billions of federal dollars to fund and expand experimental "alternatives to incarceration" programs. Strapped for cash, state and local governments were eager to slash their prison budgets, even if it meant dumping thousands of dangerous inmates back out onto the streets.

Banacek exploded again. "No way we let this pass! You all know my boy Tommy was murdered by a couple of punks who never should've been on the streets."

Kate Higgins covered her face with her hands.

Banacek saw her and pointed. "And poor Kate here, her Michael, he was—"

"George, stop it!" Jeri interrupted. "Please. This is hard enough on many of us. We'll just have to fight it when it gets to the House floor."

"What good's it going to do? Once it gets out of committee, we know they got the votes to pass it in the House. The Senate, too. And our dear president—hell, he's a lost cause. He'll sign the damned thing in a heartbeat."

"We just can't let the sentences be slashed on all the vicious criminals who did these things to us and our families," added Bob West, Jeri's husband. "Once they're out again, they'll just prey on others."

"After what that monster did to my little Loretta, I don't think I could deal with it if he got out," Lila Jackson, Morgan's wife, said in a soft voice. "I don't care if it sounds un-Christian. Those vigilante people who killed Susie and

Arthur's attackers. Whoever they are, I pray to God they would do the same thing to *him*."

"Easy, honey," Morgan said, putting his arm around her. "You know you don't mean that."

"I do! God help me, I do. But that's too much to hope for. There's just no justice in this world. No justice at all. People just don't have a clue what's going on in the legal system. We have to stop this madness."

"Maybe we can, if we bring it to public attention," Jeri said.

"How the hell we going to do that?" Banacek demanded.

"Perhaps I can help," Hunter said.

They all looked at him. He drew a slim black recorder from his sports jacket.

"If you tell me your personal stories, I'll give them the attention they deserve. I'll tell everybody how the early-release programs in this bill will lead to more crimes like those that you've experienced. Together, we can make that bill so radioactive that no politician will dare touch it."

Everyone broke into smiles and excited chatter. Kate Higgins rose unsteadily and shuffled toward him. He stood to receive her. He took in her white hair, her ravaged face. She reached out and grasped his hands; in his, hers felt tiny, delicate, and lost.

"God bless you, Mr. Hunter," she said, smiling through her tears.

He couldn't say anything.

He felt another set of eyes on him. He looked past her and saw Annie Woods watching him intently from across the room.

*

After the meeting broke up two hours later, he shook hands all around. It wasn't a coincidence that he found himself leaving at the same time she did. They said their goodbyes to Susanne at the door.

They strolled casually, side by side, toward their cars. The bright moon cast tree shadows across the pavement of the cul-de-sac. Deep in the wealthy residential neighborhood, only the sounds of their footfalls broke the eloquent silence. He felt an electric tension rising between them with each step.

She broke it first. "It's wonderful. What you're doing."

He looked at her. She wouldn't meet his eyes; hers remained focused straight ahead as she walked.

He said, "Susanne is fortunate to have someone as loyal as you in her life."

Her expression seemed to change, but she didn't reply. As she reached her car, she pulled out her keys and unlocked it remotely.

You can't get involved.

"I was wondering," he heard himself say, "if you'd like to have dinner this Friday evening."

She stopped. Didn't speak for a moment. Then turned to face him. The moonlight bared what he thought was a hint of fear in her eyes.

"Dylan, I like you. But I hardly know you. And—"

"—and when you get to know me better over dinner, maybe you *won't* like me." He knew he should stop. He couldn't. "But at least you'll have had a great dinner."

The fear was obvious now. "I really shouldn't."

Let her go.

"I really shouldn't either. But I don't seem to care."

"Tell me you're not married. Or involved with somebody."

He couldn't help but laugh. "No, Annie. I'm not married. And I'm not involved with anyone."

"Then why do you say you shouldn't?"

"For the same reason you do."

"You're scared?"

"Terrified."

"Terrified? Of what?"

"Why don't we reveal our respective fears over dinner?"

She laughed. He did, too. It broke the tension. He asked for her number and address. She told him. She asked why he didn't write them down. He told her he never had trouble remembering truly important things. She laughed again.

He loved her laugh.

He followed her around to the driver's side. It was a physical effort not to touch her as she slid into the seat. Then to refrain from touching the window when she looked up at him and smiled.

She started the car and pulled away into the night.

He stood there in the middle of the empty street, watching until the car rounded a curve and its red tail lights winked out.

On the way to his own car, he found himself humming a Cole Porter tune. In his head, he could hear Frank singing it in his iconic style.

Then Frank got to the part about the warning voice in the night, repeating in his ear.

He sat motionless behind the wheel. The voice, suppressed during the previous hours, was loud now.

Yes, you damned fool. Use your head. Face reality.

Cold logic always served him well. Cold logic now told him this couldn't end well.

But he had been alone such a long time.

He turned over the key, gunned the engine, wiped out the nagging voice.

Tonight, for once, he didn't give a damn what cold logic said.

FIFTEEN

CIA HEADQUARTERS, LANGLEY, VIRGINIA
Thursday, September 11, 9:40 a.m.

"Annie."

She was arrested by the familiar growl of Grant Garrett behind her, and she turned to face him. He stood in the hallway, feet planted apart, hands jammed in his trouser pockets, just outside the exit doors of the auditorium. His tall, lean, unmoving figure forced the crowd emerging from this year's 9-11 memorial ceremony to separate and flow around him. Like Moses parting the Red Sea, she thought.

She approached him, wading against the tide of people. "What's up?"

"Let's get some fresh air."

They wound up in the central courtyard, right outside the main cafeteria. No sooner had he left the building than he pulled out a pack of Luckies and lit up. He coughed with his first drag.

"I thought you wanted some fresh air."

He made a face at her. She kept pace as he strolled without speaking. Just as his medium gray suit matched the sky, his chilly expression seem to reflect the fall temperature.

They wandered over to the *Kryptos* sculpture. The iconic piece stood in the northwest corner of the courtyard. Twelve feet high, made of copper, petrified wood, and granite, James Sanborn's famous art work looked like an S-shaped scroll, lying on edge. Its blue-green copper surface was perforated, top to bottom, with dozens of rows of alphabetical text, which contained four encrypted messages. Since its installation in 1990, only three of the messages had been cracked by top code experts; the fourth remained unsolved.

Garrett took a seat on a red stone bench, facing the cryptic wall. He patted the bench and she sat beside him. At their feet, and driven by a hidden pump, water swirled in a bowl-shaped pool. For a while, he smoked and gazed absently at the puzzle looming before him.

"We need to rethink this thing," he said finally.

"I know. We've spent six months, and we're still going around in circles."

"There's a solution to this. But I think one or more of our basic assumptions has to be wrong."

"What are we assuming?"

"All kinds of things. First, motive: that somebody wanted to silence Muller before he talked. That would imply the Russians. But how would they find out where he was taken? That implies opportunity: another mole at

Langley, probably high-ranking, who could direct Muller's assassin to the safe house. But we assume the shooter is also almost certainly American, not Russian, because of the Barrett rifle and the hotel signature. Which implies that the shooter is probably somebody from inside the Agency— either SAD or the Office of Security—because those are the only people with the training and willingness to follow extreme orders issued by a CIA boss. Which also implies that he has to be an active-duty person. And that he could be an ex-Marine sniper, also because of that hotel signature."

"Well, I did what you asked," she said. "I went through the personnel records of SAD with a fine-toothed comb. Even if one of them had some reason to act on his own, only a handful of those guys were in this area at the time of the shooting. None with Marine sniper backgrounds. Then I discreetly checked out everybody in the Office of Security, too. Some knew about the site, of course, even though they didn't know what it was for. But Grant, the bottom line is, none of that matters. All the SAD and OS staff have air-tight alibis for that morning."

He nodded. "While you tackled it from the bottom, trying to find the shooter, I approached it from the top, trying to find the mole. And I'm dead-ending, too. To sign off on something as extreme as a hit—let alone a hit on U.S. soil, which is illegal as hell—you'd need a presidential finding. That White House order would be sent directly to the people down the hall from me, then go through me for implementation. Nobody beneath me could initiate or pull off a full-black op like that on his own, because nobody below *him* would follow orders that drastic without double-checking right back up the chain of command. There are just too many procedural sign-offs along the way."

"So if a mole set the hit in motion, it doesn't look like the shooter could be somebody in active U.S. service."

"Which would seem to lead us back to a Russian hitter, tipped off by the mole. Except for one other thing: It doesn't seem as if there *is* a mole." He stared into the swirling waters at his feet. "Annie, I've checked more ways than I could begin to tell you. The list of possible candidates isn't long, and it was easy to rule out most of them. For the few left on the list, I set some tempting traps, ones that any mole working for the Russkies wouldn't be able to resist stepping into. Info that he would've transmitted right away to Moscow, and that they would've reacted to, pronto, in ways I could track. I started laying those snares at the start of our investigation, half a year ago."

"And nothing?"

"Nothing." He rose and stepped over to a white granite block near the base of the sculpture. "We can eliminate anybody in the FBI, too, because they didn't know about the safe house until after the hit. Not even your weenie pal, Groat. So, I'm virtually sure there's no mole." He tapped the rock with the sole of his shoe. "And if there's no mole to tip off Moscow, then we can rule out a Russian hit. Just as we can rule out an American in active service, acting on his own."

"So, by process of elimination, what does that leave us? We're left looking for a skilled sniper; somebody who's not Russian; somebody who's also not on active duty in the U.S. military or in the Agency—"

"—but who still somehow could find out about a top-secret CIA safe house."

"Grant, the number of people like that would have to be vanishingly small."

"I know," he said. He tapped at the boulder harder, with his heel, while staring up at the monument to cryptology. "Damn it, I should be able to figure this out. I somehow feel the answer's staring me right in the face. But I'm missing something." He glanced at his watch. "Oh hell. I've got a meeting in the Corner Office. Look, we both have other responsibilities, but let's stay on this. At least it's a relief to know we probably don't have another mole."

"But it's no relief to know we still have an assassin."

CLAIBOURNE CORRECTIONAL FACILITY
CLAIBOURNE, VIRGINIA
Thursday, September 11, 2:59 p.m.

Adrian Wulfe didn't like Ed Cronin's face.

They sized each other up across a small round plastic table in an interview room. Both the table and the molded plastic chairs in which they sat were bolted to the floor, and Wulfe's left hand was cuffed to the arm of the chair. He knew the guards who brought him here were posted right outside the door.

Usually, these sorts of things didn't matter. He could almost always rattle somebody just by staring at them. He learned the trick when he was a kid on the streets: Don't blink. You look at somebody, but you don't blink, and after a minute or so it scares the crap out of them. He did it now.

But Cronin continued to look serene and unflappable. The guy's light-blue eyes remained locked on his own, cool and steady. And he didn't do any of those nervous things with his hands or feet or lips.

Not likely to shake a guy like this, put the fear into those eyes. Not a good idea, anyway. Not if you want to get out. Time to play nice.

"I'll be happy to help you if I can, Detective Cronin," he said in reply to the cop's previous question. "Of course, given my present circumstances"—he smiled and swept his free hand to indicate his surroundings—"I doubt that I could know much that might be useful to you."

The cop didn't respond to the smile. Just stared at him a minute before speaking.

"Oh, I don't know about that. I checked the phone records here a few minutes ago and learned you've had several recent calls from the late Mr. Valenti. So I'm figuring that maybe before he got himself whacked, he might have told you if somebody threatened him. Or Bracey." He paused. "Or you."

Wulfe made show of looking off into space, frowning, trying to think back. "No...not really. Jay-Jay didn't mention anything of the sort. No threats, no problems. He seemed happy, for once. He was looking for work, you know. He told me that he was trying to stay out of trouble and steer clear of anyone who might draw him back into it. So frankly, I was surprised to hear that he had been killed."

"Surprised? Even after Bracey's murder?"

Careful.

"Surprised and shocked. I felt right away that their deaths couldn't be a coincidence."

"That's why I wonder if anybody has threatened you lately, Wulfe."

He shook his head. "No one from outside, and no one in here."

He thought the cop would buy the lie. In fact, from the minute he'd heard about Valenti, he remembered that Hunter guy and what he said. But Hunter was just a paper-pusher, not street muscle. Even if he had the balls to try something, Valenti would've had the guy for breakfast.

Still, for a few seconds, he toyed with the idea of telling the cop about the threat, anyway. Get the prick investigated, maybe kicked off the newspaper. Payback for dissing him in print, and then to his face.

But no. Much better to take care of it personally. And much more fun. Once he was out, he'd look up the guy. Show him what happens to anyone who crosses Adrian Wulfe.

He made a mental note to add him to the list. Right along with those two bitches.

"Funny, though. You look like you're thinking of someone."

It startled him. He liked to think of himself as inscrutable. "Oh. No...not at all. I was just remembering Jay-Jay. It's depressing. Sure, like me, he had his share of problems. But he was sincerely trying to change."

Cronin threw his head back and laughed at him. "Yeah, sure. Just like you."

His wrist jerked taut against the handcuff. He was suddenly glad of the restraint. It had prevented him from hurling himself across the table and snapping the bastard's neck.

Instead, he forced himself to smile. "I know it's hard for you to believe me, Sergeant Cronin, but I—"

"No, Wulfe," Cronin interrupted, rising to leave. "It's *impossible* for me to believe you."

SIXTEEN

FALLS CHURCH, VIRGINIA
Friday, September 12, 7:35 p.m.

He parked the Forester in the driveway of the elegant two-story brick Tudor. Ivy crept up the wall, over leaded casement windows and soaring eaves. Tasteful placements of ferns, oaks, and rhododendrons graced the front yard. The style spoke of history, culture, and permanence. He smiled; it was the type of home he'd loved since childhood.

A moment after he rang the bell, she opened the door.

He knew he would be delighted. He was not prepared to be dazzled.

The crystal chandelier in the foyer outlined her in soft golden backlighting, while the lantern over the entrance cast a warm glow over her face. The light caught strands of her dark brown hair, bringing out the reddish hints. She wore a V-neck, halter-top cocktail dress, short and russet-colored, with matching heels.

"Hello?" she prompted, eyes sparkling.

He realized he'd stood staring at her for at least five seconds.

"Sorry. You've rendered me speechless."

An impish smile. "And here I was hoping for scintillating conversation."

"I'll do better. Promise. But you do look stunning."

Her smile broadened as she looked him up and down. "You dress up pretty nicely yourself, mister."

She turned to fetch a gray cashmere coat from a wall hook. As she reached up, her hemline rode even higher, making his heart skip. Though she was not especially tall, her lean legs looked impossibly long, like a model's.

"Here, let me help you." He stepped into the foyer and took the coat from her. She turned around. Except for the strap around her neck, her dress was backless to the waist; from there it flowed snugly over the swell of her hips and halfway down her thighs. Heart now racing, he opened the coat for her. Taut little muscles moved beneath the skin of her back as she slid her bare arms into the sleeves. He caught a whiff of a light fragrance.

She turned and looked up at him. Smiled again. "Shall we go?"

He could only nod.

*

She had told him she liked Italian, so he'd made reservations at La Rosa Ristorante, an intimate place just two miles away. During the small talk on the drive over, he had to make an effort not to glance down at her half-bare thighs.

Now, seated opposite her in the black leather booth, he could study her openly in the candlelight. It was the first time he'd seen her wear makeup. But she had applied it lightly, deftly, only to highlight the wide, cat-like tilt of her eyes, the high-arching brows, the height of her cheekbones, the fullness of her lips. Her naked arms and shoulders were feminine yet toned; she was clearly athletic. Her jewelry—a necklace and bracelet, with matching earrings—consisted of semi-precious stones, alternating black and dusty gray; the latter matched the color of her eyes.

After the steward took their wine order—he was pleased that she, too, preferred full-bodied reds—he noticed that those eyes seemed to be avoiding his.

"You seem a bit preoccupied. Is anything the matter?"

She looked at him. "Okay. I did have something on my mind."

"Let's have it."

"You're a very good writer, Dylan. You must have had a successful career. Well, a woman dating a strange man can't be too careful these days. I tried to check you out online. But I can't find out a thing about you that goes back more than two years."

Here it comes.

He grinned. "Oh, that. You're not the first person who has tried to dig into the dark, sordid past of Dylan Lee Hunter. In fact, the *Inquirer* editor said the same thing not long ago. And there's a reason you don't find anything. Until the past couple of years, I wrote and published everything under pseudonyms."

She frowned. "Why would you do that?"

"Self-defense," he said. He put down his glass and folded his hands on the tablecloth. "Early on in my writing career, when I was working for a paper in eastern Ohio, I wrote some things that got me into deep trouble with the Mob. They were very active in some unions over there, and I exposed it."

Her mouth was hanging open. "You took on the *Mafia?*"

He shrugged. "A former boss of mine once said I have a nose for trouble. And I have a hard time walking away. Especially when bad guys are doing bad things to good people."

She stared at him. "I believe it. Okay, so what happened?"

"One day, the FBI paid a visit to the paper and told us that a regional boss had put out a contract on me. Well, being young and cocky, I didn't mind for myself so much. But I was worried that people I cared about might get hurt if I stuck around.

"So, I figured I'd better vanish. I consulted a professional skip tracer, and he instructed me on how to disappear and leave no tracks. Things like how to obliterate personal information online, how to alter records of my contact information with banks and utility companies, and a lot more. After cutting my old ties, I applied for and got a legal change of name to Dylan Hunter. I moved away, but I didn't write under that name. Instead, to hide my tracks further, I began to write under various pen names. I telecommuted from home, moved around frequently, used post office boxes and prepaid cell phones. Like this one." He pulled out his current model and showed it to her.

She looked astonished. "You still do all this?"

"You have no idea just how much I upset them." He looked straight at her. "And as I said, I don't want anyone that I get close to, to get hurt."

She held his glance; his words hung in the air for a moment.

"That explains a few things, I suppose."

"Such as?"

"Such as the way you look around all the time. You don't seem to miss much."

"Given what I've just said, I certainly hope not."

"So you changed your name. Do you mind my asking what your name was before?"

"Go ahead and ask."

"Will you tell me what your name was?"

"No."

Her smile vanished. "So how am I supposed to trust some man when I don't know who he really is?"

Steady now....

He took a breath, released it. Pulled out his wallet and slid it across the table to her. "Go ahead. Look. No, please—I want you to. Check all the IDs and cards. You'll see they're real."

She hesitated a bit more, then took out each item and examined it.

"They all say 'Dylan Lee Hunter.'"

"And that's exactly who I am. That other guy you're asking about—he's dead and gone, Annie. As far as I'm concerned. I've forgotten about him. I hope the guys looking for me have, too."

She slid the wallet back to him. She still looked troubled. "I would hope that someday you might trust me."

"You mean: You would hope that someday you might trust *me*."

She didn't reply.

"I guess we both have some trust issues," he said.

"Mine are pretty serious. I've been betrayed before. More than once."

"Me too, Annie."

"Somebody hurt you badly?"

He had to smile. "You could say that."

"Well. What are we going to do about this, then?"

"Maybe we can work on our trust issues together."

She looked at him a long time.

Say yes.

She unfolded her napkin, spread it on her lap. Raised her head. Smiled at him.

"All right...Dylan Hunter."

*

He enjoyed the rest of their evening immensely, and she clearly did, too. Over an incredible meal featuring gnocchi, duck, and pork ravioli, she told him that she worked as a claims investigator for an insurance company in Fairfax. He asked about it, but she said she hated her boss, was hoping to find a new position soon, and didn't really want to talk shop tonight, anyway. He told her that was fine with him.

He learned that she had been raised in Colorado; that her father inherited a family fortune from a California banking chain; that he met her mother out there while she was modeling and trying to break into acting.

"So that explains where you got your looks," he said.

She didn't react as he expected. "Actually, it's best if we don't talk about my mother. She ran off with another man when I was still in my teens. I don't have any contact with her."

Trust issue.

"I'm sorry. Do you care to tell me about your father?"

She hesitated. "Well, that hasn't been easy, either. He's a very intelligent man, very idealistic. He's into all sorts of nonprofit activities. You know, social reforms. Helping the downtrodden."

Another liberal do-gooder.

"The usual liberal do-gooder stuff," she said.

He laughed. "Precisely the words I was thinking."

She laughed, too. "Don't get me wrong. I love Dad dearly. But he and I don't see eye to-eye. At all.... How about your upbringing, Dylan? Or can't you say?"

"Born and raised in the Midwest. My dad was a successful businessman; my mother was a writer. They're no longer living, but they were terrific parents. I obviously got my writing bug from Mom, but people who knew them say a lot of my personality came from Dad." He took a sip of wine. "If you must know a dark secret about me, he once said I was the most stubborn individual he'd ever met. If so, the acorn didn't fall far from the tree."

She enjoyed that. "Well, I can be pretty obstinate, too."

"'Obstinate.' And I said 'stubborn.' Maybe you should be the writer.... Anyway, we lived well. I had a happy childhood, a great education."

"Did you always want to be a writer?"

"Actually, I was first interested in government and current events. I began to dabble in writing in school and liked it, but I didn't really get my journalism career going until years after I graduated." He paused, thinking back. "Some people would say I had to find myself. Or whatever they call it when you waste a lot of time traveling down a bumpy road and reach a dead end."

"Are you working on anything special right now?"

"I meant to tell you. I've been digging into the crimes against those members of Vigilance for Victims whom we met the other night. I uncovered some explosive information about the perps, and I've just about finished a big exposé. The paper will run it on Sunday."

"Oh! Can you give me a sneak preview?"

"Sure. Here's one for you. Conrad Williams—the punk who shot Kate Higgins's son, Michael, eight years ago? That was during a robbery in a Hyattsville, Maryland convenience store that Michael managed. Do you know that Williams never should have been on the street, even then? He was on probation at the time—a suspended sentence for a previous second-degree assault, where he stabbed a guy."

"Probation—for stabbing somebody?"

"Incredible, right? For that, he should have been behind bars for attempted murder—except for a ridiculous plea bargain rubber-stamped by a lenient judge. The prosecutor pled away the presence of the weapon, in exchange for Williams paying the victim's doctor bills. Then he and the defense attorney got the judge to suspend even the two-year assault charge."

"That's horrible! Poor Kate."

"And it got worse for her. Because after something like that, she at least had the right to expect some measure of justice. But no. You see, Williams was with two other creeps when he shot Michael. But each guy blamed the other for actually pulling the trigger. The prosecutor could have pushed for felony-murder convictions for them all, meaning: They're all equally guilty of the murder, because they were all engaged in the same crime. Then he could have enhanced Williams's sentence, because of his probation violation. If he'd pushed for it, he could have put Williams away for fifteen to twenty-five years. They call that a 'life sentence' in Maryland. But again—no. Instead, the prosecutor, wanting to avoid trial, let the lot of them plead down to a lower-degree sentence. Williams got ten years, but under Maryland law, he was eligible for a parole hearing after serving only half his sentence. Bottom line? He was out in just over six years."

"That's disgraceful."

"You know what I find especially galling? The prosecutor in Williams's murder case is now a wealthy judge up in Prince George's County. He lives in a gated lakeside community with a private country club. And the defense attorney is now retired and raising horses in Kentucky."

"All that is in your article?"

"And a lot more. You should see the other cases."

She reached across the table and lay her hand on his. He hadn't noticed that he had balled it up into a fist.

"I said it before, Dylan. I just can't tell you how much I admire you for what you're doing."

He saw the look on her face as she said it. His throat tightened again.

"You can try."

*

It was past eleven when he brought her home. He went around to her side to help her from the car. They were both a bit unsteady from the Chianti, so he put his arm around her. Her thigh brushed against his as they walked toward the house.

The sky was clear, chilly, and brightly moonlit. Once again he felt the rising tension between them. The click of her heels against the pavement sounded like a ticking clock.

As they mounted the steps, she fished nervously for her keys, then turned away from him to face the door.

"Hey you," he said quietly.

She slowly turned back to face him. The light from the overhead lantern gleamed in her eyes.

"I had a lovely time, Dylan. I really did. I—"

He put his palm gently under her chin, leaned in, and kissed her lightly.

Then their arms were around each other, hands moving greedily, mouths locked with ferocious urgency.

"No," she gasped, pushing herself away.

He swayed, pulse pounding in his throat. "Why?"

"I.... It's too soon." There was naked fear in her eyes. "Dylan—we barely know each other!"

"Don't we, Annie Woods?"

She didn't reply right away. She stood there, fidgeting with her keys.

"I know. I can't believe this."

"Me either. Annie, I've never—"

She raised her fingers to his lips, stopping him. "Shhhhh. Don't say anything you might regret."

"I might regret not saying it."

That made her smile. "Not now. Not tonight. This is way too fast. I need a little time."

"And trust."

She looked up at him, her palm against his chest. "And trust."

He took the hand. "Me too." He kissed her palm.

Then he turned abruptly and walked back to his car.

*

Tired of thrashing, knowing he wouldn't sleep tonight, he sighed and turned on his bedside lamp. Squinting in the sudden brightness, he saw that the clock said it was one-fifteen in the morning.

Don't be an idiot.

But he took his cell from the nightstand, inserted the battery, and pressed the speed-dial number.

She picked up after a single ring. "Well, mister. I see you can't sleep, either."

He felt himself grinning. "Not a chance."

They remained silent for several moments. A comfortable silence. A connection more real than if she were present, here. In his bed. In his arms. Eyes closed, he listened to her breathe, drinking in the sound. Wondered if she were listening to his own breath.

"What are we going to do about this?" she asked.

"Is that an invitation?"

"No, silly," she laughed.

"What a terrible waste of this great big king bed."

"Maybe so. But not tonight."

"Damn.... At least give me a description."

"A picture present? Okay, then. I'm in a big old four-poster." He heard a rustling sound. "Lots of soft, fluffy pillows." A sigh. "Satin sheets."

He groaned. "What are you wearing?"

Hesitation. Then:

"Not a stitch. Goodnight, Dylan Hunter."

He heard her chuckle. Then she was gone.

He stared at the phone in disbelief. Then threw it at a stuffed chair across the room. It bounced off, clattered to the floor and popped open, spilling the battery.

"Maaaoowww!"

The cat jumped up on the bed, then strutted majestically toward his hand, where it lay on the covers. She nudged it with her forehead.

He sighed and scratched her between her ears. She purred contentedly, eyes closed.

"Luna, how could I let this happen?"

She opened her eyes. Looked at him disdainfully.

"No, it isn't just testosterone poisoning." He remembered how she had looked up at him, put her fingers to his lips. "This is different."

He fell back onto the pillow, covered his eyes with his forearm.

"You're insane," he said. "What in hell are you doing?"

SEVENTEEN

H STREET, N.E., WASHINGTON, D.C.
Monday, September 15, 2:55 a.m.

Two days, two nights. It had been an exercise in patience. A good thing that he was a patient man, used to lying in wait for long periods, and usually under far worse circumstances. But given everything that had happened lately, this target was cautious and didn't give him any opportunities last night.

Maybe now.

The bearded man had dressed down, far worse than usual. He wore torn, filthy clothes that reeked of the cheap liquor he'd doused them with earlier. In his hands was a paper bag; from its top emerged the mouth of a bottle, from which he occasionally pretended to sip. For most of the night, the booze smell had commingled with that of Caribbean food from the seedy bar and lounge a few doors away. It helped mask the urine stench in the recessed doorway where he sprawled, the entrance to an abandoned shop with plywood over its display window. Across the street from him stood a Salvation Army Thrift Store, a nail salon, and a hair-braiding place.

And down at the corner, leaning against the chain-link fence that surrounded a 24-hour check-cashing joint, was his target.

To put the guy at ease, he had made his presence known during both evenings, with loud, incoherent muttering. Last night, he'd even dared to weave toward him unsteadily, palm out, begging for change. He was rewarded only with a stream of f-bombs, which he returned loudly as he staggered back to his lair in the doorway. Nice touch, that. Because now, the guy wouldn't see him as any kind of threat.

The target slid away from the fence and approached an ancient Plymouth that slowed and stopped at the curb. He watched the deal go down, saw the furtive swap of coke and cash through the vehicle's open window. As it pulled away, the target glanced at his watch, then started moving down the sidewalk in his direction.

He waited, mumbling and letting his head bob about, so that he could check the streets and sidewalks. Nobody.

Show time.

As the target drew abreast of his position, he pulled the bottle from his paper bag, then hurled it at him. It hit the guy in the leg, splashing him. A calculated risk, but he knew the target's reputation: He didn't like to be dissed.

The guy stopped, looked down at his wet pants. Looked his way. Then stomped toward him, cursing.

He let him get within two strides, then launched himself to his feet, simultaneously drawing the 9mm Beretta 92FS from the bottom of the paper bag. He rammed the barrel into the guy's solar plexus. As the man doubled over, he cracked him over the head with the pistol's butt. The guy buckled and fell. He landed on the target's back with both knees, knocking the wind out of him.

While the punk lay stunned, he checked the street again. Still clear. Then he did a fast search, retrieving a knife from his baggy jeans and a .38 Colt revolver from his long coat. He flipped the guy over and shoved the muzzle of the Beretta into the guy's mouth. The whites of his eyes bugged out as he gasped for breath.

"Okay, Conrad. You and I are going to take a walk. You fight me, you yell, you do anything except what I say— you're dead, right then. Got that? Nod your goddamned head if you understand."

Conrad Williams nodded.

"Good boy. Now, get up."

He yanked the skinny man to his feet by the tangle of his long dreads, then seized his arm and pressed the gun into Williams's ribs. After retrieving his bag and bottle, he steered the guy back down the sidewalk. Doubled over, Williams could barely walk, which was good; his moans and staggering made them look like a pair of drunks. They turned the corner, then stumbled a short block, to the intersection of Florida Avenue and Holbrook. The area was completely deserted.

He hooked right, moving his quarry across the street. A wide dirt patch ran alongside the sidewalk here, serving as a parking spot for the locals. He pushed Williams to the rear of the small moving van that he'd left there hours earlier. He clipped the man again on the back of his skull, letting him collapse to the ground. After unlocking the padlock, he rolled up the rear door, then lifted the limp body inside. Climbing in after him, he quickly stuck a waiting strip of duct tape across the man's mouth, bound his hands behind his back with a plastic tie, and wrapped his feet with a cord.

Within a minute, he was driving east.

BOWIE, MARYLAND
Monday, September 15, 3:50 a.m.

Forty-five minutes northeast of D.C., he pulled off a highway onto a gravel access road and killed the lights. He eased the van back into a wooded grove at the edge of a golf course. Parking where it wouldn't be seen from the highway, he got out, then unlocked and opened the van's rear door.

Conrad Williams was awake again, cringing against the golf cart in the back of the van. In the light of the full moon, his face glistened with tears.

At least the bastard hadn't puked and choked himself. Not that it mattered.

He grabbed the cord around the man's thrashing legs and yanked him from the van, dropping him hard onto the ground. Williams lay stunned, moaning behind the duct tape.

"You know what's about to happen—don't you, Conrad?" he said, keeping his voice low.

The killer issued a muffled wail. His eyes were filled with pain and terror.

"And you know why—don't you, Conrad?" He pulled the SWR Trident 9 suppressor from his grimy jacket. Screwed the can onto the threaded barrel of the Beretta.

Williams stared in horror at the gun, breathing rapidly through his nose. He shook his head wildly, his dreadlocks whipping back and forth like panicked snakes.

He crouched beside his captive. "Oh, sure you do. Michael Higgins was a great kid. He worked his ass off, managing that convenience store at nights to support himself and his mom. And during the day, he was putting himself through community college. Do you know what he was studying, Conrad? Drug counseling. Think of the irony: He wanted to help pukes like you.... Hey, are you listening?"

Williams's eyelids were fluttering; he was about to pass out. So he backhanded him, hard.

"Stay with me, you piece of crap. One more thing: Michael's mom. She already was a widow when you and your pals took her son from her, too. I'll deal with them later. But for now, I only have you here, so you'll have to do. This is for her." He pressed the end of the suppressor against the man's chest.

Williams's eyes were like white golf balls against his dark skin. His feet scrabbled the ground frantically, and from behind the tape, he made sounds like the muffled squeals of a pig.

"Go to hell, Conrad Williams."

The sharp *snap* of the suppressed gunshot stopped the squeals and the movements.

*

He paused to think a moment before proceeding. This mission was the trickiest yet. He preferred simple and uncomplicated, but he couldn't do that here. The golf course was part of a gated community, and the only vehicle entrance was past a guard booth and cameras. No good. It had taken him a full night of recon to find an access point this close to a highway. And then a lot of thought and planning to figure out how to pull this off.

He hid the guns and knife in the cab of the truck and locked it. He would not use a weapon against anyone here. If found and challenged, he'd have to rely on his wits.

After donning a pair of work gloves, he pulled out the van's cargo ramp. It didn't make much noise as it slid to the ground; he'd made sure to oil the tracks thoroughly beforehand. Then he eased the golf cart out of the van and down the ramp, using a rope and pulley. Moving to Williams's body, he removed all the bindings he'd used and tossed them into a bag in the back of the van. Then he wrapped the corpse in a blanket, hoisted it onto the back seat of the cart, and strapped it down.

Inside the rear of the van, he stripped off his filthy clothing, wiped the grime off his face and body, then changed into clothes he'd brought, attire more suitable for a country club: slacks, polo shirt, golf shoes, cap, windbreaker, leather sports gloves. If any patrolling guard spotted him from a distance, maybe he'd think it was some crazy resident out on the course in the dark, for reasons known only to rich golfers.

During his earlier recon, he had already scoped out the home of his next target. As far as he could tell, there was no dog, and he spotted no motion detectors or cameras on the property—a testament to how secure a homeowner in this exclusive enclave must feel. He also timed the rounds of the security patrols. Like most guards, they had foolishly settled into an hourly routine, never varying their schedule during the five hours he'd observed.

He checked his watch, waiting until he knew that the latest patrol had returned to the security office. Then he climbed into the electric cart, got it going, and headed out onto the fairway.

He'd purchased this model because it had been rated as particularly quiet, and it didn't disappoint. At a distance, its soft electric hum should blend in with far-off traffic sounds. He rolled slowly and cautiously over the manicured grass expanse, staying near the trees on the perimeter of the golf course, relieved that the full moon allowed him to pick his way easily and safely.

Soon he reached a paved path. It led to a stone bridge that crossed a narrow lake and continued into the residential area. Once on the other side, he wheeled left along the water's edge, crossing the sprawling lawns of imposing mansions. Within a minute, he arrived at his destination.

Surrounded by old maples and beech trees, an immense, contemporary, gray stone edifice loomed against the night sky, its soaring lines broken into multiple gables and broad chimneys, its covered entrance flanked by tall white columns. A charming gazebo with white wicker tables and chairs graced the lawn next to the lake. All in all, a public monument to dignity and decency.

Camouflage for the moral rot within.

He stopped the cart about two hundred feet from the house. Leaving his golfer's cap on the seat, he unstrapped Williams's body from the back of the cart and lowered it to the grass. He removed another object from the cart and zipped it securely into the deep pocket of his windbreaker. Then, he slung a coil of plastic-covered cable over his shoulder.

The next tasks would be dangerous and physically punishing. Girding himself, he bent his knees, hugged his arms around the middle of the still-covered body, and heaved it onto his other shoulder. He had to stagger a bit to regain his balance. Then, placing his feet with infinite care, he advanced step by step toward the front yard.

His legs were screaming and he was sweating profusely by the time he reached the flagpole. Keeping an eye on the house, he eased the body to the ground, then unwrapped it. He took a breather while studying the top of the pole. There was no flag present at this hour, which was good: He would never dishonor Old Glory. But he knew that the pulley up there was capable of supporting only the light weight of a flag. It had taken him several hours in the shop to fashion his work-around.

Flexing his hands inside the gloves and taking a deep breath, he grabbed the flagpole and began his ascent.

From past training, he was used to shimmying up poles; but this one's metal surface was damp with dew and proved to be tougher going than he expected. He had to pause twice to rest and regain his grip before he finally reached the top.

Clinging mainly with his legs, he unzipped his windbreaker pocket and carefully extracted the gadget. About eight inches long, it was a hollow steel cylinder, slightly greater in diameter than the flagpole itself. The cylinder was closed on one end and open at the other. On the sealed end he'd welded a much-stronger pulley. He slipped the open end of the cylinder over the ball atop the flagpole, then slid it down, like a sleeve. The flagpole now was capped by a new, heavy-duty pulley.

Then he took the coiled cable from his shoulder and fed one end through the pulley. Holding that end, he let the rest of the coil drop to the ground. Then he slid down the pole, taking the end of the cable with him.

He checked his watch; just ten minutes before the next patrol.

Moving fast, he looped a free end of the cable several times between the legs of the corpse, then up and around the chest, very tightly under the arms. He tied it off securely in the back. Dragging the body to the base of the flagpole, he added a final touch. From an envelope in the other zipped pocket of his windbreaker, he extracted a clipping of the article in Sunday's *Inquirer*. He balled it up and shoved it into the mouth of the corpse.

Then, with his last great effort of the night, he braced a foot against the pole and hauled away on the cable. He had to half-wrap it around his forearms to prevent it from slipping; it bit painfully into his hands and wrists, despite the gloves. When the body at last reached the top, he tied the other end securely around the halyard fastener at the base.

He was panting hard; his hands and wrists were numb and his arms and legs quivered from the effort. With just five minutes to go, he gathered up the blanket and checked to make sure he'd left nothing more incriminating than his footprints. Then he half-trotted, half-staggered back to the cart.

As he started the engine, he took a last glance. And had to grin.

Silhouetted against the pink hints of the coming dawn, the body of a remorseless killer hung over the home of a corrupt judge.

*

Just before five a.m., the phone on the regional news desk at the *Inquirer* began to ring. Because the editor who usually sat there was off grabbing coffee, a young proofreader at the next desk picked up. Before he could say a word, he heard a metallic, distorted voice. It sounded like a recording.

Thirty seconds later, the editor returned and the kid rushed over to him, pale as raw newsprint.

"Alan, can we get a helicopter? And a photographer? I mean, *right now?*"

"Why?"

The kid told him.

His coffee sloshed onto the tile floor as he ran to his phone.

*

Judge Raymond R. Lamont was having a most pleasant dream about his mistress when he heard a thundering noise. Light, bright light, blasted against his closed eyelids. His wife, Corrine, was punching his back and yelling something.

His eyes opened to an incomprehensible scene. Outside his window, in midair, hung a large, dazzling light, accompanied by a deafening, thumping roar. He squinted and blinked.

"Ray! Wake up, dammit!" she was shrieking. "What in God's name is happening?"

Lamont was not easily shaken, but he was now. He threw off the covers and swung his bare feet to the floor. "Stay here!" he shouted to her.

He moved to the side, out of the blinding beam pouring into the room, then huddled against the wall beside the window. Trembling, he peeked around the curtain and looked outside.

Then sank to his knees.

"Ray! What is it?"

He couldn't speak. He heard her hurried footsteps padding toward him.

Then her screams, her nails digging into his shoulder, as she too saw the madness just sixty feet away.

A helicopter hovering low, a powerful spotlight aimed at their flagpole.

A man's body dangling from the pole, right at his eye level, spinning crazily in the propeller wash....

EIGHTEEN

FALLS CHURCH, VIRGINIA
Saturday, September 20, 9:35 a.m.

When she opened her door to him this time, she wore a chestnut-suede jacket over a cream-color sweater, snug brown slacks, and brown suede boots. She carried a garment bag and a look of mischief in her eyes.

"I've missed you," he said, leaning in for a kiss. She grinned and shoved the garment bag at him. "Me too. But if we expect to see any wineries today, we'd better get going."

"Sadist," he said, taking the bag. She also handed him an "accessory bag." That's what she called it. He suppressed a smile. Where he came from, they were called "overnight bags."

He helped her into the Forester, then hung her garment bag in the back, against his. As he settled into the driver's seat, he recalled the late-night phone conversation of almost a week before, when he'd invited her to spend this entire day with him, to culminate with dinner at a famous five-star inn. "You'll have to bring along some dress-up clothes for the evening," he'd told her.

She had not asked where she would change and get ready for dinner; nor did she ask when they might return. The unspoken questions and the implied answers filled a long silence before she said: "It sounds wonderful."

The unspoken hung between them now, during the quiet moments. He drove onto Route 66 and headed west. He had a jazz station playing quietly and asked if she'd prefer something different, but she smiled and said it was fine.

It was well over an hour's drive to the first of the wineries scattered along the Shenandoah Valley. During the ride, she wanted to know about the fallout from the latest killing.

"That judge up in P.G. County has taken an indefinite leave of absence and gone into seclusion with his wife someplace out of state," he answered.

"I heard on the news that several of the criminals you profiled have vanished. Apparently, they don't want to be next."

"Good thinking."

"So, Dylan Hunter, ace investigative reporter: How does it feel to be provoking all this uproar?"

He shrugged. "I have mixed feelings, Annie. I'm not weeping about what happened to those criminals. On the other hand, for an investigative reporter, it's best to maintain a low profile. But the people doing these killings—they're making that impossible for me now."

"You say 'people.' Do you think it's some kind of organized group?"

"That's what the cops think. They told my editor that, given the quote sophistication unquote of the crimes—especially the latest one in Bowie—it has to be a team. Apparently, a variety of weapons are being used, and different vehicles, too. They think that it would take several people to conduct all the surveillance, planning, logistics, and do the killings, too."

"Do they have suspects?"

"Not yet. But the theatrics with the flagpole raised this to a whole new level. I understand they've called in FBI profilers to come up with a psychological portrait of the perps. Since the shootings have taken place across several jurisdictions, they've also set up a joint task force. Perhaps by pooling their resources and information, they'll get somewhere."

"How's the management at the *Inquirer* reacting to all this? Are you in trouble?"

He shook his head. "At first, the publisher was upset. He was fielding calls from prosecutors, mayors, even police chiefs urging him to shut me up. They told him I'm inciting people to take the law into their own hands. Fortunately, though, he answers to shareholders and readers, not to public officials. And our shareholders and readers love all this. Circulation is up over twenty-five percent during the past couple of weeks. So, our dear publisher has suddenly become a champion of my First Amendment rights."

She chuckled. "How noble of him. Think he'll give you a raise?"

"I'm not doing this for the money."

"I know, Dylan."

*

They talked about music, wine, the Smithsonian museums, travel. She spoke of a week-long trip she'd taken to western Ireland. About the "fairy trees" and an old Irish storyteller; about a vast region of bare limestone known as "the Burren"; about the spectacular Cliffs of Mohar and the rugged, rock-strewn islands off the coast.

When she asked where he'd traveled, he chose to tell her of a trip ten years earlier through Switzerland, when he'd stayed in the small town of Meiringen. "That's the place Arthur Conan Doyle chose for Sherlock's fight to the death with his arch-enemy, Dr. Moriarty," he explained. He described the majestic Reichenbach Falls, where Doyle's embattled fictional antagonists supposedly plunged to their deaths. How the locals had turned the tale into a tourism bonanza, painting a white cross on the cliff to mark the spot, and opening a Sherlock Holmes museum in the basement of a quaint little church.

"Do you like to take cruises?" she asked. "I love them."

"I've never done that," he said. "But I might try it out with an experienced guide."

From the corner of his eye, he saw her smile.

THE SHENANDOAH VALLEY, VIRGINIA
Saturday, September 20, 11:10 a.m.

The first winery was a two-story wooden structure that looked like a lodge, atop a hill covered with vineyards. They went inside to the counter for a tasting. Agreeing on the merits of a Cab-Merlot blend, he bought a couple of glasses plus some French bread, cheese, and cold cuts, and they went outside to picnic on the courtyard patio.

The breeze was chilly. Gray clouds that threatened rain drifted over the distant Blue Ridge chain. Near their little table, bees darted around a trellis interwoven with flowering vines, and water tumbled over the lips of a fountain. They ate, drank, and struggled to keep straight faces at each other's jokes.

They visited another winery during the following hour and, after more sampling, bought several bottles. This one had a second-floor balcony overlooking a large willow and a duck pond. They took glasses of Syrah out there and sipped as dark clouds rolled in.

"Looks like the weather isn't going to cooperate," he said. "Perhaps we should head to the inn for an early dinner."

A beat passed. "That's probably a good idea."

They drove down winding country roads, past pastures and small cattle herds, outrunning the rain until they reached the village. He pulled into a sprawling Colonial-style complex. The main inn and restaurant were surrounded by several charming cottages and outbuildings.

He took her hand as she emerged from the car. Held it as they headed up the wide steps and into the lobby. She veered off to explore the ornate decor while he made arrangements at the front desk.

He approached behind her as she examined an antique curio cabinet. Placed a hand on her shoulder. "I made early dinner reservations. So that we can watch the rain while it's still light outside."

"That's good." She didn't look at him.

"We have about an hour. Perhaps you'd like to get ready."

"All right."

Her shyness both amused and touched him. He put his arm around her shoulders and led her back to the car.

He drove the short distance to a small outbuilding. The two-story cottage was painted deep red with cheerful yellow shutters and was dominated by a broad field-stone chimney. The entrance was through a small outdoor dining pavilion adorned with wicker furniture and hanging plants.

The first scattered drops of rain greeted them as he helped her from the car. He held out the room key, smiling. "Why don't you go on in and explore, while I bring our things."

"Okay."

She went ahead. He gathered up their bags and the wine they'd bought. When he entered, she was standing in the middle of the living room, her back to him, facing the gray stone fireplace. The staff had already prepared a cheerful fire for their arrival.

He set down the items, keeping his distance. She didn't face him.

"I know, Annie. I'm a little scared too."

"I'm more than a little scared."

"That's all right. Why don't you go upstairs and get ready. I'll use the bathroom down here."

She turned to him. She looked small and vulnerable. "It's so beautiful, Dylan. It's perfect."

"It is now that we're here."

*

The inn's five-star restaurant was renowned for its spectacular cuisine and service. All tables were filled for the Saturday night, and Hunter felt fortunate to have reserved an isolated one for two. Carved oak wainscoting embraced their corner table; a fringed silk shade muted the overhead lamp; thick, coffee-colored drapery, drawn back with golden rope ties, highlighted the window beside them.

Outside, the lawn rolled away to a distant grove of trees almost hidden in the misting rain.

Her head was turned toward the window, taking in the magical scenery. She wore a sleeveless red taffeta dress, cut low, slit to mid-thigh. A black velvet sash fell at an angle across her narrow waist; she had matched it with teardrop earrings of black tourmaline and a black velvet choker.

They feasted on lamb carpaccio, cold pear soup, filet of halibut, and braised veal. The wine pairings were superb, and by the second glass, she began to relax. Laughing and gazing into each other's eyes, they fed each other morsels from their plates and talked about things that he knew he would never later recall. By the time the dessert sampler arrived, he had slid his chair around the table to be next to hers.

He treated her to a spoonful of rum-flavored crème brûlée; it left a small dab on her lower lip.

"Miss, I'm afraid you've got some dessert on that mouth," he said, leaning close.

"Do I, now." She greeted his lips with hers.

*

They walked hand in hand under a broad hotel umbrella to their cottage. His hand shook a little as he inserted the key in the lock.

Then they were inside. He kept his eyes on her as his hand sought the switch to turn out the lights.

The burning coals in the fireplace were the only illumination. They had made the room hot. She stood unmoving, her back to him, a curving silhouette against the glowing rectangle.

He reached around from behind her and undid the clasp at her throat that held her short fur jacket. It slid to the floor; he left his palm moving over her breasts. Intoxicated by her scent, he leaned down and his lips traced the curve of her bare shoulder to the back of her neck with light kisses. She drew in a sharp breath and he felt her shiver. Still behind her, he pulled her head around and met her open mouth.

Then she was crushed against him, her breasts squeezed to his chest, her hands pushing the jacket of his tux from his shoulders. He let it fall. One hand under her, his other tight around her back, he lifted her against his body. In response, she hooked a leg around him. Somehow he carried her that way up the stairs, to the waiting canopy bed.

*

Annie did not know how many times they made love that night. It was beyond her experience, beyond even her fantasies. She could not believe his insatiability, or her own. It had begun as desire, runaway desire. But it descended into ruthless need—then into sheer savagery, into a dark place where pain and pleasure lost any distinction.

A place where there no longer was any distinction between the two of them.

Somewhere in the night, hours later, as they once again lay gasping and trembling, as she stroked the head of thick tangled hair lying heavily on her breasts, she knew that their passion at last was spent. She was beyond exhaustion; she was in physical pain from their excesses. She felt his warm breath against her belly, his big hand resting on her thigh. His breath slowed. She smiled. He was finally falling asleep.

Then he stirred. Raised his head, looked at her. In the dying light of the fire, his eyes seemed to be blazing coals, too.

He slid up her body, resting his face on the pillow next to hers. His hands moved up and down her skin, owning her. She shivered under his touch.

"My God, Dylan, I can't. Not again." She moved his hand away. "No!"

He grabbed the back of her hair. Pressed his lips into light contact with hers. His eyes, so close, bore into hers.

"You listen to me, Annie Woods. The one word that's forbidden when we're in bed is 'no.'"

She felt the power in his arms, in the thighs against hers. Impossibly, she found herself stirring once again.

"Tell me something, Annie Woods," he continued, his voice hoarse. "Is there anything you've ever imagined doing in bed with a man, that you've never gotten around to doing?"

She swallowed, felt her lips part against his.

"Yes."

*

He heard the phone purring. He opened his eyes, finding himself entangled with her. Then hers blinked open, too. She looked at him and smiled, said "mmmmm," then closed them once more.

The phone hummed again. He sighed and pushed himself away from her. The covers fell back, revealing her body to him for the first time in full light. His breath caught in his throat.

His hand groped for the phone as he drank in the sight of her. "Yes?" he said, never taking his eyes off her.

"Hello, Mr. Hunter. Sorry if I'm bothering you, sir. It's ten-thirty. Would you be joining us for breakfast this morning in the dining room? We stop serving at eleven."

He stared at the swell of her breasts, the smooth, gentle curves of her belly and hips, the impossibly long legs. "No, I don't think so. Thank you. Is it possible to have a breakfast sent to our cottage?"

"Yes, sir. All day."

"That's great. I'll call in an order later."

He slid back under the covers, drew her close. Felt the silken warmth of her flesh against his. He wrapped his arms and legs around hers.

Smiled and closed his eyes.

*

He felt something tickling his leg and woke up.

She was sitting upright in the bed, naked in the soft light, like a pale goddess. Her finger was tracing the scar on his thigh.

"Hi, you," he said. "Good morning."

She looked at him. "Hi, you. But it's afternoon."

They held each other's eyes, remembering.

"Wow," he said.

She began to giggle. "You creep. Do you have any idea how sore I am?"

He sat up, grinning. "Aw, the poor *baby*. Should I kiss it and make it better?"

She blushed and threw a pillow at him. He grabbed her and she squealed as he wrestled her back onto the thick down comforter. He held her close and they searched each other's eyes and he kissed her, long and gently.

She giggled again. "Down, boy."

"But you inspire me."

"*Please*, Dylan. I just couldn't. Besides, I'm starved."

He sighed. "Okay. I'll order room service. Besides, I guess I've gotten my money's worth from last night's dinner."

"You *bastard*," she laughed, pounding his shoulder with her fist. Then, looking serious, she held his face between her hands. "Dylan?"

"Mmmm."

"Please don't take this the wrong way. You've got a gorgeous body. But the scars. Do you mind telling me what happened?"

He buried his face against her throat. Felt its pulse against his lips.

"Automobile accident. Three years ago. Truck crossed the center line. I swerved, but he clipped me and sent me over the guard rail. My car flipped a few times. I was pretty badly carved up."

He felt her forefinger on his scalp, tracking the thin scar down and along his jawline. "My face was especially bad. The door caved in and mashed it pretty good. It took the doctors weeks to put it back together."

"They did a great job. I love this face."

"I'm glad. It took me a while to get used to the new me."

"You didn't look like this before?"

"Somebody once told me I used to look like Tom Hanks."

"Well, now you look a lot like Clive Owen."

"Who's Clive Owen?"

She kissed his cheek. "A man who looks a lot better than Tom Hanks."

*

She lay back against him in the tub, her head resting on his chest. The hot, powerful jets pounded at them, raising coils of steam into the air. He could smell the scented candles positioned around them. He tilted his head back, noticing for the first time that the ceiling of the luxurious bathroom was composed of mirrored tiles. Using his legs, he lifted her body slightly out of the water.

"What are you doing?" she said above the churning noise of the jets. "I'm getting cold."

He pointed toward the ceiling. "Look at us."

In the shimmering candlelight, the steam drifted like fog across their reflected bodies, alternately hiding and revealing.

"Oh, great. I've gotten myself involved with a voyeur."

"No jury of men would convict me." In the mirrored surface, he watched his own dark hand slide slowly over the naked, glistening curves of her torso. "I feel like Michelangelo."

She was quiet for a moment. "We are beautiful together, aren't we."

He squeezed her, then closed his eyes, letting their bodies relax and drift as one in the roiling water. He tried to push from his mind all thoughts of his past and his future. He tried to hold onto nothing but this moment of magic.

But the warning voice was whispering.

NINETEEN

ROCKVILLE, MARYLAND
Thursday, September 25, 1:02 p.m.

When the blond man with the mustache and sunglasses entered the crowded clubhouse and looked around, Barton Ames figured that it had to be the guy. He pushed away from the bar and carried his Scotch over to meet him.

"Mr. Grayson?"

The man turned to him. Smiled. "Mr. Ames. How do you do?" He held out his hand.

"That's me. Thanks for making the trip over."

"No trouble at all," Grayson said. "I am delighted that you saw my little ad here on the bulletin board."

"Me, too," Ames replied. "New carts cost an arm and a leg, so I have to stick with used. But if yours is everything you say it is, the price sure is right."

"Shall we take a look?"

"Great." He downed the rest of his drink, left the glass on a table, and they went outside.

Grayson wore brown tweed, real high-quality. He had this air about him, too, like some kind of aristocrat or something. A faint accent. Upper crust, for sure. And you couldn't see his eyes behind the mirrored shades. Ames felt a little intimidated by the guy.

"So, you said you don't have time for golf anymore?" Ames asked as they crossed the grass near the first tee.

"Not with my travel schedule. My clientele is far-flung, regrettably. I rarely stay in one place long enough to have the opportunity to work on my game. So, it's a complete waste to keep a cart."

"Investment advisor, did you say?"

"That's correct."

"Well, my sporting goods shop—business hasn't been so great this year." He grinned. "So maybe you got some hot investment tips?"

A little smile played on the man's lips. "A golf cart, perhaps?"

He laughed. Grayson was cool, for sure.

They reached a row of parked golf carts, where Grayson pointed out the pale green one with the white sun top. Ames walked around it, took a long look at the electric engine and batteries, ran his hand over the white leather seats. He liked the rear flip seat, too, since he often golfed in a foursome. He asked Grayson to start it up for him, and the thing hummed smooth and quiet.

"It's a beauty, all right. Looks brand new."

"It's three years old, but as you can see, I haven't used it much. In fact, it's been sitting idle for so long that the original tires suffered. So, I got rid of the old ones last week and put on a new set. Also, I had it cleaned thoroughly. I think it's good to go."

"And only twenty-four hundred, you say?"

"That's right."

Ames nodded. "Well, your loss is my gain."

Grayson turned to him; his mirrored sunglasses reflected the mid-day sun.

"I wouldn't say that I am losing anything," he said, smiling. "It served its purpose."

ALEXANDRIA, VIRGINIA
Thursday, September 25, 2:45 p.m.

"Got some new paper here on the forensics," Paul Erskine said, entering the office.

Cronin looked up from the piles of paperwork on his desk. "Okay, put it on that stack."

"FBI report's on top." The stocky, middle-aged detective plopped several file folders onto an already-teetering column.

"They send that stuff out to the rest of the task force yet?"

"Sure."

"Give me the talking points."

Erskine settled his bulky frame into the worn armchair next to the desk. "Let's start with the ballistics. The slug they retrieved at the scene, this time it was an Alabama Ammo Special K."

"So what have we had so far? Bracey's round was a Remington Golden Saber. Valenti's was a Fiocchi, right?"

Erskine nodded. "They've all got things in common, though. All 9 x 19's, all subsonic. But Ballistics says that from the rifling, they all came out of different barrels."

"So three different guns, then. Which tends to confirm our theory of multiple shooters. Subsonic ammo and nobody hears any shots—so figure they're using silencers, too. What else?"

"The tire prints are common Goodyears. Length and depth of the tracks, and the mark where the rear ramp came down to unload the golf cart, all consistent with a small box truck—like the ten-or-twelve-foot Ryders and U-Hauls. The *federales* ran down all the rental places within a hundred miles for the days before and after. So far, zip. If it's privately owned, we got problems, because they're not really sure about the make or year."

"Terrific. Tell me more."

"From the tracks on the lawn, they ID'd the brands of the golf cart tires and the man's golf shoes."

"Golf shoes?" He chuckled. "Clever. They dressed the part. They probably figured— Wait. Did you say 'man's'? Singular?"

"What I said. Just one set of footprints, in and out. Also, one set, the same ones, where the truck was parked. Looks like only one guy unloads Conrad and the cart from the truck. Then shoots Conrad right at the scene. Then drives him on the cart over to the house. Then lugs the stiff all the way across the yard to the flagpole. Carries him, 'cause there's no drag marks. Then climbs the pole, rigs the pulley, and hoists the body. All by his lonesome."

Cronin frowned and sat back in his swivel chair. "Jesus. He has to be hellaciously strong. What do we have here, a weightlifter?"

Erskine looked at him over the top of his half-moon reading glasses and shrugged. "You'd think, but he can't be too big. Yeah, we have deep prints tracking in—short steps, because he's carrying the body. The prints going out, though, they're much shallower and wider spaced. From that, the feebs say the depth works out to somebody no more than two hundred, max, probably lighter. And the stride suggests medium-tall height, maybe just over six feet."

"I'll be damned. Okay, what about the pole? Prints, blood, fibers?"

"Dream on."

"The pulley?"

"Homemade gadget. The tube part of it tracks back to the type of pipe used at probably half the construction sites around here. They could've bought or just swiped a chunk of it almost anywhere. The pulley itself, and the weld rod they used to make the tube, they're the most common brands out there, too. You can get them at any hardware store."

Cronin thought about it. "They had to know all about that flagpole in advance to fabricate that pulley gizmo to fit it. And the golf cart: They knew where they were going and what they needed once they got there. That means they had to be inside that community snooping around on at least one previous occasion. Just like the other hits, these guys planned this one down to the tiny details."

"Did they ever."

"They aren't making it easy for us. They're real pros." Cronin rubbed his eyes with the heels of his hands. Then looked at his partner. "Paul, you know what worries me?"

"I'm listening."

"I'm starting to think that maybe they're law enforcement. Current or ex."

"Jesus. You think?"

He sighed. "Right now I don't know what to think."

188 ROBERT BIDINOTTO

"Don't worry, Ed. Whoever they are, they're taking way too many chances. Sooner or later, they're gonna screw up."

"Sooner rather than later, I hope."

FALLS CHURCH, VIRGINIA
Friday, September 26, 6:45 p.m.

"Who the hell is this?" Bronowski answered his cell with his patented charm.

"The last great hope of Western civilization."

"Oh. Hunter. Your name didn't come up on the Caller ID."

"I would hope not."

"So, what's the occasion? Feeling lonely? Where are you? Want to come to my house and introduce yourself, at long last? Meet the wife and mooch some supper?"

"Nothing, no, none of your business, no, and no. I'm in my car, heading off on a few weeks' vacation."

"Oh."

"You sound disappointed, Bill. Haven't I caused you enough grief for the time being?"

"You have, and then some. But I was hoping you might do a follow-up on the Lamont story next week. I've gotten mail from a few people, crime victims, who want us to poke into the history of his rulings in criminal trials."

He pulled into the driveway, shut off the car. "Lamont is hiding out, for the time being. He can't do any immediate harm, so a follow-up piece will wait. Meanwhile, something else has my attention."

"Good to hear. I trust it's got a lot of potential."

He was looking at Annie's house. "Definitely."

*

Hours later, illuminated only by soft candlelight, they lay in each other's arms in her big four-poster.

He nuzzled her fragrant hair. His limbs felt heavy and relaxed. His body seemed to be floating, drifting along in a slow, languorous current.

It dawned on him that he was happy. Happy, for the first time in many years. The realization astonished him.

What did you do to yourself?

"Dylan?"

He closed his eyes and squeezed her. "Yes?"

"I know we're both private people. But the thought occurred to me again today—I don't even know where you live."

He opened his eyes. Saw shadows moving on the walls, cast by the sputtering candles.

"I mean, isn't that little strange?"

You knew it would come to this.

"I have an apartment in Bethesda. In a high-rise, right off Wisconsin Avenue. Just a couple of blocks from the Metro."

She remained quiet.

He took a deep breath, let it out slowly. *In for a penny, in for a pound.*

"I think you'll like it. Why don't we go there next weekend?"

She snuggled against him, the satin sheets whispering with her movements. "That sounds nice." He heard the smile in her voice.

Trust.

Hers and mine.

He kissed her forehead and closed his eyes again.

TWENTY

CANNON HOUSE OFFICE BUILDING
WASHINGTON, D.C.
Friday, October 3, 11:08 a.m.

Kenneth MacLean did not often have a case of nerves. But he did now as he waited in the marble rotunda of the Cannon Office Building, watching the House Majority Whip conclude a live television interview.

For his part, Congressman Morrie Horowitz seemed relaxed and comfortable under the camera lights, standing against the impressive, familiar backdrop of soaring white Corinthian columns. He toyed playfully with a well-known Capitol Hill correspondent for CNN, like a genial, horse-faced grandfather handling a naughty child. But MacLean knew that the affable appearance was an illusion. You don't get to be a party Whip if you don't enjoy hardball politics.

Echoing noise from a small group of visitors made the interview unintelligible at this distance. MacLean took the opportunity to lean over the second-floor balustrade and admire the vaulted dome, where natural light poured through the central glazed oculus. It reminded him of the one in the Pantheon in Rome, which he had toured during a vacation visit to the Vatican a few years before.

He noticed that the reporter had turned to the camera and was making what looked like concluding remarks. When he finished, a scruffy young man standing beside the camera made a knife motion across his throat. Horowitz's young aide, George, who had been leaning against a column, approached his boss and pointed in his direction. Before MacLean could even move, the politician was headed his way, led by a toothy grin that beamed as bright as the television lights.

"Ken, great to see you! So good of you to stop by," he said, pumping MacLean's hand and clapping him on the shoulder as if they were old college drinking buddies. It was only the second time they'd ever met.

"My pleasure, Congressman."

"Wish I could've met you in the office, Ken, but I have a vote coming up at eleven-thirty. Have a few minutes? Good. Walk with me."

Horowitz led the way while two aides trailed them. They made small talk until they arrived at an imposing set of bronzed elevator doors. Once inside, Horowitz didn't waste time getting to the point.

"About H.R. 207, Ken. We're all tied up with other business for the next couple of months, but we're looking good for squeezing a vote in before the Christmas recess."

"That's great to hear, Congressman." MacLean started to relax.

"But the reason I wanted to talk to you. Some people in my caucus are beginning to get a bit nervous. It's all that vigilante nonsense, and those *Inquirer* stories about crime victims."

"Oh."

"Nobody wants to be tagged as 'soft on crime.'"

"I know."

They were now walking along the broad underground passageway that linked the Cannon Building to the Capitol. Thick pipes and cable conduits ran along one wall, while the other was decorated with pictures.

"Hey now, don't worry. We're still in good shape for a floor vote. Just a few folks are wavering, that's all. I'm sure I can hold them. Especially since nobody has gone directly after the bill in the media. We do get some mail from the victims' rights groups, but so far there's no public commotion."

"I see." He understood the implication. And it caused him to remember the phone call yesterday—an interview request from some researcher with a funny name. Diffendooser, or something like that. He was glad now that he hadn't taken the call.

"So the plan is, we keep a low profile until the vote. If there's any public discussion, though, I may have to call upon you again, and your associate—what's his name?"

"Dr. Carl Frankfurt."

"That's the guy. The testimony from the two of you really impressed everybody during the hearings. Anyway, if there's any fuss, I may need you to come down here and soothe some nerves."

But who's going to settle mine?

"You can count on me, Congressman," he said. "I'll do whatever it takes. This bill represents the culmination of my life's work."

"That's the spirit. Together, we'll get it done."

They had reached the end of the passageway, where it connected to another corridor.

"Okay, this is where I have to leave you. I'll let Wendy show you upstairs to the exit." He stuck out his hand, clapped MacLean's shoulder again, turned on his one-hundred-watt smile. "It was great to see you again, Ken. Thanks so much for dropping by."

MacLean was outside of the building before he realized that Horowitz had used exactly the same words to greet him and to send him on his way.

CIA HEADQUARTERS, LANGLEY, VIRGINIA
Friday, October 3, 2:45 p.m.

"Hey there, stranger, what's the big rush?"

Annie stopped in the middle of the corridor. "Oh, Susie. I didn't see you."

Her friend laughed. "You had your eyes on your watch. You blew right past me."

"Sorry. I have my mind on other things, I guess."

"I guess, indeed." Susie took in the coat draped over Annie's arm. "Leaving so early?"

She nodded. "I've come in early the past couple days so that I could beat the Friday traffic."

"Yeah, yeah, well, you can't fool me. I bet you've got a hot date."

The joke caught her by surprise. She felt her cheeks grow warm.

Susie's eyes widened. "No. Not really."

Dammit.

Susie grabbed her arms. "Oh my God! Oh my God!" Suddenly, a huge grin spread across her face. "It's *him*, isn't it? Tell me it's him!"

She had to smile and nod. "It just...happened."

"Wow! When?"

"Two weeks ago"

"And you've been keeping this a secret from me?"

"Well, I really didn't want to say anything. I mean, you just—" She stopped.

"Oh, Annie. Did you think news like this would make me feel bad? Didn't you know I'd be thrilled for you, girlfriend?"

She could only answer with a long hug.

Susie moved back, held her at arm's length. "I should have known. You've been absolutely glowing lately. And I certainly knew *he* was interested. That night at my house— he couldn't keep his eyes off you."

"Shhh." She glanced around. "Don't you know this is the CIA? The walls have ears."

Susie laughed. "Well, when you can spare some time—*if* you can tear yourself away from him—let's get together for coffee. Then you can tell me all about it. *Everything*. I want sordid details."

"Pervert."

"Just teasing. I'm so happy for you. What a catch!" Then she looked her up and down. "No, I take that back. He's definitely getting the better of it."

"Susie, dear, you are such a treasure."

"Well, a fine treasure I am, holding you up. Now, go to your man, Annie Woods."

The words struck her with unexpected force. She leaned in to kiss her friend on the cheek, then had to turn away quickly.

WASHINGTON, D.C.
Friday, October 3, 3:45 p.m.

She reached the office building just up Connecticut from K Street. After a couple of left turns, she drove down the ramp on 18th into the underground garage. Following his instructions, she took the elevator to the tenth floor.

When she entered the reception area, a gorgeous African-American woman seated behind the counter looked up and smiled.

"May I help you?"

"Yes. I'm here to see Mr. Hunter."

The receptionist's eyes moved in an appraising, once-over glance. "You must be Ms. Woods, then."

"That's right."

"I'll let him know you're here. Why don't you have a seat?"

She felt the woman's eyes on her as she walked to a chair.

He emerged from a hallway a moment later. He was in a business suit, beautifully tailored and charcoal gray. As he approached, she noticed how the rich copper tones in his tie picked up the hazel of his eyes.

She stood to meet him. He smiled his crooked little smile and kissed her. Not long. Just long enough for her to notice the receptionist raise a brow in amusement.

Dylan took her hand and drew her to the desk as the woman stood.

"Annie Woods, this is Danika Brown. Danika handles all my business arrangements." He paused, just an instant. Looking at her, not the receptionist, he said: "Annie is my girlfriend, Danika."

The word sent a tiny shiver through her.

Danika's face lit with a dazzling smile. "I am truly pleased to meet you, Ms. Woods."

"And Dylan has said wonderful things about you, Ms. Brown."

He groaned. "Ladies, please. Cut the *Ms.* stuff. First names, shall we?"

They laughed.

"Okay—Annie," she said.

"I'm delighted to meet you, Danika."

"There. That wasn't so hard, was it? I wanted Annie to see where I work. At least, where I sometimes work."

Danika shot him a mischievous glance. "Well, Mr. Hunter, meeting this lovely lady, I understand now why I've seen so little of you lately."

He grinned. "Mainly, though, I wanted the two of you to meet. You'll be seeing a lot of each other in the future. Annie will give you her phone number before we leave today, so that if you can't otherwise reach me, you can try her. Now, if you'll excuse us, Danika, I'll show her around a bit before we head over to the Mayflower for cocktails and an early dinner."

As he walked her down the hall, Annie couldn't resist saying, "She's truly stunning."

He turned to her, eyes twinkling.

"Second most stunning woman I've ever met."

BETHESDA, MARYLAND
Friday, October 3, 8:07 p.m.

He parked the Forester in a reserved spot in the apartment's underground garage. Then he went around to help her out and carried her suitcase to one of the elevators, where they ascended to the ninth floor of the tower.

"Welcome to my secret lair," he said, pushing open the door to his apartment.

She stepped inside and wandered into the living room. "Nice digs, Mr. Hunter. Nice furniture." She looked at the walls, ran her hand over a piece of classical sculpture on a bookcase. "Fine taste in art." She went to stand at the sliding window to the balcony, her back to him. "Beautiful view."

"Beautiful view from here, too."

She turned and made a face. "You're bad."

"This is news?"

She looked at the floor. "Oh, my! What have we here?"

"The other woman in my life. Annie, meet Luna."

The cat approached her one cautious step at a time, sniffing the air.

"Well, hello, Luna." She bent over and extended a hand. The cat leaned forward, took a whiff of her fingertips, then proceeded confidently beneath her palm. Annie stroked her and the cat responded by rubbing against her legs.

"Dylan, I figured you as more of a dog guy than a cat guy."

"I like dogs, but they're too damned much work. Especially in an apartment."

"I suppose you also identify with cats because they like their independence."

He stifled the urge to smile. "There's that."

"Okay, I consider myself warned. So, who takes care of your baby when you aren't here?"

"I pay a neighbor kid to stop by and do that, and to water the plants."

She picked up the cat and scratched her head. Luna closed her eyes appreciatively.

"Now that was quick bonding. You've passed the pet test."

"And if I didn't, are you saying that you'd dump me for this cat?"

"In a heartbeat. She doesn't cost as much to feed."

TWENTY-ONE

HYATTSVILLE, MARYLAND
Wednesday, October 22, 8:40 p.m.

Too easy.

That was the thing. Car break-ins here were just too damned easy. That's why Tomas Cardenas and Manuel Maldonado liked working the parking lot at the Mall at Prince Georges.

That's what he concluded after watching the pair for the past two evenings. He'd remained hidden in his car, studying them through the SuperVision scope to get a sense of their methods and physical capabilities. Cardenas, a tall, rail-thin ex-con, covered the lot methodically with his squat, beefy partner. Maldonado was a *cholo* in the same Mexican gang and, like Cardenas, a stone-cold killer.

They showed up each night about eight-twenty, arriving from the Prince Georges Metro station across the highway. They carried empty duffle bags over their shoulders. They wandered into the parking lot, well beyond the useful range of the security cameras, and hid among the vehicles until the patrolling guards cruised past. Then they systematically checked the parked cars until they found ones with shopping bags or nice electronics. One guy would stand watch while the other broke in. Along with store purchases, they pulled out stereos, GPS devices, and any other valuables, dumping the loot into the duffle bags. When the bags were loaded, they left on foot. The whole process took just over half an hour.

The first night, he trailed them from the lot back to the pedestrian bridge that crossed over the East-West Highway and into the Metro station. At that hour, with few people around, he hung back, so they wouldn't spot him. He knew where they were headed—back to their apartments in the projects, just one Metro stop away. He'd scoped out that location previously; no good. Too many residents up all night.

The takedown would be easier here. Not easy. But easier.

Tonight, his vantage point was the second floor of the stairwell-and-elevator structure that brought shoppers up onto the pedestrian bridge—the same one the two gangsters had crossed to get here from the Metro. From this perch, he used the scope to keep an eye on them as they worked the lot.

This was where he'd intercept them when they returned.

Standing isolated at the edge of the parking lot, the drab concrete structure was like a small military blockhouse. Its walls were covered with grimy beige ceramic tiles, meant to resist graffiti; its floors were pimpled with dried wads of chewing gum and streaked with urine stains that ran from the corners. The passenger elevator was out of service, forcing anyone brave enough to enter at this hour to climb the narrow stairwell. The stairs were enclosed on both sides with thick wire mesh, which also extended out across the footbridge.

Like being trapped in a cage. A perfect spot for a predator to stalk his prey.

Somebody had trashed the stairwell security camera. Bad for public safety, but one less thing for him to worry about. He'd also taken care of the lights, so that he could remain in shadows. And he'd changed his appearance, too. The cops were looking for the bearded, red-haired guy from the Alexandria courthouse. But the rare person walking past him now saw a clean-shaven blond guy in a gray raincoat and black gloves, leaning against the wall and blathering into his cell phone about some meeting in New York.

Like the previous missions, this one had its own challenges. His chief target was Cardenas, not Maldonado, but he'd have to subdue both. He'd left his vehicle not far away, as close as he could park to this structure. Plan A was to incapacitate Maldonado and leave him here, then force Cardenas to the car at gunpoint. Plan B was to kill Maldonado on the spot, if necessary, then proceed with Plan A. Plan C was a contingency if everything went south; it had some basic elements worked out, then required a lot of improvising.

But absolutely no hesitation. That's why, before every mission, he liked to recall the criminal history of the perp. To put himself in the proper frame of mind.

Since his early teens, Tomas Ernesto Cardenas had belonged to a Mexican crime gang. At seventeen, he was charged with conspiracy to commit first-degree murder in the shooting death of a sixteen-year-old during a drug dispute. The charges were dropped a month later. The next year, Cardenas pled guilty to a firearms charge and was sentenced to a five-year prison term. But the judge suspended four years and nine months, giving him just five years of probation. Over the next two years, he was charged three times with probation violations. Yet despite the insistence of his probation officer, he was never sent back to prison.

He raised the SuperVision scope and studied the guy again. Six-three, skinny, baggy low-slung jeans, hooded sports jersey. Furtive eyes, darting around like a rat's. If the bastard *had* gone to prison, he wouldn't have been free to participate with an accomplice in that drive-by gang shooting five years ago.

The night when one of his stray bullets took the life of George Banacek's boy, Tommy.

Now, the legal system's revolving door had spun again, dumping Cardenas and Orlando Ramirez Navarro—his partner that fatal night—back onto the streets. An advocacy group appealed the manslaughter convictions of Cardenas and Navarro on grounds that the lead detective was "prejudiced," based on a record of past ethnic slurs against Mexican-Americans. The detective's testimony had been critical in getting the convictions. Now, the pair was free once more, pending a new trial.

He took a last long look at Cardenas. Then tucked the scope into a deep inner pocket of the raincoat.

He was more than ready.

*

Just before nine, he checked his watch again. This is when they'd quit the past two nights. He glanced outside and, sure enough, they were headed his way.

He crouched in the corner shadows and drew the Glock 17—the one he'd used to kill Valenti—then put on the same suppressor, the SVR.

They were babbling excitedly in Spanish when they entered the stairwell below him. He heard their scuffing footsteps as they started up the stairs. One of them made an obscene comment about some *puta*; the other hooted, his laughter echoing sharply off the concrete walls.

Deep breath. Out slow.

The street lights outside cast a bobbing shadow across the floor before him as one of the men reached the top of the stairs. It was Maldonado. Cardenas, still out of sight on the stairs, was complaining about the weight of his haul. Maldenado laughed and hoisted his duffle bag repeatedly overhead, making like a weightlifter.

He rose smoothly from his crouch. Then, just as he brought the Glock around to sight on where Cardenas would appear, Maldonado spun to face his companion.

And saw him.

"Ese!" the man yelled.

He moved the gun back toward Maldonado at the same time that the guy heaved the duffle bag at him. He fired blindly and tried to jump aside, but the heavy bag caught his legs, knocking him to his knees.

Maldonado was yanking his own pistol from under his jersey. In response, he launched himself from his knees into a side roll against the wall and came up with the Glock while Maldonado fired. The blast was deafening and stinging chips of concrete from the wall above him sprayed his back and legs. He squeezed his trigger three times, fast. He couldn't even hear his own suppressed shots through the ringing in his ears, but saw them hit—thigh-chest-face. The Mexican bucked with each impact. He collapsed, and his gun hand, in spasms, unleashed another thunderous shot that sparked off the floor and ricocheted off into the night.

Plan B.

He heard Cardenas screaming in the stairwell. He pushed himself to his feet and flattened against the wall, watching the floor at the top of the stairs for the murderer's shadow to appear.

Instead, he heard a fading rush of footsteps.

He's running.

He spun around the wall and ran to the top of the stairs. The guy was almost to the ground floor entrance, struggling awkwardly to get free of the cross-body strap of the duffle bag. He snapped off a shot at him, but it careened off the wire-mesh screens. Cardenas dumped the bag and ran outside. He hurtled down the stairs after him.

When he emerged it took a moment to spot his target. Cardenas had rounded the structure and tried to cross the highway. Blocked by the metal fence barrier running down the median strip, he turned and ran back into the parking lot.

He raced after the guy. Cardenas glanced back over his shoulder at him in terror, trying to zig-zag among the remaining parked cars and small islands of decorative trees scattered throughout the lot.

Ahead in the distance he saw a flashing yellow light at the far end of the mall. The security car. Cardenas was headed toward it.

This had to end fast, or end badly.

His panicked quarry was winded and slowing. He wasn't. He cut a direct route toward the security car, gaining rapidly. As he closed, Cardenas reached another patch of trees and half-turned to look behind him. Then his low-slung jeans caught his heel. He stumbled.

Fatal fashion *faux pas.*

He dropped to one knee and from a distance of about thirty yards fired once, center-mass. The suppressed shot wasn't loud at all. But the Fiocchi 9mm round knocked Cardenas right off his feet.

He trotted up to him. The guy lay on his back across a patch of grass under a small tree. His eyes were wide with shock and his lips sucked for air, like a fish in a bowl of dirty water. He didn't have enough breath even to moan. Blood poured from the hole in the belly of his Baltimore Orioles jersey. Cardenas would be gone in another couple of minutes.

But he didn't have a couple of minutes to wait around.

He leaned over him. Looked into his rat's eyes.

"For Tommy Banacek," he said quietly.

He pointed the end of the silencer at the middle "o" in "Orioles" and pulled the trigger.

Tomas Ernesto Cardenas stopped sucking air.

*

Unscrewing the silencer, he looked around. Incredibly, he could spot nobody looking his way.

Plan C. Leave the body here with the slug in it. They'll do a ballistics match with the one from Valenti and figure out who did it. And why.

Good. But not good enough.

Maybe you can still pull it off. All of it.

Back to *Plan A*.

He stowed the gun and suppressor in the raincoat as he walked, not ran, back to his car. It was a late-model Crown Vic with a whip antenna, rigged to look like an unmarked police car.

He got in and drove it over to the body, backing it in. He popped the trunk and went back there. Pulling up the carpeting, he clicked the hidden latch. The lid of the false bottom flipped up alongside the spare tire.

He glanced up again. The security car was drifting his way along the storefronts, getting closer.

He pulled out a body bag from the hidden compartment. Crouching under the tree, he spread it open beside the body. Flipped it inside. Zipped it up fast.

Remaining in a crouch, he waited until the security car moved behind a couple of vehicles that blocked a direct line of sight. He seized the body bag, then in one fluid motion powered by his thighs, hoisted it, spun, and dumped it into the deep well inside. He worked it into position so that the lid would close. Then noticed bloodstains on his gloves and raincoat. He ripped them off and stuffed them down there, too, along with the Glock, holster, and silencer.

He closed the hidden inner lid and smoothed the carpet over it.

He reached up to close the trunk and the high beams hit him.

*

He glanced casually toward the security car, squinting against the headlights as it rolled up. Two silhouettes inside. One held the shape of a walkie-talkie to his mouth.

He waited. Kept his hands out at his sides, where they could see them.

Both guys got out at the same time and approached, staying apart. They were young, as most security guards tend to be, still in their twenties. Also armed. Looked like Glocks on their hips. The kid to his right had a hand resting on the butt of his.

He smiled at them. "You fellas are a little late. Sure coulda used your help a few minutes ago." He motioned his thumb toward the car. "Had a flat."

The two shot glances at each other. The one on the left, a fit-looking blond kid, said, "We saw you putting something in your trunk."

He nodded. "Yep. Just finished up."

They looked uncertain. "You mind if we asked for some identification?"

He forced himself to grin. "Hell no, 'course not. Left my wallet in the glove compartment. Mind if I fetch it for you?"

They were edgy. The kid on the right, dark hair, played it well. "I'd actually prefer if you let me get it, sir. If you don't mind, that is."

Keep the grin. "Hey, sure. Be my guest. It's unlocked."

He watched the dark-haired guard circle the long way, behind the car, so that he could take a glance inside the open trunk as he passed. He hoped that the kid wouldn't look the other way, at the ground behind the car, and spot all that blood.

After a moment, the guard emerged from the passenger side with the wallet in hand. Hustled back to them, this time around the front of the car.

"I'm really sorry to have troubled you, sir," the kid said, looking anxious. He handed over the wallet, opened to reveal the gold badge so that his partner could see it, too. "You should have said something, Detective Talionis."

He laughed. "Nah, no trouble at all, fellas. Just wanted to play along and see how you performed. And you know what? You guys are really on your game. We don't see enough of this kind of professionalism with private security. I'll have to write a letter to your boss, tell him how impressed I am."

"Well, thank you, sir. We try to keep an eye on things, but it's tough covering all these lots. We get more than our share of trouble around here. As you know."

Right then, they heard the first siren.

He laughed. "As I know too well. Well, I better find out what the hell *that* is all about."

"Yes sir," said the blond guard. "Stay safe."

"You too," he replied. He walked back and slammed the trunk lid. "As for me, I've had all the action I need tonight, right here."

They laughed with him again as he got into the car and drove away.

COLLEGE PARK, MARYLAND
Thursday, October 23, 8:25 a.m.

Maurice Juliette pulled off Route 1 and into the parking lot of the run-down office building. Normally he didn't arrive at work until nine, but he needed to get a jump on the day. The grant proposal would take hours, and he had a lot of other stuff to do, besides.

Juliette grabbed his worn leather briefcase and brown tweed jacket from the back seat of his old Volvo. The door squeaked loudly when he closed it. He had to bang it twice before it stayed shut. Piece of junk. He wished he could afford better. But you don't get rich working in a nonprofit.

Not even if you're an attorney. Not even if you're the executive director.

Staring at the faded beige finish of the heap, he felt familiar pangs of resentment. He thought about how well so many of his classmates from Georgetown U Law Center were doing these days. Most had taken "Curriculum A" and gone into commercial and corporate law. Where the big bucks were. They'd all sold out. They lined their pockets helping the rich get richer by exploiting the underprivileged.

Not him, though. He was an idealist. He'd gone the "B" route, busted his ass learning from some of the foremost scholars in Critical Legal Studies. And he wound up here, running Class Justice Legal Services.

The breeze was chilly. He put down the briefcase to slip into the jacket.

Yeah, they had lots of money and material things and trophy wives, sure. But legal services had other compensations. Emotional rewards. *Moral* rewards they would never know. You get to help so many of this rotten society's victims. People who never have a chance in life. Poor, disadvantaged people and minorities who get screwed by the system—by the same corporations his old fraternity pals now protect.

He thought of all the prisoners that Class Justice Legal Services represented *pro bono*. Victims of racism and injustice at the hands of the power structure. Treated like society's refuse and warehoused out of sight. And what were their real crimes, anyway? Being poor or the wrong color or nationality in white, patriarchal, capitalist Amerika.

Okay, so maybe he wasn't rich. But being the champion of social victims earned you prestige. Street cred out in the community and in the media, but lots of respect on the Hill, too, where the progressives *got it*. Like the call he'd gotten returned yesterday from Congressman

Horowitz's office. The chief of staff said Horowitz would be delighted to lend his name as a reference for his grant proposal to the MacLean Family Foundation.

And ultimately, connections like that brought in whatever money CJLS really needed. Sometimes federal money, but mostly foundation cash. Now, planning next year's budget, they *really* needed the MacLean money. The administrator there promised to fast-track his grant proposal if he submitted it by Friday. That was tomorrow. Where the hell did the week go?

He picked up his briefcase and headed for the entrance. Saw his approaching reflection as he reached the glass entrance. To himself, he looked skinny and kinky-haired and nerdy. Sheila told him he looked like a young Alan Dershowitz. Yeah, wish I had his bank balance.

He pulled out his key and was surprised to find the door already unlocked. He knew nobody else would have arrived this early. Goddamned cleaning crew. They always forgot something. Anybody could walk right in.

When he opened the door, he caught a faint, unpleasant smell. Great. Not only do they leave the place wide open, they don't even clean it right. First thing, he'd call their super and chew him out. What are we paying them for?

He thought of stopping first at the kitchen and putting on some coffee, but he needed to get to that proposal. He crossed the small, shabby reception area to the hallway and headed back toward his office. The smell got worse with every step. Jesus, did the toilet overflow or something?

He pushed open his office door and stopped, startled.

He immediately recognized the client's face. Tomas Cardenas. Sitting in his chair, behind his desk, nice as you please. Staring back at him arrogantly, holding an open newspaper spread across his chest.

"What the hell?"

But Cardenas was staring slightly to his left. And not reacting.

Then his skin crawled as he realized from the frozen, sleepy expression that *the guy was dead.*

And he knew what the smell was.

The briefcase fell from his nerveless fingers. His knees went wobbly and his face got warm and he turned and stumbled out into the hallway, hand against his mouth, staggering toward the bathroom and knowing that he wouldn't make it in time....

TWENTY-TWO

SILVER SPRING, MARYLAND
Saturday, November 15, 1:17 p.m.

The rest of the investigators from the task force had been at the crime scene a while when Cronin and Erskine got there. They badged the uniforms standing outside, ducked under the yellow strand of tape, and went inside the high-rise office building. Another cop in the lobby directed them to the elevator bay and the twentieth floor. More crime-scene tape was strung across one of the elevators, so they took the freight car to the top. Its door opened onto a wide reception area of soft lighting and expensive wood-and-leather furniture.

Cronin stepped outside and looked around. The walls were paneled in polished mahogany and large Impressionist paintings adorned them. The place was crawling with about a dozen CSI. Off to the left, behind a wall of glass, a large conference room was adorned festively with colorful crepe ribbons and balloons. About two dozen well-dressed people, men and women, huddled there in small groups, looking stricken. A couple of the women were crying and being consoled by others.

Marty Abrams, the task force's lead investigator, was talking to another detective near the reception desk and spotted them. He made a show of looking at his watch.

"Nice of you to join us, ladies," he called out.

They went over. "Come on, Marty. It's a long ride from Alexandria," Cronin said. He glanced back at the other elevator, where three CSI and a photographer worked the scene. "What do we have this time?"

Abrams said, "Even cuter than College Park last month. Or the one in Fairfax last week. We don't have a positive on the stiff yet, but it looks like a Darone Antoine Wallace, gang-banger from the District, northeast. At least that's what the newspaper clip on the body says. Looks like our vigilantes whacked him last night, brought him up here this morning."

Erskine raised his eyebrows. "This morning? You mean in broad daylight?"

"Yeah. Take a look. You're gonna love this."

They walked to the elevator and asked the crime-scene investigators to take five. Everyone backed out, and they stepped up to the open door.

Inside, secured with ropes onto a high-backed swivel chair, sat a dead African-American guy who appeared to be in his late twenties. He'd been shot between the eyes at close range. Tracks of dried blood ran from his ears and nose, and what they could see of the back of his head looked like a mass of dark jelly. The guy wore no shoes or socks, just jeans and a white t-shirt—or it had been white: Now it was covered with patches of blood, gone rusty brown. His right hand was clamped around a newspaper clipping and rested on his lap.

"He's sure not dressed for the weather," Cronin added.

"Nope," Abrams said. "And notice his mouth."

They leaned forward. "Is that food?" Erskine asked.

"Uh huh. That, plus how he's dressed, makes me think they caught him right in the middle of supper last night. Probably at his place. I'm betting that when we find out where he lives, we'll find the rest of his brains on the floor around his front door. You know: 'Ding-dong, Avon calling.' He opens up. *Boom.*"

"So what's the rest of this staging all about?"

"See, this is a private elevator, key-card-operated." Abrams pointed to the elevator buttons. A panel around the card reader had been unscrewed and removed, exposing a tangle of wires. "It only goes up to the law firm here— Ellis, Lehman, and Rogers."

"*Those* bastards," Cronin said, looking over at the distraught faces in the conference room.

"Yeah. *Those* bastards. So today they're throwing this small luncheon for the partners, their biggest clients, and their wives. They tell us that this elevator has an 'out of order' sign on it when they get here this morning, around eleven. So everybody takes the freight elevator up here. The party starts about noon. Then, about twelve-twenty, they hear the elevator alarm go off. All of a sudden, this door opens up. The alarm is real loud, now, so some of them go to check it out, and this is what they find."

Erskine smiled. "This could cost them a few of those big clients."

"I think that was the idea, Paul," Cronin said. "So how did this go down?"

The older veteran ran his palm over his bare scalp, like he was smoothing hair that wasn't there anymore.

"This building has private underground parking. No guard in the booth late nights and weekends, just an electronic card reader to raise the gate. This being Saturday, almost nobody is going in and out, except for the people coming to the party.

"So I'm figuring they drive in there with the stiff sometime before the party. Then they stick 'out of service' signs on the elevator doors, down there in the garage and in the first-floor lobby. Then they go back to their vehicle and wait. After noon, when everybody's here and the coast is clear, they rig up our gang-banger in his chair. Then they fiddle with the electronics in the elevator, as you can see, to bypass the card reader. They press the alarm and push the number-twenty button. The door opens up here. 'Surprise, everybody!'"

"Yeah," Erskine said. "Having a naked broad jump out of a cake is so *yesterday*."

Abrams ignored it. "They needed a key card to get into the garage, but I can't imagine they had somebody on the inside working with them."

"They wouldn't need that," Erskine said. "They could've used one of those electronic 'skimmer' things. It's a hacker device. They sneak in here late one night, after the guard leaves, and attach it inside the card reader on the gate, then leave it in place. It records the codes whenever anybody swipes his card. Sometime later, they come back, stick a different gizmo into the card slot, and the skimmer transmits the stored card data right into that. Then they remove the skimmer from the gate, leaving no trace. Now they have the data to program their own key card."

"Great. Maybe the security-camera video will show something."

"Security cams haven't helped us so far," Cronin said. He pointed at the body. "So what's with the news clipping? Another article by Hunter?"

Abrams shook his head. "It's several years old, and it's from the *Post*. Just like the one on the stiff in Fairfax last week. Forensics don't want us to touch it yet, but from what I could read of it, this guy Wallace jacked a car four years back, killed the owner." He indicated a tall, thin man in the conference room, wearing an expensive suit and a look of shock. "Dwight Rogers over there, one of the partners, represented him. He got most of the evidence tossed on a *Miranda*. So Wallace walked."

"Prick lawyer."

"That's redundant, Paul," Cronin said. "Well, then, the pattern hasn't changed. These guys, whoever the hell they are, have hard-ons for defense attorneys, liberal judges, lefty legal-aid groups. And prosecutors who do plea deals."

"Don't forget politicians," Abrams reminded him.

"Oh, right. That child molester last week, Smith, they dumped him on that state rep's lawn in Fairfax—what was that guy's name?"

"Dinsmore," Erskine answered. "The jerk-off who blocked the bill about enhanced sentences for baby-rapers."

"Which let Smith get out after just six months of some bullshit therapy," Abrams said. "I gotta say, I liked how they crammed Smith's pockets full of the kiddie porn they took from his apartment. Wind blew it all over Dinsmore's yard and into the neighbor's. And the feds checked Smith's email. You know that dirt bag was grooming two other young boys from his town?"

"Say what you will about these shooters," Erskine said, "but they're sure as hell taking out the garbage."

Abrams nodded. "Feeb profilers figure them as super-conservative, super-pissed-off at 'leniency in the legal system.' Their words. They think one or more of them lost a person they loved because some punk went through the revolving door. So this is payback time."

Cronin shook his head. "Maybe that's part of it. But I have a feeling this is more than personal revenge."

"Why?"

"If it was only revenge, then they would've hit only the perps responsible for their own losses, and maybe those judges or defense attorneys, but that would be all. I think they would've stopped by now. But they haven't. Besides, we've been looking hard at all the victim families in every case, and drawing blanks. None of them are good for this stuff."

"So if it's not personal revenge, where does that leave us?"

"Well, look at what they're doing, even here. These guys are getting back not just at specific perps, but at the people who turned them loose. And they seem to be operating by some sort of code. They whack only the killers and sex predators. But they don't kill anybody in the legal system or in any of those criminal-sympathizer groups."

"At least they haven't so far," Erskine said. "They just embarrass the hell out of them."

"Exactly. They're doing what the system should've done to the perps. But then they bring the criminals right back to the doorsteps of the people who freed them. Literally. Plus the records of their crimes. These newspaper clippings, starting with the Hunter columns: It's like they're prosecutors building an indictment—only they're indicting the whole system. They're holding everybody accountable."

"Justice for all," Erskine said.

"There you go. So I don't see this as being about private revenge. It's bigger than that. It's about retribution. These guys don't think the *legal* system is a *justice* system anymore."

"Well, they got that right," Abrams said. He paused, lowering his voice. "So, you still suspect this could be a team of cops or ex-cops, Ed?"

"It fits. The shooter at Prince George's Mall badged the two guards and drove a Crown Vic—"

"But he was a fake cop. There's no 'Detective Lex Talionis.' The name's a joke—Latin for 'eye for an eye.' The badge number didn't check out legit, the car's plate was phony, and the security camera down the road showed the Crown Vic was civilian, not a P71. Come on, Ed, all that proves is that these people are good at masquerading and flashing fake IDs. We already knew that, from the Alexandria courthouse."

"That's not my point, Marty. I'm only saying the guy knew enough police procedure to convince the guards he was the real deal. Besides that, they know how to pick locks, bypass alarms and security gates, rig electronics, keep a crime scene clean. And they get in and out of places without arousing suspicion. Especially that. If they're police, that would explain it. Who stops a cop from going anywhere?"

Erskine was studying the exposed wiring around the elevator buttons. "I'm with Ed on this. We've already established they have a pile of money, multiple vehicles, a bunch of guns, plus people experienced in planning, logistics, surveillance, and conducting hits. Who else except cops would know all that stuff?"

Abrams shrugged. "People in government. Military, ex-military. Former SWAT or Navy SEALs or something."

"So what's their motive?" Cronin asked.

They looked at each other blankly.

Abrams turned to stare at the corpse. He sighed and his shoulders slumped. "Yeah. We still got jack shit."

BETHESDA, MARYLAND
Sunday, November 16, 9:35 a.m.

She drifted awake, wondering if she had been dreaming or if something had touched her bare shoulder. She kept her eyes closed and pulled the comforter higher around her.

Seconds later, a light tap on her cheek.

She opened an eye. Luna was a foot away from her face, paw extended.

"No," she groaned.

She felt Dylan stir somewhere behind her.

"We don't use that word here. Remember?"

"Not you. Your cat."

"Luna, let the lady sleep."

"Mrrrroww."

"Get your paw away from my face!"

"She's probably out of food. I'll take care of it."

She felt the bed quiver as he got up. Heard the thump of the departing cat hitting the floor. Felt herself drift off again....

*

She awoke some vague time later to the smell of coffee. After stopping in the bathroom, she padded out in her bathrobe and bare feet.

Dylan was also in his bathrobe, reading the Sunday paper at the dining table. He looked up at her and smiled.

"Hi, you."

"Hi, you," she answered. "Thanks for letting me sleep. At least this *morning*."

He chuckled, raised his mug. "Made another pot. You have first dibs."

"Great." She went into the kitchen, poured a cup, fetched a container of yogurt from the fridge, then joined him at the table.

"So where's Luna?"

"Curled up on my office chair."

"Ah. What's in the news today?"

He gave her that crooked grin she loved. "Only the greatest piece of writing in the history of investigative journalism."

"Oh Dylan! You didn't tell me! Another big crime exposé?"

"See for yourself." He slid the editorial section over to her, then got up with his empty mug and headed for the kitchen.

She spun it around, saw the headline spread across the front page of the section.

Felt her smile fade and blood drain from her face.

MACLEAN FAMILY FOUNDATION: THE CRIMINAL'S BEST FRIEND

News and Commentary by Dylan Lee Hunter

It is a tax-exempt charity, controlling over a billion dollars in assets.

Every day, without fanfare, it serves and defends a clientele that it characterizes as "society's stigmatized victims."

But its furtive, publicity-shy ways are completely understandable. After all, it is responsible for some of the most heinous crimes of the past decade.

Let me introduce you to the MacLean Family Foundation: the nation's most influential champion of murderers, rapists, and assorted predators.

It's the source of endless studies that excuse criminal behavior, and of countless policies that turn loose convicted criminals to prey on others.

It's the pillar that supports what I'll call "the Excuse-Making Industry."

She stopped reading. Her eyes drifted to the middle of the page.

To the large photo of her father.

She felt disembodied, unreal.

She was staring at the handsome, smiling face—her father.

Steps away, whistling in the kitchen, was his enemy— her lover.

Well, what did you expect? You knew it had to come to this.

"Wonk? You up?" He was on his cell with somebody. "Good, you already saw it, then.... Well, thanks. But you outdid yourself, too. Can't thank you enough for all the research." He paused, then laughed. "For sure. We've turned over a rock, my friend. Now all the roaches will be scurrying around, looking for cover.... Oh yes. The fireworks this time will be incredible..."

She closed her eyes.

"...No, not today. I expect they'll issue some response tomorrow, though. They'll have to. And thanks to you, I'm ready for it. You'll get a bonus for this one, Wonk. I'm doubling your usual rate.... Absolutely, I'm serious. The check will go out tomorrow.... No, you deserve it.... You, too. Now go enjoy your afternoon."

She felt as if the walls in the apartment were shrinking, threatening to crush her.

You've been living a lie.

How could you do this to him?

And how could you do this to your own father?

"What's wrong?"

She realized she was shaking. With a great effort, she forced herself to raise her head, meet his eyes. He stood near, staring at her, his eyes wide with alarm.

She couldn't tell him. Not yet. She needed time to think.

"I don't feel very well."

"I can see that. You're all white! I should call a doctor."

"No, no! It's not that bad. I just.... It must be all the Mexican we ate last night. My stomach isn't right and I just had a dizzy spell.... Maybe I should lie down a bit."

He took her arm as she got up and he led her back into the bedroom. He helped her under the covers, pulled them up around her.

"Are you sure I can't get you anything?"

"No, I'll be okay. Really, Dylan. Just let me be for a bit."

"All right." He bent and kissed her cheek. Then went to the window and drew the heavy curtains closed.

Each act of tenderness made her feel more guilty. She blinked back tears as he turned to leave.

"Dylan."

"Yes?"

She had to say it. Now. Whatever happened later, he had to hear it.

"I love you.... I want you to know that. I really do love you."

He didn't move for a moment. Then he approached the bed. Leaned down, took her face in his big, strong hands. His eyes, usually so intense, were soft now.

"And I love you, Annie Woods. I really do love you."

It was the first time they had said it.

He kissed her, gently.

Then he straightened, smiled down at her, and left, closing the door softly.

She turned into the pillow to muffle her sobs.

*

After about an hour, she left the bed and went into the bathroom. She looked in the mirror.

You fraud.

Her eyes were red-rimmed and bloodshot. It would be obvious she'd been crying.

First, a shower.

Then she had to make an excuse and get out of here. Get away for awhile. Think.

She had deceived him. And he would hate her for it.

She ran the water as cold as she could stand. Stepped in and stood there, taking it.

You fraud.

TWENTY-THREE

ALEXANDRIA, VIRGINIA
Monday, November 17, 9:45 a.m.

"You look like you just ate a crap sandwich," Erskine said.

From behind his desk, Erskine stared up at him over his half-moon glasses.

"Just did," Cronin said. He tilted his head toward the chief's glassed-in office.

"Let's have it."

Cronin flopped into Erskine's visitor chair. Around them, the other desks were half-occupied by uniforms and investigators working leads and catching up on weekend paperwork. As usual, they had to talk over a steady din of chatter, chirping phones, and questions shouted and answered across the room.

"Read the latest Hunter article in the *Inquirer* yesterday?"

"Naw, I'm illiterate, Ed. Of course I did. He really laid it out, didn't he?"

"Too well. He's been pissing people off for weeks. People with clout. Judges, prosecutors, attorneys, prison officials. Now this MacLean guy, who's politically connected and has boatloads of money. Going after him seems to have been the last straw. Chief got a call last night, he wouldn't say who. He told me the Powers That Be want us to lean on Hunter and get him to shut up."

Erskine's mouth fell open. "Lean on a reporter? That's nuts!"

"Of course it is. It shows how desperate they're getting. They tried to talk to his bosses at the newspaper, but it didn't work. So now they're telling us to play hardball with him. They're pretending it's because he's encouraging the vigilantes. 'Every time he writes, somebody dies,' is the official line. But it's really because he's embarrassing a lot of suits."

"But why ask Alexandria PD to go after him? We're small potatoes."

"I asked. Chief says he owes a big favor to some guy, and now the guy's calling it in. He was told they don't want the whole task force to be implicated if it goes bad. So, guess who's our department's designated hitter?"

Erskine stared at him. "You're kidding."

"I wish. Chief told me, 'Nose into his background a bit. Find something we can use to persuade him to back off.'"

"Jesus. That sucks."

"Tell me about it."

His eyes drifted around the room, watching his friends work. Most of their faces looked like he felt. Worn. Tired. He thought of his rookie days, when he showed up here every day full of piss and vinegar and pride and idealism. He hadn't felt any of that for—hell, he couldn't remember how long. And he knew why. Too many days like this one.

He faced his partner. "Dammit, Paul. I like the guy. I even told him the whole department was behind what he's doing."

"He's saying all the things that need to be said."

"And now I'm being ordered to go back on what I said to him."

"I'm sorry, Ed.... So what are you going to do?"

"I don't know." He moved a paperweight on Erskine's desk in small circles. "I'll start poking into his background this morning. Go through the motions, anyway. Just enough to keep the brass and the mayor from breathing down my neck. Hell, it's not like I don't have enough to do already."

"Ed. You know I'll cover for you, if you need me to."

He met his partner's eyes. "Thanks, Paul. But I'll be okay." He sighed and rose to his feet. "It's just that, days like this, I wonder whose side we're really on."

CLAIBOURNE CORRECTIONAL FACILITY
CLAIBOURNE, VIRGINIA
Monday, November 17, 10:35 a.m.

As always, the dozen men sat in a circle in the second-floor meeting room. As always, each of them spoke in turn, and to all appearances, spontaneously and sincerely.

As always, they'd rehearsed their lines together ahead of time.

Adrian Wulfe looked around at his fellow inmates. At all the jutting jaws, the bulging biceps, the scars, the tats, the dreads. At the feigned expressions of interest and contrition, masking boredom. He glanced at the clock for the third time in a minute, wishing the hands to move faster toward eleven.

Frankfurt's group counseling sessions were scheduled twice a week. Almost all of them hated being here. Except for Preacher Jim, of course. The gaunt-faced old-timer with the stringy gray hair sat across from him, rocking back and forth in his chair, looking up at the ceiling periodically, like he was waiting for Jesus or something. Whenever anybody spoke, Preacher would mumble to himself, then say "Amen!" when they were done.

The others, though, were here for the same reasons he was. They volunteered for Group only to get good-behavior credits and knock some time off their prison terms. Occasionally, if you impressed The Hairball with your "progress," he'd put in a good word and you'd get some perks, too. More free time in the music room or library, better jobs. And you made him feel important, like he was accomplishing something. A win-win situation. Sure, they all hated sucking up to him, but you did what you had to do.

His eyes followed The Hairball, who strolled in the center of the ring, like a lion tamer. He didn't know who had come up with Frankfurt's nickname, but it stuck. The shrink's frizzy, unkempt hair and beard did kind of remind you of something a cat coughed up.

Wulfe was one of the few in the joint who had some college, so they all came to him when they needed something to be written, or for help in what to say in situations like this. He traded on his education and literacy for favors, cash, and contraband. For Group, he coached

them to think of it like an acting class. You're putting on a
show, a performance. You have to seem credible. And if
you can impress The Hairball, you could probably snow
parole and probation people later, too.

They listened to him, not only because he was smart,
but because he'd actually taken two semesters of drama in
college. Mainly to get near the theater girls, because he'd
been told that artsy bitches would do pretty much anything,
in bed or out. So he took acting classes and learned some
Stanislavsky bullshit, before the college tossed him out on
his ass near the end of his sophomore year. But he could
still cry on cue, if he wanted to. Not here, of course, or
they'd think you were a pussy, which could be fatal. But
outside, it came in handy, sometimes. Like if you wanted to
get in some broad's pants, and maybe there were people
nearby, so you couldn't just force her, and you had to do
the Mr. Sensitivity act. Sure, it was better when you just
forced them, but sometimes you had to make do.

Bo Weller, the Aryan Brotherhood enforcer, was into
his routine, now. It was all Wulfe could do to keep from
laughing. Here's this three-hundred-pound dude with a
broken nose and all those gang tats bullshitting Hairball
about how his parents' divorce when he was thirteen left a
"hole in his emotions." Wulfe had given Weller that line
yesterday, in exchange for a couple of cigarettes. Weller was
a moron, and Wulfe wasn't sure if Hairball would see right
through a line that lame; but he could tell that the shrink
was eating it up. People believe what they want to believe.
So, you feed them what they want to hear, and you own
them.

But he could tell that Hairball was sulking today. He
didn't seem to be paying much attention to what the guys
were saying. He had a grim expression on his face and a

faraway look in his eyes while he paced in the middle of the circle.

Wulfe knew it was the article in yesterday's paper by that smart-mouthed prick Hunter. He was pissed off when he read it, so he could only imagine how pissed The Hairball was. It was bringing all sorts of unwanted attention to the shrink's programs, including this one.

That could screw his own chances to get out early. He had to try and move the ball down the field now, if he could.

"Excuse me, Bo," he said, "I'm sorry for interrupting. But I wanted to ask Dr. Frankfurt something."

The dude blinked. "Ah...okay."

The shrink frowned at him. "Mr. Wulfe?"

"I hope I'm not being out of line, doctor—and please tell me to mind my own business if I am. But you seem—I don't know, a bit distracted today. I just wonder if there's a problem?"

Frankfurt blinked in surprise. Then his eyes narrowed and his mouth began to work before he finally spoke. "Yes. As a matter of fact, there *is* a problem."

It was as if Wulfe had lanced a boil. The shrink started to pace more rapidly around the middle of the circle, his words pouring out in a torrent.

"Perhaps some of you saw the *Inquirer* yesterday. That horrible article about the MacLean Foundation and its inmate rehabilitation programs?" The guys looked at each other and some nodded. "Well, as you may know, I head the Psychological Services Program for the foundation. And this outrageous attack cuts at the heart of everything we're trying to do. Including this counseling program."

Everybody made the appropriate faces and angry noises.

"The author, some hack writer named Dylan Hunter, who must think of himself as the Lone Ranger, has been riding his 'crime-fighter' hobby horse for months. He's doing tremendous damage to years of work serving clients like you, undermining our public and political support. I just spoke to Kenneth MacLean himself about an hour ago, and he's extremely worried that some key backing we've had for the sentencing reform bill in Congress might now be in jeopardy. In fact, immediately after this session, I have to drive to Washington for a press conference with him. We're going to set the record straight."

Wulfe nodded sympathetically at the jerk. "I'm truly sorry, doctor. Your work has been such a big help to all of us, and I'm sure to many others."

"Thank you, Mr. Wulfe. I appreciate that more than you could know."

Oh, I'm sure of that, Hairball.

"It's really an either-or choice for society," the pompous ass continued. "We can dwell in the bitter past, looking behind us down the path of retribution and recrimination. Or we can look forward and take a new path to personal rehabilitation and restoration."

"What he's writing, if you ask me, it's downright un-Christian," Wulfe interjected. "It's contrary to the virtues of forgiveness and trust as rewards for sincere repentance."

"Amen, brother!" Preacher Jim chimed in.

"Precisely!" The Hairball said, nodding enthusiastically.

Encouraged, Wulfe stood and kept going, taking care to keep his voice restrained. "I think it all comes down to this: How do the American people want to see themselves when they look in the mirror? As cold-blooded, Old-Testament, eye-for-an-eye savages? As an angry lynch mob looking for revenge for every slight against them? Or do they want to look into that mirror and see a reflection of the New Testament virtues of mercy and compassion and human salvation?"

He nodded as he said it, looking around the room at the others. They caught on and nodded in agreement, and Preacher "amened" him twice more.

"What I've learned here from you, Dr. Frankfurt," he concluded, "is that the lessons of psychology are really the same lessons that we can find in the Sermon on the Mount. And I'm grateful to you for teaching me that."

The Hairball stared at him, blinking rapidly. For a minute, he thought crazily that the idiot was going to rush across the room and hug him; it seemed all he could do to contain himself.

"Thank *you*, Mr. Wulfe!" he said at last. "As I mentioned, I have to go to Washington now, so I'm going to cut this session short today. I hope we've all learned something from Mr. Wulfe's heartfelt words. I want us to ponder them until we meet again on Thursday. That will be all for now."

The men looked at each other and got up to leave.

"Adrian, if I could have a word with you for a moment."

So it's *Adrian* now. Wulfe sat back down as the room cleared.

"Let me tell you how much I was moved by your eloquent statement just now. I want to thank you for that, and also share with you how impressed I am by your progress."

"I certainly couldn't have gotten this far without your help, doctor."

"You've already demonstrated your maturity in so many ways over these many months. I've shared with my colleagues the story of your enormous restraint, compassion, and dignity during your meeting with Mrs. Copeland two months ago. You've also taken a leadership role here in Group, and your behavioral record in Claibourne has been spotless. Adrian, I want to say that I consider you to be an exemplary client."

"Dr. Frankfurt...I just don't know what to say to that."

"I know that it's highly unusual, given the crime for which you were convicted, but there's no question in my mind, none at all, that you've earned placement in the Accelerated Community Reintegration Track."

Yes. Wulfe's heart was pounding. He did his best to push his face into a humble expression of speechless gratitude.

"Given the current circumstances," The Hairball went on, "with all this media sensationalism and vigilante rubbish, I'm not sure how much longer we'll even have enlightened programs such as this one. So I want to make sure that I initiate your transition right away. And as a first step in your reintegration, Adrian, I'm recommending you for your initial community furlough this coming Christmas."

Nobody else was in the room, so it was time for Stanislavsky. The first tears began to flow as he reached out and clutched the shrink's hand.

"Dr. Frankfurt, you can't begin to imagine how important this opportunity is to me. And let me assure you, I know how to take full advantage of it."

TWENTY-FOUR

WASHINGTON, D.C.
Monday, November 17, 2:02 p.m.

Kenneth MacLean checked his watch as a straggler entered the room at the back, found a chair, and sat down. He turned and smiled reassuringly at Dr. Frankfurt, who was seated beside him, sweating and tapping his foot. Then he rose from his chair and took position behind the podium.

Before him, nearly three dozen seats in the Murrow Room on the thirteenth floor of the National Press Club were filled with reporters, and no less than five television cameras faced him from the back and sides of the room. It was exactly the kind of media circus he'd done his best to prevent, all along. But the "D.C. vigilantes" story had gone national weeks before, and now the *Inquirer* had tried to link those lurid stories directly to his foundation.

To *him*.

He fought down his anger while he shuffled his notes. It would be counterproductive to lose his temper here, in spite of how unfair the smear campaign was. He had to remain calm and focus on the facts. For the facts were on his side. He raised his eyes. Many of the reporters were reading the materials in the press packets they had distributed. Good. He knew that much of that information would find its way into the stories they filed this evening.

He spotted George and Wendy, Congressman Horowitz's aides, sitting near the back. They would be reporting back to their boss on how it went. He took a deep breath, knowing that his life's work was on the line. He let it out slowly, smiled, and began.

"Good afternoon. Thank you for coming. My name is Ken MacLean, and I'm president of the MacLean Family Foundation. Seated to my right is Dr. Carl Frankfurt, chief of the Psychological Services Unit in our Justice Program. We're here to set the record straight concerning a host of misrepresentations in the media about us. So, we'll begin by having Dr. Frankfurt give you a PowerPoint presentation to clarify who we are, what we do, and why."

Frankfurt took his place at the podium and flipped a switch to shut off the lights in the room. For the next ten minutes, he clicked through the slides, explaining the foundation's history, objectives, and projects in the criminal justice area. At one point, the door in the back of the room briefly opened and closed. MacLean turned to look, but the brightness from outside the darkened room prevented him from seeing who had entered.

"As you see, then, the MacLean Family Foundation has developed safe, cost-effective, ground-breaking alternatives to incarceration for minor and nonviolent offenders," Frankfurt concluded, pausing on a final slide. It showed a group of smiling young men, mostly African-American and Hispanic, posing with him on the sidewalk outside the main entrance to the foundation. "We've pioneered inmate therapeutic programs that have reduced their recidivism. We've championed the cause of diversionary sentencing, to ease the burden of prison and jail overcrowding. We've persuaded many governors and state legislatures to repeal the mindless get-tough crime laws and mandatory-minimum sentencing statutes that they passed in recent years. Besides being the humane thing to do, it's simply good economics. States are going bankrupt due to an orgy of expensive prison construction."

He clicked the lights back on.

MacLean rose from his seat to stand beside him. "Thank you, Carl. Ladies and gentlemen, we've shown that we can manage tens of thousands of convicted offenders safely, and far more economically, outside of prison walls. But what primarily motivates us at the MacLean Family Foundation is the moral dimension of our work."

He smiled again, his eyes scanning the faces before him. "Our overriding concern is improving conditions for people who are badly served by the established institutions of society. We *must* turn away from the excessive use of prisons. Our cherished humanitarian values are being corroded by our excessive focus on vindictiveness. And now we'll be happy to entertain your questions."

A forest of hands shot up.

"Yes, you first."

"Andrea O'Donnell, A.P. Dr. Frankfurt, you make a convincing case about the high cure rates of your therapy programs. But how do you answer those critics who point to horror stories like those in the recent *Inquirer* series:

offenders who participated in your programs, were released early, then committed horrible new crimes?"

MacLean saw Frankfurt's lips press into a hard line as the psychologist leaned toward the microphone.

"You're referring to inflammatory lies and misrepresentations spread by a sleazy, tabloid journalist. Well, all he has managed to accomplish is to encourage a wave of vigilante violence. But let me answer your question directly. Of course, no rehabilitation program, no matter how good, can be one hundred percent effective. You'll always have tragic exceptions. But wise policy-makers have to weigh their many social benefits against some unfortunate individual costs. And here, I think the conclusion is clear: The good of society, as a whole, must take precedence over these isolated exceptions, because—"

"—because individual crime victims are expendable."

MacLean wheeled around, his eyes searching for whoever had made the loud comment. The reporters swiveled in their seats, looking toward the back of the room.

He stood leaning casually against the wall between two TV cameras, arms folded across his chest.

"Excuse me," MacLean said. "You know the rules here, sir. And Dr. Frankfurt wasn't addressing you."

"Oh, but he was."

The dark-haired man stepped forward as all the TV cameras swung his way. "I'm the sleazy tabloid journalist to whom he was referring."

MacLean felt something fall in the pit of his stomach.

Don't let this spin out of control.

"So, you are Mr. Hunter, then," he said, noticing that his voice sounded tight.

"That's right. And since this news conference is supposed to be about setting the record straight about your foundation, I knew that I'd better be here."

MacLean gripped the podium. "You have your own media platform, sir," he said, trying to keep his voice even. "This is ours. You are permitted here as a member of the press. However, if you won't follow basic journalistic etiquette, I'll have you escorted out."

"And be perfectly within your rights to do so," Hunter said, smiling. Hands in his trouser pockets, he began to stroll slowly down the outside aisle, moving toward him. "But then, all these fine reporters would have every right to believe that you're ducking the tough questions. The kind of questions that only I can ask."

"Get out of here!" Frankfurt yelled, his face red. "You've caused enough trouble!"

"Easy, Carl," MacLean interrupted, placing his hand on the man's shoulder. "We have nothing to hide or be ashamed of. Remember: We have the facts on our side."

"Do you, now?" Hunter said. "I wasn't taking notes, but I recall a number of—well, let's call them 'errors' in your presentation."

"Such as?"

"Such as your claims about your success in rehabilitating criminals, Mr. MacLean. Your re-offense statistics—they're garbage."

Frankfurt shouted, "Only four percent of the clients participating in our reintegration programs are convicted of a serious new offense. That's a *fact!*"

Hunter stopped about ten feet from where they stood. A slightly crooked smile formed on his lips. "Doctor, please. I read the study where you make that statistical claim. And it's phony."

"What do you mean, 'phony'?" MacLean demanded, hearing the edge in his voice.

"First of all, that four-percent failure rate is based on only one year of tracking your 'clients,' after they're freed—and not three years, as in most recidivism studies.

"Second, you only track new *convictions* in a court of law. You don't bother to count the much higher number of new *arrests*.

"Third, you didn't mention that most of those caught re-offending aren't even arrested or sent into a courtroom: They're just returned behind bars for parole and probation violations."

"But you—"

"Fourth and finally, you define 'serious offense' so that it excludes all new property crimes, gang participation, illegal possession of weapons and drugs, most domestic abuse reports, and a host of other criminal activity that you people call 'nonviolent.' So you don't bother to count any of those, either."

He chuckled, shaking his head. "I've recalculated the numbers, gentlemen. And here's the bottom line. If you include everything I just mentioned, the actual re-offense rate from your program graduates isn't four percent; it's over seventy percent."

Frankfurt opened and closed his mouth. MacLean jumped in.

"Mr. Hunter, I don't know how you do *your* calculations, but the efficacy of our programs has been independently reviewed by scholars and criminal-justice organizations across the nation. And they emphatically do *not* support your conclusions."

"I'm not surprised, Mr. MacLean. Three of the groups conducting those so-called 'independent' reviews were funded by your own foundation. And their statistical manipulations are similar to what I've just described."

Hunter turned to face the room. "I encourage you gentlemen and ladies to do your own checking, your own arithmetic. I believe you're in for a few surprises."

"Why are you doing this?" Frankfurt yelled. "Why are you targeting programs that help society's victims?"

Hunter turned back to look at them both. "Victims?" he said, his voice quiet, cold. "Is that how you think of your criminal clientele, Doctor? Well, they certainly have many champions. Your billion-dollar foundation, for one—and many more like it. Also, defense attorneys and bar associations. Plea-bargaining prosecutors and lenient judges. Psychiatrists. Ministers. Politicians. Charities and advocacy groups. And even more: Criminals get all sorts of taxpayer-funded benefits and help, inside of prison and outside. Yet you call them 'victims.'

"Well, I've been spending time with a different group of victims. *Crime victims.* Victims of the predators that you represent. Victims of the thugs that you recycle back onto the streets. You ask why I'm doing this. Because it's time that somebody represented *them.*"

MacLean saw the reporters scribbling furiously on their notepads; saw the operators shifting their cameras back and forth, from Hunter to them; knew they were transmitting the dramatic images down to the satellite trucks on the street outside, and from there to their stations and networks. He noticed the expressions on the faces of Congressman Horowitz's two young staffers, and he cringed inside, knowing how their boss would react when he saw this disaster unfold on television.

The whole news conference was slipping away from him. He had to say something, stop the bleeding.

"Mr. Hunter," he said as calmly as he could, "you seem to believe that we have no concern for crime victims. But we do. In your article yesterday, you attacked H.R. 207, the model legislation that we helped to frame. Are you aware that this bill will add billions of dollars in grants from the federal government to the states, earmarked to aid crime victims?"

He saw a glint in the man's eye.

"That's great, Mr. MacLean," Hunter said. "Because if Congress passes your early-release bill, there will be thousands more crime victims. And they will need every penny of that aid."

CIA HEADQUARTERS, LANGLEY, VIRGINIA
Monday, November 17, 2:35 p.m.

"And they will need every penny of that aid."

She felt the impact of his words like an electric shock, transmitted to her right through the TV screen by the stunned look on her father's face. She watched in helpless, unblinking anguish, witnessing his dreams, his ideals, *his soul* being crushed.

Crushed ruthlessly by the man she loved.

Dylan—stop! Please stop!

She had slipped away from her office to this small conference room to watch the live broadcast of the news conference, which was being carried by a national cable news channel. She had hoped that her father could somehow reclaim the personal reputation that Dylan's article had so badly damaged. And for a while the whole event went smoothly—until she was startled by the familiar voice, strong and deep:

"...because individual crime victims are expendable."

She gasped at the words, disbelieving. Then stared at the screen as the camera swung to him.

She saw the familiar tangle of thick, dark curls, the hollow cheeks, the proud thrust of his chin. Saw the fearless flash in those eyes, the mocking twist of those lips. Then the camera pulled back to reveal his body, lean and relaxed, the body she knew so well, now moving forward slowly, deliberately toward her father, like a prowling panther stalking its prey.

She had jumped to her feet and approached the screen. She hung onto every word of their exchanges, terrified to see what would happen, unable to tear her eyes away as the horror unfolded.

Now there was a commotion. Reporters stood and shouted over each other, directing questions at the three of them. Frankfurt was yelling something at Dylan; her father, his face blank, stood mute and unmoving behind the podium.

Then Dylan turned toward the reporters approaching him and made a dismissive motion, brushing off their questions. "I've given you plenty to chew on."

He walked swiftly back in the direction of the camera, his image growing larger until his face nearly filled the screen before swerving past. The camera swung back toward the front of the room, zooming in on her father, who was now gathering his notes and refusing further questions. Then it spun toward Frankfurt, who had stopped halfway down the aisle, where he was surrounded by reporters. He was gesturing wildly and saying things that she couldn't make out in the din.

The TV network's reporter moved into the frame, holding a microphone. "A stunning turn of events here at the National Press Club as Dylan Hunter—the *Inquirer* reporter at the center of the firestorm of controversy about the criminal justice system and the D.C. vigilantes—crashes the MacLean news conference and confronts him face to face. Let's take a moment just to recap what we've just witnessed...."

She pressed the remote button, extinguishing the program.

She knew what she had just witnessed.

WASHINGTON, D.C.
Monday, November 17, 4:02 p.m.

The phone chirped, and Danika glanced down at the console. Saw that the incoming call was for Dylan Hunter's line.

"Mr. Hunter's answering service. May I help you?"

"Hello, this is Detective Sergeant Cronin of the Alexandria Police."

She recalled the sexy cop with the bright blue eyes and smiled to herself. "I remember you, Detective. How may I help you?"

"It's Danika, right?"

She felt a little twinge of pleasure. "Why, yes, sir."

"Well, Danika, I was hoping to catch Mr. Hunter, if he's in."

"No sir, I'm afraid he's not. He's rarely here, as you probably know. He usually calls in for his messages once a day, and he did that just a few minutes ago. I'm afraid I don't have a way to reach him, probably until tomorrow."

"I see. That's too bad. This is pretty time-sensitive."

"I'm really sorry. I can take your message and—" The thought struck her. "Oh! I just remembered. He gave me a number. His girlfriend's, actually. He said he might be reachable through her."

"He has a girlfriend then?"

"Oh yes," she said, chuckling. "They just met, not too long ago. She's a real beauty, too."

He was silent a moment. "Tell you what, Danika. I'd really appreciate it if you would share the number with me. It's pretty urgent."

She hesitated, feeling torn. The procedure was for her to reach him herself, not to let out his contact information. Still...he was a police officer, after all, and they seemed to get along really well when she'd seen them together. And Dylan *was working* on crime stories....

"Danika?"

"I'm sorry, Detective Cronin. I was just thinking how I should handle this. You're both working on some of the same crime cases, I guess?"

"Why yes. You could say that."

"Well...I guess it would be all right, then." She looked up and read off Annie's number to him.

"Thanks so much, Danika. I really appreciate this."

"Well, you're welcome. I hope you can reach him through her, maybe after she gets off work this evening.... He's really gotten into this crime stuff lately, hasn't he?"

"Up to his ears, Danika."

TWENTY-FIVE

TYSONS CORNER, VIRGINIA
Monday, November 17, 4:55 p.m.

The Galleria at Tysons Corner was a familiar haunt for CIA employees. Because the mall was so close to headquarters, many people who worked for the Agency and lived nearby shopped here. Occasionally, young CSTs—Clandestine Service Trainees—were turned loose on the premises to practice surveillance detection and dead drops with concealment devices, or to arrange "clandestine" meetings at one of the restaurants with trainers posing as "foreign assets."

Now, here she was, having a clandestine meeting with a cop to discuss her lover.

Ironic.

She sat at a small dining table near the Starbuck's kiosk on the ground floor of the upscale mall, sipping a hot latte as she waited. She'd received the detective's call on her private cell at work, while she was still reeling from the televised debacle. The guy, Cronin, explained how he'd gotten her number, then was cryptic but insistent about needing to talk to her about Dylan. Which worried her. She suggested this place because of its proximity to the "insurance company" where she worked.

She checked her watch, then pulled out her cell and tried her father's number again. It still routed her to his voice mail.

"Dad, me again. Sorry to keep calling, but I'm worried about you. I know how hard it was for you today. I just want you to know I love you and I'm here for you. I'd like to come by and see you tonight, if you're home. So please call me back when you hear this."

She closed her phone. Then waited.

The cop showed up just a minute after five, dressed as he had described: gray coat over gray sports jacket and slacks. She stood as he approached.

"Ms. Woods? Ed Cronin, Alexandria P.D." Lean-faced. Intense blue eyes. Definitely good-looking.

"How do you do, Detective," she said, extending her hand.

He took it and smiled. "Please, sit. I realize you have things to do, so I won't be long."

"Thank you. I've had a difficult day. I hope what you're going to discuss with me isn't about to make it more so."

"I hope not, either. It's in connection with a case I'm working on. Today I stumbled across something puzzling concerning your"—he paused—"concerning Dylan Hunter.

I understand that you two are close, so perhaps you might help clear it up for me."

"You just said a 'case.' Is he involved in something I should know about?"

"No, not at all. You see, I'm a member of what the media calls 'the Vigilantes Task Force.' The first of those incidents took place on my turf, in Alexandria, which is how I got involved. And I met Mr. Hunter through his newspaper articles on the subject."

"Oh," she said, relaxing. "For a minute, there, you had me worried. So, what's the problem, or puzzle, then?"

He leaned forward, placing his palms flat on the table. "Let me be up front with you, Ms. Woods. Mr. Hunter has aggravated some prominent and powerful people with what he's been writing."

"I know."

"I can see it bothers you, too. Look, personally speaking, I applaud what he's doing. He's telling it like it is about the legal system. That article he wrote yesterday, for instance. He really opened a can of worms. I wish—"

"Excuse me, Detective," she interrupted, "exactly how might I help you?"

"I'm sorry. Forgive my babbling. As I said, because he's upset some V.I.P.'s, I've been asked to find out a bit more about him. You know—what makes him tick, why he's doing this. That sort of thing. But when I started to do that this morning, certain things just didn't add up."

"What do you mean?"

"Ms. Woods, when I started running background on him, I couldn't find any history anywhere for a 'Dylan Lee Hunter.' The name, it just materialized out of thin air two, three years ago. It doesn't lead back anywhere. It's like this guy is a ghost."

She laughed. "Oh, that! Okay, I see your problem. I encountered the same thing when we first started dating a couple of months ago, Detective Cronin. You see, I'm an investigator, too. Insurance claims. When we met, I did a bit of research to find out more about him. I also hit nothing but dead ends."

"So why are you laughing about it?"

"He explained it to me." She spent the next five minutes repeating to Cronin what Dylan had told her about his background. "So, you see," she concluded, "you probably can't find him because he legally changed his name to Dylan Lee Hunter. He showed me his IDs under that name, including his Maryland driver's license. I'm trained to judge such things, and they were completely authentic."

Cronin still looked skeptical. "I already guessed he might be using a pen name. Or even that he might have changed his name a few years back. But a *legal* name change leaves tracks. The new name would be linked to the old one in state records. We have access to their databases, and I ran checks this afternoon. Every state. Nada. We came up dry."

"There must be an explanation." She tried to remember exactly what he had told her. "He said he talked to some skip tracer, who coached him on how to disappear. He cut all his old ties, deleted and altered personal information on his old accounts before he closed them. Then he applied for a legal change of name and moved from place to place, job to job."

Cronin rapped his fingertips rhythmically on the table, looking off into the distance. "But that wouldn't be enough to erase all tracks from our databases that would tie him back to his old identity. For one thing, he'd still have the same Social Security number. That would link his new name to his old one."

A group of loud kids wandered by, horsing around. Her eyes rested on them, automatically, but not her mind. She was thinking of their first date, of how relaxed he looked while he explained it all to her. It had sounded so reasonable. Now, she felt her early uncertainty about him creeping back, like a slow-acting poison in her veins.

Cronin continued. "To really vanish as whoever he was, and establish a new identity as Dylan Hunter, he almost certainly would need a new SSN in that name." He stared off into space as he thought it through. "He couldn't function anywhere without one—get a job, buy a house, open bank accounts, or obtain other legit IDs, like a driver's license. But the Social Security Administration doesn't issue somebody a new number."

"What about a fake SSN? Maybe he got one and used that to obtain all his new IDs."

"Not likely. Not anymore. Since 9-11, the states have really tightened security on issuing copies of birth certificates and new drivers' licenses. A fake SSN would be flagged during their routine record checks. But you say he had authentic IDs. That suggests to me that he also has a real SSN, issued to Dylan Hunter. So how could *that* happen?"

"Well, illegal aliens seem to get all sorts of ID documents right on the streets. Don't they get Social Security cards, too?"

"People who want to hide their pasts, like illegal aliens, don't get government-issued SSNs. They usually rely on fake IDs. Fakes won't pass close inspections, so that limits what they can do without getting caught. That's why they typically work for cash at day jobs, where nobody bothers to check their IDs too closely. They keep a low profile.

They avoid attention and encounters with the law. Well, does that sound like Mr. Hunter? Instead, he's hiding in plain sight, right out in the open, and getting lots of public attention. And if you're right, he has managed to get legitimate government IDs for what he admits isn't his real name."

He paused. His cool blue eyes were direct and unsparing.

"Ms. Woods, what he told you just can't be the whole story. How well do you really know him?"

She felt a pang of anxiety. "What do you mean, 'how well'?"

"You don't really know much more about him than what he told you—right? From what you say, he's put up a wall between you and his past. You're a professional investigator. But even you haven't been able to confirm a single thing he's told you about his history."

Her mouth was going dry. She licked her lips. "So, what are you suggesting?"

"Nothing in particular. I certainly don't have reason to think he's involved in anything criminal, if that's what you mean. Maybe there is another perfectly reasonable explanation, like you say. I hope so. I like him. And I love what he's been doing. But the details of his story just don't add up. So far, we've been accepting him on blind trust."

The words struck her like a slap in the face.

"I'm sorry, I didn't mean that like it sounded."

"No. It's okay. You've just taken me off guard.... So, what are you going to do now?"

"First, I think I need to pay him a visit and get some answers."

"Maybe I should, too," she said.

"Not yet. That might be counterproductive. Look, why don't you let me poke into this a bit more before you do or say anything?"

He rose to his feet; she followed suit.

"Please let me know what you find out," she said.

"Will do. Meanwhile, here's my card. Just—well, just keep your eyes and ears open. Call me if you discover anything that might clear this up. And thanks for all your help."

*

She sat down again after he left. After a few minutes, she raised the cup to her lips; her hand shook as she sipped the coffee, now cold and bitter.

How can you really know someone?

How can you really trust anyone?

She replayed their conversations in her mind, seeking clues in his words to answer the questions now looming before her. But his words faded in her memory.

Instead, she saw his face. The firm, proud set of his mouth and chin, the direct intensity of his gaze—these seemed to banish all questions and doubts. She remembered the night they had met with the crime victims. Recalled the compassion of his gaze as he listened to them, the righteous anger in his eyes as he vowed to help them.

And today—that same fearless passion for justice in his words, in his bearing, when he confronted—

She closed her eyes.

No. He couldn't fake that. He *couldn't*. He could not be capable of anything dishonest or dishonorable.

Not a man who could look, act, and speak as he did.

Not a man who could love her as she knew he did.

No. She would not doubt him.

There had to be some good explanation.

WASHINGTON, D.C.
Monday, November 17, 6:15 p.m.

"Sweetie, I'm sorry I couldn't return your calls sooner. I know you've been worried, but I've been in meetings all afternoon.... Yes, and I appreciate your daughterly concern. But I'm all right. Really.... No, you don't have to do that. Besides, I won't be back home until late tonight.... We're just doing damage control. Right now, we're trying to salvage the House bill.... Sure. It's *very* difficult right now. This Hunter fellow has messed things up terribly. I just don't get it. He seems to have some kind of personal vendetta against us.... I hear what you're saying, but that's a debate for another time. At the moment, I have to get back to my dinner companions.... I will.... Love you, too."

MacLean left the alcove outside the restrooms and returned to his table. He liked the Old Ebbitt Grill, one of the better places for seafood and steaks. But tonight he had little appetite; coming here had been Carl Frankfurt's choice, and since it was so close to the Press Club, he didn't argue.

He slid into the plush green velvet seat on his side of the mahogany booth, facing both Frankfurt and Charlie Alexander, Congressman Horowitz's white-haired chief of staff. "Sorry again. My daughter was worried."

Alexander waved off the interruption. "No problem. Carl and I were talking about this situation while you were taking her call. It couldn't have come at a worse time, Ken."

MacLean knew that. So did Carl, whose morose expression was not improved by a half bottle of Cabernet.

"We're willing to do whatever it takes, Charlie."

The patrician-looking veteran of decades of Capitol Hill battles nodded and finished chewing a piece of his pork chop. "Sure," he said. "But we're gonna have to wait a while now. Till after the holidays, when all this hopefully blows over."

It stung him. "I was really hoping we could get in a vote this year, before the recess."

"No go, Ken. The congressman wanted that, too. But word is out all over the Hill about the news conference. MSNBC ran it live, and I'm sure Fox and CNN and everybody else will show clips tonight. We were counting noses this afternoon. Right now, we have less than a forty-sixty shot at passage. Odds are probably gonna go lower than that by tomorrow. We have to let all the hysteria die down a bit."

"I understand." He felt desolate, for the first time in years. The dream had been within his grasp, only to be snatched away. Torn from him by some self-absorbed fear-monger, pandering to society's basest instincts.

Alexander poked at the last piece of meat on his plate, then held it up on the end of his fork, gesturing with it to emphasize his points. "Look, Ken, I know how you feel. But Morrie warned you to keep a low profile on this, didn't he? I know, I know, you had to respond to that *Inquirer* hit job, I understand. But you shoulda just issued a written rebuttal. Not held a frickin' news conference. You never do that on something this emotional. These things can turn into sideshows."

"Tell me about it," Carl mumbled, his body sagging low over his plate.

"All right, then," MacLean said. "So, how do we play this from here?"

Alexander took a big gulp of red to wash down the last morsel, then smacked his lips appreciatively. "At this point, I don't think it does us any good for you to put out some kinda written reply. It only keeps this in the headlines. We need to turn down the volume, let this fade from people's memories. And it will, trust me. So, you go about your business quietly. You do what Morrie told you before: You stay out of the limelight. Do whatever it is you people do, but don't make a big public issue about it."

"We won't. The only thing we have coming up is our annual Christmas party. It's black tie, invitation only. So there's no chance of that reporter being admitted."

"Good.... Ah, look, Ken, I know Morrie has attended that in the past. But circumstances being what they are, I'm guessing he may take a pass this year. Now, I'm not gonna speak for him and say that's definite; just don't be surprised if it turns out that way."

He gritted his teeth, forced a smile. "I'll understand if he can't be there. Although please convey to him my hope that he will."

"Absolutely. He'll consider it, sure. We've got, what, over a month. If everything's calmed down by then, he'll probably show." He wiped his mouth with his white linen napkin, leaving a pink stain, then dropped it in a heap on his plate. "Look, Ken, I know how tough this is for you, but we gotta face realities. The congressman is one of the most progressive Members. He's on your side. This bill means a lot to him, too. Morrie'll do everything he can to get everybody in the caucus back on board right after the holidays, and then we'll stick it back on the calendar. I figure we can get this through in early March. Just be patient a bit longer."

He slid awkwardly out of his seat and stood. He was a big guy: big belly, big lips, big red nose, big booming voice. MacLean also got up and shook hands. Alexander nodded at Carl, who remained seated and sullen.

MacLean returned to his seat. He looked at his half-eaten portion of Alaskan halibut. He wasn't in the mood. Instead, he picked up his glass of Spanish white, an Albariño.

"Well, Carl. It looks as if we have to recalculate our priorities for the next month."

The psychologist bobbed his head. "Yes, I've been thinking about that for the past hour."

"I'm listening." He took a sip.

"The way I see it, Ken, some of our flagship programs are now in jeopardy. I'm especially worried about the Accelerated Community Reintegration Track."

"Yes, it would be a prime target in this poisoned atmosphere, wouldn't it? A lot of our sponsoring partners in the communities are likely to back away from us when our contracts come up for renewal in January."

"So if we're going to meet next year's quotas and mandates from the board, we'd better act now and put a lot more clients into the pipeline before it might be shut off."

MacLean twirled the glass; the pale gold liquid shimmered in the light of the table lamp. "That makes sense to me. There are so many who have earned their chance. It would be cruel if their hopes were dashed because of all this."

"Anyway, I have a list of candidates for placement. I can have it on your desk in the morning. And I'd like at least four of them to have Christmas furlough opportunities this year."

"I've always trusted your judgment about such things, Carl. You know these clients better than anyone. I'll sign off on the list and submit their names, along with our recommendation, to the various state corrections departments." He was about to take another sip, then paused. "Remember, though—we were just warned to stay out of the spotlight. Is there anyone on your list who might provoke any more public controversy?"

Carl Frankfurt picked up his fork and broke off a piece of trout parmesan. "Of course not. My furlough candidates, especially, are model clients. You wouldn't believe how much they've grown. Ken, I would trust every one of those guys with my life."

TWENTY-SIX

BETHESDA, MARYLAND
Tuesday, November 18, 1:25 p.m.

"It's me, Danika."

"Hi there, Mr. Hunter! How are you this afternoon?"

"Great. Any calls or messages?"

"Not since yesterday's call from that detective, um, Mr. Cronin."

He stopped pacing his kitchen floor. "Call?"

"Didn't he get in touch with you last night?"

"Why, no. How was he supposed to do that?"

Pause.

"Well, sir—you gave me Ms. Woods's number, and you told me to use it to contact you if I couldn't reach you. Detective Cronin, he called yesterday and said it was an urgent matter, so—Well, I gave him that number.... He told me he'd be calling Ms. Woods right away to reach you."

His mind raced, considering possible implications.

"Mr. Hunter? I hope I wasn't out of line, doing that."

He forced a smile, hoping she'd hear it in his voice. "Oh, no. Not at all, Danika. That's fine. I'm afraid I didn't get his message, though. Perhaps she had her phone off. I'll call him back right away. Any mail?"

"Nothing today."

"All right. Thanks. You have a nice afternoon, now."

"You too, Mr. Hunter."

He closed the phone.

Thought some more.

He took the cell into his den, pulled Cronin's business card from the small stack on his desk, then thumbed in the number.

"Cronin."

"Dylan Hunter. You were trying to reach me?"

"Oh.... Yes. That's right, Mr. Hunter. I was."

But you're surprised to hear from me.

"So what's up, Detective?"

"I was...just going through some things and was hoping we could sit down and chat. Are you able to meet me later this afternoon?"

Forced casualness.

"No problem. How about my office? Three o'clock okay?"

"Sure. That'll be fine. See you then."

He snapped the phone shut. Flipped it over, thumbed off the cover, removed the battery. He'd dump this one on the way into town.

Something was off.

He thought about how Annie had left so abruptly late Sunday morning. And how she hadn't wanted to talk that evening. Okay, she was sick. But then there was their phone chat last night. She seemed to be responding mechanically, volunteering little, with forced cheerfulness. Something like the way Cronin's voice sounded now.

He tapped the battery against the desk top.

Felt Luna rub against his shin.

"Hello, girl." He picked her up, put her on his lap. Began to pet her, soothing his own nerves.

"If Cronin wanted her number so badly," he said aloud, "he must have either spoken to her, or left a message for me. Then why didn't she tell me?"

The cat purred in response to his voice and the strokes down her back.

What if he had talked to her, though? About what?

"Maybe he said something that upset her."

"Mrrrr."

"That could explain why she sounded so strange on the phone last night." He swiveled the chair gently from side to side. "But it wouldn't explain why she seemed upset the day before."

He tried to recall the sequence of events. Everything had been great on Saturday, and it seemed fine when she got up on Sunday morning. Then she got some coffee and sat at the table. He remembered how she looked when he told her that he had written a new piece. Authentically excited, even thrilled. Then he left her to read the paper, went into the kitchen for a refill, and phoned Wonk.

And when he returned to the table, she was sick.

Or upset by something she read?

"Okay, let's assume she really was sick. What about last night, then?"

He tried to remember the details of that call. Her voice seemed too flat at first, as if she didn't want to really be talking to him. Then, abruptly, too cheery. He asked how she was. Better, she said. What was she doing? Oh, just cleaning up after dinner. Want to come here and stay over on Tuesday night, Annie? Sure.

It had gone like that for several minutes. Usually, she was eager to hear his voice, eager to chat. This time it was like pulling teeth.

Another thing: She hadn't mentioned that she'd seen or heard about his confrontation at the MacLean news conference. Not until he brought it up and asked her. She said she had. Then she added only: "You made your points very well."

He remembered feeling a bit let down. In the past, she'd been excited about his writing, always telling him how much she admired him for fighting for crime victims. And this was his biggest coup so far. Yet her response was oddly muted—as if she were just trying to be polite.

"As if she really didn't mean it," he said aloud.

The cat tapped his hand with her paw. He started to pet her again.

Something had happened. His gut now told him it started on Sunday morning. When she sat at the table and started to read his article.

What was it about the article?

He looked at the cell phone lying on his desk. He was tempted to call her, ask bluntly what was wrong.

No. It was better to wait until tonight. When he could see her reactions, read her eyes.

Whatever it was, it couldn't be good.

WASHINGTON, D.C.
Tuesday, November 18, 3:02 p.m.

"Mr. Hunter?"

He glanced up from the papers on his desk. "Come on in, Detective Cronin." He motioned to the guest chair.

Cronin smiled and was just settling in when Hunter spoke first.

"You're concerned about something, Detective."

It took him off-guard. As intended. But Cronin was good. He took his time making himself comfortable, all the while looking at him steadily.

"I am."

Hunter nodded and waited him out.

Cronin gave it up. "So let me get to the point. I've been checking into your background, Mr."—he paused a second, just to lay emphasis on the next word—"Hunter. And I'm having a bit of trouble."

He smiled at the cop. "I'm not surprised."

Cronin didn't expect that, either. "No?"

"First, may I ask what prompted you to want to check my background?"

Cronin hesitated, obviously weighing his words. Then said, "You've managed to get under the skin of a lot of important people."

"You don't say."

"And they want to know why you're doing this stuff. I've been asked to find out more about you."

"Asked?"

That made the cop smile—against his will, he could tell.

"Okay. Not exactly asked."

"I appreciate the position you're in, Detective Cronin. So, let me guess: You want to know why all information about Dylan Lee Hunter goes back only a couple of years, then dead-ends."

Cronin stared at him, again thrown off-balance. Good.

"Well, it does arouse my curiosity."

"I changed my name. Quite legally, I may add."

"From what?"

Hunter held his eyes. "From a name that only I need to know."

"Maybe I do, too."

"Not unless I'm a suspect in some kind of a criminal investigation."

"Maybe you are."

He leaned back and laughed. "No, I'm not. You're fishing, Detective. I know you have your orders, but that's all this is. A fishing expedition. You said it yourself: I've gotten a lot of veddy, veddy important people's panties in a bunch, and now they're looking to get something on me. To shut me up."

The cop looked uncomfortable. Obviously, this wasn't going the way he'd planned. "You mind showing me some current ID?"

"Not at all." He drew his wallet from his sports jacket and handed it over.

Cronin inspected it, starting with the Maryland driver's license. Glanced up at him. Pulled out a small spiral-bound notepad and a gold pen and jotted down some details. "I'm wondering if the Chevy Chase address on this license is valid," he asked.

"You might find me there. Sometimes."

"Where else might I find you?"

Hunter spread his hands. "Here. There."

"Give me your Social."

He rattled off the number. "For what good it will do you."

Cronin stopped writing, raised his cold blue eyes from the pad. "You mean it's a phony?"

"Oh, it's real, all right. But it won't help you go back more than about two years, either."

"You mind telling me why?"

Hunter sighed. "Okay. Maybe once you hear it, you'll understand. And get off my back." He repeated what he had told Annie—about being a young investigative journalist in Ohio, falling afoul of the Mob, having to get out of state and change his identity.

Cronin listened, keeping a poker face. When Hunter finished, he could tell something was still bugging the cop.

"You say you changed your name legally to Dylan Lee Hunter. But you still didn't explain why I won't get your real name when I run your Social. Nobody ever gets a new SSN," he said. Then his expression changed. "Unless—"

"Bingo. WITSEC." He used the insider acronym.

"You're telling me you're in the Witness Protection program? So you testified against the Mob, then."

"No. I just shared my information with the feds. I never got into court. But they were kind enough to enter me into the program, anyway. New identity, with a new SSN. So if you run the number, you'll find it on file at the Social Security Administration. But that's all you'll get from them."

Cronin regarded him for a moment, then rested an elbow on the table. "You want me to believe this wild story, but you still don't want to tell me who you really are."

He slammed his palm on the table. "Come on, Cronin! You've already admitted you're under orders to dig up dirt on me for the people holding your leash, dirt they'll use to try to muzzle me. So, I'm supposed to trust you to keep my real identity secret? While there's still a standing Mob contract out on me? Don't make me laugh."

Cronin's face softened. "Look, Hunter—whoever the hell you are. I meant it last time, when I said that a lot of us like what you've been doing."

"I don't like what you've been doing to me in return."

"This isn't my idea. Anyway, why didn't you just tell me all this stuff last time? Save us all a lot of misunderstandings?"

Time to toss him a bone. He sighed, lowered his voice.

"Look. I do appreciate your position, Detective Cronin. But you see how I make enemies. And if you keep poking around and asking questions about me, the people I've been trying to avoid all these years might hear about it. And put two and two together. And then I could wind up dead."

Cronin watched him, unblinking, for a long time. Then nodded. "Okay. I'll try to tread lightly in the future."

Hunter nodded, stood, and offered his hand. "I'd appreciate that. So would some far-off relatives. They don't like me much, but they'd feel obligated to show up at my funeral."

Cronin smiled and shook his hand.

FALLS CHURCH, VIRGINIA
Tuesday, November 18, 6:10 p.m.

"Okay, I talked to him," was the first sentence out of Cronin's mouth.

She tightened her grip on the phone. "Go ahead."

He told her. It surprised her. Then disturbed her.

"I don't understand. He never said a thing about being in the federal Witness Security program. He told me that other story—about consulting a skip tracer, then doing it all himself."

"Maybe he was trying to protect you in some way. Or himself. I don't know. Maybe he thought telling you that the feds were hiding him might scare you off."

"Why would being in Witness Protection be any scarier than what he told me?"

"Yeah, you're right. That doesn't make a lot of sense, does it."

How could he lie to her?

She began to pace in front of her fireplace. "Tell me honestly, Detective," she said, trying to keep her voice steady. "Do you believe him?"

He was silent a moment. She heard a ringing phone and voices in the background.

"Ms. Woods, I deal in facts. I can only tell you what I know. I know his SSN is real, and that it's issued to his current name—I confirmed that with Social Security in Baltimore. His IDs—driver's license, credit cards—they're all real, too, just as you thought. And all the dates of issue conform to his story."

"You didn't answer my question."

She heard him sigh. "Okay, let me put it this way: Nothing so far contradicts him being in Witness Protection. But, could he be conning us? Sure. It's possible. He's very smart. Very cagey."

Not what she wanted to hear. "Can't you check out his story with the feds?"

"I can try. Maybe get somebody in the U.S. Marshals to talk. They run Witness Protection. But I'm not optimistic. It would take a court order to force them to open up his records. And to get court paper, I'd need to give the judge a damned good reason. Right now, I've got jack."

"I understand."

Her eyes tracked around her living room, pausing on furnishings that she and Frank had picked out and purchased years before. She suddenly felt as she did in the days after he left. Small. Exposed.

"I'm sorry I can't tell you something definitive," Cronin was saying. "Ms. Woods, in my experience, everybody has baggage. But your guy—he's carrying more than Amtrak."

She had to laugh. "All right. Thanks for telling me what you've found out, Detective. It's a relief to know this much."

He was silent.

"Is there something else?" she prompted.

He took his time before replying. "You're on the job this many years, you get feelings about things. This somehow doesn't feel right."

"I know." Her throat felt tight.

"So, you feel it, too.... Okay, tell you what: I'm going to stay on this. And I suggest you try to keep an eye on him, too. Jot down notes of his comings and goings. You never know when a timeline might come in handy."

"Yes," she said, trying to ignore the quivering knot in the pit of her stomach. "You never know."

"I haven't asked you before. But it would help if you told me where he lives."

She took a slow breath. "I'm not ready to do that," she said. Then added: "Not yet."

BETHESDA, MARYLAND
Tuesday, November 18, 8:25 p.m.

"Hi, you," he said.

She stood in his doorway with an overnight bag and a little smile. "Hi, you."

He searched her eyes for an instant, then drew her close and kissed her.

"Missed you last night," he murmured.

"Me, too." She squeezed him.

He took the bag from her, then her coat. "Feeling better today?"

"Much. Thanks."

His eyes followed her as she wandered into the living room, then stopped to pet Luna, who was sprawled on the sofa. She wore a brown pantsuit. It was the first time she had dressed in anything other than a skirt or dress in his presence.

"Have you eaten?" he asked, hanging the coat in the entryway closet.

She tossed her purse on the sofa and sat. "Yes.... No. I mean, I'm not hungry. Some wine would be nice, though."

"Relax there and I'll fetch some."

He observed her out of the corner of his eye from the kitchen while he pulled a Chardonnay from the refrigerator, uncorked, then poured it. She was stroking the cat, but watching his reflected image in the dark window of the balcony's sliding door.

He felt the tension.

He pasted on a grin and brought their glasses over. Handed her one, clinked it with his, then took a nearby armchair instead of sitting beside her. So that he could watch her.

"How was work today?" he asked.

"Oh. All right. Not as bad as usual."

"Want to talk about it?"

"Not really." She took a sip.

He had debated whether to wait her out or simply confront her. Her eyes remained focused on the cat, not him. That decided it for him. She was trying to gloss over whatever it was.

But he never let anyone gloss over anything.

As she raised her wine glass again, he asked: "Then what else could be bothering you, Annie Woods?"

Her glass paused in mid-air; her eyes shot to his, startled. "What do you mean?"

He held her glance and very deliberately lowered his own glass to the coffee table. "Something's been bugging you. Since Sunday morning. And it wasn't just the Mexican food from Saturday night. Don't you think we should talk about it?"

She took a deep breath, her breasts rising against her suit jacket, then falling.

"All right. It was your article. That started it."

"Figured as much. What about it?"

She put down her glass, sat back. Her eyes were— what? Worried?

No. Wary.

"Dylan," she said carefully, "you know that I've believed in what you're doing. For crime victims. They didn't have a voice until you came along." She stopped.

"But...."

"Yes. *But.* But I think you've gone a bit too far."

"Annie, if anyone else on the planet said that to me, I'd answer: 'Why should I give a damn what you think?' But because it's you, I'll bite: How have I gone too far?"

"You've gone beyond attacking criminals and the people in the legal system who free them. Yes, they deserve to be exposed. And I'm proud of you for doing that. But now—now you're targeting private individuals. Reformers. People who sincerely believe in rehabilitation and are only trying to do what they think is the right thing. Okay, maybe they're naïve do-gooders; but their only real sin seems to be an excess of idealism."

"Idealism," he repeated. "And what are their 'ideals'?"

She shrugged. "Turning criminals away from crime."

"By making excuses for them?"

"Maybe some of them are trying to understand *why* they commit crimes. Perhaps they're looking for explanations."

"Tell me: What, exactly, is the difference between an 'explanation' for crime and an 'excuse' for crime?"

"Look, Dylan, you know that I don't agree with them. I'm not trying to defend what they advocate."

"Aren't you?" he asked. "You seem to be saying that I'm attacking them unfairly."

She looked away. "But why focus attention on them? I just don't see how *they* are responsible for what those in charge of the courts and jails do."

"You don't? Annie, my article laid it out. The MacLean Foundation has supported or engineered everything that's wrong in the system. They're professional excuse-makers for criminals. Politicians quote their studies and statistics when they gut tough sentencing laws. Lawyers and judges rely on their excuses and recommendations when they turn criminals loose."

"But the counselors, the people running the programs—they're not the ones actually freeing the criminals. They're just talkers."

"Talkers who empower the bad actors."

"Empower? What do you mean?"

"I'm saying that Edmund Burke was wrong."

"Now you're speaking in riddles."

He had to stand, move. He went to the window of the balcony. Stared into the night.

"Burke famously stated, 'All that is necessary for the triumph of evil is for good men to do nothing.'"

"How true."

"*Not* true. He made it sound as if evil people are powerful. But they're not. Evil people are nothing more than parasites who feed on others. They're losers. Most can barely survive on their own, let alone triumph on their own."

"But that's silly! Bad people *are* powerful. They're thriving. Sometimes, I think they run the world."

He turned to her. "Ask yourself why, Annie. Ask yourself why there are such things as 'career criminals'— losers like Bracey and Valenti, with rap sheets a mile long. Why weren't they stopped cold after their first few crimes? And how did they get out again, even after what they did to Susie and Arthur Copeland? It's not because they're powerful; it's because they've been *empowered*. They have millions of eager, do-gooder accomplices. All those 'nice' people who blabber about mercy and forgiveness, instead of simple justice. All those 'nice' folks who feel so sad and sorry for bad people—then feel so holy and self-righteous whenever they give monsters 'second chances.' Third chances. Tenth chances, fifty-ninth chances. Endless chances to hurt more innocent people. People like Susie and Arthur. And George Banacek's boy. And Kate Higgins's kid."

Her gaze was directed at the floor; he went on.

"Yes, Annie, evil people do triumph, too often. But it's not because 'good people' do nothing; it's because of what they *do*. They actively *encourage* evil. While kidding themselves that they're engaging in saintly acts of virtue. If I were into psychobabble, I'd call them 'enablers.' Enablers of predators. Do-gooders like that MacLean guy—they're giving aid and comfort to society's enemies."

"That's a really harsh view of the world." Her voice sounded strained.

"The world is a harsh place. But who makes it that way? That's why Edmund Burke had it wrong. He should have said: 'All that is necessary for the triumph of evil is an enabler.'"

Abruptly, she stood. "Dylan, this conversation—it's really upsetting me."

"I see that. I can't see why, though. You've never reacted this way to my earlier articles."

"It's just.... I don't know. And watching you at that news conference.... It was.... I saw things I didn't expect to see."

Her words were uprooting something inside him, leaving him feeling hollow.

"Annie," he said quietly, "you saw exactly who I am."

She approached him. He saw anguish in her eyes. "I know," she said. She stood on tip-toes to kiss his cheek. Then pushed back. "I wish I could explain it to you, Dylan."

"Why can't you?"

"I'm sorry." She blinked, seeming to be on the edge of tears. "This was a bad idea."

She turned away and went back to the sofa. Picked up her purse.

"You're not staying."

She shook her head. "I have some things to sort out."

He followed her to the closet, helped her on with her coat. She opened the apartment door, then turned to him.

He touched her face, ran his thumb lightly across her cheek. Watching her closely, he said: "You say you have 'some things' to sort out. 'Things,' plural. So, what else is bothering you, Annie?"

He caught it, a little flicker in her eyes. She closed them, turned her lips into his palm. Kissed it.

Then pulled away and headed down the hallway, toward the elevator. She didn't look back.

He closed the door.

Stood there a moment, his palm resting flat against the cool surface.

He returned to the sofa. Looked down at her wine glass. Saw the faint trace of her lipstick on the rim.

He settled back into his armchair. Reached for his own glass. Took a large swallow.

So incoherent. So unlike her.

And it all started with his article.

The cat leaped from the sofa onto the stuffed arm of his chair, then slinked down into his lap. He rested his hand on the soft fur of her back. Felt her begin to purr.

But the article wasn't all of it. One other thing he now knew for certain, from her startled reaction in the doorway.

She and Cronin *had* talked.

Talked about his past.

He pressed the chilled glass against his temple.

"I think they may be on to us, Luna."

TWENTY-SEVEN

CIA HEADQUARTERS, LANGLEY, VIRGINIA
Friday, November 21, 12:15 p.m.

"You don't seem to be hungry today," Grant Garrett said.

She stopped moving the meat around on her plate and set down her fork. "I guess not."

They sat by themselves inside the cafeteria at a table on the stairway landing that led to the second level. Employees who usually claimed the area for daily socializing saw who was seated there and gave them a wide berth.

She felt his gaze weighing on her. She turned her eyes from her tray to the main floor below them, where people wandered between the food stations and chatted at tables.

"Hey. I'm over here."

She looked at him, feeling awkward. "Sorry. I didn't mean to ignore you."

"You seem distracted lately," he continued. "Anything you care to talk about, Annie?"

She forced herself to look into his eyes. "No. Not really."

He put down his coffee cup, dabbed his lips with his napkin. "A man, then."

It caught her by surprise. She opened her mouth to deny it. Then sighed.

"I've been seeing someone, yes. For a couple of months."

"From the look on your face, it doesn't seem to be going well."

"It's not."

"Fixable?"

"I hope so."

"Need a little time off?"

"No. Absolutely not."

"Don't get defensive. I was just asking. We seem to be at a bit of a standstill, anyway, so maybe a break might do you some good."

She shook her head. "I'll be all right. Really." Time to change the subject. "Have you had any fresh thoughts?"

He knew what she meant. He raised a gnarled forefinger, tapped his gray temple. "The answer's in here."

"What's that supposed to mean?"

"It means I know the answer to this, Annie. I *know* that I know it. I've felt it for months—that I have all the pieces to figure this out. But I'm still not putting the pieces together right."

"Maybe we should brainstorm some more. Go over everything we know, try—"

"No, we've done plenty of that. We've been trying consciously to force all the puzzle pieces to fit. But I'm thinking that's going about this the wrong way. Maybe the better way is for us to give it a rest for a little while, let it simmer. I think the answer is sitting here in my own skull, in my subconscious. Something tells me it has to do with a past operation. There are times when I feel I almost have it. Like something you sense in your peripheral vision. Then when you look straight at it, it vanishes, like a ghost." He folded his napkin neatly, placed it back onto the tray. "Maybe I'm the one who needs the break. I should take a few days off, visit friends or something."

"That doesn't sound like the Grant Garrett I know. You'll ruin your reputation."

"It couldn't get any worse."

BETHESDA, MARYLAND
Friday, November 21, 8:05 p.m.

Trust.

Her wipers swept intermittently to clear the windshield of the light drizzle and the spray from the cars around her. She gripped the wheel tightly, trying to stay alert for unexpected maneuvers by the crazy drivers on the Capital Beltway. They were even crazier in the rain.

But it was hard to concentrate.

Trust. The word had haunted her since her first conversation with Cronin. That's when the doubts had begun.

Or had they?

Be honest with yourself. It was before then. And you know it.

She recalled their first date. When, sitting across from each other in the Italian restaurant, they had talked about his fears, and hers.

"I would hope that someday you might trust me."

"You mean: You would hope that someday you might trust me."

"I guess we both have some trust issues."

No, this mess didn't start because she hadn't trusted him. It began when she realized that he couldn't trust *her*.

It began when she saw what he'd written about her father. That's when she finally admitted to herself that she'd been hiding from him who her father was. That's when she knew she was living a lie.

When you realized you were a fraud.

She braked for a traffic light. Waiting for it to change, she gathered her resolve.

Tonight, the deception would end. She had to trust again. And she had to make herself trustworthy, too.

She would tell him the truth. About her father. And about her job.

He deserved to know everything. He *had* to know—whatever the cost.

Then, she would ask him to reveal the whole truth about his own past. If they were to continue together, she deserved to know that, too.

And after that, they would see what they could salvage.

"Well. What are we going to do about this, then?"

"Maybe we can work on our trust issues together."

"All right...Dylan Hunter."

Yes, Dylan. Let's try.

She hadn't told him she'd be coming tonight. Somehow, it would be better if she just showed up, unannounced. She hoped he'd be there when she arrived, but if not, she'd wait. She glanced at the overnight bag on the passenger seat. Wishful thinking?

"We'll see," she said, aloud.

*

She made the sharp left onto Wisconsin and headed north, approaching his high-rise. About a block ahead, in front of his building, she noticed a man crossing Wisconsin, right to left. He wore a dark hat and raincoat. In the middle of the street, he broke stride with a funny little skip-hop, then began to run to avoid oncoming traffic.

She caught her breath. She couldn't remember exactly when she'd seen him do that little hop—maybe while they were out at dinner one night—but it had imprinted somewhere in her memory. She watched him run easily, then leap a puddle, graceful a gazelle, to reach the sidewalk.

Damn. If she didn't hurry, she'd miss him.

She turned into the street beside his building, pulled into the curb, and hit the four-way flashers. Then she jumped out and ran after him, awkward in her heels, dodging traffic to cross the broad highway.

He had about a thirty second lead and had disappeared down an alley between two buildings. She ran after him, emerging on Woodmont Avenue. She halted and spun, bewildered. He had vanished. There were no open stores or restaurants—only two parking garages on opposite sides of the street. Not there. Dylan had reserved parking for his Forester beneath his own apartment building, so he wouldn't need to—

But then she spotted him, trotting up the glassed-enclosed stairwell of the garage on this side of the street. Before she could shout, he turned off the fourth-level landing and disappeared back inside the garage.

Maybe she could still catch him.

She ran to the pedestrian entrance of the garage, then up the stairs as fast as she could manage, cursing her heels with every step. By the time she reached the third-level landing, she heard a car engine rev somewhere above. Figuring that she might intercept him as he descended past her, she yanked open the stairwell door, emerging into the parking area.

Then saw that the car exit ramp was all the way at the other end of the building.

She ran toward it, but was only halfway there when the vehicle whipped into view around the descending curve in the distance.

It was not the Forester, however. It was a white pizza delivery van. It rolled quickly around the ramp and down.

She stopped, not bothering to shout. That couldn't be him, he had to be upstairs yet. She might still catch him. She began to run again toward the exit ramp. She arrived about thirty seconds later, gasping, her ankles aching and toes screaming from the narrow shoes. She paused and listened.

Nothing but the sound of her own heavy breathing.

Apparently, he hadn't even started his car yet. She began to relax. He had to come down this way, so she would definitely connect with him, now. She walked up the curving ramp to the fourth level. Then paused again to catch her breath and scan the parked vehicles.

She heard nothing. Saw no one. Saw no car that looked like his Forester.

It was crazy. She *knew* he'd entered this level of the garage. Even if he'd walked up or down a flight, she would have seen or heard his vehicle depart.

She moved slowly through the rows of cars, her footsteps echoing sharp and hollow, thinking he had to be sitting in one. But they were all empty.

She waited there another five minutes before heading back to his building.

There was only one explanation. She'd been mistaken; the man had only looked like Dylan. He was probably at his apartment.

She fetched her car where she'd abandoned it and drove down into his building's underground garage. Then she laughed in relief when she pulled up to his reserved spots and saw the Forester sitting there.

Idiot. He'll have a good laugh, too, when you tell him.

Knowing it would be a presumption, she left her overnight bag in the car. On the way over to the elevator, she felt damp from the drizzle and sweaty from the running. Her hair would be a frizzy mess, too. Great.

She used the key card he'd given her to enter the elevator and ride up to his floor. Walking down the hallway toward his door, though, she felt her anxiety growing again. She tried to remember some of the words she had thought of to explain things to him—then gave it up. No, she had to be spontaneous about this. Authentic. And just hope for the best.

She paused outside his door to gather herself. Then pressed the bell and waited.

After thirty seconds, she tried again.

Nothing.

Well, he has to be here; his car is downstairs. Maybe he's in the shower.

She pressed the bell again.

No answer. Then a faint *meow* from the other side of the door.

She knocked, long and hard. "Dylan? Are you there?" No response. "Dylan?"

Then she heard a door unlatch, just down the hall. A distinguished-looking older woman with well-coiffed white curls poked her head outside, frowning slightly.

"Oh! I'm sorry if I disturbed you," she said to the woman. "I was just trying to let Mr. Hunter know I'm here."

The woman smiled. "Ah. Well, it won't do you any good, my dear. He's not in. I arrived home about fifteen minutes ago, and he was just leaving. If he's expecting you, though, I'm sure he'll be back presently."

She forced a smile, tried to say it calmly. "Perhaps I saw him outside when I drove up a little while ago. Do you remember what was he wearing?"

"Mmmm.... Dark hat, dark trench coat or raincoat, I think."

"Yes. That was him.... Thank you."

"You have a nice evening, my dear." The woman closed her door.

She stood there a moment, trying to make sense of it. The only sound was Luna scratching at the door.

FALLS CHURCH, VIRGINIA
Saturday, November 22, 9:15 a.m.

Even her third cup of coffee couldn't compensate for the lack of sleep. And nothing she told herself could tamp down the rising tide of fear that had kept her awake.

She knew what she had seen. She spent all night trying to force it to fit into her conception of a sane world. But she couldn't.

She had seen him leave his building, on foot—his departure confirmed by another eyewitness. She had seen him enter a public parking garage. And she had seen only one vehicle leaving that garage, right after he entered.

When they were training her in investigations, they made a big deal of Occam's Razor: the principle that the simplest explanation for a given phenomenon was almost always the valid one. Now, Mr. Occam was telling her something both mysterious and ominous.

The simplest explanation was that a man known to her only by an admittedly false name, Dylan Hunter, had left his own car parked in the garage of his residence, and had taken instead a second vehicle—*a pizza delivery van*—from a parking place at a nearby garage that he could reach quickly, on foot. Occam told her that the van had to belong to Dylan, and that he was parking it there because he didn't want it to be linked to him.

She didn't know why. But she couldn't imagine any reason that wasn't criminal.

His false name. His secrecy about his past.

How well do you really know him? So far, we've been accepting him on blind trust.

Trust.

She knew so little. But what little she did know now shattered her resolution to confide in him.

During the night, she ordered herself to begin to detach from him, emotionally. She knew she had to put aside her feelings, now. She had to reclaim her objectivity. She had to use her skills as an investigator, if she were ever to find out the truth about the man calling himself Dylan Lee Hunter.

She went to the kitchen counter, where she had dropped her purse last night. She opened it and removed her cell and the business card. She tapped in the number.

"Cronin here."

"Oh. Annie Woods here, Detective. I didn't expect you to be at your desk on a Saturday. I figured I'd have to leave a voice mail."

"Yeah, well, duty calls and I'm not at my desk. What can I do for you, Ms. Woods?"

"You said to call if I had any further information about Dylan. Well, I'm afraid I do."

"'Afraid.' That doesn't sound good. Look, I'm kind of busy right now. Can you give me the headlines?"

She did. She wondered why he remained silent after she finished speaking.

"Ms. Woods," he said, his words sounding measured, "is there any chance we could meet today? Like, in an hour or two?"

"Why, sure. I suppose so. I have to warn you, though, I'm running on fumes. I didn't get much sleep last night."

"Me either. We had another vigilante murder late last night."

The way he said it bothered her. "Well, it sounds as if we both had busy nights. Before we meet, though—" She stopped.

"What?"

Just say it.

"I want to give you Dylan's home address."

BETHESDA, MARYLAND
Saturday, November 22, 9:55 a.m.

The sky had cleared from last night's rain, so, still in his bathrobe, he took his coffee out onto his balcony. He bent and rested his elbows on the damp railing, sipping the hot liquid. That, combined with the chilly November air, helped to restore his alertness.

He was thinking about the events of the previous night when he heard the slider door open on the next balcony. Sarah Oglethorpe emerged, bundled in a long coat and carrying a black garbage bag, which she crammed into the trash bin she kept out there.

"Morning, Sarah," he said, nodding.

She looked over, her face brightening. "Oh, good morning, Dylan. Did you have a nice evening?"

"Yes. You could say that."

She looked impish. "I'll bet you did. She is certainly adorable."

"Excuse me?"

"Your lady friend. My, she's lovely!"

He lowered the cup to the railing, steadying it there. "Are you referring to the woman I've been dating recently?"

"Well, before last night I didn't know you were seeing anyone. But she certainly was eager to see *you*."

Keep smiling. "I didn't know you two had crossed paths."

"Just after I came home. You remember that you and I passed each other near the elevator? Well, she happened along just a few minutes later. I heard her banging on your door and calling for you, so I told her you'd just left. She mentioned that she thought she saw you go, but wasn't sure. Anyway, I told her that you'd probably be right back, then. I'm so glad she waited."

Whatever you do, keep smiling. "Me, too. I really appreciate that, Sarah." Confirm it was her. "So. I gather that you approve. Did you like her new hairstyle?"

"Oh, yes! So cute, those shorter cuts. They go so well on brunettes with wavy hair like hers."

"That's what I told her, too.... Well, Sarah, it's a bit cold out here. Perhaps I'll see you later this weekend."

"You give the lady my regards, now."

Smile. "I will."

The smile vanished the second he got inside.

TWENTY-EIGHT

BETHESDA, MARYLAND
Thursday, November 27, 8:07 p.m.

For a special task force, they really weren't very good.

The trick to surveillance detection is to never let them know that you've made them. Let them think they're observing you undetected. Meanwhile, to make them start to doubt that you're really a viable suspect, you do nothing but innocuous things. You bore them to death.

He'd picked up the team following him the minute he left his apartment, just before six o'clock. He drove over to the city lot across from the Barnes & Noble and parked. Then he spent half an hour browsing its bookshelves, before taking the thriller he'd purchased to a restaurant right around the corner. He sat there reading and eating for a bit, forcing the plainclothes cop they sent in to keep an eye on him nurse a beer at the bar. Finally, he led them on a grocery-shopping expedition before returning home.

There were two more unmarkeds staking out his building tonight, parked in spots different from the ones they occupied last night. He made them the minute he turned into the short side street running alongside the highrise. Never glancing in their direction, he swung down the ramp into the garage, leaving the Forester in its usual space.

Tonight, like all the previous nights since Annie had tipped them to his address, he'd been working to lull them into thinking that he wasn't going anywhere.

He flipped on all the lights when he entered the apartment, left all the curtains wide open, too. See, fellows? Nothing to hide. Even though he swept his car and apartment and found no bugs, so far, he whistled while he put away the groceries and fed the cat—just in case they'd installed some while he was out.

The absence of bugs told him they didn't have enough on him to get a court order. So this was still just a fishing expedition. Cronin and his buddies had suspicions, but nothing solid. Tonight, though, his goal was to satisfy them that they could rule him out as a suspect.

He turned on the TV in the living room, cranked up the volume a bit. Poured a glass of wine and made a show of walking past his windows with it in hand. Yep, just another lonely single dude, dumped by his girlfriend, spending another quiet, pathetic evening home alone with his cat. Nothing to see here, folks. Move along....

He collapsed onto the sofa, not bothering to watch the popular amateur dance competition on the tube. Luna had disappeared somewhere else in the apartment, leaving him alone with his plans. And his demons.

His "girlfriend." He remembered when he'd called her that. He fought down his anger as her image flashed into his consciousness. It had been so long since he'd let anyone in. He'd let her in, all right. He had to admit it: He'd fallen in love. Hard. Like he'd never fallen for anyone before. Yes, he had opened himself, even admitting to her that he had been betrayed before.

And he'd been prepared to open up even more. All the way. To tell her everything, past and present. He had understood from the beginning that if this were to grow into something important, he couldn't keep her in the dark. Eventually, she'd have to know.

For him, it *had* become something important. So important, that he was ready to walk away from everything else. Ready to let all the chips fall as they might, when he told her. Ready, because he thought she was worth it.

And look where it had gotten him.

She'd been playing him. How long, he wasn't sure. But it didn't matter. And it didn't matter that she loved him, either. Of that, he had no doubt; he could tell how conflicted she was. But he didn't give a damn about her conflicts. You either love someone, or you don't. You either trust somebody all the way, or you don't. And she had betrayed him. That was all that mattered. She was working with the cops to bring him down. Why, he didn't know. And couldn't care less.

Not anymore.

Okay, so if she wanted to play him, he'd play her right back. She'd become part of his alibi for this evening.

He pulled a cell from his pocket, inserted its battery, and keyed in her number.

"Hello?"

He felt in icy control. "Hi, you."

Hesitation. "Hi, you."

"I'm just calling to tell you how much I miss you, Annie."

Silence. Then: "Oh, Dylan. Me, too.... I wish I could be there tonight.... I'm so confused."

Sure you are. "You still haven't told me about what."

"It's so complicated." She paused, then added: "There's so much that we don't know about each other."

"Apparently not." He heard the edge creeping into his voice. Careful.

"Remember what we talked about on our first date? That we both have trust issues?"

"I remember. Very well, in fact."

"I...I just can't seem to get past mine."

He found himself gritting his teeth. "Well, I thought I'd gotten past mine. But maybe not."

"Dylan—I keep going back and forth on this in my mind. Some days, I want desperately to see you. But other days, I just want to run away."

"I know how you feel."

A long pause.

"You sound so distant," she said.

The undertow of anger began to tug at him. He didn't want to say it, but he had to.

"I thought we had something very special, Annie. I don't exactly know what happened. I feel blindsided, though. It still sounds as if you have some things to sort out. 'Things,' plural."

She didn't respond.

"Okay, so how about we leave it this way: Let's take a bit of a break, a couple of weeks. Take the time to try to figure out what we each need. And whether what we each need can mesh together."

"If that's what you want." Her voice sounded soft. Tentative.

"It doesn't have anything to do with what I want. It's what I think we need, though. You need some time. I do, too."

"Okay."

"I'll call you again in a few weeks. Right now, though, I feel like crap. I think I'm going to wrap things up here, then turn in early."

"All right," she said. Then: "You promise you will call me, won't you?"

"I promise," he found himself saying.

"Dylan?"

"Yes?"

Her breath was coming in short, broken gasps. He realized she was crying.

"Dylan...I do love you."

Someone was squeezing his chest, so tight that he could hardly breathe. He clenched his jaw tight. No, he wouldn't say it. He had vowed to himself that he would never say that again. To her. To anyone.

He closed his eyes. "I love you, too, Annie."

He had to snap the phone shut.

He cursed himself for his weakness. Cursed her for her hold on him.

This was no time to be a pussy. He had to focus on tonight's mission. He knew he could always control his emotions when he focused on the mission.

After a few minutes, he felt the coldness return. She was just an alibi, now. Nothing more.

He checked his watch. Just after nine. Time to move.

He removed the battery from the cell, then went through the same routine he'd established on the previous nights. He clicked off the television, rose from the sofa, stood in front of the balcony door, and stretched. Then drew the curtains shut and turned off the living room lamps.

He went into the kitchen and filled Luna's water bowl and food dish. She heard the noises and emerged from her hiding place to feast.

Entering the bedroom, he flipped on the lights and the other TV, then shut the curtains there, too. Unseen now, he spent the next five minutes sweeping the whole apartment for bugs. It was still clear.

He entered the walk-in closet, changed clothes, then went into the bathroom to do the rest of his prep. When he was done, he stood in front of the full-length mirror on its door, making sure everything looked just right.

At nine-forty, he set the timers on the circuits in the bedroom. He left the lights and TV on when he left the room, closing the door behind him.

It was dark in the living room, now. He sat down to wait. After a moment, Luna joined him on the sofa. She pranced back and forth under his hand as he pet her.

"Well, girl," he said softly, "I've had to make some substitutions on the team. Since Hyattsville, things have gotten a little too hot for Lex, so I've benched him. Maybe permanently. Tonight will be Shane Stone's turn again." He smiled. "As we know, he's every bit as good."

He felt her flop against him, purring. He reached down, found and scratched her head. Sat there, thinking. Recalling the Vigilance for Victims meeting. Remembering the haunted faces.

Remembering his silent vow to them.

"You can't walk away," he repeated, aloud to himself. "You have to finish this. But there's more to do, yet. A lot more."

He felt the cat lick his hand with her sandpaper tongue. Felt himself smile in response.

"So, you still up for this?"

He heard a contented purr in the darkness.

"Glad you're still on the team."

*

He kept checking his illuminated watch. At nine minutes before ten, he rose, opened the door to the apartment, and checked outside. The hallway was clear. He slipped out, closing the door softly behind him, then moved quickly to the fire door onto the emergency stairwell. It took him a couple of minutes to descend to the garage level. From behind the door there, he peered outside. Watched an arriving couple get out of their car and walk toward the elevator. When its doors closed, he left the stairwell and walked without hurry over to the car.

It wasn't the Forester, which remained in its spot on the other side of the garage. This one was a black 2007 BMW 7 Series High Security sedan. Dark-tinted windows and lots of useful toys. He got in, not worrying about the garage's security cameras. Their tapes, if ever checked, would reveal the vehicle's registered owner: the older, wealthy, seldom-seen occupant of unit 7D.

*

At two minutes before ten, Cronin nudged his partner. A vehicle's headlights were visible inside the garage's entrance.

They watched a sleek black BMW emerge. "Nice wheels," he said.

"Not his, though," Erskine answered.

"Don't assume. Remember, he had that pizza truck in the garage over there across the street."

Erskine pointed at the building and raised his binoculars. "Not him, though. I just saw his bedroom lights go off, this very second."

Cronin looked. The bedroom window to his apartment, lit brightly just seconds ago, had gone almost dark; only the intermittent flickering of his television screen was visible through the linen curtains.

"See? He can't be in two places at the same time. He's up there watching TV, like he always does before he goes to sleep."

At that moment, Cronin felt the vibration in his jacket pocket. He took out his cell and noticed the Caller ID. "It's our girl," he said, then flipped it open. "Ed Cronin here."

"Sorry to bother you this late, Detective Cronin," she said. Her voice sounded stressed.

"No bother at all, Ms. Woods. We're watching his place. But you sound upset. Is everything all right?"

He heard her draw a deep breath. "I'm just calling to say that I can't do this anymore."

Erskine threw him a questioning look. Cronin put his finger to his lips, then put her on speaker, so his partner could listen in. "Tell me what's the matter," he said, keeping his voice gentle.

"He called tonight. Just a little while ago. We talked only briefly. But I could tell how hurt he was. He doesn't think he can trust me."

Erskine rolled his eyes.

"Ms. Woods, I understand you're upset. But think about it. If he's guilty of something, *of course* he would be angry if he thought he couldn't continue to con you."

"You didn't hear me. I said *hurt*, not angry. Detective Cronin, I *know* him. And yes, I realize he's not telling me everything about his past, and yes, some things still don't add up. But I also know that he's a decent man. And a compassionate one, in so many ways. He has the strongest code of personal honor of any man I've ever known. So I just can't buy your theory about him. I don't think he's involved."

"My theory doesn't contradict anything you said, though. If I'm right, he's probably the brains behind the vigilante team. He's certainly intelligent enough. And as for his code of honor—Ms. Woods, have you ever heard the term 'righteous slaughter'?"

"No. What's that?"

"It's when somebody kills a bunch of people because he's convinced himself that they deserve it. You see it all the time with mass murderers—the guys who walk into some fast-food joint or post office and mow down everybody in sight. They always have some grand excuse for it, some grievance or injustice they think rationalizes their revenge. The people they shot all had it coming to them. Well, that's not much different from the way vigilantes think, is it?"

"Except that in this case, the people getting shot really *do* deserve it."

Erskine grinned and gave a thumb's-up; Cronin scowled at him.

"Well, miss, that's not for us to decide. We just can't let individuals decide for themselves who lives and who dies, and for what reason. But you're forgetting things. Like that pizza van you're sure he was in. How do we explain things like that?"

"Detective, we both know he takes elaborate security precautions. He has to. That was probably part of it: something he does so that people can't follow him. Have you asked yourself how much of his behavior can be explained by simple paranoia?"

"Fair point, I suppose. But why would he have to be paranoid about us? We're on his side. But he's not been fully honest, either with me or with you."

"You know exactly why he's not been open with you—he told you himself. He knows you're associated with the people who want to silence him. And I know why he can't trust me, either. It's because *I've* been deceiving *him*, almost since the day we met. About important things that he has a right to know. I think he senses it. And I think that's why he's holding back. He has damned good reason not to trust me. Not to trust either of us, Detective. Maybe if we give him more reasons to believe in us, he'll open up and tell us the things we need to know."

He gave up. "Okay. So how did you leave it with him?"

"He said we probably both need a little break from each other. A couple of weeks. Then he wants to try to work things out."

"Anything else?"

"Just that he was really beat tonight and wanted to turn in early."

He glanced up at the window, watched the light from the TV moving on the curtain.

"Ms. Woods, I told you that I'd love to believe this guy. I really would. So you trust him, then."

"With my life."

TWENTY-NINE

**COLUMBIA HEIGHTS,
WASHINGTON, D.C.
Thursday, November 27, 11:10 p.m.**

From his vantage point in the SUV parked next to the kids' playground, he could see into the rear yard behind the apartment buildings. At eleven-ten, an Hispanic kid in his early teens clambered down the steps of the building to his left, being dragged along by a big Doberman on a leash. The dog couldn't wait to get out into the small yard the before lifting his leg against a bush.

During his recons the past few nights, he'd watched the kid walk the dog several times around eleven. He was relieved that the kid, and not his target, owned the dog: No way he'd break into an apartment and face down a guard dog. Still, even though the animal would be in another apartment, he might bark up a storm when he entered.

In addition, the target, Orlando Navarro, was obviously on guard, keeping out of sight for the most part, and staying close to other people whenever he emerged from his apartment. From all reports, Navarro—a beefy bodybuilder covered with gang tats—was no genius. But it didn't take genius to figure out that murderers whose names appeared in the newspapers were vigilante targets.

And the fact that his old *amigo*, Tomas Cardenas, had been whacked must have scared the hell out of him. Navarro had gone into hiding immediately after Cardenas was killed, changing his residence, with permission of the court. However, he had a problem staying hidden. Though free on appeal for the killing of Tommy Banacek, he was still on the hook with his probation officer for past crimes. Navarro had to show up at the office once a week to check in with the Man and take a urine test. And his P.O. knew where he lived.

So it really wasn't too hard to track him down. From a disposable cell phone, he'd called a low-level clerk in the probation department, routing the call through an online Caller ID "spoofing" service. The service allowed his phone to "spoof" the local courthouse's phone number, so that it appeared on the clerk's Caller ID. The service was even programmed to alter his voice as he spoke.

All it took, then, was a little "pretexting": prying privileged information from an unsuspecting source by impersonating somebody with a legitimate need to know. His pretext was that he was a records manager at the courthouse. He told the probation clerk that the judge needed to know if one Orlando Ramirez Navarro had been complying fully with the terms of his probation. Could the clerk look up his records, please?.... Great. Now, at what day and time are Mr. Navarro's weekly appointments with his P.O.?.... Uh-huh. And have his urine tests been coming back clean?.... Good. By the way, let me read off the contact information we have, just to make sure it's all correct in our records.... Oh, you say that's his *old* address? Well, please give me the new one, so that I can update our files.... Thank you very much for your time, Mr. Jones.

Piece of cake.

So, the guileless clerk had pointed him to Navarro's new digs in this public-housing complex in Columbia Heights. A lot of Hispanics lived in the area, and his target no doubt hoped that he would blend right in. From his recons, during which he used a different vehicle each night, he was sure that the guy lived alone. Gang pals sometimes showed up in the evening, allowing him to note which second-floor apartment lights went on and off when they arrived and left. That gave him an idea of the layout of the place. Tonight, a couple of them showed up around eight and left at ten-thirty. One set of windows, which he'd figured for the living room, went dark about eleven, and immediately the window to its left lit up. The bedroom. He'd be in there by himself, now.

For this job, he'd use a combo from the Eastern Shore weapons cache that already had been used previously: the Beretta 92FS with SWR Trident suppressor, popping Alabama Ammo 147 grain Special Ks. Reliable, accurate, and most importantly, very quiet.

But this couldn't be like any of the previous missions; that had already been decided. The plan was to leave the target here, with the news clipping on him. It was just too difficult to remove the body, unseen, and deposit it where it might be more symbolically appropriate.

Still, this guy—the second gang-banger involved in the death of George Banacek's kid—just had to go. For one thing, he was unfinished business. For another, after he was taken out, the other murderers in the news stories would know that none of them could hide anywhere.

He waited for the kid to drag the Doberman back inside, then gave it another two minutes for everyone to settle in. His watch said eleven-fifteen. Time to go hunting.

Once the traffic cleared, he rolled the Chevy Trailblazer out from the curb, down the street past the front of the building, then into the driveway that led behind the complex. He backed into a parking spot close to the building, leaving the engine running. The silenced Beretta and newspaper clipping were inside the deep, right-hand pocket of his long leather coat. A small lock-pick gun was inside the left one.

There were no security cameras to worry about, but he wore a broad-brimmed leather hat, anyway, and kept his head down as he moved down the sidewalk and up the short steps to the building entrance. He also wore brown leather gloves to match his coat and hat. A good gangster look that wouldn't be out of place here.

The door lock was no problem; the electronic pick got him inside within ten seconds. Against the wall to his right, stairs led to the second- and third-floor apartments. He made sure to keep himself physically oriented as he crept up to the second-floor hallway. Estimating the distances from what he'd seen from the front of the building, he knew that Navarro occupied the second apartment to his left.

He stepped quietly to that door. Listened. Noise from a TV or stereo from within, probably the bedroom. More bass thumping from somewhere else down the hall. Good. The racket would mask any sounds of his entry.

He glanced down the hallway in both directions. Clear. Then drew the Beretta from his coat. One in the chamber, full mag, hammer down. He thumbed off the safety. With his left hand, he carefully inserted the pick into the upper dead-bolt lock and pressed the button. Even the soft buzz-rattle of the pick made him cringe. Then stuck it into the door-knob keyhole. Another brief buzz. He withdrew the pick, dropped it back into his coat pocket.

Pointing the gun upward in his right hand, he leaned against the door with his left shoulder. Carefully turned the doorknob with his left hand. Eased the door open, just enough so that he could slip quickly into the darkened room and swing it almost shut behind him, leaving it slightly ajar for a fast exit.

For just a second, he saw the bright rectangle of the bedroom entrance, ahead and to his right.

Then there was a rustle and blur of motion on his left.

The big Doberman, barely visible in the weak light from the bedroom, was so fast that he only had an instant to jerk up his left arm to shield himself as it leaped. Its weight and momentum knocked him back against the apartment door, slamming it shut loudly.

His hand banged against something and he dropped the gun.

He fought to retain his balance as the dog snarled and clamped down on his left forearm. It shook its head violently, its sharp teeth tearing right through the thick leather and into his arm. The pain was excruciating.

He regained his footing, straightening his body and lifting hard with his arm. But the animal, growling savagely, wasn't about to let loose; he only succeeded in pulling it upright, flat against his body. Barely a foot from his face, its wild eyes glinted darkly into his.

Then his peripheral vision caught a huge silhouette in the bedroom doorway.

"*Matar!*" Navarro yelled. Then lunged toward him.

One chance.

He pushed out with his left forearm, forcing the Doberman's head back vertically, while simultaneously crashing his right forearm down like an axe against the back of the dog's neck. He heard the snap, felt the jaws release. He kneed the dying creature hard, propelling it into the path of the charging giant. Navarro stumbled over its body, staggering toward him, off-balance.

He took a step forward to meet him, grabbed his huge, flailing left arm, then pivoted, pulling him and accelerating his forward momentum. The big man slammed head-first into the wall, sinking to his knees.

He snapped out a front kick; his boot caught the back of Navarro's head, banging it again into the wall. Stunned, the guy slid farther down the wall—then stopped, propping himself with his huge arms, planted like quivering tree trunks on the floor.

He pivoted again and snapped out a side kick, this time against the guy's left elbow. Heard the *crunch*. Navarro toppled, rolled over onto his back, then seized his elbow with his other hand and started screaming.

He stopped that by dropping on the guy's throat with his knee. Navarro's limbs shook and twitched.

He stood, swaying, and groped for the light switch on the wall near the door. Found and snapped it on.

With a crushed larynx, Navarro couldn't breathe. The big man's eyes bugged out; his bear-like right hand now pawed helplessly at this throat, his face turning blue. The twitching of his legs was slowing. He'd be unconscious in seconds. Then die.

Not that way.

He looked around, found the Beretta near the door. Went to Navarro and bent over him. The guy's bulging eyes still tracked him.

"This is for Tommy Banacek, you bastard." He stood back, aimed at his head, and pulled the trigger. Then shoved the gun back into the coat pocket, pulled out the newspaper clipping, and dropped it onto his chest.

Only then did he notice the rising din of shouts in the building. Of doors opening down the hallway. He leaped to the door and flipped the deadbolt back in place. Looked around the scene for anything he may have dropped. His hat. He picked it up and put it back on. What else?

That's when he saw the spatters of blood.

He looked at his left arm for the first time. The leather was stained dark; a trickle flowed from the end of the sleeve, dripping onto the floor and into his glove.

His blood. His DNA.

Not good.

Elevating the arm, which hurt like hell, he pawed his coat open with his other hand. A zippered pouch was sewn inside. He yanked open the zipper, drew out a small spray bottle from among its other contents. Then crouched and began to spray the blood drops everywhere he saw them.

Excited voices at the door, now, babbling in Spanish.

He wheeled around, bloody arm pressed against his body, looking everywhere for stains he'd missed. Found a few more and sprayed.

Knocking. *"Orlando? ¿Estás bien amigo?"*

He had to get out. Now.

He shoved the bottle back into the coat pouch. Killed the lights again. In the glow from the bedroom, he jumped over the dog's body, then headed over there and flipped off those lights, too. The whole place was dark, now.

Somebody rattling the doorknob, then pounding the door. *"Orlando! Abre la puerta!"*

He ran to the sliding glass door at the front of the apartment. Unlatched and yanked it open, went outside onto the second-floor patio balcony. Felt the clamminess in his left glove. If he touched anything, he'd leave blood traces. If he removed it, he'd leave fingerprints. He scanned the yard below him. He'd have to get down from here one-handed.

He waited until a car passed on the street, then clambered awkwardly over the iron railing. Holding on with his right hand, he knelt at the edge. Then gripping the bottom of the railing one-handed, he let one leg at a time slide over the edge. He dangled a second, then let go.

He landed in a half-roll, holding his left arm crushed against his body, hoping like hell that he wouldn't leave blood on the grass. Rising to his feet, he ran in a crouch, staying in the shadows close to the wall, then darting around the corner. He slowed to a walk as he approached the parking area. Heard muted shouts from somewhere inside the building.

Crossing the small lot at a steady pace, he kept his head down under the lights until he reached the SUV. He climbed inside, pulled the door shut.

Then grunted under the searing pain. He'd forgotten and used his left hand.

He put the idling vehicle in gear and pulled away, driving and shifting clumsily, one-handed, relieved only that it was his left arm that was damaged, not his right.

So it *was* Navarro's Doberman, after all. Probably paid the kid to walk the dog, so that he could stay inside. Where he thought he'd be safe.

He had to put a few miles behind him before digging into the first-aid kit. But he knew the dog had inflicted some real damage. His forearm felt ripped to hell, maybe some torn tendons in there. It would require professional attention. He had to get to a doctor, pronto. The right kind of doctor, the kind that would take a big wad of cash and ask no questions. He knew a few of those.

If he could get to one before he passed out.

He fought off waves of shakes and dizziness. Adrenalin crash.... Okay, maybe even shock.

So, *focus*, you son of a bitch. Don't blow it all now.

After you get yourself patched up, you'll need to go to ground for a while. You need the R&R. You're losing your edge.

But right now, you need to stay clear-headed. *Focus*.

You can do this.... You've handled lots worse than this.... Come on, stay in your own lane.... Just a few more miles....

BETHESDA, MARYLAND
Thursday, November 27, 11:55 p.m.

"His TV finally went off," Erskine said, lowering his binoculars.

Cronin looked up, saw the darkened bedroom window. He checked his watch. "Eleven fifty-five. Maybe he stayed up to watch a 'Frasier' rerun."

"Why don't we call it a night, Ed?"

"I'm with you. I don't see him going anywhere now. Chief's on my case about all the overtime, anyway."

He had just turned over the ignition when he felt the vibration. "Who the hell is calling at this hour?" He pulled out the cell, saw the display. "Oh great. Abrams."

Erskine launched into a string of profanity, and Cronin had to wave him to silence.

"Yeah, Marty.... Where?.... Can't Bancroft handle it?" He shut his eyes. "Yeah, okay. Give us forty-five." He clicked off the phone, then, exhausted, lay his forehead against the steering wheel.

"Don't tell me!"

"Okay, Paul. I'll just take you there and let it be a surprise."

COLUMBIA HEIGHTS, WASHINGTON, D.C.
Friday, November 28, 12:52 a.m.

After a quick stop for coffee and doughnuts, it was closer to one in the morning that they got to the scene. Abrams met them in the hallway and gave them the preliminaries, then led them inside. They took in the dog, then the body.

Cronin whistled. "Holy hell, Navarro is huge."

"Was," Abrams corrected. "Well, nothing much for him to do in the joint but lift weights all day."

"So, you're telling me somebody actually beat the crap out of *this* dude before he shot him?"

"And then some. M.E. took a quick look and guesses at least a fractured skull, elbow, and crushed throat. Maybe more will show in the autopsy. And look closer at the dog. See the way the head's twisted? Broken neck."

Erskine stood with his mouth half-open, disbelieving.

Cronin's gaze shifted from one body to the other. "So our perp has a gun, but he doesn't use it on the dog. He doesn't even use it on Navarro, not at first. Instead, he takes on and kills the Doberman, bare-handed. And then, for all practical purposes, he kills this gorilla, also bare-handed, before finishing him off with one tap in the forehead." He turned to his colleagues. "Remember the hit up in Bowie, that deal with the flagpole? I'm guessing this perp is the same shooter. Whoever the hell he is, he's inhumanly strong to do all this stuff."

"What's with the smell?" Erskine asked, wrinkling his nose. "Somebody started cleaning the joint already?"

"That's ammonia, all right," Abrams said. "But it's not from us. And that's even more interesting. Look down there. See those smears on the tile? And the little beads of spray over there? Our shooter sprayed ammonia around here." He pointed to a young CSI tech who was bending over the Doberman. "Jeff thinks the perp was using it to break down blood stains. Destroy any DNA."

"*His* blood, then," Cronin said. "Our boy was injured."

"That's how I see it. Only thing that makes sense. You don't take on two monsters like these and walk away without a scratch."

"So where's the ammonia?" Erskine asked, looking around in the kitchen.

"There isn't any. None that we found yet, anyway."

"You mean he took it with him?" Erskine asked.

"Maybe he *brought* it here with him," Cronin said. "For exactly these kinds of situations."

Abrams said, "These guys think of everything."

"Which means we won't find the shooter's DNA here," Cronin said wearily.

"Oh, I wouldn't say that," said a nearby voice.

They turned. It was Jeff, the tech. He was grinning. He wore white latex gloves, and he had lifted dog's head, displaying its muzzle and teeth and hanging tongue.

All covered with blood.

"Gentlemen," Abrams said slowly, a smile crossing his lips, "Maybe we just got our first big break."

PART III

"And oftentimes excusing of a fault doth make the fault the worse by the excuse."

—William Shakespeare, *King John*, Act IV, Scene 2

THIRTY

The hot, pulsing spray from the shower beat down onto the back of his neck and shoulders. After five minutes, he felt the tight knots slowly loosening.

This morning's workout in the gym downstairs had been exceptionally long and hard, the first good one he'd had in a while. But he knew that wasn't the only reason for the tension in his body.

He was tense about the call he was about to make.

He'd thought a couple of weeks away from her would allow him to detach completely. He hadn't expected how difficult that would be. It used to be easy for him to acquire and hold an Olympian perspective on things. He was always able to climb to a kind of cold, watchful height, a place above it all, where he could look down upon the world below with an icy calm. That habit or skill or discipline, whatever it was, let him maintain objective control whenever it was necessary to confront circumstances or do things that others found to be stressful, distasteful, even overwhelming.

But something had changed after he met her. From the beginning, she was an exception, the one element in his universe about which he could not maintain emotional distance. He seemed to have no will in the matter, and he didn't understand it. And what he couldn't understand or control unsettled him. He'd been honest enough to admit that fear to her, at the beginning.

Now he felt exposed. At a time when he needed to do everything possible to protect himself.

All the facts, looked at objectively, told him that she was working with Cronin and the other cops to bring him down. Only one fact stood against the growing pile of evidence: her eyes. Or, rather, what he saw in them, when she looked at him. What he saw in her eyes, and what he felt from her body when she was in his arms. That response couldn't be an act, couldn't be faked.

Try as he might, he simply couldn't make himself believe that she was betraying him. Or ultimately would.

He flipped the shower faucet to cold, hoping to shake himself out of this mood—to escape this emotional straitjacket that threatened to immobilize him, stop him from doing what he had to do.

What he had to do was use her. Use her, in order to find out what the cops knew and what they were planning. And to accomplish that, he had to resume his relationship with her. Pretend to be in love with her.

Then hope, for his own sake, that it *was* mere pretense.

*

After he'd toweled off and dressed, he went into the den. Put a fresh battery into a fresh phone. Steeled himself. Keyed in her cell number.

"Hello?"

"Hi, you," he said.

He felt five heartbeats before she spoke.

"Hi, you." Cautious pleasure in the voice.

"I said I'd call."

"And you kept your word. I knew you would, Dylan."

It disarmed him. After a few seconds: "I've been busy and still have things going on all this week, evenings included. But I hoped we might get together next weekend."

"I'd like that."

"My place, Saturday? Luna misses you."

She laughed; it sounded wonderful. "I miss Luna. And you."

"I miss you, too, Annie Woods," he said, knowing it was true.

He heard voices over the phone in the distant background. "Am I interrupting a meeting?"

"Just some co-workers outside my office on coffee break."

"When we get together, you'll finally have to tell me about the company."

She burst out laughing. "The company.... Yes, of course, Dylan. It's time I told you all about the company."

"Private joke?"

"Very private." She giggled again. "I'll let you in on it next Saturday. I have some chores during the day. I can get to your place in the early evening. Is that okay?"

"Perfect," he said. "Can't wait."

"Me, too."

WASHINGTON, D.C.
Monday, December 12, 3:05 p.m.

"Ken, take a look at this."

Startled, MacLean looked up from his desk. Carl Frankfurt had barged into his office without knocking and marched right over to his desk, holding a white business envelope between his thumb and forefinger. His eyes were wide with excitement.

MacLean pushed aside his irritation at the interruption and took the envelope from Frankfurt's hand. It was unsealed. He reached inside and extracted a light blue-colored check and a business card. He flipped over the check and looked at it.

Then stared.

It was made out to the order of the MacLean Family Foundation in the amount of $150,000.

He looked up at Frankfurt, astonished. "What's this all about?"

Frankfurt was grinning. "Why don't you ask him yourself? I left him in the conference room."

He glanced down at the pile of papers on his desk. They would keep.

He looked at the check. He'd been stiffed before. "Carl, could you call his bank and make sure this is legitimate? Then please join us."

When he reached the conference room, a distinguished-looking middle-aged man rose from a seat at the table.

"How do you do, sir," the man said. "Wayne Grayson."

"Hello, I'm Ken MacLean," he replied, shaking the gentleman's hand. "Please, have a seat, Mr. Grayson."

"Thank you." The man had blonde hair, an impressive mustache, a deep suntan, and a suit that must have cost at least one-tenth of the amount of his check. "It's generous of you to make time for me, Mr. MacLean." There was a faint accent, perhaps Boston.

"Let's not speak of my generosity, but yours. Am I correct in understanding that you wish to make a donation to our foundation?"

"You are."

"Frankly, I'm at a loss for words, Mr. Grayson. 'Thank you' seems inadequate, given the size of your gift."

He waved it off nonchalantly. "I have witnessed first-hand the powerful impact of your foundation's work on many lives, sir. You may consider this as only the beginning of a personal campaign to repay you for all that you have done."

"You're most kind. Tell me: How are you familiar with us?"

The man smiled. "Individuals close to me have undergone life-changing experiences, directly as a result of your programs—especially those run by Dr. Frankfurt. I just can't tell you what his efforts have meant for them."

"Would you mind my asking who these people are? I'm sure he would want to know."

"Well, I'm not at liberty to reveal any names at the moment. However, I'm certain that their feelings will be conveyed back to him in due course."

Frankfurt entered the room at that moment, catching his eye with a smile and nod. He sat opposite Grayson.

"Mr. Grayson was just telling me that his gift is largely in response to your work, Carl."

Frankfurt beamed. "I don't know what to say."

"Doctor, words are inadequate to encompass the reach of your deeds," Grayson said.

MacLean glanced down at Grayson's business card, which he'd placed on the table at his fingertips. "I see you're headquartered in Los Angeles."

"It is just a place to hang my hat. My financial-services consultations take me all over the country. One of my regrets is about Christmas this year. I have heard about your gala annual holiday party, and I would have loved to attend," he said. Then grinned. "Assuming that my donation would have been sufficient to purchase a ticket."

MacLean and Frankfurt laughed with him. He really liked this man. More than a bit stuffy, but obviously a kind soul. You found so few like him in the business world these days.

MacLean said, "That's too bad. Our trustees will be attending, and I have no doubt they would have wanted to meet you."

"Yes, it is regrettable," he said. Then his face brightened. "However, perhaps I might contribute a little something to your celebration?"

MacLean exchanged glances with Frankfurt, whose face reflected his astonishment. "Oh, but Mr. Grayson, you've already been more than generous!"

The man leaned forward, his eyes intense and eager. "No, really. If you would please permit me—perhaps introduce me to your event planners—I would *love* the opportunity to participate. I have been involved in planning a number of high-profile, even theatrical, events. I am certain that I could add some creative touches to your celebration, as well. Since I will not be able to be in the room with you in person, it would be my pleasure to join you in spirit."

MacLean looked again at Frankfurt. "What do you think, Carl?"

"I could him put him in touch with the people over at the hotel."

"That would be splendid," Grayson said, smiling broadly. "I have about another free hour today—assuming that your schedule permits, Dr. Frankfurt."

"Oh, of course. I'd be delighted."

MacLean rose from his seat. "Mr. Grayson, I'm just flabbergasted. In all my years of charity work, I've never had an encounter quite like this one—so unexpected, and so delightful. I can't begin to thank you enough. I hope to see much more of you."

Grayson shook hands with him. "Oh, you will, sir. And again, your gratitude is quite unnecessary. If you will forgive me a familiar platitude, just think of this as my way of 'giving back.'"

THIRTY-ONE

CIA HEADQUARTERS, LANGLEY, VIRGINIA
Friday, December 19, 1:01 p.m.

She rapped on the door.

"It's unlocked."

She entered Garrett's office. He stood near the coffee table and club chairs with an elderly, distinguished-looking gentleman in gray tweed. Both men smiled as she approached.

"Annie Woods, I'd like you to meet my old friend, Professor Donald Kessler of Princeton University."

"Professor *emeritus*, actually; my teaching days are long past."

She smiled and shook hands with him. He was in his seventies and blade-thin. But he still had a full head of wavy white hair and a matching goatee. She thought, amused, that he could do ads for a fried chicken chain.

Garrett gestured for them to sit. Annie poured some coffee from the waiting pot while he began.

"Don taught undergrad Politics at Princeton's Woodrow Wilson School for Public Policy. Also, grad courses in International Studies, if I'm not mistaken."

"You're not," Kessler replied.

"But years before that, and just after he finished his doctorate, he spent about seven years with us as a case officer. Damned good one, I might add."

"Until I met the girl of my dreams," the old man said.

Garrett smiled at him gently. "She sure was something, Don."

"She was." The soft way he said it told her the rest of the story.

"Anyway, after Don left the Agency and started teaching at Princeton, we kept him on the payroll as an outside consultant. Among his little assignments over the years was to spot talent for us."

Kessler turned to her. "In the old days, the Company recruited many officers straight from the Ivy League. I was one of those recruits, and later, one of the recruiters."

"Which brings us to why I called you in," Garrett said. "Annie, I was right. I've been blind. I had it all in my head, all along. But it didn't come together for me until Don came by to visit. He asked what I was working on, and no sooner did I begin to tell him, than it hit me."

She leaned forward. "What?"

"Remember our conversation a few months ago about our assumptions? About how one or more of them had to be wrong?"

She nodded.

"Well, our very first assumption was wrong. *Motive.*"

"What do you mean?"

"We knew the Russians would want to stop Muller from spilling his guts about their operations. That's motive. So when he was taken out, we followed a chain of very reasonable inferences. Because Muller was killed at a top-secret safe house, we figured somebody had to tip the sniper about the location. And that implied a source on the inside—another Agency mole. Yet, we were baffled because the crime-scene evidence didn't suggest a Russian sniper, but an American."

"Right," she said. "So we deduced that our Agency mole must have enlisted an Agency sniper. And then we went on a wild goose chase looking for somebody in SAD or OS who might have done it."

"Just as my mole-hunt proved to be a wild goose chase. Because we never double-checked our initial premise. *Motive*, Annie. We, the FBI, everybody—we all simply assumed that the Russians were the only people who might want James Muller dead."

The thought startled her. "Well, who else, then?"

He reached for a small manila envelope lying on the coffee table and handed it to her.

"Annie Woods—meet Matt Malone."

*

She opened the flap and withdrew a 5 x 7 photo. It showed a dark-haired, bearded man in rough clothing. He sat on a flat-topped boulder in a harsh, stony landscape with jagged mountains in the background. Across his lap lay what looked to be an AK-47. She couldn't make out much of his face: The grainy shot had been taken at a distance, and he was in profile, looking at something off-camera. If she hadn't been told his name, she would have guessed that he was an Afghan or Paki tribesman.

"Let me guess," she said. "He's one of ours."

"He *was* one of ours. The best damned officer I ever ran."

"The best damned officer I ever *recruited*," added Kessler.

Garrett got up, rolled his shoulders, then headed for his desk drawer. He came back with two packs of Luckies and his electronic smoke filter.

"Grant, you're incorrigible," Kessler said.

"Screw you." He clicked a button, got the gadget humming.

She asked, "So what can you tell me about this man?"

Kessler took a sip of black coffee, put down the cup. Spread his pale, bony hands on the thighs of his trousers, then closed his eyes, remembering.

"Matthew Everett Malone. Born 5 June 1969 in Pittsburgh. An only child. His father, Michael Henry Malone. A hugely successful building contractor whose business took off in the 1950s. That was the initial phase of Pittsburgh's 'Renaissance' redevelopment. Helen Cassini, Matthew's mother by Malone's second marriage, was with a Pittsburgh newspaper. She met Malone while on assignment. They married and she left the paper when she became pregnant with Matthew."

He paused for another sip. "Matthew idolized his father. He described Mike as a man's man with a strict code of honor and a strong drive to achieve. Clearly, he was a brilliant entrepreneur. Before he died, Malone Commercial Development had branches in ten states, and the family fortune was estimated at over a half-billion dollars."

Garrett whistled. "I didn't know it was *that* much."

"Oh yes. The Malones lived in an upscale Pittsburgh suburb, Fox Chapel. Matthew didn't want for material things or opportunities, including foreign travel and a great private school. And thanks to his mother, there were plenty of books in the house to pique the curiosity of a little boy with a restless, inquisitive mind. He told me that current events and politics were frequent topics around the dinner table."

Kessler looked off into space. "Well, Matthew could have turned out to be just another spoiled rich kid. But instead he grew into a well-educated, athletic young man with unusual poise and self-confidence. And he had a charming, dry sense of humor, too."

"I envy his girlfriends," she said, interrupting his reverie. "He must have been the most popular guy in school."

Kessler shook his head. "You would think so. But actually, he was a loner. Not antisocial, just not really very social, if you get what I mean. Serious, solitary, self-sufficient. He told me once that he had been so captivated by the world of ideas that he felt little kinship with his more conventional peers." He smiled. "I could relate to that. Perhaps that's why we hit it off when we met, and why he eventually opened up to me."

Garrett got up and began to pace near the windows as Kessler continued.

"He might have become a scholar. But his father wanted to temper his cerebral preoccupations with involvement in the real world. So, in addition to getting his son's hands dirty on his construction sites, Mike insisted that he take up at least one competitive sport each school year. Predictably, he avoided team sports and chose the individual ones: swimming, gymnastics, martial arts. He told me he preferred to be the only person responsible for his success or failure."

"How did you get to know him so well?"

"We met by sheer serendipity, Annie. I was into martial arts, too, and we had both signed up for a hapkido class not long after he arrived as a freshman. That was in '87. Well, after one sparring session, I found that we shared many philosophical views, and he was extraordinarily articulate about his. I learned that he was majoring in Politics, with a focus in political theory, and it turned out that he'd be taking a lot of my classes.

"I liked him immediately, so I invited him to a party at our home for some grad students. These were some of the smartest young intellectuals at Princeton—which means some of the smartest in America. Anyway, some hot political argument started up, as they often did among those kids. But even though he was about six years younger than most of them, he held his own. Let me tell you, I was impressed. So much so that I arranged to become his faculty advisor. Over time, we became friends, and I continued to invite him to our home. Jill became quite fond of him, too."

He paused, just an instant. The loss seemed fresh. "Anyway, Princeton is quite tough on Politics undergrads. But his grades were exceptional, and somehow, despite his course load, he still managed to keep up competitive swimming and martial arts. He even did some reporting and columns for the campus paper."

She picked up and studied his photo again. She tried to reconcile what she was hearing with the bearded, rough-looking thug cradling the rifle.

"When he graduated in 1990," Kessler went on, "I encouraged him to pursue a Master's in international affairs and also to take some Middle Eastern languages. I told him that the Middle East was where the important action in the world would be centered for the foreseeable future. He agreed and jumped right in. He became my preceptor—I'm sorry, that's Princetonese for 'teaching assistant'—and he enrolled in the local Berlitz courses in Farsi and Arabic. That's when I discovered another remarkable thing about him: Matthew had an incredible facility for languages."

"You were grooming him."

He held her eyes. "And I make no apologies for it. Matthew was highly patriotic, and he had all the talents and aptitudes that would make him a great case officer."

"So, how did you make the pitch?"

"Before I could, there was an interruption. In 1992, Mike Malone was diagnosed with pancreatic cancer. It hit Matthew hard. He took off the spring semester—which would have been his last—to care for his dying father and help his mother cope. Mike died that summer, and Matthew returned to complete his last semester in the fall."

"Which brings us up to the first World Trade Center bombing."

He pointed a thin finger at her and smiled. "Good girl. February 26, 1993. Yes, that was the turning point. I immediately took a month's leave to do some consulting here at Langley and over at the Pentagon."

Garrett approached, cigarette in hand. "After that bombing, Congress leaned hard on us to put more officers in the field and try to recruit agents inside the terrorist networks. That's when I finally got the green light to ramp up our own recruiting here in Ops. So, when Don showed up here in my office and started raving about this potential NOC superstar–" He spread his hands.

"NOC?" It surprised her. She knew most CIA case officer candidates were trained for eventual "official cover" status in a foreign embassy, usually with a transparently fake job title. They had the protection of official diplomatic status. A "non-official cover" officer, however, was a different breed. NOCs lived under deep cover, out in the cold, operating largely on their own and without diplomatic immunity. Typically, they held a cover job with a private company. "How did you peg him as a NOC so early?"

"Think about it, Annie," Garrett said, ticking off the points on his fingers. "Loner—completely self-reliant and utterly self-confident. Super smart. Fluent in the right languages. Skilled in martial arts. Experienced with firearms. Patriotic. Self-disciplined. Highly motivated. Hell, I never thought twice about putting him into the usual training track down on the Farm. I knew that after a couple years, he'd wind up making paper airplanes behind some desk in Madrid. Just another total waste of talent."

He took a puff, blew a stream of smoke before continuing. "And we just couldn't afford that. Not anymore. Not with the terrorist threat spinning out of control. I needed people who could be trained to operate without anybody holding their hands. People who would be willing and able to go out and mix it up with the *hajis*."

She had to smile. Nobody ever accused Garrett of being Politically Correct. "So you signed off on it."

"And sent Don right back home to make the pitch."

Kessler picked up the tale again. "I invited Matthew to discuss something over drinks down in D-Bar—that's a watering hole in a basement at the Grad College. After some small talk, I brought up the World Trade Center bombing. The implications. Where it was all headed. I remember saying, 'The next time will be much worse.' My God, I had no idea, then.... Well, Matthew agreed with me. He was passionately opposed to radical Islam and keenly understood the dangers that it poses to the West."

"So over beers, you pitched him."

"I did. I told him my history with the Company; that one of my jobs was to find qualified candidates to help fight the war against violent Islamic fundamentalists; that I thought he had an extraordinary set of abilities to bring to the defense of America."

"I bet he was floored."

"He's pretty reserved about showing his feelings. But let's say that it was not at all what he had planned to be doing with his life. Over the next hour, I explained—as honestly and graphically as I could—the sort of contributions he might make. And the personal costs. He listened without saying a word, looking straight into my eyes the whole time. When I finished, I told him to sleep on it, and I called the waitress over for the bill.

"I'll never forget the expression that came over his face. It had been tight, completely intense. All of a sudden, it relaxed. He looked slowly around the room, at things on the walls, at his fellow students. Then he picked up his mug of beer, drained it, and set it back down on the table, very deliberately. He held my eyes, stuck out his hand, and said: 'I don't have to sleep on it, Don. I'm in.'"

She glanced again at the photo, now lying on the coffee table. "As you say, an extraordinary young man. And now—he's gone?"

"But not forgotten. His subsequent career in the Agency—if we could tell it—would be the stuff of legends."

It baffled her. "How does a man like that go rogue and become an assassin?"

"That brings us back to motive," Garrett answered, sitting down again. "Matt Malone had every reason in the world to hate and want to kill James Muller. You see, Malone was one of the officers that Muller betrayed to Moscow."

"Oh!"

"So that's motive. He also had opportunity—because he knew about the safe house. In fact, he'd been there himself once, to conduct an interrogation."

Kessler said, "And also believe us when we say: He had the means. Many times, he had proven in the field just how lethal he could be."

She paused, turning it over in her mind. "Okay. I believe you. Still, I'm having trouble getting my head around this. His motivation, mainly. Sure, Muller blew his cover, and he was pissed off. But *assassination*? That seems a bit over the top."

The two men exchanged glances.

"It's more than just being blown," Garrett said. "After Muller tipped off the Russians, they tried to assassinate Malone. That was almost three years ago, March. He was in Afghanistan as an interrogator attached to a black ops team. The Russkies lured him into an ambush. They had a bomb waiting. Malone barely survived it. His face in particular was a mess. We flew him back to Walter Reed. He underwent extensive reconstructive plastic surgery." He looked at her, said quietly: "Your late friend, Dr. Copeland, did the surgery himself."

"Arthur?" she said. "I suppose I shouldn't be surprised. He was the best."

"Imagine what that must have been like, Annie," Kessler said. "Sure, we all take risks in this business. It's part of the game. But you don't expect to be betrayed by one of your own. You don't expect to have your career, let alone your appearance, annihilated by a traitor."

She stared at the face in the photo, hating the memory of James Muller even more. "So you're sure he did it."

"Malone is a stellar marksman. It all fits. No other explanation does."

"We had it all wrong, then," she said, sighing. She turned the photo around to face them. "You say he had plastic surgery, but this is an old shot. What does he look like now?"

Garrett shrugged. "I'd like to show you something more recent, but I can't."

"Why not?"

"There isn't one."

"But don't we——"

"Not for him." He leaned back and propped a foot against the edge of the coffee table. "There's no file, either. We have nothing on him. Not even fingerprints. I'll explain in a moment. In fact, it's sheer dumb luck we have this single photo. It shouldn't exist. It was taken surreptitiously by a Special Ops Group team member in Afghanistan. To impress his girlfriend, he admitted later. We canned the idiot for that; but he should consider himself lucky, because if Malone had known, he would've probably killed him. Anyway, it wound up at the bottom of the SOG guy's file, and it turned up only after we began searching for anything that could help us find Malone."

"Find him?"

Garrett said, "Two months after his admission to Walter Reed, he vanished from his hospital bed. That was the night before Dr. Copeland was going to remove the bandages from his final round of plastic surgery."

THIRTY-TWO

**ALLEGHENY NATIONAL FOREST
TIONESTA, PENNSYLVANIA
Thirty-one Months Earlier—May 15, 3:45 p.m.**

"Who are you?"

The lips on the stranger's face in the bathroom mirror moved, perfectly in synch with his own.

He stood frozen in place, unable to make sense of what he was seeing.

For weeks, he thought he'd accepted what had happened to him. With his usual cockiness, he figured he was prepared. In fact, he'd been eager for this moment.

But that was before he stared into this mirror—into the haunted eyes of a pale, swollen, bruised, unshaven face that he no longer recognized.

He exhaled loudly, suddenly aware that he'd been holding his breath. He shook his head—but stopped when the stranger shook his, too.

"Who the hell are you?" he demanded, louder.

The stranger's lips had moved again. And this time the voice registered. Deeper than his own. Not quite raspy, but huskier. The same trauma that had done this to his face had done something funny to his vocal cords, too.

He stopped.

His face? *His* voice?

His heart was pounding and his head began to spin. He had to look away. He lurched to the bathroom doorway and leaned against the frame, stomach churning, fighting down the bitter taste rising in his throat.

The rustic living room swam before him dimly, gloomy from the towering oaks and pines that cloaked the cabin in perpetual shadow.

He noticed his duffle bag on the bare planks of the floor, where he'd dropped it a few minutes ago. Nearby, his worn leather jacket, draped over the back of an old wooden chair.

His eyes drifted to the double-barreled Mossberg he'd propped near the screen door that led onto the front porch.

Outside, the wind hissed through the leaves of the forest. Somewhere in the distance, a crow cawed.

A faint medicinal smell reminded him that he still gripped the remnants of the bandages he'd just cut from his face. He lifted the white tangle and noticed brown streaks of dried blood on it. Instinctively, he opened his hand to drop it, but the surgical tape stuck to his fingers. He waved his hand, but it still clung tightly. He shook his hand wildly, two, three times, grunting like an animal. The stained white wad finally spun off into the middle of the room, landing beneath the knotty-pine coffee table.

He was sweating now, and shivering. His tongue felt like a thick rag. He knew he was losing it. As he'd been trained, he closed his eyes, imagined himself on a puffy cloud, counted slowly as he struggled to control his breathing.

He wanted to step into the living room. But he couldn't move. He knew he had to look again. Had to force himself to come to terms with what he had become.

He turned slowly. At first, he didn't dare look into the mirror. He bent over the sink, propping himself on shaky arms. He remained that way for a moment, eyes down, staring at the rough floorboards beneath his boots. Until the knots and swirls in the wood grain arranged themselves into an Edvard Munch image of a distorted, howling face.

He clenched his teeth. Raised his gaze to the mirror.

The haunted stranger with the bruised jaw and swollen cheeks still stared back at him.

"Who am I?" the stranger whispered at him.

*

For several days after he arrived, he could barely muster the will to unpack necessities, which he left scattered around the cabin. He didn't eat much or go out. Didn't read or listen to the radio. Didn't bother to clean up or shave, either. He didn't want to look again into the bathroom mirror.

Each morning, he put on a pot of coffee. Wrapped in a gray flannel bathrobe, he sat on the porch in the old, creaking rocker. Sipped coffee in the morning, wine in the afternoon and evening.

Sipping. Rocking. Staring off into the Allegheny National Forest. Watching the oak leaves flail helplessly in the grip of the rising wind, as a cool low front moved in. Watching gray squirrels scramble and dig in last fall's brown, rotting drifts. Watching flocks of black birds wheel under the gunmetal sky and scudding clouds.

Watching. Rocking. Trying to reconcile himself to the face in the mirror.

At dusk, sluggish from the wine, he limped up the stairs to the loft and stretched out under the scratchy olive Army blanket on the bed under the eaves. He slept without sheets, right on the bare mattress pad. He slept at least ten hours every night, his dreams haunted by images of violence.

*

Rocking on the porch and sipping Malbec during the afternoon of the fourth day, he thought about his first time here.

He was twelve years old when Dad—the tall, beefy man everyone else called "Big Mike"—brought him here for a week during deer-hunting season. They'd driven a couple of hours north of their sprawling home near Pittsburgh, taking the big Chevy pickup. Along the way, Dad revealed that the cabin was his private retreat; not even Mom knew about it. He went up here each November, he said, to get away from his high-pressure construction business and "recharge the batteries."

The first day, Dad showed him how to clean and shoot his Remington "thirty-ought-six." It was his first experience with guns. Dad patiently demonstrated how to safely carry, load, aim, fire, and clear the rifle. Then he set some empty soup cans out on the grass, with the slope of a steep hill as the backstop.

The first time he shot his father's rifle from a standing position, the kick nearly knocked him down and left his ears ringing, despite the ear plugs he wore. But the blast sent a can tumbling.

Dad laughed and clapped. "Nice shooting, Mr. Boone! Now, try again. But this time, lean a bit more, like I showed you. And pull the stock tighter to your shoulder."

The second day, Dad led him into the forest to show him how to stalk deer. He explained the difference between "up-wind" and "down-wind." How to find a good spot and keep still. How to wait and let the animals come to you.

That night, a snowstorm blew in. When it cleared the next morning, Dad took him out to do some tracking. They crunched through the powdery drifts about a half mile from the cabin, picked up the tracks of three deer and followed them to a half-frozen pond. But the animals had already gone.

Dad pointed to a nearby grove of trees surrounded by tall bushes. "There's a good place to set up. The wind is right, and we'll watch the pond right through those bushes."

The plastic-covered Pennsylvania hunting license pinned to Dad's camo jacket flapped in an icy gust, and he shivered as a cold finger of the wind poked down the neck of his own jacket. His father seemed to notice.

"Problem, Matt?" he asked.

"Uh—no."

Dad looked at him, his pale blue eyes twinkling.

"Too cold?"

"I'm fine."

His father smiled that slight, crooked smile of his and nodded.

They took up a spot behind the bushes about thirty yards away, sitting on a fallen tree trunk after brushing off the snow.

And waited.

The wind swirled through the white-crusted bushes and drove tiny stinging crystals into his face. His eyes watered, his nose ran, and his breath raised a frosty fog. Even through thick woolen gloves and heavy boots, his toes and fingertips were going numb. Within fifteen minutes, his teeth were chattering. Ashamed, he clenched his jaw to try to make them stop.

After half an hour, he thought he was going to freeze to death.

But Dad didn't seem to notice either him or the cold. He remained still and watchful, straddling the log with the left side of his body angled toward the pond; his Remington lay across his knees with its muzzle pointed in that direction. His big, bare hands were tucked into a fur hand-warmer on his lap. His eyes, squinting against the wind under the brim of his hunting cap, were the only things that moved, constantly scanning the area in front of him.

After forty-five minutes, he finally couldn't take it anymore and turned to say something—but stopped when Dad suddenly raised his hand, demanding silence. Then he pointed.

Out of a line of pines on the opposite side of the pond a large buck emerged, moving one halting step at a time. It turned its head in brief jerks, its large rack of antlers tilting with each move, its nostrils testing the air.

He felt his heart begin to race. All awareness of the cold vanished.

Dad again motioned him to remain still. Moving with infinite patience and precision, he smoothly drew his bare left hand out of the fur, then, very deliberately, raised the rifle to his right shoulder. Suddenly it became apparent why he'd sat with his left side toward the pond: All he had to do now was lift and aim the weapon without turning or shifting his body, perhaps alerting the nervous animal.

Dad didn't have a scope on his old Remington. He simply looked down the fixed sights on the barrel, slowly drew in a breath, then let out a little white cloud through his nostrils and held the rest.

He remembered turning to watch the deer when the unexpected blast in his ear caused him to flinch and slide right off the log into the snow. He saw the buck spasm, partly rear up, then fall. Its legs twitched twice and then it was still.

"Clean shot." Dad said it to himself, quietly, simply.

"Wow!" Bounding to his feet, he caught the amusement in Dad's eyes, and he charged over the powdery surface to where the deer lay. A crimson stain was spreading in the snow beneath its tawny shoulder. His father came up beside him, leaned over the antlers and moved his forefinger, counting.

"Twelve points. This old guy's been around a while." Dad straightened, towering over his son. "Now, we earn the privilege of taking his life."

They muscled the carcass back to the cabin—or rather, his father did most of the muscling. Still, it was a long trek, and when they arrived, he was sweating despite the cold, his aching lungs gasping for breath. He watched in squeamish fascination as Dad strung up the buck from a tree branch and demonstrated how to gut and clean it.

"I could truck it up the highway and have somebody else do this first part," he explained, wiping his long, sharp knife on a rag. "But I want you to see what's involved. Meat doesn't just come out of a grocery store in plastic wrap. Somebody has to kill an animal before we can eat it...."

When we're done here, we'll drive it down to Tionesta. A guy there will finish the job, and in a day or two we'll pick up our venison."

Dad paused and looked at him.

"Still cold?"

"Huh?" He had completely forgotten about the frigid temperature.

Big Mike grinned. "I know you were freezing your ass off out there. But you didn't moan and groan about it, and you kept still. And you see? Patience was rewarded." Dad punched him lightly on the shoulder. "I'm proud of you, son."

His father went back to work, but continued to speak.

"Proud because you're not a whiner. That's important.... First thing I watch for when I hire a guy is: Does he make things happen, or does he make excuses?"

He reached into the buck's abdominal cavity, pulled out a bloody, lumpy mess and dropped it onto the plastic sheet he'd spread under the deer.

"See, Matt, there's two kinds of people," he went on. "And the difference is in how they see themselves. One guy says to himself, 'I'm the boss of circumstances.' The other guy says, 'I'm the victim of circumstances.'"

He paused and straightened. Looked into his eyes. "And you know what?"

"What?"

"They're both right."

*

He sat in the rocker, eyes unfocused, twirling the wine in the glass. After a few more minutes, he drained what was left. Got up and limped inside.

He went to the kitchen, poured himself another glass. Grabbed a wooden chair and dragged it up the creaking stairs to the loft. Planted it in front of the dusty mirror on the vanity and sat down.

Raised his eyes to meet the stranger's.

The guy in the mirror looked as if he'd been waiting.

So, he began to talk to him.

He spoke quietly, for a long time. Spoke about things he had never told anyone. Things he'd seen.

Things he'd done.

Told him why he was doing this crazy thing now.

His voice was growing hoarse and the white square of the skylight had gone gray when he stopped. He suddenly realized that it was no longer a stranger's face in the mirror. Nor was it a stranger's voice uttering his words.

He leaned forward in the dim light. Closer than he'd yet dared.

Beneath the beard stubble, the swelling on the guy's face was down, now, and the bruising almost gone. He was surprised that he could barely notice any surgical scars.

Not such a bad face. Maybe even better than the one I had.

The guy smiled at that.

It'll be okay. I can build a new life with that face. And it's a good one to match the name on the Social Security card.

He stood, raising his almost-empty glass to his new friend.

"Hello, Brad Flynn."

THIRTY-THREE

CIA HEADQUARTERS, LANGLEY, VIRGINIA
Friday, December 19, 1:29 p.m.

"So, nobody knows what he looks like, then," Annie said.

"We certainly don't," Kessler replied.

"Didn't you try to find him?"

The men looked at each other and chuckled.

"First, you don't find Matthew Malone unless he wants to be found," Kessler said. "Second, it seems that Matthew had been preparing to leave the Agency for some time."

Garrett broke in. "As you know, several years before then, we began to suspect there was a mole here in Langley. Missions around the Middle East were blown, for no apparent reason. Then a couple of our case officers turned up dead in Pakistan, and another disappeared in Afghanistan. In fact, back in May 2005, Malone himself survived an earlier attempt on his life."

"So they were on to him even then."

"Uh huh. And what was more troubling was that Malone wasn't an obvious case officer, attached to an embassy under some transparent diplomatic cover. He was a NOC, working as a stringer for the Associated Press. His reporting was credible and there was no reason for anybody to suspect him. And being a NOC, sometimes working with black ops teams from the Special Activities Division, we of course didn't even keep any files on him here. But the attempted hit reeked of Moscow. So how the hell was he blown, except by somebody here at Langley, with unusual access?"

"He kept in touch with me during visits stateside," Kessler interjected. "He was worried about more than the mole. He hated the office politics at Langley. The Company"—she had noticed that he preferred the more dated term—"was always playing it safe. Many senior people, starting on this floor, but extending all the way to the station chiefs, were afraid to put case officers in the field. Too many opportunities for blowback if operations went sour, they always said. So they put handcuffs on Grant and his people. That's why the number of officers in the field *gathering* intelligence has been minuscule compared with the number of people here *analyzing* it."

"And Malone wasn't one to put up with bureaucratic crap," Garrett said. "I can't tell you how many times he went off the reservation, breaking rules, pissing off station chiefs. Even a few ambassadors. I had to pull his ass out of the fire more than once. But it was getting harder to do as time went on. He could see the handwriting on the wall. So

I think after that first attempted hit, he began planning his exit strategy."

"Strategy?"

"Annie, it was really incredible, what he did. We found out only later that he'd been quietly liquidating his family's holdings, piecemeal. He sold all his shares of their company. He sold the estate outside Pittsburgh, and all the contents. Cars, boats, vacation properties—the works. He must have set up accounts abroad while he traveled, because we're sure a lot of it wound up offshore."

"How could he move and hide half a billion dollars without leaving tracks?"

"Dummy companies. And aliases."

"Come on, Grant. You can't tell me he set up dummy companies and accounts with a few fake IDs from Central Cover."

"Not fake. Not from Central Cover. And not a few, either. I don't know how many. Maybe dozens."

"How could he get so many *authentic* IDs?"

"He scammed the Social Security Administration. He used a spoof phone to call their headquarters in Baltimore; the Caller ID number tracked right back here. He identified himself and said he was coming over with a written request. When he got there, he showed a supervisor his ID, then handed him a signed letter on the director's letterhead asking for access to their computers, on a matter of national security."

Kessler laughed. "That is so very like Matthew."

"He told the supervisor that we were trying to penetrate some domestic terrorist cells, and we needed to establish deep-cover aliases for a team of operatives. He talked the guy into issuing him about a hundred random Social Security numbers. Then, ballsy as you please, Malone sat at the guy's keyboard for about an hour and typed in fake names and birth dates for all the SSNs. Finally, he actually got the guy to delete those SSNs from the queue of numbers to be issued in the future. That supervisor was so eager to do his patriotic duty that he even brought in a computer specialist to help tangle up the records, so that nobody could ever know which numbers were issued."

"You're telling me that he walked out of there with scores of authentic but *untraceable* Social Security numbers?"

"All connected to equally untraceable and unknown names. And of course, then he could use them to get other IDs. Drivers licenses. Credit cards. Library cards, pocket litter. You name it. From there, he could set up bank accounts, corporations, whatever he wanted."

"I can't believe this."

"Believe it. He's that good. He even conned me into giving him some alias IDs."

"He conned *you?*"

Kessler laughed harder.

"Yeah, me," Garrett growled, stabbing his latest butt into an ashtray. "He used several schemes. After the attempt on his life, he convinced me to delete all Agency records on them. And to contact other federal agencies, and have them delete all *their* records on Matt Malone, too."

"You did that?"

"I know it sounds stupid in retrospect. But the Russians were on to him, they wanted him dead very badly, and we knew they would try again. So his only chance was to completely erase his tracks and set up a new identity."

"But you haven't said *why* the Russians wanted to kill him."

He looked at his friend. "Don, this is 'need to know.' You want to give us five minutes?"

"Sure. I'll take a walk down the hall." The older man grinned. "Clear my lungs."

After he left, Garrett leaned forward. "What I'm going to tell you is classified way above Top Secret—SCI, in fact—so you never heard it, okay? When Malone was on a mission in Afghanistan, he heard a rumor that Moscow was funding and supplying the Taliban with weapons to use against our troops and NATO allies."

"*What?*"

"Yep. He risked his neck a dozen ways to run the story down. The trail led to a Russkie in Islamabad, one of the money guys. Being Malone, he didn't play nice with Ivan. He snatched the guy from his digs, dragged him off somewhere, and tortured the bastard. He got Ivan to sing like Josh Groban. Malone got names, dates, details of the shipments, contents, and transactions. The guy told him that the Kremlin wanted to bleed us dry by arming and financing the Taliban. That Putin himself considered it to be payback for when Reagan backed the jihadists against the Red Army, back in the Eighties."

"Malone got actual proof of this?"

Garrett nodded. "Taped confession and some damning paperwork. He managed to deliver it to our station chief before he went back into the field."

"But that's—"

"—political dynamite," he finished. "As Malone would soon discover. When the Russians missed their man, they followed the same trail of informants backwards, to Malone. They convinced one of the informants to tell Malone there was a meeting planned between Russian embassy personnel and some top Taliban. They knew he'd want to witness and record it. Malone took along a SOG guy for backup. But when they got to the place, all that was waiting inside was an IED."

"God!"

"Only because he was so careful opening the door did he survive at all. He stood to the side, but the blast still blew the door right back into him, smashing his face. He took a few pieces of shrapnel, too. The SOG guy was out covering the alley, so he was okay. He picked up Malone and drove him out of there. We got Special Forces medics to stabilize him and we flew him to Germany, then back here to Walter Reed."

She tried to process it all. "Russia—backing the Taliban! Grant, why is this is the first time I'm hearing about this?"

His face was drawn into bitter creases. "Because after risking his life to get that explosive information, Matt Malone was betrayed once again. This time, by his own commander-in-chief. While Dr. Copeland was piecing his face back together, just a few miles south, our dear president decided that it would be far better for his future relationship with Putin to sweep the whole thing under the rug."

"Do you mean to tell me that American troops are dying over there, thanks to the Russians—but nobody's doing a damned thing about it?"

"If you're angry, imagine how Malone felt when he found out."

Once again, she looked at the photo on the coffee table. "How could they do that to him?"

"Can you see now why he would've been angry enough to blow Muller's brains out?"

*

She sat in her office, hunched over a few sheets of paper and a man's photo.

The papers were notes she'd been scribbling since the meeting with Garrett and Kessler ended an hour earlier. The photo was the one of Matt Malone.

She kept going back to the photo. Maybe if she could come to understand him better, she might be able to find him. Though now that they knew what they were up against, it seemed almost hopeless. Clearly, he was a genius in the clandestine arts. Probably a genius, period.

She tried to imagine the intensity of the idealism that could compel someone to such extremes. For she had no doubt, based on what they had said, that Matt Malone was a passionate idealist. A man so idealistic that he could lay down his life for his principles. Or, if necessary, kill for them.

It caused her to wonder about the depth of her own principles, and what she would or wouldn't do in their name. What is the boundary line between a man of principle and a fanatic? Between a person moved to violence by a passion for justice, and a person motivated to violence by blood-lust and nihilism? Surely there was a difference, not in degree but in kind, between someone like Matt Malone and a typical terrorist. A moral difference. He seemed a reluctant warrior, someone for whom violence had become a last resort, not a preferred alternative.

She tried to put herself in his shoes, tried to fathom the sheer depths of his loneliness and isolation. She thought of his life history, of its promise, of what he could have become. Of what he *should* have become. He was a man of enormous talent, courage, and integrity. The sort of man who, in a just world, would be making headlines with his deeds.

What a tragic waste.

She heard the faint tone of her cell phone and dug it out of her purse. Frowned when she saw who it was.

"Yes, Detective Cronin," she answered.

He chuckled. "I wonder how many heavy breathers have been put out of business by Caller ID?"

"Better living through technology. What's up?"

"We haven't talked for a while. Just wondered if anything new had developed?"

"Not really. He contacted me again. We're going to get together this weekend."

"Well, that's something, at least. We lost track of him a couple of weeks ago. I don't know how; we had his place staked out pretty well. Anyway, I called his editor at the *Inquirer*, and he said that Mr. Hunter told him he was off researching another crime piece."

"No doubt. I wonder what new surprises he has in store for us?"

"You sound a bit negative. I thought you liked what he is writing."

"Oh. Well, yes. I guess I'm just a bit tired."

"Don't lose your idealism, Ms. Woods. I like that about you. And, truth be told, I like your boyfriend's idealism, too."

"So do I," she said. She glanced at Malone's photo. Another idealist. She smiled to herself. *I can't seem to escape them.*

"Well, as long as I have you on the line," he continued, "I might as well bring you up to speed on the investigation. Don't spread this around, but we have a blood sample of one of the shooters."

It perked her interest. "Really. That's great news. How did that happen?"

"We didn't let it out to the press. But remember that Navarro killing a couple weeks ago? The guy owned a Doberman. It bit the shooter before he killed it and Navarro. We got the shooter's blood sample off the dog. It had to be his blood, because it didn't match Navarro's. It's our first real break, because when we eventually get a shooter suspect, we can check for a DNA match or maybe scars from dog bites."

"That's at least some progress."

"The longer they do this, the more chances they take, the more mistakes they make, and the more clues they leave behind. And the people around them start to notice things, too. All the sneaking around."

"It's a shame you don't have more than the blood to go on, so far."

"Not much. Just that and the symbolic names."

"Symbolic names?"

"Oh. Sorry. That hasn't gotten out, either. The vigilante team has been using symbolic aliases."

"I still don't get what you mean."

"You know, names like 'Lex Talionis' and 'Edmond Dantes.' Lex Talionis, that's Latin for 'eye for an eye.' Old Testament justice, you see. They used that in Hyattsville, when a—"

Something froze inside her. "Did you say Edmond Dantes?"

"Yeah. One of our guys looked it up. That's the hero in a classic revenge novel, *Count of Monte Cristo*. That guy was also a vigilante. So the way we—"

"Billy Joe Stoddard," she mumbled.

"Excuse me?"

The walls seemed to be spinning.

Suddenly, things began to crash together.

Malone assassinates Muller, out of revenge.

And leaves behind the name of a fictional avenger as his signature.

The vigilantes assassinate criminals, also for revenge.

And leave behind the name of fictional avengers.

Matt Malone is a vigilante?

"Ms. Woods?"

She stared in shock at the photo on her desk.

It couldn't be.

It *couldn't* be.

But then everything else began to tumble into place.

Matt Malone, CIA master of assassination and disguise...and of surveillance detection.

Matt Malone, *idealist...who had plastic surgery...who left his old identity behind...living now under a false identity...seeking justice....*

"You still there? Ms. Woods?"

Arthur Copeland rebuilds Matt Malone's face....

Her pulse was hammering.

Dylan Hunter—with a rebuilt face and a new identity—shows up at Arthur Copeland's funeral....

She stared at the photo of the dark-haired man. Began to shake.

No—God no!

She felt a crushing weight on her chest, making it hard to breathe.

Matt Malone...Dylan Hunter...

You've been hunting your own lover!

"Annie! Is anything wrong?"

"I...have to go...."

She clicked off the phone. It fell from her shaking hand to her desk.

THIRTY-FOUR

FALLS CHURCH, VIRGINIA
Saturday, December 20, 4:25 p.m.

The sight of her lingerie in the overnight bag caused her to shudder.

She had to stop packing and sit on her bed, trying once again to settle her nerves.

Since yesterday, the fear had come upon her in sudden waves. It prevented her from sleeping last night, until she finally took a pill that relaxed her enough for a fitful few hours of semi-consciousness.

Throughout the day, though, the thought of facing him again terrified her. All the facts, all the logical inferences she could draw from them, told her that Matt Malone, CIA assassin, had become Dylan Hunter, leader of a team of vigilantes.

But those same facts—and mistaken logical inferences drawn from them—had led her and Garrett astray for the past six months. The same facts and erroneous inferences had propelled them into futile manhunts for imaginary Russian moles and military snipers.

Well, were her inferences any more valid this time? Everything she felt, everything she knew, told her that she was right about this. But did she really know *everything?*

Before she would say anything to Garrett or Cronin, she needed proof. Iron-clad proof. She could not destroy Dylan's life because of some terrible mistake or misinterpretation.

She ran her hand over the smooth fabric of the bed's comforter.

Nor could she destroy their relationship because of some tragic error.

So she had to face him tonight. Had to pretend to him that she had resolved her doubts and fears. Had to play-act long enough to get the proof she needed. Or evidence that would exonerate him, once and for all.

She stood again, started to zip the bag. But stopped once more at the sight of the lingerie.

How could she possibly get through the next twenty-four hours? She would have to sleep with him. Lie in the arms of a possible assassin that she had sworn to bring to justice. Allow herself to be touched by the hands of a possible killer hunted by the police.

How could she do that?

She entered the bathroom. Ran cold water over a face cloth. Pressed it to her eyes and cheeks. Let the chill dampness penetrate her skin.

Eyes shut, she thought of the man in the photo. The man named Matt Malone. Of his idealism and bravery. Of the obscene betrayals and the horrific trauma he had endured, and that had fueled his desire for retribution. Of his rebirth under the skilled, caring hands of Arthur Copeland.

Then, she thought of what it had to be like for him to learn that a trio of sadistic savages had destroyed the man who saved him.

And what of the man she knew only as Dylan Hunter?

All right, suppose he *was* Malone, resurrected. Suppose he *had* taken on the role of a vigilante, retaliating against those monsters in order to avenge the ruined lives of people like Arthur and Susie. And against other monsters, on behalf of Kate Higgins and George Banacek.

How could she blame him?

She removed the cloth from her face. In the mirror, her eyes were tired, gray, desolate.

No, that wasn't the question. The real question was: *How could she betray him?*

After all, if she were honest with herself, that's what she was planning to do. She was a government security officer. She had sworn an oath to abide by and to protect the nation's laws. To shield a killer from the reach of the law would dishonor that pledge.

Now, she had to choose.

She could betray the law that she had vowed to uphold, and end her career.

Or she could betray the man she loved, and end their relationship.

But she could no longer remain loyal to both.

She tossed the cloth onto the sink. Began to gather the last of her toiletries.

It would be so much easier if only she had some valid reason to hate him, a motive strong enough to tip the balance, to commit her to stopping him. Then, turning him in would not be a betrayal. It would not be fraud this time, either. It would be an act of loyalty.

But what reason could turn her against the man she loved?

Unbidden, an image arose in her mind.

Her father's face.

She remembered the night at his home, not so long ago. Remembered how he had responded to her anger with his patient, deep, gentle faith. Recalled the hurt in his eyes at her harsh parting words.

Then she remembered the news conference. Remembered how Dylan had stalked up the aisle, his face cold, his accusations merciless. Recalled the look of shocked vulnerability on Dad's face....

She looked again into her reflected eyes in the mirror. Saw a measure of resolve return.

Then she strode back to her overnight bag, tossed in the rest of the items, and tugged the zipper closed.

She would spend the weekend with him. She would sleep with him. She would force herself to do these things, in order to learn the truth.

And if, at last, she found him to be responsible for these crimes, then she would turn him in to the authorities.

Yes, he might have his high ideals and principles.

But she had hers.

BETHESDA, MARYLAND
Saturday, December 20, 6:20 p.m.

She had managed to hold onto her sense of cool control during the drive over, during the elevator ride to his floor, during the walk down the hallway to his door. As she rang his doorbell, she reminded herself of her father and of her oath.

The door opened on his face. The thick dark curly hair, the cleft chin, the green-brown eyes. The eyes looked hard, for just an instant, then softened. That funny little twisted smile formed on his lips.

"Hi, you."

She felt her resolution soften, felt herself smiling.

"Hi, you."

He lay his big hand on her arm, guided her inside, closed the door. He lifted the overnight bag from her shoulder, set it down on the floor. They stood in the tiny foyer, looking at each other, not touching. She felt the tension build between them.

He raised his hand to her chin. Gently tilted it up, leaned down and kissed her.

It was like the first time, the night of their first date, outside her door. She felt his strong arm move around her, felt herself leaning back under the pressure of his lips, felt her arms rise to grip his powerful shoulders, felt everything else falling away. She was molded to his body, responding helplessly, her knowledge and will obliterated.

He pulled back first, his face hovering just above hers. He stroked her hair with the back of his hand and stared, unblinking and serious, into her eyes.

"We're going to get through this, Annie Woods."

The words, so unexpected, so right. She had to blink rapidly to keep from crying. "I hope so, Dylan," she whispered.

He held her at arm's length, looked her up and down. "Better than I remembered."

She laughed in spite of herself, relieved to release the tension without tears. Then she did the same to him, taking in his sports jacket, cord slacks, and short boots, all deep tan. "You look great, too. Are we going somewhere?"

"We always seem to do better when the evening begins with a good dinner," he said. "I've got seven o'clock reservations at a nice little French bistro."

"Do I get to change first?"

His eyes roamed her body again. He shook his head. "You'll do."

*

Though the place was jammed, their table was set apart in an alcove filled with hanging plants. The wall was exposed brick and adorned with an Impressionist landscape. They ate meats baked in puffed pastries and shared a good bottle of Cabernet Franc.

She felt surprisingly relaxed. Looking at him study the painting in the candlelight, she couldn't make her suspicions real. Garrett and Kessler had led her to believe that Matt Malone was a tragic victim of circumstances. But the man before her was their confident master. His light-hearted gaiety, his serene self-assurance...this was not a brooding, damaged soul, striking out in blind, bitter anger.

He turned to her. Then grinned. "Still trying to figure me out, I see."

"Am I that transparent?"

"To me."

"I'll have to remember that." She searched his face. "I'm just wondering how you got to be you."

He sipped his wine, not breaking eye contact. Then: "Long story."

"We have the weekend."

He put down the wine. "So, what specifically do you want to know?"

"In my experience, most men are cynics. You're not. You don't seem to have a cynical bone in your body. You're an idealist."

"My idealism does get tested, from time to time. As I'm sure you know." He paused, his expression now serious. "Because you're an idealist, too, Annie Woods."

She tried not to show a reaction. "Maybe. But this is about you, Dylan. I know that justice means everything to you. What interests me is why. How did that develop?"

"Maybe it's not something that develops. Maybe it's something that people have, but lose."

"That sounds clever, but I'm not sure I understand."

He gestured toward their fellow diners. "See all these people? How many of them start out their lives as cynics? How many of them, as little kids under five years old, have no dreams or ideals? How many identify with the bad guys?"

"Okay. I get that."

"But by the time they're in their teens, a lot of them have. They've already given up. Why? Face it, idealism is hard. It's hard to adhere to some standard. Selling out is so much easier."

"Then you're saying that a cynic is just a coward?"

"Yes. But so are a lot of those fake 'idealists' out there, who turn their cowardice into virtues."

"What do you mean?"

His eyes rested on the chandelier above their table; they flashed in its light. "Annie, it's not easy to live with yourself when you sell out. When you give in, just to 'belong,' just to 'keep the peace,' 'not make waves,' 'go along to get along,' and all the other common euphemisms for cowardice. Because that's what it is. Cowardice. And at some level, the person doing that knows that he's a coward. And he feels guilty."

"So, cynics are *guilty* cowards, then."

"Which is why they need to rationalize. They even make virtues out of 'humility' and 'turning the other cheek' and 'loving everybody.' Why? Because it alleviates their guilt. It's much nicer to pretend to yourself that your passivity makes you a saint, rather than just another gutless puke who won't take a stand for what's right."

She tried to mask her discomfort. "Don't you think some people who preach such things are sincere, though? Not cowards, but true idealists?"

"I don't doubt it. But it's like I said to you once before: Those types become enablers. Foolish enablers of evil, whether they intend to or not."

"Let's get back to you. When did justice become so important to you?"

He remained silent a moment, as if he were weighing something.

"All right. I've never told this to anyone. When I was about ten or eleven, I was on the playground at school. I saw this gang of kids in a circle, hollering, and I went over to see what was going on. A couple of bigger kids, bullies, were picking on this smaller boy, Joe. No teachers were around, and the others were just egging the bullies on. I liked Joe. He was nerdy, but smart and funny. Anyway, he was terrified and crying and—" He stopped. "I just couldn't walk away."

"You got involved?"

"At first, I just told them to stop. Then the pair turned on me. They were a lot bigger than me. One of them grabbed me, ripped the pocket of my shirt. I looked down at that, and I saw red. So I just swung at him, bashed him on the cheek. Then they started to hit back. We really started going at it. All the kids started yelling and cheering. For a minute, every time they hit me, I just got angrier.

"But then I tasted blood in my mouth. My blood. It was like somebody flipped a switch. I wasn't enraged anymore. I just turned icy cold. I became like a machine. After that, nothing they did to me hurt at all. I didn't feel anything."

His gaze was fixed somewhere far away. "I just pounded them, knocked both of them down, first one, then the other. Then I jumped on them, kept pounding until they screamed for me to stop. I grabbed both of them by the hair, turned their bloody faces toward Joe, and told them to apologize. They apologized."

He blinked, coming back to the present. "But I wasn't done. I stood up and turned on one of the kids who'd been mocking Joe, and I demanded that he apologize, too. He looked scared to death and did. Then I faced down all the rest of them. Hell, it was a yard full of kids. I said, 'Who wants to be next?' There was dead silence, except for the two kids wailing on the ground. I pointed at them and said, 'Any one of the rest of you ever bothers Joe again, *that's* what will happen to you.' And then I took him by the arm and led him away."

She saw the imprint of the memory etched on his face as he raised his glass again.

"You went after the bullies," she said. "And then you confronted their enablers, too."

The glass paused at his lips.

"I hadn't thought of it that way before," he said. "But yes. I suppose that's true."

"That day changed you," she said softly.

He placed the glass on the table and nodded slowly. "It was kind of a turning point. A moment of self-definition." He suddenly looked at her. Smiled, breaking his reverie. "Okay. Now, it's my turn to ask a question."

"Oh. Well, okay, fair is fair, I suppose."

"Trust."

She licked her lips. "What about it?"

"What happened, Annie?"

She drew a long breath. "Actually, I had a conversation not long ago about that. Somebody close to me pointed out that I'd been betrayed twice. The first time, when my mother left my father and me to run off with another man. The second time, when I caught my ex screwing another woman."

"I'm sorry. How long were you married?"

"Since July 2002." She suddenly felt the need to unburden herself. "Frank was a commercial pilot. I met him at a hotel during a business trip, not long after 9-11. There was instant chemistry. And my dad liked him and insisted on throwing a big wedding in Georgetown. After the honeymoon, we resumed our careers. He traveled a lot, of course, and I was pretty wrapped up in my work, too. But we made the most of our time together. Or thought we did."

"Until when?"

"Until last year. When I accidentally found the emails from his babe in Denver." She paused to take a sip of wine, moisten her lips. "Ergo, my trust issues. Just so that you know, I'm officially divorced. Since January."

"You had mentioned your mother on our first date. I didn't know about your husband."

"I didn't want to bring it up, then. I figured it might scare you off."

He covered her hand with his. "I'm still here, Annie."

She looked at his hand on hers. "Me too."

*

They were both a bit tipsy when they arrived back at the apartment. She could not completely relax and sensed that he could not, either. There was still a slight wariness, a dull edge of caution, in their interaction. She could not suppress her awareness of her suspicions about him; but neither could she suppress her knowledge of his motives, of the reasons that may have turned him into an outlaw.

Inside the door, he drew her into his arms again. Her mouth responding to his, she felt as if she were spinning dangerously, deliriously, deliciously out of control. She was overpowered by it, by the restored feeling of oneness with him, by the sheer power of him and how it possessed her. For a fleeting instant, she knew that the danger that he represented only added to her intoxication, and to the intensity of the passionate tension between them.

If everything would only freeze in place, right here, right now. If only it would go on forever this way....

They stumbled, laughing, toward the bedroom, toward the waiting bed. She tugged off his jacket and dumped it on the floor. Then he pulled her to the bed and sat on it, facing her. Holding her eyes, he undid the buttons at her throat, then down the front of her blouse. He slid the straps of her bra down her arms, then reached behind her to release it. As it fell, he buried his face between her breasts.

But she pushed him back, then held up her hand to stop him. With deliberate slowness, she unbuttoned his shirt. She ran her flat palms over the hair of his chest, up to his shoulders, then down his arms to free his sleeves—

—and exposed the bandage wrapping his left arm.

*

In an instant, he saw her half-closed eyes snap open, her half-parted lips widen in a gasp. Saw the shock as she gazed at his arm.

He had to cover it, give her the excuse he had prepared.

"Don't worry about that. It's nothing. I just had a run-in last week with a friend's pet poodle."

The shock didn't vanish as her eyes turned to his. For a moment, she didn't speak. Then: "You say a dog did this?"

He tried to keep the smile fixed in place. "A poodle. If you count them as real dogs."

But she didn't smile. He watched closely as something faded in her eyes.

She knows.

*

Their love-making had a frantic quality, he thought, as if both of them were trying desperately to convince themselves that what they knew could not be true.

At first, he almost felt as if he was forcing himself upon her. She seemed to be fighting him, as she had in the past, when it had been only playful; but for a few moments it seemed real as she twisted away, seeming to recoil from him, to reject him.

"No," she gasped, flailing at his shoulders with her fists.

At the word, he felt anger rise within him, and he grabbed her hair, pulling her head back.

"Yes," he said. He began to kiss her naked shoulders, then breasts, then throat. He heard her gasp again, and he covered her open mouth with his.

In a moment, something changed. She began to return his kisses and to move with him. She drew up her legs and wrapped them around him; her arms snaked around his back and she began to rake his skin with her nails....

*

Afterward, they lay quietly, wrapped in each other's arms. He stroked her hair with his fingers, feeling his pulse slow, feeling the heat rising from their bodies.

Yet as close as they held each other, he felt a widening chasm between them.

His hand touched her cheek. It was damp.

She knows.

*

He didn't sleep. Hours later, when her breathing at last became long and steady, he slid carefully from beneath the sheets. Gathering his bathrobe from a hook on the door, he stole from the room, drawing the door shut behind him. Then he entered the den. In the dark, he felt for the hidden latch at the bottom of his bookcase and eased open the panel. His fingers probed inside for what he needed. He withdrew it, then clicked the drawer back into place.

In the living room, he pulled his key card from his wallet, then carefully opened the door to his apartment and headed for the elevators.

Three minutes later, his task completed, he returned.

Then sat alone in the dark on the living room sofa, stroking the cat.

He knew that tomorrow, they would engage in a complex minuet of forced affection. Both would try to be light and frivolous, pretending that everything was normal.

And of course it would not be. Could not be.

Until morning, he would sit here and try to learn to live with this new pain.

THIRTY-FIVE

BETHESDA, MARYLAND
Monday, December 22, 5:02 a.m.

He arose at five in the morning. He pulled on his sweats and went down to the gym on the first floor. After warming up with some *katas*, he hit the machines and free weights, using the ultra-slow-repetition routines that he'd practiced for many years—the kind of high-intensity workouts that build the most muscle in the shortest amount of time.

After just over half an hour, sweating profusely, he went back to his apartment and headed directly into the shower. He winced as the hot water stung the places on his back where she had scratched him. In spite of everything, he had to smile, marveling at the intensity of her passion even after she had discovered the truth about him. Some things about women, he thought, would always remain a mystery to him.

After feeding Luna, he dressed, sat at his desk in the den, and went back to puzzling it all out.

She had left yesterday in the early evening, telling him that she had to get ready for work on Monday morning. He'd expected that; keeping up the charade any longer was just too awkward for both of them.

There was no way he'd fool her again, of course. Her reaction to the dog bite made it clear that Cronin had told her about the Doberman. Now she had confirmed, at least in her own mind, not only that he was a vigilante; she also knew, specifically, that he had to be Navarro's shooter. She'd tell Cronin all about it later today. They still wouldn't have proof, of course, but with their suspicions now confirmed, they would be all over him like fleas on a dog.

He would still have ways of eluding them, even while they were watching him closely. However, before he disappeared, he had some unfinished business to take care of.

For now, though, he had to put himself in their shoes. How would it go down today? He had begun to work it out on Saturday night, while lying awake next to her in the dark.

It was unlikely that she'd tell Cronin much by phone; he would need a detailed report from her, and that would take at least an hour, plus travel time. And other members of the task force would probably attend, too.

But where and when? Maybe at police headquarters in Alexandria, though possibly somewhere else. And probably after work—unless she was so upset that she'd take the day off and go see them in the middle of the day.

Timing was important. To make sure he had enough time to react before they arrived later today, he had to know exactly when she left her house or workplace and went to meet them.

Which is why he had sneaked from bed on Saturday night while she was asleep, gone down to the garage, and hidden the real-time GPS tracker in her car.

*

He was filling another coffee cup at 7:47 a.m. when he heard the computer program for the tracker start to beep. It automatically activated a computer alert when the subject vehicle was in motion. He went back into the den, sat, and zoomed in on the screen map.

The flashing red dot representing her car entered the maze of highways in Falls Church, moving east toward Route 29. He remembered that she worked for an insurance company in Fairfax; so she'd probably get on 29 and shoot straight west. Once he was sure she was on her way to work, he'd probably be okay for hours, maybe all day.

He sipped his coffee and watched. Watched her turn onto 29 *east*.

He sighed. It was looking as if her meeting with Cronin & Company would be first thing in the morning. That didn't give him as much time as he'd like. He watched for a while as the red dot continued on 29. If she were meeting the cops in Alexandria, she might next take 120— Glebe Road—south, cutting off a lot of miles.

The red dot intersected 120 on the map.

But turned *north*.

What the hell?

He watched the red dot track along Glebe all the way past the George Washington Parkway, where it picked up the end of Route 123 and veered north again.

Probably heading now for the big cloverleaf entrance onto the GW, just a mile ahead.

He sipped more coffee, staring at the screen.

But the dot kept moving past the GW intersection.

He clicked the mouse several times, enlarging the street map.

Then the hair began to stand up on the back of his neck as he watched the red dot approach a place that he knew very well.

He put down his cup.

Surely she would continue right on by.

But she didn't. Annie Woods's car made the right turn off 123.

And onto the access road the led into the headquarters of the Central Intelligence Agency.

Stunned, he zoomed in to the maximum magnification. Watched the red dot pause at the security entrance, then move on, entering the Agency campus. Then loop around to an area he knew was set aside for employee parking.

Where it stopped moving.

*

He stood on his balcony, staring blankly at the neighborhood.

He wracked his brain for something, anything, that could make sense of what he had just seen. But came up empty. It was as if all the laws of nature had been repealed—as if up and down were suddenly reversed, while gravity and inertia no longer existed. Everything he knew was coming apart, spinning crazily into chaos. And he had no idea why.

Start with what you know about her.

He realized then that he actually *knew* very little. Nothing but what she had *told* him. Except for the house in Falls Church, which was real enough; he had been there. But what else did he really know?

She was young, extremely smart, very athletic. She claimed to be an insurance claims investigator, obviously false.

What about her name? The crime victims he had met, including Susanne Copeland, all called her Annie Woods. But was it real? Could she have fooled them, too?

The funeral. He recalled all the Agency faces there. Of course, Arthur Copeland had worked for Langley as a contractor. But what if there was more to it?

The thought occurred to him: *How did Annie know Susanne?*

He went back inside. He needed answers.

He spent a few minutes working out his pretext. Then pulled a fresh phone and battery from his desk drawer, dialed into the "spoof" website, and programmed in an internal Agency phone number he knew by heart. That one would show up on the Caller ID when he dialed the main number.

"This is Mel Riggins in DS&T," he told the Agency operator. "I need a couple of updated phone numbers, if you would?"

"Certainly, Mr. Riggins. Could you give me the employee names, please?"

"First is Susanne Copeland. Second, Ann Woods. That's Ann with no 'e.'"

"A moment, sir."

There were a few clicks, then the woman came back on the line. "Are you ready for those numbers, sir?"

"Go ahead," he said. He took down the numbers, then said, "Wait a minute. Isn't Susanne Copeland in D.I., Middle East?"

"Mmmm...yes, Directorate of Intelligence, but actually with Eastern Europe."

"I see. Maybe they transferred her. And Ann Woods, where is she now?"

"Let me see.... I have her in the Office of Security, special investigations.... No, wait a minute. There's a notation that she transferred some months ago.... Okay, yes, she's now working out of the office of the NCS deputy director."

Suddenly, he could no longer speak.

"Will there be anything else, Mr. Riggins?"

"No," he managed to say. "Thanks much."

He broke the connection. Set the phone down and gripped the edge of the desk.

"Garrett," he said through clenched teeth.

It had been bad enough dealing with the police.

*

He sat at his desk with a notepad and pen, drawing those lines and circles they call "mind maps." He liked the technique; it helped him visualize connections between all sorts of random data and ideas. It took another hour before he thought he had sorted it out.

First, there was the CIA and Grant Garrett, plus Annie Woods—an OS investigator now working for Garrett. That looked as if it could be about Matt Malone.

Second, though, there was Annie Woods and Cronin. That was completely separate. It was all about the vigilante killings.

He looked at the linked bubbles of names. The one and only connection between both investigations was Annie Woods. And—as insane and ironic as it was—it looked as if her presence in both of them was all *his* fault.

After all, *she* hadn't known he was going to show up at that funeral. In fact, she had no idea who he was, then. Or even later, when he also turned up at the prison. Or at the victims meeting. Since then, *he* had been pursuing *her*—not the other way around.

He remembered strolling outside with her on the street after that meeting. How she'd tried to brush him off; how he'd insisted.

It had been an incredible breach of mission security. He recalled, with bitter irony, that Sinatra song about the warning voice in the night. *Don't you know, you fool?* No, he didn't know. How could he have known? But he'd been a fool, all right. He had not simply walked into a trap; he had set the damned trap for himself. Set it by falling in love, by ignoring the fact that any woman with half a brain would want to know his background.

How could he have been that big of an idiot? So it served him right that, of all the women on the planet, he had picked the one woman who would be most dangerous to him.

And now she knew all about his ties to the vigilante killings. What would happen if she also found out about his connection to Matt Malone? Or did she already know?

Did Garrett?

He took the sheets of note paper he had been scribbling on and fed them, one by one, into his shredder.

The loud whirring and grinding sent Luna scurrying from her hiding place under his desk and out of the room.

Intel. He needed more information. Most immediately, he needed to know more about her. Who she really was, what she was really up to.

He dialed in Wonk's number. After the social preliminaries, he explained what he wanted.

"Let me read this back to you, Dylan. This lady friend of yours lives at a home in Alexandria, and she works for an agency which, on this open line, shall remain nameless. She was married in July 2002 in Georgetown to a man, first name Frank, and was divorced from that gentleman in January of this year. Do you have anything else?"

"I wish."

The researcher chuckled. "I am certain it will be enough. Call me at noon."

*

A couple of hours later, he dialed back. Wonk answered at the first ring. "Dylan?"

"Yes."

Silence.

"Well? What did you find out?"

"Dylan...are you sitting down?"

"What's wrong?"

"You simply are not going to believe this."

"Believe what?"

"In fact, you will not like it one bit."

"Wonk! For God's sake, will you get to the point?"

"Ann Woods is her married name. Her ex-husband's name is Frank Woods. She kept his surname, most probably for career reasons."

"All right, so what's her maiden name, then?"

He hesitated again, just for a few seconds. "Ann MacLean."

It felt as if something were crawling up his back. "Did you say 'MacLean'?"

"Dylan...she is his daughter. Kenneth MacLean's daughter."

CLAIBOURNE CORRECTIONAL FACILITY
CLAIBOURNE, VIRGINIA
Monday, December 22, 12:05 p.m.

Dr. Carl Frankfurt led his client through the final security checkpoint, and then to the front doors. Parked near the sidewalk was an old white Chrysler with its four-way flashers on.

"That must be your sister. Why didn't she just come into the lobby?"

"She's afraid of prisons, Doctor. And who could blame her?"

"Oh, that's right. I forgot. She didn't even visit you since you've been here."

"Well, she's a good soul. She's never denied me help when I've asked."

"You're fortunate. I wish that every other resident here had support like that." Frankfurt faced the man and stuck out his hand. "This is a big step for you. Enjoy the next few days."

His client took the hand and clasped it in both of his. "Thank you, Doctor."

"Merry Christmas, Adrian."

"Oh, it will be that."

CIA HEADQUARTERS, LANGLEY, VIRGINIA
Monday, December 22, 4:32 p.m.

She emerged from the Old Headquarters Building and pulled her coat tight around her, trying to shield herself against the frigid, buffeting wind. Snow was in the forecast. The thin bare limbs of the trees around the CIA campus clawed at the darkening sky like black, skeletal fingers. The clouds reminded her of dirty padding spilling from a torn mattress.

Head bent forward against the wind, she walked rapidly toward the lot where her car awaited her.

And her decision.

Of all the days of the past weeks, this one had been the most difficult. She had not been able to eat breakfast or lunch. She drank coffee only to relieve the headache from caffeine deprivation—and the stress. She avoided Garrett, hunkering down in her office, going through the motions of working, but accomplishing nothing.

All because she had been dreading this moment. This decision.

As she reached her car, she pressed the key fob button. The vehicle's lights flashed twice in response. She entered, tossing her purse onto the passenger-side floor. Because there was a manila envelope on the seat itself.

She sat motionless for a moment, gloved hands on her lap. She listened to the wind rising and falling, felt it rock the car, almost imperceptibly.

She took off her thin gloves deliberately, one finger at a time. Placed them carefully on the seat beside her, next to the envelope. Looked at it for a moment, then picked it up and held it a few seconds.

She had to face this now. Once and for all.

She straightened the metal clasp on the envelope. Opened it. Withdrew the sealed plastic sandwich bag and held it before her, staring at its contents.

Eight small, dark, half-moon shapes.

Her gaze moved automatically to her fingertips. To the nails that she had clipped short on Sunday morning. At his place. Before she showered.

She looked at the clock on the dash. Cronin would be in his office until five. She could call him, right now. And when she told him what she had, he would wait.

She reached up to adjust the rearview mirror and caught her reflection. Just her eyes, imprisoned in a horizontal rectangle. They were like the sky: dull gray, bleak, empty.

You have to decide.

Whom and what will you betray today?

She shut her eyes. Held them closed a moment more.

Decided.

She replaced the plastic bag within the envelope. Fastened the clasp. Placed the envelope on the seat again.

Then she keyed over the ignition. Backed out of her parking space. Headed for the exit.

She did not look into the rearview mirror again.

THIRTY-SIX

BETHESDA, MARYLAND
Wednesday, December 24, 11:21 a.m.

Hunter stood in the middle of the living room, going over things in his head one more time, just in case he missed anything.

He'd never kept much here in the way of personal items, and he'd moved a lot of it out, a bit at a time, in recent weeks. What little was left now was in the trunk of the car downstairs.

He had already packed his bug-out bag and had Luna's pet carrier ready to go. He'd shredded the files from the hidden drawer in the bookcase, stuck the other items in the bug-out bag. Though the computer was still up and running, he planned to take it with him. But just in case he couldn't, the hard drive was ready to be pulled out and transported. Or destroyed at the touch of a button, if it came to that.

He had also moved his other vehicles late last night to one of his other safe locations before returning here by Metro. That left only the BMW downstairs, which they still didn't know about, and which he'd use to make his escape.

Today, after rising before dawn, he packed the last towels and bed sheets. Then he scrubbed down everything, every surface, and followed up by vacuuming floors, curtains, rugs, and upholstery. He had a garbage bag waiting for Luna's litter box and food dish, which he'd take with him tonight and dump somewhere.

This afternoon, the professional cleaning company would come in and do the whole thing again, including the carpets. Whistle-clean for the holidays—that's what he'd told them he needed. And a big bonus if you do an absolutely immaculate job, everywhere. Don't leave a crumb. I have a sister with life-threatening allergies, you see....

That about covered things. The rest, he could handle by phone and mail, from remote locations.

He took a seat on a wooden bar stool at the kitchen counter, making sure not to touch any surface with his hands. Now, to think about the hours ahead.

They were up to something; that was certain.

He had left the GPS tracker program open on the computer. She had not gone to work back at the Agency on Tuesday or today. In fact, her car had not left her driveway since Monday night. Nor had the police stakeout resumed here.

That made no sense. No sense at all. They were preparing something, and no doubt trying to lull him into lowering his guard.

But he was one step ahead of them. He would bail out of here before they arrived, and vanish again. Right after tonight's mission.

The cat wandered in, stopping to look at him and sniff the air, wondering about the lingering ammonia smell. She made a small *rrrr* noise; it sounded like an inquiry.

"I know, girl. I liked it here, too. But remember: There's always Grayson's place downstairs."

WASHINGTON, D.C.
Wednesday, December 24, 2:14 p.m.

He walked up to the front desk of the Hotel Royal Summit and smiled at the pretty young clerk.

"Hi. My name is Shane Stone, and I'm here regarding the MacLean function this evening. They told me to talk to Sarah in event planning."

The girl smiled. "I'll call her," she said, reaching for the house phone.

After she made the call, he added, "Also, I believe you have a guest room key card for tonight, reserved for me by Mr. Wayne Grayson?"

"Let me check, sir.... Here it is," she said, handing it over. "Number 315. I see that it's prepaid for you, Mr. Stone. I hope you'll enjoy your evening."

"I'm sure I will. Merry Christmas."

Within moments, a thin, middle-aged woman with short, bleached-blonde hair marched across the lobby and up to them, her heels making clip-clop sounds on the marble floor.

"Yes, sir. I'm Sarah Wright. May I help you?"

He smiled at her, too. "Shane Stone. Wayne Grayson contracted with my company to prepare the multimedia video they'll be playing tonight. I'm here to check out and augment the audio-visual system. He told me the two of you met and made the arrangements."

"That's right. I'm glad you're here early. Let me show you to the Grand Ballroom."

He followed her down the hallway, and they turned through open double doors into a vast function room.

Huge chandeliers blazed over a sea of round tables covered with white linen cloths, alternating red and green napkins, and glittering crystal and dinnerware. Twisted strands of green and red crepe paper ribbons stretched across the expanse of the ceiling. An enormous, decorated Christmas tree stood in the right front corner of the ballroom. On the left, workmen were laying down sections of a parquet dance floor over the blue-and-gold-patterned carpet.

"This is really great," he said, surveying the place.

She smiled. "Well, Mr. Stone, do you need any help from us? Or are you able to handle things on your own?"

"Thanks, Ms. Wright, but I think we'll manage. We appreciate all your help."

*

He went outside to where he had parked the panel truck near the delivery entrance. Snow was already falling, though the temperature was not yet cold enough for it to stick. That made his work less problematic.

He opened the back doors of the vehicle, lowered the rear ramp, then rolled out a utility cart. He brought it in through the delivery entrance, down the hallway, and into the ballroom. He put on work gloves. Then, he pushed the cart over to the corner platform housing the sound board, microphones, computerized audio-visual equipment, and video cameras.

For the next hour, he strung cables, fiddled with the equipment, enlisted the staff for sound checks and lighting levels. At one point, he opened a tool kit on the cart and bent over the laptop computer running the audio-visual system. He also borrowed a long ladder from the maintenance staff and climbed up to the ceiling near the back, installing several electronics components on some high braces.

Just before 4:30, he left as he had come.

*

At 5:30, the hotel's event technicians entered. The head of the wait staff paused to watch them work, wondering why they were performing the same sound and light checks all over again.

These rich people, he thought; for them, everything has to be just so. He sighed, then went to see how things were going back in the kitchen.

*

At 6:45, a black 2007 BMW 7 Series rolled into the hotel parking lot. The driver didn't leave it with the valets, but parked it himself, front facing outward, at the side of the building, not far from the delivery entrance.

A dark-haired man with a goatee emerged, wearing an expensive black wool coat over a tuxedo, and carrying a large black-leather briefcase. He walked through the falling snowflakes to the front entrance, then headed straight to the elevators, where he pressed the button for the third floor.

*

When Annie entered the ballroom at 7:30, she spotted her father in the midst of a knot of guests near the dais. She threaded her way through the tables and arriving guests.

His eyes lit up when he saw her. "There she is!" he said, spreading his arms for her.

With his strong features and boyish shock of strawberry hair, he was still movie-star handsome, and his tuxedo revealed a body that was still tall, lean, and erect. Yet she saw in his face what the recent months had cost him. There was something different about his eyes—a missing sparkle, perhaps—and his cheeks looked drawn, as if he had lost weight.

"Hi, Dad." She stepped into his embrace.

"I'm so grateful you decided to come," he whispered in her ear. "It means so much to me, especially right now."

"I know," she whispered back. "I'm here only for you, Dad."

In fact, she hated being here. She didn't believe in his cause. During the past few months, she had come to despise it. And she wouldn't have attended, except for his pleas.

*

In Room 315, he had tossed his overcoat on the bed and hung his tuxedo jacket on the back of a chair. Now he sat at the room's desk, watching the screen of the powerful wireless laptop that he had removed from the boxy briefcase.

The image on the screen was being transmitted from the tiny, battery-powered, wireless-operated video camera that he had installed overhead in the ballroom a few hours ago. He could use his laptop mouse to direct the movable lens of the camera, panning or zooming in and out. The whole setup was expensive and hard for most people to obtain.

For most people.

He spotted her almost immediately when she entered the ballroom. He was not particularly surprised that she was present. Nothing much surprised him anymore.

He zoomed in on her, then panned the camera to follow as she and her father walked up the steps onto the dais and took seats next to each other in the center of the long table. She wore a long, pale yellow evening gown. Her beauty was breathtaking. But his appreciation felt abstract and remote, as if he were in a museum looking at some ancient sculpture of a beautiful woman.

He glanced at his watch. It would still be a while before it was his turn to participate in the festivities. He sat back to watch.

*

She had insisted to her father, as a condition of her attendance, that she would be seated as far as possible from Carl Frankfurt. She was relieved that the shrink was sandwiched between two dowagers near the end of the dais.

The older man to her right, a trustee, had given up on her quickly when she responded monosyllabically to his attempts at small talk. And her father, on her left, was engrossed in conversation with the politician next to him.

For the moment, she could be alone with her thoughts.

Thoughts of him.

She still could not come to grips with the chaos that had engulfed them. It was as if they were trapped between two colliding realities: one, a sane, joyous world that they inhabited together; the other, a nightmarish, paranoid universe where no one could be trusted and nothing understood. And it felt as if they had been slipping back and forth, unpredictably and disastrously, through some black hole that connected those incompatible worlds.

She had tried countless times to resign herself to the impossibility of their relationship. Yet something deep within her rebelled. Rebelled at the indignity of being a victim of circumstance. She had never submitted to "fate" in her entire life, about anything else.

How could she surrender to it now, over something this important?

How could two people, so close and so right for each other, have allowed outside circumstances to drive them apart?

*

The wait staff had cleared the main course, poured more wine, and served dessert. Ken MacLean saw the hotel's event coordinator nod at him from below the dais. He checked his watch; just after nine. He returned the nod, then turned to the guest of honor. "It's about that time. We'll run the film first, then I'll introduce you."

"That's fine, Ken," said Congressman Morrie Horowitz.

MacLean got up and went to the podium. He looked out upon the eight hundred faces that turned to him expectantly. He let their conversations die down, then spoke.

"Ladies and gentlemen, I do hope you've enjoyed your dinner. Now it's time for us to reflect upon and celebrate the foundation's many achievements over the past year. It has been a year of both triumphs and challenges. But thanks to your faithful support and participation, the MacLean Family Foundation is poised to make the coming year our best ever."

He smiled and waited for the applause to end.

"To remind you of where we have been, and to excite you about where we are headed, a new foundation benefactor, Mr. Wayne Grayson of Los Angeles, has prepared a short film. I've not yet seen it, but he assures me that it will help us remember this very special occasion. If we could have the lights lowered a bit, please?"

MacLean returned to his seat. His daughter smiled at him and patted his knee. The lights went down in the ballroom. He turned to the big screen.

*

In Room 315, he moved the computer's mouse and clicked two icons on the screen.

The first click sent a wireless command to a device he'd placed inside in the master computer in the ballroom, shutting it down. The dummy video he'd provided the staff would not play.

The second click sent a wireless command to activate a DVD player he'd hidden under the dais. It began to run his video, transmitting it through a cable he'd connected to the giant screen.

*

Annie watched the name of the foundation fill the screen.

"Good evening, ladies and gentlemen," said a booming, electronically distorted voice. "As supporters of the MacLean Family Foundation, we have gathered here to celebrate Christmas...."

The screen abruptly filled with a horrifying image of a woman's body, half-naked and bound, sprawled in a field.

"Oh my God!" a man's voice pierced the darkness from somewhere in the audience.

A woman shrieked.

Then a rising chorus of muttering, punctuated by angry shouts.

The booming voice went on, overpowering the cries from the audience.

"But unfortunately, *this* beneficiary of the Foundation's programs won't be celebrating Christmas with her husband and children. Because Julie Madison was murdered by"—the photo changed to a mug shot of a bald man with tattoos on his cheek—"Richard Garney, a serial rapist who was granted parole early this year, thanks to the testimony of"—the slide changed again—"*this* man. That's right, it's our very own Dr. Carl Frankfurt! Dr. Frankfurt, you see—"

Shocked, she turned to her father. In the light from the screen she could make out his mouth hanging open, his eyes wide in disbelief.

"Hey! What is this?" shouted the congressman seated next to him.

"Stop this!" screamed Frankfurt, leaping to his feet. "Shut that off!"

"...And this next beneficiary of the foundation's work this past year was little Tommy Atkinson," the unstoppable metallic voice thundered. "He doesn't look too good in this photo, though, does he? That's because one day, Tommy, age eight, met *this* man, Rory Miller—a pedophile who managed to avoid prison. How? By entering a foundation-funded treatment program—"

As the din from the audience rose, her father jumped up, knocking over his chair. He stumbled and pushed his way past others on the dais to reach the podium.

"Let's have the house lights—and please, turn off that TV screen!"

The chandeliers suddenly blazed, exposing a scene of bedlam: hundreds on their feet, shouting, screaming—others staring at the screen in mute, open-mouthed horror—women covering their eyes—one throwing up convulsively at her table—couples rushing toward the exits—wine glasses falling—people yelling at the tech crew in the back, who were shaking their heads frantically and waving their arms in helpless frustration....

"Friends! Please! Don't panic! Don't run!"

Her father, standing helplessly at the podium, shouting into the microphone, unheeded, his ashen face reflecting the horror of the spectacle before him.

She had remained rooted to her chair, feeling as if all the blood in her body had been drained, leaving her paralyzed.

Then she rose slowly to her feet. She scanned the room, from one side to the other.

After a moment, a nearby sound penetrated her consciousness. She turned and saw her father crumpled in a chair on the now-empty dais, his body hunched forward, sobbing uncontrollably as he gazed out at the wreckage of his life.

She walked over to him, knelt. Let him bury his face on her shoulder. Stroked his thick, unruly hair.

*

In room 315, he watched the horror unfold.

It was the horror that he was simply reflecting back upon them.

The horror that *they* had caused for so many others.

He felt not a shred of pity for them. He thought instead of their victims. The countless victims that these self-righteous, sanctimonious bastards preferred to forget.

Well, he would not let them forget. This night was their reminder.

He watched as they scrambled for the exits, like roaches caught in the light and scurrying for cover.

Then, amid the chaos, he noticed one point of calm.

He saw her rise slowly from her chair. Then, just as slowly, scan the audience from one side of the room to the other.

He knew the face she was looking for.

He watched her move to her father. Kneel and hold him.

After four minutes, he stopped the DVD. Closed the laptop and slid it back into the briefcase.

Slipped on his tuxedo jacket, then his coat and gloves.

When the police searched for Shane Stone, they would find only this empty room.

When they checked for Wayne Grayson, they would find that he had paid for this with cash and prepaid, store-bought credit cards. All untraceable.

When they examined the equipment he left behind, they would find nothing that would lead them anywhere, either.

He paused at the open door to take one last look around.

"Merry Christmas to all, and to all a good night," he said aloud.

He closed the door behind him.

THIRTY-SEVEN

BETHESDA, MARYLAND
Wednesday, December 24, 10:47 p.m.

He backed the BMW into its slot in the garage. Before leaving the car, he took a moment to strip off the fake goatee. He left the groceries in the trunk; he wouldn't be long, and they'd keep a while. Gas and groceries had been the last items on his long mental checklist. Now, he and the cat would be able to cover some distance, then stay out of sight for a couple of weeks while the manhunt was most intense.

He entered the elevator, pressed 9. The door hissed shut.

As he ascended to his apartment, he considered once again what he was leaving behind.

Then angrily dismissed it.

It was all an illusion. A fantasy. Get over it.

You were kidding yourself that you could ever have that kind of life. That kind of love. You never have. You never will. And you were an idiot to imagine that you could.

The elevator door opened and he headed down the hallway toward his apartment.

Now, to change out of this tux. Get Luna into the carrier—which won't be fun. Dump her litter box and food into the garbage bag, seal it up. Grab that, her carrier, the bug-out bag, and you're out of here.

He stuck the key card in his lock and pushed open the door.

"Hello, Dylan Lee Hunter," she snapped. "Or should I say: Matthew Everett Malone?"

*

She stood in the foyer, arms crossed, feet apart. Still in her gown from the party.

Eyes blazing. Cheeks livid.

He stood still for a moment in the entrance, key in hand.

Then took a step inside and let the door swing shut behind him.

Well, well.

"Hello, Annie Woods. Or should I say *Ann MacLean of the CIA's Office of Security?*"

She blinked, startled.

"Oops. I'm sorry, but I just can't quite keep up with you. You're working for Garrett, now—aren't you, *Miss MacLean?*"

Shock replaced the fury in her eyes.

"Oh yes. I know all about you," he went on. "Although I must confess, you were way ahead of me. I only learned the truth over the past few days. But what a small world it is! Why, we shared the same employer. Then, I'm tricked into sleeping with the daughter of my worst enemy. Speaking of the devil, how's *Daddy* feeling tonight?"

She flared up again. "You bastard! You fake!" she shouted, trying to regain her advantage. "You're a fraud and a liar—"

"Oh please!" He spat the words out. "It's not as if I'm the only liar here. Or even the biggest. In fact, I'm a rank amateur compared with you, Annie what's-your-name. So: How long has the Agency been on to me? Months? Just how long have you been working to set me up?"

The last words seemed to startle her.

"I have to say, though, they did choose well in sending *you* after me." He yanked off his overcoat and threw it at a wingback chair. "I never thought much of shrinks, but whichever one at Langley selected you deserves a raise. He obviously knew my type better than I did. Tell me: Did you enjoy your performance as the phony little seductress?"

"That's not true!" she gasped.

"*True?* Who the hell are you to lecture me about truth? About *trust?*" A sadistic desire to hurt her was pulling him recklessly past some kind of inner barrier. "Hell, I'm no saint. For sure. Yes, I lied to you. Sure, I did. I lied to protect my life. But at least I never lied about the one thing that I thought really mattered between us: how I felt about you. But you took that and used it against me."

She was shaking her head slowly, eyes wide.

"I know, I know: You were just doing it to protect Daddy, right?"

"No! It wasn't that!"

"No? Well, what else, then? Money?"

"How can you say——"

"Who was it easier to betray me to: Cronin or Garrett? Were they in a bidding war for your services? Did they offer you bonuses for seducing me?"

"Dylan!" She began to cry.

But he was too furious now to stop. "No, seriously. You're very good, you know. Did you undergo special physical training at the Farm for this little Mata Hari role?"

"Dylan!" she screamed, sobbing. "Stop!.... Please stop!.... Please!"

He stopped.

She stumbled to the sofa, collapsed onto it, her face buried in her hands.

He stared at her a long time.

What is happening here?

He went to the sink, drew some water in a paper cup, took it to her and offered it wordlessly. She took it, sipped, and looked up at him, shivering. The despair in her eyes could not be feigned.

He sat in the chair across from her. Leaned forward, elbows on his knees. He saw every word of his cruelty etched in her face.

What have I done?

When he could trust his voice, he said:

"We've both been living lies too long, Annie. We need to know what was real."

She looked at the floor a moment, then back into his eyes.

"No. We need to know what *is* real."

TYSONS CORNER, VIRGINIA
Wednesday, December 24, 11:07 p.m.

She gazed at their framed wedding portrait hanging above the fireplace, and she fought down the urge to cry again.

She had told her friends that she didn't want to go out and celebrate with them tonight, that she'd prefer to remain home by herself. They'd tried hard to convince her, even threatening to show up and visit her, anyway. But she was firm about it.

She had to get used to her first Christmas without him.

She hadn't put up the tree or any decorations, nor had she displayed any of the many Christmas cards she'd received. There were several hundred this year, many more than they had ever received in years past. People were trying to be nice, they meant well. But their gestures of caring were still reminders. And reminders were painful.

She had plenty of reminders here.

She sat in her favorite chair in the living room, sipping a Coke. She had sworn off wine and any alcohol after that night, several years ago. And she had not been tempted even after Arthur's death. She had seen what happened to people when they tried to numb pain and escape memories in booze. Not her.

It had been so hard at first. Both times. Losing Arthur had been harder. But you took it one day at a time. She had learned the truth of the saying: "That which doesn't kill you, strengthens you." She felt herself a bit stronger each day, now.

Her eyes roamed, taking in their furnishings, their framed prints, their hanging plants, their photos on the end tables. *Their.* She could accept that word. At first, she'd been tempted to redecorate. But that felt like running away, too. Learning to accept his ongoing presence in the things they'd shared strengthened her.

The doorbell rang.

She looked at the wall clock in disbelief. After eleven! She had *told* them she preferred to be alone tonight. But as she went to the door, she had to smile to herself, suppressing her irritation. She should feel lucky to have friends like this.

She flipped on the switch for the outside light next to the door, but it remained dark outside. She'd have to replace the bulb.

"Yes?" she called through the door.

She heard faint whistling, then made out the tune.

We wish you a Merry Christmas.

She chuckled as she unlocked the door, pulled it open.

"Merry Christmas, Susanne," he said, a sick grin on his lips.

The shock paralyzed her. Before she could move a muscle or open her mouth to scream, he rushed in, smashing into her, lifting her right off the floor with one arm around her back, clamping his other huge hand over her mouth and nose. Holding her crushed against him, he kicked backward, slamming the door shut behind him.

He swept forward like a giant wave, carrying her with him through the entryway, out of the living room, down the hall. She flailed helplessly, uselessly, trying to scream through the pressure of his fingers, unable to breathe, walls and doors flashing by, lights, then no lights no air I'm falling I can't breathe God I'm dying my lungs the pain...

*

Something smacked her across the face, jerking her head to the side. Stinging pain. Her eyes twitched open. Light, shadows, blurred. Something over her mouth. Something tight on her wrists, pulling her arms behind her, setting her shoulders on fire. The room fuzzy, out of focus, spinning.

A face.

His face.

She tried to scream, but the thing across her mouth made it a muffled moan.

"Now that's silly, Susanne. No one can hear you down here."

Her head snapped around. She was in her basement den.

"See? There's no point in yelling, calling for help. No point in fighting me, no point in cursing me, blessing me, begging me. No point at all, Susanne."

She began to cry, her eyes blurring with tears.

"Poor, poor Susanne. The big bad man is back, isn't he?"

She sobbed, breathing only through her nose. Then started to choke.

He knelt and leaned close, inches from her face, frowning. "No, don't die on me, Susanne." He raised his hand; she felt the pressure of his finger tips against her cheek; then his hand tugged across her face. She felt a tearing sensation across her lips.

Suddenly her mouth was free and she gasped, filling her lungs with a rush of air. She started to cough uncontrollably.

"Better? Be nice, now, or the duct tape goes right back on." He grabbed her hair. "Understand?"

She nodded weakly. Began to cry softly.

"Good girl! Now remember: No carrying on. Nobody is going to hear you, anyway, but if you irritate me, you're going to be punished. And you wouldn't like that."

He stood, a giant, his head almost touching the basement ceiling. He had taken off whatever jacket he had worn, and now towered above her in a red flannel shirt and jeans. He began to wander around the den, idly examining the bookcases, the photos on the wall. He paused in front of the display of their vacation photos. Pulled one off the wall.

She closed her eyes.

"What is this? London? How nice. You were quite the romantic couple, weren't you?"

"Please...."

She heard his sudden footsteps closing on her. Snapped her eyes open. He bent over her. Seized her shoulder near the neck and squeezed with his forefinger and thumb.

She screamed.

"You broke the rule, Susanne. You begged. I told you not to do that. You don't ask for anything, you don't beg for anything, you don't speak unless you're spoken to. Understand?"

She nodded frantically, biting her lip.

He took his hand away. "Good." He knelt again, leaned right into her, rested his forehead against hers. She closed her eyes. His breath was foul, like onions.

"Now, before we get cozy," he said quietly, "there's a phone call you are going to make. And there are going to be rules for that, too, Susanne. You say exactly what I tell you to say. And if you say anything else—if I even begin to suspect you're trying to warn the person—"

She felt his heavy palm on her shoulder again. His fingers lightly stroked the place where he had just squeezed.

"—then the pain you'll feel will be nothing like you have ever imagined. Okay?"

She felt dizzy, as if she were about to pass out again. How was he free? How was he here? How could this happen?

She could not think. There was no will left in her.

Kill me now, get it over with, be done with it. Let me see my Arthur again....

"Stay with me, now, Susanne. We're going to call your dear friend, Annie. And here is what you're going to say...."

BETHESDA, MARYLAND
Wednesday, December 24, 11:20 p.m.

They had been quiet for a while.

"I'm sorry," he said at last.

She glanced up at him, clutching the small paper cup in both hands.

"It wasn't true," he said. "Any of what I said. I knew it when I said it. Look, you *couldn't* have known who I was when we first met. And I went after *you*. So I know that what happened between us—and what we felt—none of that could be a lie. We weren't faking our feelings. It was all real."

"Then how could you say those things?"

It was hard for him to admit it. So he knew he had to.

"I wanted to hurt you."

"But why?"

"Because *I* was hurt. Because I wanted so much to make this work. Because I loved you, but all the lies were killing it."

"Loved?" she asked.

He saw her struggle to suppress any more tears, to regain control, to reassert her dignity. He suddenly understood the courage that it had required for her to get this far with him. Of the terrible price she had been willing to pay for her love. Of the price she had paid tonight. And even now.

He searched her eyes and searched his feelings.

"Love," he answered.

Her chin trembled. But she did not cry again.

"I needed to know that," she said. "Because if you hadn't said that, then I couldn't do *this*."

She rose from the sofa, went to the kitchen counter, where she had left her purse. Brought it back with her to the sofa.

"I needed to hear that first, because I had to know that you trust me enough to still love me. That you trust me not to betray you. I needed your absolute trust—*before* I offer you proof that I wouldn't betray you."

"Proof? I don't understand."

"Dylan, there's something important you don't know. And if I truly wanted to betray you, I wouldn't tell you this. The police—Cronin and his people—they have a sample of your blood. Of your DNA. They got it off that dog." She looked at his arm, smiling weakly. "You know—that 'poodle' that bit you."

A chill touched his spine.

"I didn't know about the DNA," he said. "I could tell you knew about the dog bite, though, from the way you reacted when you saw my arm. From that, I deduced that Cronin had told you about the dog." He paused, thinking it through. "But now I realize that I completely missed something. It never occurred to me to ask myself: How the hell would he, or you, know that the dog had *bitten* me? Unless, of course, I'd left my blood behind?"

She nodded. "On the dog. That's how they knew."

"So they have my DNA."

"No. They have some *vigilante's* DNA."

He saw what she meant. "Of course. They don't know it's mine. Because they don't have a sample of mine to match it."

"But I do."

He watched as she poked into her purse. Came up with a small plastic bag. From where he sat, it looked empty. She looked at him and smiled.

"And now you can have it back," she said, tossing it onto the coffee table.

He picked up bag. Held it up to the light.

Saw the fingernail clippings.

It took him a few seconds to get it.

She laughed. "Close your mouth. You look like an idiot."

He stared at her, feeling numb. "You could have handed them my ass."

She was still grinning. "True. And for a while there, I wanted to." The grin faded. "Oh, *how* I wanted to. I was furious. You told me so many lies, from the beginning. You were lying to me even then, about the dog bite."

He had to swallow hard. "Okay. So why didn't you?"

She suddenly looked as if she were about to cry again. "You really *are* an idiot."

He put the bag down on the table. Got up and moved to sit beside her on the sofa. Put his arm around her shoulders. She turned and pressed her face into his chest. He rested his cheek against her hair.

"Yes I am," he said, holding her tightly.

After a while, she turned her face up to him. This time, the color of her eyes reminded him of steel.

"No more lies," she said.

He nodded. "No more lies."

*

They sat that way another moment. Just holding each other in silence. Restoring trust. Reconnecting.

A faint high-pitched tone broke the spell.

She straightened. "My cell."

"Let it go."

She put her hand on his cheek. "My father was in a bad way tonight." She didn't add: *And I'm here with you, not him.*

He kissed her fingertips. "I understand."

She pulled it out and flipped it open. "Hello?"

Then looked surprised. "Oh. Susie! Hi. I was expecting–" She stopped, listened. Then looked concerned. "Right now?" She looked at Hunter. "I don't know, I'm—" She listened some more. "Yes...no, not too long, maybe half an hour.... I will.... Sure, just hold on tight, girlfriend. Bye."

She closed the phone. "That was Susie. She was in tears, really sobbing. She said something terrible has happened, and she needs me to come right away." She stopped. "Dylan, I'm so sorry. I don't want to leave you, not now, not tonight. It's just—"

"Don't be silly. I think we're fine, now. You should go to her. In fact, maybe I should come, too."

She shook her head. "No, let me see what this is all about first. If I need some help, I'll call you, okay?"

"All right."

He followed her to the door, helped her on with the long fox fur coat she'd left on a chair. He rested his hand on her shoulder as she buttoned the coat over her pale yellow evening gown.

"You're not exactly dressed for an emergency," he teased.

She smiled. Then they kissed. Clung to each other tightly, neither wanting to let go.

"We're going to get through this, Annie Woods," he whispered.

He saw that she remembered. This time, her eyes shone.

"Yes, we will."

THIRTY-EIGHT

TYSONS CORNER, VIRGINIA
Wednesday, December 24, 11:53 p.m.

Because it was Christmas Eve, traffic was almost nonexistent. Though snow had been falling for hours, leaving several inches on the ground, the plows and salt trucks had kept the main roads clear. So she made good time getting over to the Capital Beltway, then great time on it, heading south.

She got off on the Georgetown Pike, headed west about a minute, then south a couple of miles into the tangle of residential neighborhoods north of Tysons Corner.

Susie's house was in a tony cul-de-sac. Expensive homes, their faces, yards, and trees blazing with Christmas lights, surrounded the circle at the end of the street, their driveways spreading out from it like spokes from a wheel hub. A solitary car was parked in the circle—an old white Chrysler that looked out of place. Probably some college kid home for the holidays.

The exception to the seasonal cheer was Susie's house. It was completely undecorated, and from outside it barely seemed inhabited. Pulling into her drive, she saw that the first-floor curtains were drawn. The foyer inside was lit, but the front door light wasn't on.

Strange. She knows I'm coming.

She's starting to act like a recluse. Must be a delayed reaction to Arthur's suicide. I'll have to help her through this....

She parked, then got out and headed for the front door, not even bothering to lock the car. No risk of auto theft in this neighborhood, especially on Christmas Eve. The drive and sidewalk were heated and free of snow and ice—a blessing for a lady in heels. At the door, she saw the reason for the darkness outside: There was no bulb in the socket above the entrance.

Damn. She's really letting things slide.

She was about to ring the bell when she noticed a scrawled note taped to the door. She leaned forward to read the block letters in the glow from the neighborhood lights.

IT'S OPEN
I'M IN THE BASEMENT

Must be serious for her not to greet me at the door.

Entering, she paused just inside. "Susie.... It's me, Annie."

No response. She heard only faint classical music. It sounded as if it were coming from the den.

Probably can't hear me down there with the stereo going.

Closing the door behind her, she unbuttoned her fur coat. Then walked toward the door at the head of the stairs that led down to her den. It was ajar only a dark sliver. As she approached, the symphonic strains from downstairs sounded louder.

She put her hand on the knob and opened it onto the dark silhouette of a huge man at the top of the stairs. She had almost no time to react as he grabbed for her. She instinctively jerked up her arms to protect herself, taking a step back. The giant charged her, grabbing the lapels of her coat, stepping into the light and revealing his face.

Wulfe.

The shock was almost paralyzing.

Almost. Her training kicked in and she spun as he bore in, drawing him toward her even faster, pulling him off-balance so that she could put him down and begin the strikes.

But with surprising agility he countered, hooking his long left leg around both of hers even as he fell, dragging her with him to the floor. She broke her fall with her arms to prevent her face from smashing into the marble surface.

They were prone, now, side by side, with his heavy left leg pinning both of hers inside the long gown. He grabbed the back of her coat so that she couldn't get up or roll away. In response, she whipped her right elbow down, aiming for the bridge of his nose. But he jerked his head back just enough so that the blow grazed his cheek and struck his collarbone instead.

He grunted in pain. Enraged, he released his left hand from her coat and seized the back of her hair. He jerked it toward him, causing her to cry out, and he simultaneously wrapped his left leg around her thighs, rolling her into him and onto her side.

Her hair in his grip, her legs trapped, she flailed wildly with both hands, reaching blindly behind her for his face and eyes. But suddenly she felt his right arm shoot forward just over her shoulder, then circle back around her exposed neck.

With her throat in the crook of his elbow, he bore down with his huge forearm and bicep in a pincer against the sides of her neck.

She had scant seconds to think: *Sleeper hold...he's an expert.* Then her energy faded and everything went fuzzy, then dark....

BETHESDA, MARYLAND
Wednesday, December 24, 11:53 p.m.

He changed into the jeans and the black sweater he'd brought up from the car, leaving the pieces of his tux scattered on the bare mattress. It was okay. He wouldn't be going anywhere.

Now, he didn't have to.

He pulled open the sliding door, stepped onto the balcony, hands in his pockets, his short boots sinking into the soft snow.

It didn't feel that cold. There was not a breath of breeze. Big, delicate flakes drifted and tumbled down slowly, silently, from invisible heights, creating glowing cones of light beneath the street lamps below. Off in the surrounding neighborhood, Christmas lights illuminated the falling snow, wrapping each house in what looked like light fog. The snow clung to the bare branches of the trees, creating frosted web-work patterns against the white ground.

It was a rare, magical moment of serenity. Even here, in the city, there was no traffic noise. Not at this hour. Not on this night. Everyone was home with family, now. Children were asleep, dreaming of the presents they would find under the tree in the morning. Parents were tip-toeing around in the dark, bearing armloads of dolls and video games and clothes—willing conscripts performing their traditional roles and rites in a grand, benevolent game of inter-generational deception.

It was an interesting thought. A season of goodwill and generosity, bringing joy to so many. Yet resting on lies. On deceiving small children.

Do we really mind this, though, when we're old enough to learn that we've been fooled? That our parents deceived us for years—but only to make us happy?

So, are all lies harmful, then? Isn't there truly such a thing as noble deception?

Or don't all lies—black ones or white ones—erode the bonds of trust that we all depend upon?

He didn't know the answers, or how to begin to find them. He had been living lies for most of his adult life. He was a man enmeshed, probably inextricably, in a world of falsehood: a world of aliases and cover stories, of disinformation and dishonesty, of trickery and pretext.

He had enrolled in that world of untruth as an eager volunteer. It had been for a vital cause: to protect his country and its people. Because our enemies use clandestine and covert methods against us, we would be insane to handicap ourselves and risk our very survival by foreswearing such measures in self-defense.

There's a difference between deception and treachery. Sometimes, we must use deception to protect the innocent from evil.

He brushed off some snow from the metal railing, grasped its cold surface, leaned out to survey the world around him.

It had become so easy, so natural. He was so damned good at it. So good at it that he had performed many critical but deniable missions on America's behalf that would forever remain unknown and unsung. So good at it that he now used those same manipulative skills to deliver justice to monsters—monsters that a corrupt legal system only enabled and encouraged.

So good at it that his life of lies threatened the most important relationship that he'd ever known.

He moved back from the railing, then watched a large snowflake flutter down to the bare spot where he'd gripped the railing. He leaned over to inspect it. Saw its deviously intricate crystal patterns slowly melt against the reality of the warmer surface. Then vanish.

As if it had never been real.

He had made his peace with his mission. But he had not made peace with martyrdom.

Could he ever reconcile the professional and personal aspects of the life he'd chosen?

Could he somehow erect a firewall between his covert life and his personal life?

Could he shield her from his world of deceit?

*

He looked his watch. Midnight.
Christmas.

He remembered another person, probably as lonely as he on this night.

He went inside, stomping his shoes on the mat to knock off the snow, then went to the desk in the den. Pulled a phone out of the drawer, inserted a battery. Sat. Tapped in the number.

"Hello?"

He felt himself smile. "Hey there, Wonk. Merry Christmas."

"Dylan! My God, I am so relieved you called!"

Something in his voice. "Relieved?"

"Yes! I have sent you repeated emails, all evening. Did you get them?"

"No," he said, looking at the bare surface of his desk. "Wonk, what's wrong?"

"It is all over the news! He tied up his sister and took her car...and they are all looking for him, now...but they believe he...is on the run!"

"Wonk, settle down. Take a breath. Okay, now tell me. Who are we talking about?"

"Wulfe! Adrian Wulfe! Dylan, they gave him a furlough, and—"

"What?" He shot to his feet.

"A Christmas furlough. From his prison. Apparently on Monday. He was to stay with his sister. She told the police that he had wanted to borrow her car. She refused, and then he beat her, tied her up, and then left in the stolen car. That was last night. A friend found her like that this afternoon."

Those bastards.

"Imagine! His own *sister!* Dylan, he is so dangerous. There is no telling how many people he will harm before they find him."

"I know, I know.... Look, we need to think this through. Maybe we have some nugget of information that will lead me to him."

"You?"

"I mean the police. Listen, you start going over his files again, and maybe we'll talk in a few hours."

"All right, I shall start right away.... Oh—and Dylan?"

"Yes?"

"Thank you for thinking of me and calling." His voice quavering.

"Merry Christmas, Wonk," he said gently.

"Merry Christmas, Dylan."

*

He set down the phone on the desk. Checked his watch. Just after midnight, now.

Dammit.

He thought of that shrink, Frankfurt. That prick. This had to be his doing. He couldn't care less about the victims of sadists like Wulfe. They didn't count. How could he possibly sit there with Wulfe beside him, and look someone like Susanne Copeland in the face, while—

The cold sensation started on his skin, then crawled inside his body.

Susanne's desperate call....

Annie.

No.

No, God no—

He snatched up the phone, punched in her cell phone number.

Held his breath, waiting for the connection.

Maybe she was still on the road.... Maybe he could still reach her...stop her in time....

Heard the chirp of the first ring tone in his ears.

Pick up, Annie....

The cat, sitting at his feet. Staring at him....

Another chirp.

Pick it up!

Another chirp.

Closed his eyes.

Annie, please answer....

TYSONS CORNER, VIRGINIA
Thursday, December 25, 12:03 a.m.

The quiet sobs brought her around. That, and the feeling of something jerking her arms.

It took several blinks for her eyes to fully open and focus. Her head was hanging down and she was seeing her lap. A narrow band of blue cloth crossed over her dress at the waist and disappeared somewhere behind her, at both sides. Her arms were drawn behind her, her hands felt squeezed together. Someone was tugging on her wrists.

She remembered....

She raised her head. She was in the den. She saw her fur coat in a heap on a nearby chair. Her purse was open, and its contents had been dumped on the floor.

She turned to the source of the sobs.

Susie. Beside her, about six feet away, in a wooden chair. Her legs tied to its legs, with colored strips of cloth...men's ties. Her arms pulled behind the back of the chair, hands bound together. Her white blouse torn, exposing her bra. Her dark red hair unclasped, wild, disheveled. A red welt on her cheek, tears welling from eyes filled with despair.

"Annie...I am so sorry," she whispered.

Movement behind her.

He stepped into view, moved in front of them, stopped and faced them both.

Adrian Wulfe smiled.

"Now Susanne, there's no need to apologize. Annie, you should know that your loyal friend here truly *tried* to resist. She didn't want to make that phone call. She really didn't. But I made it so that she just couldn't help herself. Isn't that right, Susanne?"

"I'm sorry, Annie," she repeated.

"It's okay, Susie."

"'Susie,'" he repeated. "Not 'Susanne.' All right, Susie and Annie, we'll dispense with the formalities, then. Call me 'Addie.' My bitch mother did."

She looked up at him. "So, *Addie*, is this how you're working out your issues with Mommy?"

He lost the smile. Reached her in one giant stride. Drew his huge left hand up to his waist, then back across his body, then whipped it forward, backhanding her across her face.

Seeing it coming, she jerked her head to the right and leaned as it struck, trying to diminish the impact. Still, it hit with the force of a jackhammer, a loud banging *crack* that rattled her teeth and sent a spear of pain through her skull. She felt her chair falling to the right, but his hand snatched her arm and pulled her back to vertical.

Her head throbbed and swayed. She just couldn't quite keep it upright and centered. Somewhere, Susie was screaming.

Wulfe knelt before her, his face spinning and drifting crazily in front of her half-closed eyes. He grabbed her chin, steadying her head. His dead gray eyes bored into hers.

"Ever since that day, I've been waiting for this one," his voice rumbled, barely above a whisper. "You two thought you were so high and mighty, so unreachable. Especially you. I remember every word you and your dear friend here said to me. Every word. I didn't have much to do all day in prison. So, do you know how I filled my time? I wrote out those words of yours. Then I counted them. Then, I imagined a specific penalty for each word."

He released her chin, then stood.

"None of the penalties will be fatal. But after a short time, Annie and Susie, you will wish they were. We're going to be here for a long, long time, you and I."

He turned away, went to an end table holding a large brown paper bag. He picked it up and there was the sound of metallic *chinking*. He set it on a coffee table, then dragged the table and positioned it before them.

Then he dumped the bag's contents onto the table top.

Kitchen knives. Garden tools. Screwdrivers. Hammers. Nails....

"Susie, you and Arthur certainly kept your home well-supplied."

She shrieked. It became a long, low keening wail.

Annie had to close her eyes. She felt herself start to shiver. She had expected to be raped. Then to be murdered. She had already begun to prepare herself, to try to detach herself from her body, to let whatever happened, happen, until it stopped forever.

But *this*....

The shivering became uncontrollable. She tried to think of something to say, something that would stop him—even delay this, if only for a moment. But her brain was paralyzed, overwhelmed with the horror and the pounding pain in her head.

"You don't have to do this," she could only manage to croak.

He picked up a box cutter. Twisted his head around to look at her. Bounced it in his palm. Smiled.

"Oh, but I do."

Then he paused. "You know, there's something missing." He snapped his fingers. "I know! We need a witness to these proceedings."

He turned and went to the bookcase. Found a framed photo of Arthur Copeland. Brought it back to the coffee table. Put it down on the table, facing Susie.

"No!" She was panting rapidly, gasping, her breathing out of control, hyperventilating. Her eyes, enormous in terror, moved back and forth wildly, from the box cutter in his hand to the photo.

He stood, looked at the photo. Rubbed his chin. Then reached down to reposition it.

"There, Susie. That's better."

He turned to face her.

Her lips parted, her eyes lost their focus, and her head slumped forward on her chest.

He went to her, felt her neck with his fingers.

"Why, the little minx has fainted dead away. Oh, well. She'll keep."

He turned to face her. "Let's start with you, then. Just look at you, all dressed up. What a nice Christmas present for me. Let's unwrap the package and see what's inside."

She closed her eyes again, gritting her teeth.

Heard the cell phone.

Her eyes snapped open.

He looked at where it lay, flashing on the floor. "What's this? A holiday well-wisher? Well, he or she will keep, too."

Then she knew who it was.

It chirped a second time.

Only chance....

"You really should answer that, you know."

He raised a brow. "And why should I do that, love?"

"Don't you want to talk to the man who's coming right now to kill you?"

Third chirp.

He looked amused. "And just who might that be?"

"Dylan Hunter."

Fourth chirp.

A sneer twisted across his face.

"Do tell."

Fifth chirp.

He reached down an ape-like arm for the phone.

THIRTY-NINE

BETHESDA, MARYLAND
Thursday, December 25, 12:06 a.m.

Fifth chirp.

He was shaking, now.

I'm too late....

A soft click.

"Ho, ho, ho!" said the low, unmistakable voice. "Merry Christmas, Mr. Hunter!"

He reached out a hand to steady himself against the desk.

"This *is* the great Dylan Hunter, isn't it?"

The name.

It reminded him of who he was.

He straightened. Went into his cold mission mode.

First, gather intel.

"Oh, excuse me. I must have misdialed. I was trying to reach a human being."

Wulfe laughed.

"Well played, Mr. Hunter! I thought the sound of my voice on this lady's phone would shock you to your core. But you sound so blasé about it."

He's a sociopath. So manipulate his inflated ego. Keep him talking.

"You don't surprise me at all, Wulfe. You're entirely predictable. And that's a fatal flaw."

Pause.

"Oh really?" A tiny edge in the voice. "The little lady here seems to be under the delusion that you're going to rescue her and her friend, and then somehow kill me."

They're still alive.

He grabbed his car keys, ran to the apartment door.

"You should have believed her, Wulfe. The little lady is right."

Moved outside, into the hallway.

"My, my! Such bravado from a mere journalist."

Not the elevator—the cell signal will cut out.

"A journalist deals only in facts, Wulfe. You're as good as dead."

He pushed through the emergency door, then hit the stairs, trying to keep his footsteps as quiet as possible while he flew down, two steps at a time.

Eighth floor....

"You know, you're beginning to irritate me, Mr. Hunter. Perhaps as punishment for your disrespect, I'll let you listen in while I begin having a bit of fun with Annie and Susie."

Seventh floor....

Hasn't started to torture them yet.

"Sorry, Wulfe. That's just not going to happen."

Sixth floor....

"You don't think so? Well, then, just keep listening. I'll put it on speakerphone for you."

Fifth floor....

"Then you're about as stupid as I figured."

"Me, stupid?" Angry now. "Who's really the stupid one, Mr. Hunter?"

Fourth floor....

"After all, you're wherever you are, while I'm here with your two lovely friends...."

Third floor....

"And so, Mr. Hunter, much as I'm enjoying our friendly banter, I think I should return to my Christmas party and guests."

You'll never make it in time. Neither will the cops.

Second floor....

"Let me start with Annie...."

Have to stop him right now.

"Well, it's going to be a very brief party, Wulfe."

"You're bluffing. I can hear the stress in your voice."

Watch your breathing....

First floor....

"Not at all, moron. I figure you've got—oh, maybe five minutes."

Pause.

"And how do you figure that, Mr. Hunter?"

Basement.

Thighs on fire, he shoved open the stairwell door, ran into the underground parking garage. Pushed his legs to move faster, toward the BMW.

"Because I know where you are, Wulfe."

Pause.

"So where am I?"

He reached the car.

"Why, you're at the Copeland residence, of course."

Silence.

He unlocked the door, slid inside.

"Isn't that right, Wulfe?"

Silence.

He closed the door quietly. Inserted the key into the ignition.

Don't turn it over yet. He'll hear.

"So, you really don't want to start anything that you can't finish, Wulfe. In fact, I think that if you don't leave those ladies and run for it, you'll be in handcuffs in...oh, let's make that about four-and-a-half minutes, now."

Silence.

"Unless I get to you first, that is. Don't you remember what I promised you, Wulfe?"

Pause.

"All right, Mr. Hunter. I'll be leaving now. But I do believe I still have enough time to take the lovely ladies with me."

The phone went dead.

He turned the key and gunned the engine.

TYSONS CORNER, VIRGINIA
Thursday, December 25, 12:11 a.m.

She watched him raise her cell phone above his head, then smash it to the floor. Pieces bounced in every direction.

He looked at her, his face a mask of cold fury.

He grabbed a large kitchen knife from the coffee table. Rushed to Susie and slashed through the bonds at her feet, freeing her legs. Then he grabbed her by the waist and lifted, raising her entire body so that her arms, with her hands still tied together behind her, cleared the back of the chair. He set her down on the seat again and began to slap her.

"Time to wake up, Susie.... There's my good girl."

She began to moan, then struggled to hold herself upright.

He left her and moved quickly to Annie. Standing to the side of the chair so that she couldn't kick him, he severed the bindings on her feet. Then the one around her midsection.

He returned to Susie, grabbed her by the hair, and dragged her out of the chair, over to where he had dumped the contents of Annie's purse. Reached down and pawed through the mess until he found her car keys. Grabbed some of the cut-up ties.

Then stood and pressed the long edge of the knife to Susie's throat.

"Now, Annie, you're going to stand up and clear your hands from the back of the chair, just as I did for Susie. And then we're all going upstairs, very fast, and out to your car. And if you try to run or resist or slow me down, I will cut her goddamned head off."

12:11 a.m.

His custom BMW 7 Series High Security sedan surged out of the garage entrance.

He cut the wheel hard right, playing the gears and brakes as he had been trained in the Agency's "crash and burn" courses over the years. Glancing to his left to make sure there was no traffic, he darted out onto Wisconsin, ripping another right.

He hit the buttons that lit up the blue-and-white strobes in the grill and rear windows and set off the police siren. Then punched it, accelerating up to Norfolk. Braking hard and working the wheel, he forced the heavy rear end of the armored car to skid around on the wet pavement so that it was sideways in the intersection, facing left.

Flooring it, he pushed it down Norfolk, whipping past the side streets with barely a glance, hoping his lights and siren would stop anyone from getting in his path.

Downshift, brake...hard left onto St. Elmo's. Punch it again. Cross Old Georgetown.

Flying now down Wilson Lane...the high-performance V-12 engine climbing in seconds to eighty, ninety, one hundred...barreling right through stop signs and lights toward River Road and then the Beltway....

Verbal command to activate the onboard communication system.... State the memorized phone number....

"Cronin," said the familiar voice in the dash speaker.

"This is Hunter. Adrian Wulfe has kidnapped Annie Woods and Susanne Copeland at the Copeland home." He gave the address. "Get the locals there, fast. I mean *now*, Cronin." He cut it off before the cop could utter a word.

12:16 a.m.

He forced her to drive.

Her hands and feet were free, now, but useless to her. He sat behind her in the back seat, belted in securely with a shoulder strap. But he ordered her to keep hers off. If she tried to crash the car, he'd survive. She might not.

And Susie definitely would not. He held her across his lap, on her back, face up, with the knife lying across her throat. Susie's eyes were squeezed tight. Her lips were moving. Praying....

They were only three minutes from Susie's house when she saw the first of the police lights up ahead, blue-and-white flashers growing as they raced toward her.

"Keep driving straight and steady. Let them go past. No tricks—or Susie's head will be sitting beside you in the passenger seat."

The lights sped toward her, seeming to get faster by the second. The car drew abreast, and the high-pitched squeal of its siren died off octaves lower as it blew by.

"Good girl."

If she were alone, she would have crashed the car anyway. Suicide would be infinitely preferable to whatever he might do to her. But she had no right to make that decision for her friend.

And maybe they could still get out of this.

Dylan....

He'd survived governments and their hit teams. He'd stymied the combined investigative talents of scores of police agencies. He'd bested cold-blooded killers, both armed and bare-handed.

And he was coming for her.

She glanced into the rearview mirror. Wulfe was staring at her, unblinking—a dead, blank, malignant stare, like that of a snake.

She stared back at him.

"He is going to kill you, you know."

He lifted one of Susie's hands, now untied. Tapped it with the tip of the blade. "One more word, and Susie will lose this thumb."

She turned her eyes back to the road.

*

After another minute, she made a right onto 694, heading southeast toward the destination he had ordered. She approached the Capital Beltway and passed over it.

"I don't want us to take any side trips, my dear. Show me what the GPS tells us to do."

She came to an intersection and stopped at the light. She flipped on the GPS.

"I'll program the most direct route." She hit the right buttons. "Okay, there are the instructions. See for yourself."

The screen displayed printed instructions to stay on Route 694 all the way into Falls Church.

He leaned forward and looked.

"Good. Just keep going straight."

She continued down 694. They reached the second traffic light within thirty seconds. After a minute, she proceeded. In another half-minute they stopped again at the intersection of Route 123.

She had programmed the most direct route.

Not the fastest.

12:18 a.m.

Lights flashing, siren blaring, the powerful car raced down the Capital Beltway at well over one hundred miles per hour. He glanced at the dashboard clock and said, "Redial previous number."

"Cronin here."

"Me again. What do you know?"

"I'm on my way there now. Just got a call from the Fairfax County P.D. They and the staties are on scene. They would've waited for SWAT, but the front door was wide open, so they chanced it and went in. It's empty. Looks like they just missed them."

He didn't say anything.

"They couldn't have gotten far, though. And it looks like he dumped the car he stole from his sister at the scene. Copeland's is in the garage. So he's got a fresh set of wheels, maybe whatever Ms. Woods was driving. Do you know what her car is?"

"Yes." He told him.

"Okay, we'll put out an alert. Copeland's place is real close to the Beltway, and my guess is they're on it and trying to get out of the area."

"Right."

"Sorry, Hunter."

He cut off the call. Downshifted and braked hard, pulling off the road.

Annie's car.

He popped the trunk, ran back there and grabbed his bug-out bag and a laptop computer. Slammed it and jumped back inside. Opened the laptop on the passenger seat, hit the "on" button.

While it was powering up, he popped the stick into gear and hit the gas, kicking a spray of slush behind him as he fishtailed back onto the highway.

He wished he kept a gun in this car.

12:24 a.m.

"Goddammit, I've never seen so many red lights," he thundered. "Isn't there a better way?"

"This is the way I always go home from Susie's. It's the most direct—almost straight to my door. You can see it on the GPS. Everything else takes you out of the way."

The light changed, and she moved forward, staying in the speed limit.

"Two lanes. Twenty-five, thirty-five miles per hour, the whole way. Couldn't we get on a thruway?"

"You know he called the cops. The big highways are the first places they'll be looking."

She cast a quick look in the mirror. His face now looked strained. She noticed the red streak on his cheek where she grazed him with her elbow.

She glanced again at the digital clock.

I'm trying to buy you time, Dylan.

But how could he possibly know where they were going? It was the last place anyone would dream to look.

She gripped the wheel tightly. Saw a sign for a curve in the road ahead, marked for twenty-five miles per hour.

Took her foot off the gas.

12:25 a.m.

He was doing over one twenty-five, zig-zagging through the rare vehicles he overtook, passing them as if they were parked.

He couldn't bring in the cops, not now. If they got involved, Wulfe would use the women as hostages, then kill them if things went south.

He had to do this his way.

His eyes darted from the highway to the laptop as the program loaded. Then, using his forefinger, he tapped in the numerical code for the device. Hit "Enter."

On the screen, a flashing red dot appeared on the map.

There you are....

He watched the dot heading southeast on 694. But to where? His eyes tracked ahead, moving down the line on the map.

Why, you devious son of a bitch.

He estimated the distance, did a quick mental calculation of comparative speeds.

He accelerated even more, heading south toward the Dulles Toll Road. A four-lane highway, with no traffic lights, running parallel to 694.

He glanced at the dashboard clock.

It was going to be close....

12:34 a.m.

"All right. Pull the car into the garage."

She reached for the button on the visor that opened her garage door. It rose slowly and the inner lights came on. She looked up the expanse of the driveway. In her headlights, the snow on the ground was unmarked by any tire or footprints.

She began to tremble again.

You'll have to find a way out of this yourself.

She eased the car into the garage.

"Now, lower the garage door."

She did as she was told.

"Shut off the car, and toss the keys to me. Gently, please. Remember that this knife is right on her pretty neck.... Put your hands on the steering wheel where I can see them, and keep them there."

In the mirror, she saw him lift Susie to a sitting position on his lap. Her eyes were vacant. She was like a rag doll in his arms. He hauled her out of the passenger side.

"Now, get out of the car.... Put your hands on your head and walk to the house door."

Her legs were wobbly and she stumbled as she approached the door. Her eyes searched for anything nearby that she could grab and use as a weapon.

"Stop there. Now, understand something, my dear," he said, as if reading her mind. "You surprised me back at Susie's. I won't be surprised again. I see that you've trained in martial arts. But don't even dream of it. I have fourth- and fifth-degree black belts in several of them and competed as a mixed martial artist for a while. Retired undefeated."

She knew she was trembling visibly now, and hated herself for it. She didn't want to give him that satisfaction. But she couldn't help it.

"Do you keep this door locked?"

She shook her head.

"Silly girl. All right, you're going to disarm your home alarm when we go inside. Open the door, then stand right there."

She did. He shoved her unexpectedly, causing her to stumble and fall to her knees. He dumped Susie on the floor next to her, then grabbed her by the hair, putting the knife to her throat.

"Get up.... Now where is the alarm?"

"Over there."

He marched her to the keypad on the wall. Her legs were like rubber, her arms like lead. She'd never be able to move fast enough to disarm him now.

"Key in the code."

She raised her eyes and hand to the alarm box. And stopped.

The alarm was already off.

Her pulse began to pound.

"What's the matter?"

"I must have forgotten to set it," she said, her voice quavering.

He laughed. "You really *are* stupid. Don't you know there are dangerous men prowling the neighborhood?"

*

Flipping lights on as they went, he nudged them along from behind with his body, his knife never leaving Annie's throat. Their perfume excited him almost as much as their fear. Still, as he passed the kitchen, he was suddenly aware that he hadn't eaten all day.

"All this running around has worked up my appetite," he murmured in the redhead's ear. "So before we celebrate the holiday, let's grab a bite, shall we?"

He pushed them inside. It was bright, modern, spacious. White cabinets with small-paned glass doors hung over marble countertops. Bowls, a carving set, and a container of large kitchen utensils sat on an island with a butcher block top. On the opposite end of the kitchen was a breakfast area with a small rectangular table and high-backed chairs.

"All right, let's seat you ladies here at the table. Annie, please help Susie into her chair.... Now, pull her arms behind it, like before, and tie this around her wrists." He reached into his pocket and tossed her one of Arthur's ties that he had brought with him.

When she finished, he pushed her to the facing chair at the table. From behind, he dropped another tie onto her lap. "Put one end around your left wrist, and tie it tightly.... Okay, now put both hands behind the back of the chair."

Still behind her, the knife at her throat, he used his free hand to tie her wrists together. It was hard, but he managed. Then stepped around in front of her.

"There. You're not going anywhere." He looked at the other one. "Oh dear, it looks as if Susie has passed out again. Poor thing must be as starved as I am. Well, time to see what's in the fridge."

He crossed the room toward the refrigerator, dropping his knife on the island. It landed beside a newspaper resting there. He glanced at it in passing, then did a double-take and stopped.

The Hunter article about the MacLean Foundation.

Annoyed, he picked it up and shook it at the brunette bitch.

"A big fan of Mr. Hunter, aren't you?"

She smiled. "Want to know why?" Her eyes turned toward the hallway.

*

He stepped into the kitchen, quiet as a panther.

Stopped between Wulfe and the women.

"You want me to autograph that for you, Wulfe?"

It stunned him. "Well, I'll be damned," he said softly.

"You are," Hunter said.

The cocky bastard seemed to be unarmed, too. Incredible.

Wulfe snatched up his knife from the counter. Then grabbed a carving knife.

I'll skin that smirk right off his face.

"I'm going to enjoy this, Mr. Hunter."

"No you're not."

*

She knew that he was in the house, from the instant she saw that the alarm was off. She'd shown him how to do that when he had stayed here, weeks before. And she knew then that he would lie in wait for the right moment, when Wulfe no longer hovered near them with the knife.

She saw him make his move when the monster went toward the fridge: saw first his spectral shadow slide across the wall and floor of the hallway, then watched how he glided in noiselessly, like some dark ghost—a ghost loosed years ago to haunt and hunt faraway enemies in stinking alleys and high-mountain deserts.

She saw him wink at her, then turn to face this new enemy: a malignant Goliath who had shattered lives here, in the homeland he'd so deeply loved and gallantly defended. She saw him for what he always had been: a shadow soldier, performing unsung a sacred duty that had been abdicated by those hired and sworn to perform it.

She knew then that, whatever happened now, he had always deserved her trust and loyalty. And she was honored to have lived to have his love, if only for weeks—and if only for a few minutes more.

"I love you, Dylan Hunter," she said.

He did not turn; he continued to face the monster across the room; but he seemed to stand taller, and she heard him reply:

"I love you, Annie Woods."

*

He watched the slow sneer form on the Target's face across the kitchen.

"Oh—silly me! I should have known," the Target said. He swung out his gorilla arms in wide circles, loosening his shoulders, the blades glinting beneath the lights. "So you've come to rescue your lady love. Mr. Hunter, you've just doubled my pleasure."

"Enjoy it while it lasts."

He was no longer distracted by fear or fury. He had climbed to that cold Olympian summit, the place where he always went at these moments, where he could look down at the Target with chill, clinical detachment.

The Target stood beside the island, grinning arrogantly, whirling the knives before him in a blinding fog of motion, trying to reduce him to cringing, terrified paralysis.

But he had analyzed this Target's vulnerabilities, and he knew how to strike them. For his apparent strengths—his menacing size, his intimidating bravado, his lust to overpower—masked the pathetic reality. Like all sociopaths, this one had an eggshell ego. Like those bullies so long ago, on the playground of his childhood, this Target's unquenchable craving for power over others was a measure of his utter sense of impotence. His desperate quest to demonstrate his power to himself and others was proof that he didn't have it.

Hunter had that knowledge. And it was his first weapon.

"Are you having fun way over there, Mr. Wulfe?" he mocked.

He watched the arrogant grin erode into an angry grimace. Wulfe stepped out in front of the island, moving the knives around more deliberately, his feet sliding into patterns and then setting into a stance that revealed martial arts training.

Good to know.

Time to employ his other weapon. A weapon he had mastered.

Deception.

Don't reveal your own martial arts expertise. Let him think you're no threat.

Hunter took a step forward. Stood casually, hands down at his sides.

He saw the Target's faint smile in response. He's thinking, *This will be too easy.*

Now goad him some more.

"You're boring me, Mr. Wulfe."

Saw the anger blaze in his eyes.

Now, combine mockery *with* deception.

Hunter turned to the side, swinging his right arm behind him.

"See? I'll fight you with one arm behind my back."

Watched the anger in the eyes boil over into rage, uncontrollable—and uncontrolled.

The Target lunged toward him, technique forgotten, one knife drawn back to deliver a spear thrust, the other raised to slash down on him.

Deception.

In one motion, Hunter drew the combat knife from its sheath on the belt at his back, leaped to the right to avoid the onrushing Target, and slashed down on the spearing forearm.

That knife fell from the Target's nerveless fingers.

Hunter turned to press the attack from behind, but the Target's own combat reflexes took over, and he spun to face him again.

Now positioned between Hunter and the women.

Not good.

Deception.

Hunter feinted his own lunge, forcing the surprised Target to recoil a step, but instead he leaped to his side, then two quick steps past him toward the women, then pivoting to face him.

Again between them and the Target.

Mock him. Goad him. Use details from his file....

"What's the matter, *Addie*," he said. "Did I give you a boo-boo?"

The Target glanced at his left sleeve, shock in his eyes. A slash across the red flannel was turning a deeper shade, and crimson drops fell from the tips of fingers that now dangled uselessly.

Then his eyes narrowed. He danced back into the center of the room, retreating.

"Again, Mr. Hunter, well played. I believe I under-estimated you. As I did your little whore there," he said, nodding toward Annie. "But you will find that I never make the same mistake twice."

Hunter knew that he'd lost the initial advantage of surprise. But now the Target was injured and his confidence rattled.

Time to finish this.

He danced out to meet him.

They moved from side to side, warily now, jockeying for position and advantage, looking for openings and mistakes to exploit.

Goad him some more.

"Does *Addie* want *Mommy* to come kiss his boo-boo and make it better?"

Watched the anger flare.

But then die. Saw the Target's eyes grow cold.

Sociopath or not, he had been well-trained. That training was now in control.

He realized he'd lost a psychological weapon, too.

Now it was just a matter of skill. And determination.

He flipped his knife from his right hand to his left, feinted a thrust and snapped it back.

The Target slashed at it, hitting empty air.

He'd hoped for that, and lunged in again, stabbing the tip toward the Target's exposed chest.

Then everything went wrong.

The Target had anticipated too. Astonishingly quick, he hopped back onto his left foot and leaned away from the blade while snapping a cobra-fast kick with his right, into his left forearm.

Into the still-healing tendons from the dog bite.

The combat knife sailed across the room, clattering off the wall and onto the floor.

He was now exposed, wide open to the Target's blade.

"Dylan!"

The natural impulse was to jump back. But in an instant calculation born of years of combat training and experience—and before the Target could straighten and recover his two-footed balance, then move in for the kill—he continued his forward momentum instead, rushing into him, seizing him and propelling him backward into a crashing impact against the island. Their bodies fell onto its top, spilling everything onto the floor.

His body was now pressed down upon the Target's atop the island, their faces inches apart, eye to eye. He looked down into the blank gray depths, sensing fear.

Then something else.

Suddenly he felt searing pain in his left thigh. His breath left him as the agony coursed through him. A look of triumph blazed in the Target's eyes.

He had to stop a second thrust.

He snapped his forehead down hard, a stunning blow against the bridge of the the Target's nose. Then again, a crunching smash against his mouth.

Then pushed back, feeling the blade tear out of his leg.

"Dylan!"

Someone's voice again, far away.

He heard the Target's bellows of pain but he was dealing with his own. He hopped back, mostly on his right leg, empty-handed, needing to play for time, now, trying to recover his advantage.

Then felt the pulsing in his left thigh, the hot spurts soaking the inside of his jeans, and he knew that time was one thing he wouldn't have.

He looked up. All the deadly kitchen utensils were scattered around the island, behind the Target.

Who raised himself from the top of the island, his useless left hand pawing at his nose and mouth. His nose was bleeding profusely, his lips a crushed pulp. He spat a bloody mess and Hunter heard the rattle of teeth hitting the floor.

Hunter's left leg and hand were out of commission.

His right hand was empty.

Only one good leg.

And he started to feel dizzy.

"Dylan!" Another scream.

Annie....

What could he do?

Do what you know best.

Deception.

He staggered back, hopping on his right leg, leaving a trail of blood from his left along the floor. Then stopped. Stood there, tottering. A crimson puddle formed on the floor around his left foot.

He looked at the Target. Saw his eyes follow the smear of blood from the island, across the polished wood floor, to the rapidly growing pool at his feet.

Then Hunter's left leg buckled beneath him, and he sagged to the floor.

He was sitting, now. Only his upper body and right knee remained upright. He leaned against the raised thigh, his right hand clasping his ankle to keep from falling over.

He was getting dizzier. He knew he was bleeding out.

He raised his head.

He saw that the Target knew it, too. He leaned back against the island on unsteady legs, but his bloodied mouth bore a twisted grin.

Waiting now for him to bleed to death.

Goad him.

"You should see what I did to you, you puke," Hunter said. "I really did a number on that ugly face of yours."

Saw the grin vanish.

Hurry....

"What's the matter, you pussy? Afraid to finish me? I figured you were going to kick the crap out of me."

The Target's eyes, so long dead, came to life. Even across the room, he could see the towering rage building in them.

"Dylan!"

"Where are your balls, Wulfe?"

The Target approached him, now, stumbling, still half-stunned, with one immobilized arm, but on two powerful legs and with a long knife in his perfectly good right hand. Coming to finish him.

Deception.

"So go ahead, you worthless piece of shit. Come and stomp me."

"Dylan! Dylan!"

Hunter clung to the cold, high place.

Hurry....

The Target loomed above him. His face was a ghastly red mask. Savage hatred burned in the once-dead eyes. He paused, weaving slightly.

"Stomp you?" his voice rumbled. "It will be a pleasure."

He raised a heavy boot to crush his skull.

Just before it reached its apex, Hunter swept up his left arm, batting the foot outward—

—while his right hand shot up and slammed the smaller combat knife from his ankle sheath into the man's groin.

*

Adrian Wulfe felt a giant spike of incredible pain shoot from his groin upward and outward, a shockwave that reverberated jarringly throughout his entire body. He screamed, an endless scream, dropping the knife, his hands clawing madly below his waist, trying to find the source of the red-hot spike, trying to make it stop, anything to make it stop and he was up on his toes, staggering backward away from the man, away from the source of that pain and he was about to fall....

*

With a last surge of adrenalin, Hunter pushed himself off the floor. He stood, feeling nothing now, watching the strange figure dancing frantically in front of him, then making mincing little steps backward.

He reeled toward that figure, the Target, his Target, the beast who had taken Annie, and now he would put an end to him because he was no longer on that high cold Olympus anymore, he was right down there in some savage place, a place where suppressed rage and controlled violence were now unleashed to rule....

He followed that retreating figure on legs that seemed unreliable, that seemed mired in mud, hurtling through fog, someone yelling his name, eyes on the Target....

And now he caught the Target and was pushing him back, once again bending him backward over that island countertop, collapsing onto him, staring into that mangled face. And then he remembered what he had just done, and he lifted himself enough to see the hilt protruding and blood pouring around it, and then he looked into those eyes, those hateful, bulging, agony-filled eyes, and recalled something else....

"Remember what I promised, Wulfe?" he heard someone's rasping voice. "I said this face would be the last thing you ever saw. Look at it while you die, Wulfe."

Then he gripped him by the shoulders and roaring with his final burst of unleashed rage, he smashed upward with his right knee, driving the hilt all the way into the Target's body.

Watched the Target's eyes snap open impossibly wide, then roll back somewhere into his skull.

Felt the body beneath him grow limp.

He pushed away and staggered and fell onto his back.

Raised his head. Watched the Target slowly slide off the island, down onto his knees, then face forward onto the floor.

The Target's head landed on a newspaper. A red stain began to spread over it.

Then everything started to fade....

*

"Dylan!.... Dylan!.... Wake up goddamn you wake up Dylan!"
He knew that voice.
Oh yes. Annie. Where are you, Annie?

"Dylan!"

Something clicked somewhere far down in his brain.

He tried to say her name. Couldn't.

Knew that somehow he had to find her.

Couldn't let her go.

Opened his eyes.

A ceiling. Spinning around.

"Dylan! Please, Dylan!"

He rolled onto his side. His head was swaying, as if disconnected from his shoulders. He tried to see where the voice was coming from.

Oh. There she is. Way over there. How did you get way over there?

"Dylan. Darling, you have to come to me. You have to crawl to me."

Of course, Annie. Just let me rest here a minute....

"Dylan!" A scream. "Wake up! Now crawl over here. Hurry, Dylan!"

Okay, Annie. I love you, you know....

He clawed his hands along the floor. It was so slippery. What is that, blood? Yes, I remember. Annie, I'm coming....

Saw the wooden boards under him moving. One at a time.

"That's it, my love.... Yes, keep coming.... You're getting closer now."

So hard.... Why is this so hard.... No energy.... Everything so numb....

"Don't stop! That's right.... You're almost here.... Dylan.... Listen. Do you see that knife there beside you? The knife, Dylan! Bring me the knife!"

What knife? Oh, there it is. I'm trying, Annie....

"There! You have the knife. Now bring it to me, Dylan."

Everything so crazy. Light one minute, dark the next. Maybe when I get to Annie we can sleep....

"Okay, Dylan darling, I need you to do one more thing. Just one more, okay?"

There you are. You're so beautiful. One more thing.

"Take the knife, Dylan. See, behind the chair? My hands are tied. I need you to cut that thing off my hands. Do it, Dylan...*Do it now!*"

Yes, I see it. I'll try, Annie.... It's so hard, though....

"I feel it, Dylan, keep going, you're doing fine, just keep cutting!"

Everything swimming. Knife. Back and forth. So hard.

He watched the funny piece of cloth part just as he lost his grip on the knife.

Then it was dark.

Then he felt himself being rolled over.

A face over his.

Hello, Annie.

He closed his eyes again.

Something pressing on his leg, squeezing.

Poking into his jeans pocket.

Somebody talking.

Grant! Shut up and listen to me....

Grant.

I know that name....

FORTY

Ed Cronin didn't often see this much blood at a crime scene.

The metallic smell of it hung thick in the air. Before long, he knew, it would have a slightly rancid edge, before they cleaned it up. The CSI boys and photographer were having trouble navigating it while working over the body.

He stood once again in the hallway entrance, just to survey the scene and try to get a sense of what had gone down.

Somebody had called it in to the locals about 1:20 a.m., anonymously, and when the first black-and-whites arrived, it was just like the Copeland place: front door open, tire tracks everywhere, but nobody home.

Except the stiff. He could tell it was Wulfe.

He couldn't read the newspaper underneath the guy's head, but he had little doubt it was related to the vigilantes.

When he got here about ten minutes ago, the neighbors huddled outside the tape told him what they'd seen. Just a couple minutes past one, flashing lights and car engine noise woke them up. They looked out and saw three black SUVs and an orange-and-white ambulance with its strobes going. Their neighbor, Annie Woods, was standing at the front door of her house, wearing what looked like a gown, and she was waving frantically at them. About a dozen people spilled out of the cars and ran inside while the EMTs followed with a couple of stretchers.

Then, barely a minute later, about six of them came charging out with one of the stretchers and somebody on it. They carried it, not rolled it, very fast over to the back of the ambulance. One of the people was Annie, and she looked like she was running barefoot through the snow alongside the stretcher. Then the other stretcher came out, just as fast, with somebody else on it, and they brought that to the ambulance, too. Then they moved aside and one of them slapped the side of the ambulance and they heard him yelling *Go! Go! Go!*

Then they jumped in two of the SUVs and hauled ass out of there, following the ambulance. About one-fifteen, two guys came out of the house with a bunch of stuff in their hands—no telling what—and got into the last SUV. Then they sped away, too.

What the hell is going on here?

Annie Woods.

Wulfe.

Then who was on the stretcher?

Susanne Copeland?

Who else?

And those SUVs—what is *that* all about?

Watching his steps, he went over to one of the CSIs who was kneeling over the body.

"All that blood. Looks like whoever did this really butchered him," he said.

The tech looked up, glanced back at the pool and smear across the floor. "That blood's not from this guy. He's mashed up and bleeding, all right, but not leaking *that* bad."

Whose, then? Copeland? Jesus, I hope not. The poor woman.

Then he remembered the dog.

Blood from one of the vigilantes?

"Make sure to get plenty of samples, then."

"Let's not do that," said a voice behind him.

In the entranceway, Marty Abrams was standing next to some tall, older guy in a gray suit.

He went over to them.

"What are you talking about, Marty? And who's this?"

The guy had steel-gray hair to match his suit, and a hard face. He held up credentials.

Cronin looked close. Felt something turn over inside of him.

"Grant Garrett," the man said. "Please come out to my car. We've got to talk."

WALTER REED MEDICAL CENTER
BETHESDA, MARYLAND
Thursday, December 25, 10:09 a.m.

The first thing he was conscious of was the familiar smells of antiseptics and bandages. Then the familiar feeling of pain, all over his body.

Then he opened his eyes on the equally familiar sight of a hospital room.

"Hello, Matt," said a gravelly voice. Also familiar.

He turned his head and saw Garrett, legs crossed, fingers entwined across his middle, sitting in a chair next to the window.

"We've got to stop meeting like this," the spymaster added, gesturing toward the surroundings.

"So you found me."

"Nope. She called me. Lucky thing, too, because of how close by we are. Another minute or two and you'd have been room temperature."

Then he remembered. "Annie! Is she okay?"

He raised a hand. "Fine, fine. Take it easy. From what she told me, you saved her neck, just in time. And Susanne's, too."

He closed his eyes.

"They're down the hall a ways. Under sedation. They've apparently been through hell, but they'll be okay.... What Annie told me before they put her under, though— it's pretty damned incredible. Even for you."

"You know it all, then."

"Probably not. But enough." He leaned forward and lowered his voice. "So why in hell did you get mixed up in all this vigilante stuff?"

Hunter turned away, his gaze fixing on the ceiling.

"I never intended to. It just happened. When I bugged out after the plastic surgery and went to ground, I figured I'd just resurface as somebody else, and try to live a normal life."

"You? Normal?"

"Okay. As normal as I can be. But then I heard about Arthur Copeland and his wife."

He stopped. His eyes rested on the drip bag next to the bed. He had trouble getting the rest out.

"I owed that man, Grant. I owed him everything. He gave me this face. A chance at a new life. So when I heard that the animals that attacked them had been set free—"

He turned back to him. "I just couldn't let it go. I couldn't walk away."

Something softened in Garrett's face. "You never could."

He shut his eyes again. The two of them were quiet for a while. He listened to the faint sound of voices somewhere out in the hall. He felt the tightness of the wrap around his thigh under the sheets. Felt the heavy bandage on his left forearm. The dull aches in other places that he didn't know had been hurt.

"Seeing as how I just saved your sorry ass again," Garrett said, "I'd like to know a few things. If you don't mind, that is."

"Fire away."

"I know you've got reasons, lots of reasons, to be pissed at the Agency."

"Whatever gave you that idea."

"So. You took out Muller, right?"

"Of course."

"Of course." Garrett paused. Then: "Are you willing to let it go at that?"

He thought about it. About everything he'd been through. About what they allowed to happen to him. About the betrayals, at the highest levels.

Then he thought about what he had now. And about what might be ahead for him.

"I'll let it go."

Garrett got up, stood over him. Extended his hand.

"Then so will we."

He looked up at his old boss, took the hand, and shook it.

Garrett didn't release it. "Matt, I know this is a stupid question. You wouldn't think of coming back and working for us, again, would you?"

"You're right. It's a stupid question."

"Then how about working directly for me?"

He smiled. "That's not a stupid question. And thank you, Grant. But no."

Garrett looked sad. "You know, son, there are many days that I envy you."

"Don't. I'm glad you're there. You're holding it all together, Grant. I shudder to think of how bad things would get if you weren't."

Garrett coughed.

"Still smoking?"

Garrett shrugged.

"Please stop."

Garrett shrugged again. "I'll check on you later. You'll be here for a bit. Not too long, maybe a week. But you've been busted up pretty badly, and they have to put you back together again. Don't worry, it's on the Company's tab."

He picked up his overcoat from the other chair. "Don't run off again, Matt. You won't have to do that anymore. Promise?"

He smiled again. "I promise." Then added: "Grant?"

"Yes?"

"Call me Dylan."

They looked at each other. A moment passed.

Grant Garrett smiled. Actually smiled.

"See you later, Dylan Hunter."

Then turned and left.

He shut his eyes again.

*

Felt something.

Someone lifting the sheets from his body. He opened his eyes.

She was climbing into the bed with him.

He seized her, and she him.

They clung to each other and looked into each other's eyes.

Then, like her, he began to tremble.

Then, like her—and for the first time since his father died—he cried.

*

The morning sun had moved, leaving only a soft afterglow in the window. It framed her as she sat in the chair next to his bed. She held his right hand in both of hers, neither of them wanting to let go. After a while, she said:

"My father visited me here this morning."

He knew they had to face this together. "Yes?"

"This was even harder for him, you know. He almost lost me. To somebody from one of his own programs. The guilt over this is almost killing him."

He could only listen.

"I tried to calm him down. We talked a long time. He's not sure what he's going to do, now. But I know there will be big changes in the foundation. For one thing, what he saw on the screen at the Christmas party...it really opened his eyes about Frankfurt. That, and now Wulfe. He told me that he was going to call Frankfurt today and fire him."

"On Christmas Day?"

"He said he couldn't do it fast enough. Then he's going to cut off funding of Frankfurt's programs and others like it. He doesn't want to be responsible for any more things like...what happened."

"I'm glad."

"I suggested that maybe he could direct money toward victims of crime, instead. Groups such as Vigilance for Victims. He liked that."

"That's a great idea." He paused. "Annie?"

"Yes?"

"I think there's a big difference between people like Frankfurt, and people like your father. Frankfurt and his kind actually sympathize with the monsters. But your father and those like him—I don't think they're malicious. They just seem to be terribly confused about justice and compassion. They don't realize that you can't grant compassion toward bad people without committing injustices against their victims. You have to save your compassion for those who have earned it. Compassion without justice is just enabling."

"I see that a lot more clearly since I met you, Dylan."

"Maybe you can help him see it, too."

*

The sound of soft rapping on the door.

"Excuse me. I don't mean to intrude."

Cronin stood in the doorway.

He felt Annie's hands squeeze his tighter.

"Not at all," he replied. "Come in and have a seat."

Cronin did. He didn't bother to take off his coat.

"Just thought I'd check in and see how both of you were doing," he said.

"Much better now, thanks. They say I should be out of here in five days or so, a week tops. And Annie is all right."

He smiled. "So I see. I'm relieved.... How's Mrs. Copeland doing?"

Annie answered. "A few bumps and bruises. The main damage is psychological. It will take a long time for her to process this. To believe it's really all over."

"I'm sure. But she has a lot of good friends like you to help her."

No point in dancing around it.

"So, what's happening with the investigation, Detective?"

Cronin looked straight at him.

"Of course, I'll need a statement from you. When you're feeling up to it. But I think the facts are pretty clear-cut. The way we reconstruct things, Ms. Woods managed to sneak a phone call to you and let you know where they were. You showed up and fought with Wulfe, and both of you grabbed knives from the kitchen. He almost killed you, but after you were stabbed in the leg, you picked up this combat knife that he'd dropped, and you managed to stab him fatally. Isn't that the way it was, Mr."—he paused—"Hunter?"

He didn't answer. Just held the cop's eyes.

"That's exactly the way it was," Annie interjected, fighting a smile.

Cronin turned to her. "And, of course, you'll sign a statement to that effect, won't you, Ms. Woods?"

"Why, of course, Detective."

"What about you, Mr....Hunter?"

"Gee, it all happened so fast. But that seems to be about right."

"There. I figured it was pretty cut and dried. Nothing at the crime scene appears to contradict that interpretation."

"How convenient for you."

"And that's one dead criminal I won't have to chalk up to the vigilantes, either."

"What a relief for you."

"Sure is. I'm glad we don't have Wulfe around to worry about anymore. He was a scary dude. I mean, with all his advanced belts in hand-to-hand combat—why, it's a damned miracle that a mere newspaper reporter like you was somehow able to overpower and kill him."

"It had to be a miracle."

"You're lucky you survived. And you left a lot of your blood there, Mr. Hunter. Lucky for you that Ms. Woods works for the CIA, so close by, and could have them send help so quickly."

"As you say, I'm lucky."

"You sure are."

"Speaking of blood, Detective: Annie told me about the DNA matching you're trying to do from one of the vigilante crime scenes. How's that going?"

Cronin's eyes lost their glimmer of amusement. "Funniest thing about that. Last night I happened to be talking to Ms. Woods's boss at the CIA—a Mr. Garrett. And he said they have a priority need for that DNA sample.

Something about some highly classified national security investigation involving an assassination. So, it looks like we'll be turning that DNA sample over to them."

Annie squeezed his hand harder.

"How unlucky for you."

"Yes. How unlucky." The cop leaned forward in the chair. "You know, Mr. Hunter, those vigilantes must really like you. If they ever try to contact you, I wonder if I might count on you to let me know?"

"Why, Detective Cronin! I'm a journalist. I have to protect my sources." He turned to look at Annie. "After all, you wouldn't want me to violate a trust, would you?"

She beamed at him.

"No, I suppose not." He got up. "Well, it's time I got back to the wife and kids. I only had a couple hours with them this morning to open the presents. I hope both of you get better real soon. Merry Christmas, Ms. Woods. And Mr....Hunter."

"Merry Christmas, Detective Cronin," Hunter said.

Annie stood and went to Cronin. Kissed him on the cheek.

"Thank you," she said.

He nodded.

He moved to the door, then stopped. Not turning to face them, he said:

"Hunter?"

"Yes?"

"Stay the hell away from Alexandria."

He walked out.

They looked at each other and broke out laughing.

CONNOR'S POINT
MARYLAND'S EASTERN SHORE
Tuesday, December 30, 10:32 a.m.

When Billie Rutherford opened the front door, she was surprised to see Vic Rostand standing there in heavy winter clothes, holding a gaily wrapped box.

"Hi there, Billie."

"My God! How are you, stranger? Jim—it's Vic! Come on in out of the cold, it's freezing out there."

"No, I'm afraid I can't. I was just checking in on things here, making sure they shoveled the walk and saved the mail. I'm going to be gone again for about six weeks. But before I go, I just wanted to drop off a belated Christmas present, since I've been out of town."

Jim came up behind her. "Again? So soon? Don't you ever get a break?"

"Actually, that's what this is about. I need some R & R. I took a spill while skiing last weekend and the doc says it's going to take my arm and leg a while to heal properly."

She saw that he was shifting uncomfortably and balancing mostly on his right leg.

"Well, it's about time you had a vacation. You work too hard."

He laughed; she wished she could see his eyes better, behind those tinted glasses. "Well, Billie, as they say, 'an idle mind is the devil's playground.'"

She had to ask. "Were you alone on that ski trip, Vic? Or were you with anyone special?"

He grinned. "Well, yes. There *is* someone special. I'll introduce her sometime. She's quite a lady. And she owns an interesting cat." He handed them the package. "Anyway, Merry Christmas. And Happy New Year. I'll see you again sometime in early February."

"Same to you, Vic. Drive safe."

She closed the door and through the window they watched him limp back to his Honda CR-V.

"What a nice, sweet man," Billie said. "I hope she's good enough for him."

*

"Bronowski." The impatient growl over the phone.

"And happy holidays to you, too, Bill."

"Where the hell have you been these weeks? I thought you'd fallen off the planet! It's been nuts around here since you left."

"I know a little about that."

"Well, thank God you're back. Just today, all kinds of fallout from your last piece and that Adrian Wulfe escape. Here's from A.P. this morning: 'Prominent charity benefactor Kenneth MacLean issued a statement today that he is initiating reorganization of his foundation, with a focus on advocacy for crime victims.'"

"It's about time."

"Hunter, you have the inside track on this stuff. I need you to follow up, now."

He gazed down at the iron expanse of the Chesapeake from the lofty height of the Bay Bridge as his car sped westward.

"Your coverage has been just great without me, Bill. In fact, I'm just calling to wish you happy holidays and let you know I'll be gone till the beginning of February."

"What! *Now?*" Bronowski moaned. "You're kidding me!"

"Don't worry. I promise you lots of fresh meat when I get back."

TIONESTA, PENNSYLVANIA
Tuesday, December 30, 8:13 p.m.

His bouncing headlights illuminated the rutted, snow-covered drive leading to the cabin. He pulled up and parked near the door, in the clearing embraced by the pines and oaks. Left the engine running until he could go unlock the door and turn on the lights.

Then he came back for her.

"You're going to love it here."

He brought her inside. Then he turned her loose to explore.

At first Luna stood outside her carrier bag, hunched nervously, sniffing the bare planks of the cabin floor. Then, after a few tentative steps, during which no beasts of prey leaped from hiding places, she straightened and began to trot from item to item, checking them out.

He let her wander and went back outside to bring in and store the rest of their gear.

He kicked off his boots and hung his parka on the deer antlers next to the door—the trophy of a hunting trip so long ago.

He went to the kitchen area and, after uncorking and pouring some wine, sat on the couch. Put his stocking feet up on the knotty pine coffee table. Looked around at the bare wood walls. At the empty mantelpiece over the big stone fireplace.

It hurt not to be able to put out photos. But at least he had his memories, and particularly fond ones of this place.

He knew that he had undergone an important passage in his life since he was here last. That a new chapter was beginning. He knew he had to mark it now, alone.

He had to answer the question that he had asked himself here, not quite three years earlier.

He drank the glass. Then another.
Poured a third.

                              *

Once again, he limped up the stairs, carrying his duffle bag and a glass of wine. Luna scampered up after him and immediately found a place on the bare mattress. He used a rag to wipe the gathered dust from the vanity mirror. Then he sat down on the mattress beside the cat. He sipped the wine, stroked the cat, and looked into the mirror.

"Okay. So, who are you?"

The face that was now his own stared back at him, not answering.

He took another sip. Placed the glass on the floor.

Reached into the top of his duffle and extracted a leather pouch.

Opened it and pulled out the drivers' licenses.

Spread them on the mattress next to him.

> Brad Roark Flynn
> Victor Edward Rostand
> Wayne Alan Grayson
> Shane Michael Stone
> Edmond Dantes
> Lex Talionis

Then pulled out his wallet. Removed his driver's license. Tossed it next to them.

> Dylan Lee Hunter

He looked into the mirror, then down at all the cards.

On several, the resemblance was close to the face in the mirror.

But there were beards and wigs and mustaches on others, different colors.

And makeup.

And a great latex mask on one.

He picked up the wine glass from the floor. Stood, unsteady now.

Lifted his glass to the mirror.

"Gentlemen—a toast now to our sire: the late, great Matt Malone. Mr. Malone, here we are. Your bastard offspring, standing in your shadow. Living not as real men, but as ghosts."

He took a last big swallow. Stared at himself.

His face in the mirror looked sad.

He sat again.

"Who are you?" he asked softly.

*

He heard the sound of a car engine approach, then die.

Heard quick steps marching up the porch stairs.

Heard the cabin door creak open.

Heard her call out:

"Dylan?"

And knew.

About the Author

Robert Bidinotto earned a national reputation as an authority on criminal justice while writing investigative articles as a former Staff Writer for *Reader's Digest*. His famous 1988 article "Getting Away with Murder" stirred a national controversy about crime and prison furlough programs during that year's presidential campaign, and it is widely credited with having affected the outcome of the election. It was honored by the American Society of Magazine Editors as one of five finalists for the National Magazine Award for "Best Magazine Article in the Public Interest Category."

Robert is author of the acclaimed book *Criminal Justice? The Legal System vs. Individual Responsibility*, with a foreword by John Walsh of the "America's Most Wanted" television show, and of *Freed to Kill*—a compendium of horror stories exposing the failings of the justice system.

His many articles, essays, book and film reviews also have appeared in the *Washington Times,* the *Boston Herald, Success, The American Spectator, Writer's Digest,* and other publications. Robert was awarded the Free Press Association's Mencken Award in 1985 for "Best Feature Story," and he has been honored by the National Victim Center and other victim-rights organizations for his outspoken public advocacy on behalf of crime victims. As an editor, in 2007, he won the magazine industry's top honor for editorial excellence—the *Folio* gold "Eddie" Award. A popular speaker, he has appeared as a guest on scores of major talk programs.

With his wife, Cynthia, and their stridently individualistic cat, Luna, Robert makes his home on the Chesapeake Bay, where he is working on the further adventures of Dylan Hunter.

A Note to Readers

Did you enjoy *HUNTER*? Would you like to see more stories featuring Dylan, Annie, Wonk, Danika, Garrett, and, of course, Luna?

Then I'd be grateful if you'd recommend *HUNTER* to your friends, on social-networking sites and blogs, and in "reader reviews" on Amazon, Smashwords, and other online book retailers. And tell your local bookstore that they should stock the print edition.

The success of this, Dylan Hunter's first adventure, will determine his future. Surely you wouldn't want the vigilante to *retire*, would you? Don't you want to know what happens in future tales, such as *Crusader*, *Bad Deeds*, and *Blind Copy*?

Then, please spread the word that *HUNTER* is available as an ebook and as a print book.

This book has been released in ebook formats for the Kindle, Nook, Sony Reader, Kobo, iPad, and others. If you don't have an ebook reader, you can download free "Kindle apps" from the Amazon Kindle website, then read the ebook on your own preferred device.

HUNTER also has been published as a trade paperback by Avenger Books, available on Amazon.com. You can obtain a personally inscribed copy—either for yourself or as a gift for someone special—at the Avenger Books website (link below). When you make your purchase there, please tell me how you want me to inscribe it. It will be shipped to you within 24 hours.

Bookstores and retail outlets interested in carrying *HUNTER* should contact:

Avenger Books
P.O. Box 555
Chester, MD 21619
www.AvengerBooks.com

If you'd like to contact me, drop me an email at:
RobertTheWriter@gmail.com
I comment on thrillers, "indie" publishing, and fiction generally at "The Vigilante Author" blog:
   www.bidinotto.com
And if you're intrigued by the provocative viewpoints expressed in *HUNTER*, check out my *non*fiction blog:
http://bidinotto.blogspot.com
You also can find me on Facebook:
https://www.facebook.com/bidinotto
And on Twitter: **@RobertBidinotto**

Behind the Scenes

Like the story of its title character, the story of *HUNTER* grew from incidents in my own life. And while I hope the tale provides readers with grand entertainment, my purpose in writing this novel could not be more serious.

For six years during the late 1980s and early 1990s, I was an investigative journalist for *Reader's Digest*, specializing in "true crime" stories. That preoccupation began when I investigated, then wrote, the now-famous article in the July 1988 issue about the Massachusetts prison furlough program. Titled "Getting Away with Murder," the article made the name "Willie Horton" famous during that year's presidential election. Political historians say that it had a major impact on the outcome of the election between George H.W. Bush and Michael Dukakis.

But its major impact on *me* was to raise my awareness about the plight of crime victims, and how they were routinely abused, ignored, and further victimized by the criminal justice system.

During the course of that investigation, I met rape victims. Parents of murdered children. Countless targets of thugs who had been released, irresponsibly and prematurely, into halfway houses—into unsupervised "furloughs" from prison—into early parole and "diversionary" probation "supervision"—a host of other "alternatives to incarceration."

The faces of those victims haunted me during many sleepless nights.

Their faces haunt me still.

During subsequent investigations, I learned little-known truths about the systemic leniency of the criminal justice system—and about those who made it so. I wrote investigative articles under such titles as "Freed to Rape Again," "Revolving-Door Justice," "The Law Criminals Love," and "When Criminals Go Free."

I learned that there was an "Excuse-Making Industry" of intellectuals in the social-science establishment: philosophers, psychologists, political scientists, legal scholars, sociologists, criminologists, economists, and historians, whose theories have shaped our modern legal system. That "industry" also consists of an activist wing of social workers, counselors, therapists, legal-aid and civil-liberties lawyers, "inmate rights" advocates, "progressive" politicians, and activists.

It was this industry which, in the Sixties and Seventies, initiated a quiet revolution in the criminal justice system, and routed the last of those who believed that the legal system's purpose should be to apprehend and punish criminals. Instead, the Excuse-Making Industry—united in the belief that the criminal isn't responsible for his actions—rejected the fundamental premise of the justice system: *justice.*

In 1994, I published a book, *Criminal Justice? The Legal System vs. Individual Responsibility*—an anthology of articles by me, and by legal scholars, exposing this corruption. I also wrote a short book of horror stories documenting the bloody consequences of the Excuse-Making Industry's policies, titled *Freed to Kill.*

I tell you this, because you should know that the descriptions in *HUNTER* of the workings of the legal system, of "alternatives to incarceration," of "diversionary sentences," of crimes by predators recycled constantly from prisons to streets and back, and of the hideous personal impact on crime victims, *are accurate accounts of the actual workings of today's legal system.*

For example, the criminal histories in *HUNTER* are composites of many real individuals. The memo on the bulletin board in Chapter 10, listing all the sports opportunities in one prison, is a verbatim transcript of an actual memo, in my possession, posted at the Massachusetts Correctional Institution in Norfolk (sent to me by an outraged corrections officer). Descriptions of inmate amenities are drawn from my personal observations during visits to prisons all over the United States, while researching my November 1994 *Digest* article, "Must Our Prisons Be Resorts?" The meeting of the crime-victims group in Chapter 14 was inspired by a dinner meeting I had with members of Parents of Murdered Children in Massachusetts.

So, if you think the presentation in *HUNTER* of criminals, outrages in the legal system, and horrors inflicted on victims is in any way exaggerated, I will only say: I wish.

I hope that *HUNTER* helps to bring public attention to this enduring, despicable state of affairs, and to bring to crime victims a measure of the justice owed to them by our legal system.

The criminal justice system was one of the two major settings for the novel. The other was the shadow world of the CIA and intelligence agencies—a setting I know far less about, none of it from personal experience. Here, I make fewer claims for authenticity. But I wasn't striving for journalistic accuracy: I was hoping only to create fictional persuasiveness.

Still, I'm delighted that several professionals in the intelligence community—some of whom offered input during my research and editing—assure me that my rendition of the activities, skills, and methods of spymasters, NOCs, CIA paramilitary teams, and even Dylan Hunter himself seem plausible. Two intelligence veterans from two different agencies thought that Matt Malone's imaginative method of acquiring his many aliases appeared to be *possible*. Regarding the details of spycraft—and the problems within the CIA—I relied heavily on published sources, including books by former Agency case officers.

While many of the locations in *HUNTER* actually exist, I've treated them creatively, oftentimes making up details to enhance the story. For example, I hope that no reader makes a pilgrimage to Linden, Virginia, and pesters the good residents there. I assure you that the "government road," the "CIA safe house," and the sniper location are all complete fabrications. The same goes for the romantic inn where Dylan and Annie launch their relationship: It's a composite, borrowed from several places, and with invented ambiance.

As for other aspects of the story and characters, I'll address them in time on my blog, "The Vigilante Author": www.bidinotto.com

Writing this, my first novel, has been a lifelong dream. The enthusiastic advance response to HUNTER has been better than I had dared to anticipate. I'm grateful to you for welcoming my fictional avatar into your homes, and, I hope, into your hearts.

Acknowledgments

If you're tempted to skip this section—please don't. Allow me to introduce you to this book's legion of uncredited co-authors.

HUNTER was graced by input and inspiration from many people—some of whom don't yet even know it. It's time that they did.

Let me begin with the thriller authors who, over the decades, helped to fuel my imagination and fashion my values. As a young man, I was captivated by the tales from seminal action writers Alistair MacLean, Desmond Bagley, Donald Hamilton, and Mickey Spillane. A long list of others contributed to my understanding of thriller-writing, but I'll limit this accounting to some best-selling authors with whom I've had personal interactions.

Foremost among them, let me single out Brad Thor. Not only is Brad a first-rate thriller writer; he is also a gentleman of profound convictions, intellectual depth, personal charm, and enormous generosity of spirit. His quiet, unsung gifts of time, counsel, and personal donations to worthy causes proves that good guys finish *first*.

The same can be said of Vince Flynn, another great American patriot, great writer, and great human being. I was privileged to interview him for a magazine article some years back, and Vince's life story is an inspiration to any author facing formidable personal challenges.

Thriller master Lee Child also graciously gave me a full afternoon of his valuable time—while on deadline, no less—for a long magazine interview in 2007. His keen intelligence, delightfully dry wit, and sage advice made the occasion memorable. But I thank him most of all for creating the iconic action hero Jack Reacher.

Over a year ago, I ran into another legendary thriller writer at a book signing in Annapolis: Stephen Hunter. I am in awe of this man's writing ability: He simply has no authorial weaknesses. His "Bob Lee Swagger" has become another fiction icon. I paid homage to Mr. Hunter and his sniper hero in the pages of this novel, in some pretty obvious ways.

But that applies to the others I've just mentioned—in case you didn't notice (check out Matt Malone's aliases). I trust that none of them objects to my none-too-subtle tributes. I also treasure the fact that they inscribed their own books to me with admonitions to finish mine. As Stephen Hunter elegantly put it: "Robert—Finish your goddamned novel." Yes, sir.

Then there's the mistress of spy thrillers, Gayle Lynds, whom I met at a writers' conference. Not only did Gayle boost my morale, she also introduced me to a CIA source that proved hugely helpful. Thank-yous also go to wonderful thriller writers Mark Greaney and Neil Russell, both of whom contributed kind words and the stellar examples of their own work.

If you aren't yet reading these authors, you don't know what you're missing.

Many other people deserve kudos for anything that's good in this novel.

My great appreciation to Alan C. More, who managed to walk me through the seventh floor at Langley—metaphorically speaking—without revealing a single national-security secret, while providing the kind of descriptive detail that every thriller author cherishes. Also, my gratitude to a couple of buddies at intelligence agencies that will go nameless, for their input, advice, corrections, and reassurance that I haven't *totally* misrepresented the spy biz.

To Sally Torbert, who spent an afternoon years ago vividly re-creating for me the Princeton campus and its atmosphere, thereby helping Matt Malone get an Ivy League education and wander into the campus bar where he was recruited into the CIA. America thanks you, Sally.

To the late philosopher and novelist Ayn Rand, for having been the most profound influence on my philosophy, values, and literary preferences. Some may even see a wee bit of her own fictional vigilante, Ragnar Danneskjöld, in Dylan Hunter.

To the individuals who inspired and educated me about taking the "indie" route to publish this book: self-publishing gurus Joe Konrath, Robin Sullivan, and Dean

Wesley Smith. Special thanks to Robin and her talented author-husband, Michael J. Sullivan, for their personal advice and encouragement.

To graphic designer Allen Chiu for a *fantastic* book cover and header for my fiction blog. If you need a great graphic designer, contact Allen at: pealwah@hotmail.com. And to Joshua Zader of Atlas Web Development (http://www.atlaswebdev.com/), who designed the blog to my own quirky requirements.

To Nick Ambrose at www.everything-indie.com, for formatting and designing the interior for this book and ebook. And to Rick Hogan, a first-rate artist and designer, for his gracious support and generous encouragement.

Howard Dickman, now of the editorial staff at the *Wall Street Journal,* gave me my first break as a writer by bringing me into the pages of *Reader's Digest.* Then, as my editor, he shepherded all my articles through the editorial minefields to publication. Eternal gratitude unto you, Howard.

Kudos, too, to the designers of the amazing creative-writing software package I used, "WriteItNow." It proved to be indispensable. (www.ravensheadservices.com)

Then there are the folks who saved my butt during the editing of this book: my "beta" readers. Their wisdom, input, and critical reading of various versions of the manuscript have spared me endless embarrassments. Some volunteered their time despite difficult personal circumstances. There's not enough space to detail their individual contributions, so just let me list their names here: Shawn Reynolds, Larry Abrams, Frank Schulwolf, Rose Robbins Schild, Jeanette Traeg, Mark Gardner, Sean Killian, Gregory Wall, Karen O'Shea, Gabrielle Suglia, Francisco Villalobos, and Robert L. Jones. Friends, there's no way to thank you enough.

Finally, to family and friends who have encouraged and endured me over the years:

To the Slate family and their spouses, for their love and support: Don and Barbara; Steve and Janice; Candy and Ray; Shelley and Steve; Mike and Jan; Pete and Melissa; and all their kids. Thanks for welcoming this congenital loner into your tribe.

To my old pal Don Heath, a great friend when I needed one, and just as valuable a "beta reader." Thanks forever, Don. And to Margaret Bidinotto, for all the things too personal to mention here. I'm grateful, Margaret.

To Chris Doffing, who wanted me to write more books, and who assisted me generously on another book project—thank you, Chris.

To my dear, long-time friends Henry Scuoteguazza and Claudia Leone. Given your recent personal circumstances, I'm deeply moved that you took out time to read the novel in advance and give me your kind verdicts. You're the best. Hugs to you both.

To another college buddy, Steve Lord, and his lovely wife Cindy. Steve has been a cheerleader to me, and much more, throughout my adult life. Well, I finally did it, my friend.

To my closest confidant, Alan Paul. In my worst, most isolated moments, you've been there to toss a lifeline. In my happiest, most joyous moments, you've been there to celebrate with me. I'm grateful for every moment of our friendship, Alan. I don't know what my life would have been without you, but it surely would have been a lesser life.

To my late parents, who wanted better opportunities for me than they'd had for themselves—and who struggled to make sure I got them: my loving memories.

And to Luna. Yep, she's real, folks. I'll post a photo on the blog.

No man could boast a finer brother than mine. A lifetime of love goes across the miles to Colorado, and to Ed Bidinotto. We've come a long way, you and I, haven't we? Congratulations on your own recent book, and I hope you enjoy this one. And love to your fiancée, Connie.

No man could boast a better daughter than the one I've got, either. Katrina, dear, I'll never be able to fully express just how proud I am of you. I love you and wish you and Jason every happiness—wishes I also extend to my granddaughter, Doria, and to the new baby on its way. (I can't wait!)

Finally, to the most important person in my life: the woman who made this book possible.

I've dedicated *HUNTER* to one named person, my wife Cynthia. At a time of turmoil in both our lives—a period when most wives would have been pushing their husbands to chase the phantom of "financial security"—Cynthia stood behind me and pushed me to go for my dreams, instead. It was an act of love, of respect, of trust, and of remarkable bravery.

I don't know what I've done to deserve you, my Cyn—or even if I have. All I know is that you bring out the best in me.

And that's why this one's for you.

—Robert Bidinotto
June 2011

Made in the USA
Lexington, KY
08 September 2012